I 5.00

MW01711555

MURDER in the FOURTH

Ruth anne Wicker

Jill Martin

Murder in the Fourth is a work of creative non-fiction. The events around the murder of Georgia Jackson are factual. All characters, except for the Revivalist preachers and Jehovah's Witness leaders, are creations of the authors.

Murder in the Fourth

tellwell

Tellwell Talent

www.tellwell.ca

ISBN

978-1-77370-892-8 (Hardcover)

978-1-77370-891-1 (Paperback)

978-1-77370-893-5 (eBook)

This book is dedicated to
all those who have the courage
to break free.

Murder in the fourth degree will not be found in any book of law. Murder of minds in Cults is both insidious and cancerous. Cults brainwash the poor, the sick, the lonely and those on the periphery of normalized society. They isolate and threaten their followers with fear of eternal damnation and rejection by God. Hiding behind the walls of their belief systems, the perpetrators enact these crimes with impunity.

"Foul deeds will rise..."
Hamlet (1.2.37)

Acknowledgements

There are many people to thank for their assistance with the final production of this book. Surviving a cult brings us together as we find each other, share stories and heal. Those people know who they are.

Thank you to our first readers — Marilyn Keddy, Nancy Wilson and Catherine Norman-Donovan. All three of you offered your feedback and urged us to continue with this project.

To the production team at Tellwell Publishing in bringing *Murder in the Fourth* to the public.

To friend and musician Mark Haines who listened to this story and, when asked if he would like to write a song that reflects it, wrote "We are Free." This song will be sung by many who have found freedom from the shackles of any cult.

To Judith Carey for unending support in creating our cover.

To John McIntyre at McIntyre Purcell Publishing for your mentorship and big picture advice.

To the Elgin County Archives for their assistance in locating the newspaper articles from 1966 and 1972 that recount the story of Georgia Jackson from her disappearance to justice being served. To the perseverant staff at the Aylmer Cemetery who, despite having little to go on, found Georgia Jackson's final resting place.

To our friends and family: thank you for listening. It has been three long years. You are patient and understanding beyond belief.

Table of Contents

PART ONE

DISCOVERY

"Pre-trial disclosure of pertinent facts or documents"

Lorraine

1

Daytime Nightmare

Lorraine pulled into the nearly vacant lot. Always ample parking at the nursing home, she thought wryly.

The previous weeks' visiting restrictions had finally been lifted that morning. For ten days, the home warned family members about widespread pneumonia, the Angel of Death, which was threatening the residents. Luckily, it passed over her mom, but it did land on the chests of Bert Tripp and Esther Grant. Their family cars would not be in the parking lot anymore. Bert and Esther's kids and grandkids had been regulars.

Others rarely came.

Lorraine locked her car and headed to the front door, her mother's home for the past five years. Her bag slung haphazardly over her shoulder, she hurried across the parking lot.

The heavy scent of the sea caught her attention. She paused to steal a glimpse of the Lunenburg Back Harbour's calm and pristine waters. *Maybe I'll be able to take her onto the upper terrace for a bit if she's not too tired. I know she loves the view and the sea smells.*

As she had done for years, Lorraine walked down the long outer hall and passed through the keyed entry toward the elevator.

Her mother's fall five years earlier had necessitated moving her from her lovely bedroom in Lorraine's house to the Home. And since then it had been a daily ritual. Every afternoon at four, she went to see her mom. This past year her mother had lost even more weight. She looked like a baby bird with see-through skin pulled over a tiny face of protruding cheeks and a prominent nose — a bird-like beak. Her long, beautiful blond hair was gone, replaced with sparse grey tendrils trailing down her sloped back. She was frail and weak. Profound deafness had also taken over and now she hardly spoke.

Lorraine turned into the cramped room where she found her mother in a deep sleep. Rather than wake her, she took advantage of the respite of a quiet visit and sat down in the hard visitor's chair by her bedside.

She looked the same as yesterday and the day before that and the day before that. The cancerous growth on her forehead was still there, a shiny red bump, right in the middle. It looked like bluish-red broccoli, so, Lorraine called that lump "broccoli" and the one on her cheek "grape." Grape and Broccoli were already two years old, stubbornly growing on her bird-like face.

Mom "minded" them, as they say in Nova Scotia.

They bothered her. She picked at them constantly. Bloodied hands and face became the norm. Lorraine started each visit by getting a warm wash cloth and wiping away the dry blood, but today she was too tired to consider that ritual. She hadn't slept much the night before, but it wasn't lack of sleep that had bowed her. She couldn't wipe the horror of the morning from her mind.

*

On Nova Scotia's South Shore, a rich palette of orange and yellow accompanied with unseasonably warm temperatures mocked the calendar which read November. Other places in the country had already seen snow, but Lunenburg hadn't had a sniff of the white stuff. A few days before, Lorraine had planned to clean up her flower pots in preparation for the hard winter that they were predicting for 2016, but when she got on her gloves and headed out in the garden, she changed her mind.

The red geraniums were blooming profusely and the white alyssum, still full and vibrant, cascaded over the pot in a triumph of cotton fluff. She just couldn't do it. Instead, Lorraine dragged the pots across the flagstone patio and put them right beside the window outside her kitchen table. There she could enjoy them. They would be a beautiful backdrop for her morning coffee.

As she did every morning, she placed her laptop on the table, made her Keurig dark roast and settled down to catch up on world events. The election in the States was just days away, so she could be guaranteed something interesting to read. With one click on Firefox, the MSN news feed popped up on the screen.

It wasn't election coverage, however, that caught her eye. It was the opening byline of a story covered by CBC. A story that was very close to her heart. She quickly scanned the article. Her body began to tremble. She felt a massive wave of nausea fill her core.

Lorraine read the facts in a deathly whisper. Two women, one aged 27 and the other 30, died following caesarian sections. Both were Jehovah's Witnesses and in each case, they were cited as making informed and free decisions to refuse the blood transfusions. Both newborns lived and both young mothers died.

Lorraine couldn't think straight. *No mother in her right mind would choose to let her own child die in order to follow Jehovah. To never hold the life she had carried joyfully and expectantly for nine months. No. Never.*

The blood-red geraniums, happily blooming outside the window, stared back at her. She covered her face.

"No, no. This can't still be happening," she wailed aloud.

Lorraine knew all too well the power of the cult, the rulings of the Governing Body and their stand against taking the Blood. She shivered with the tragic recollections in her own family and how fifty years later those trapped and bowed by the indoctrinating machinations of the cult were still dying due to the narrow-minded ideology of the Organization.

*

Lorraine slumped in the hard chair and gazed long and wistfully at her mom. The morning had taken her hostage. She recalled the smiling face of the young mother from the article. She took a deep breath and buried her face in her hands.

How the fuck did we get to this? Why is she holding on at 96? Heart disease, cancer, dementia, not to mention incontinence — she's had them all. The cruel indignities of growing old.

Lorraine glanced at the brochure on her mother's night table. It was an invitation to a Care for the Caregiver Conference.

Intended for me, no doubt, she thought, picking it up. The first topic caught her attention: "Caregiver Stress and How to Cope."

"What a joke. I'm the only one who's totally burnt out. No help for this caregiver. Peter's so far away and little brother Dougie," she sneered, "well, he could be dead for all we know."

Deborah had not heard from her youngest son in over twenty years. Following Jehovah God's direction, he checked out of the family both physically and emotionally when his mother left the Hall. The Shunning of his mother and his siblings was complete.

The tiny form in the middle of the bed remained quiet and peaceful. Lorraine whispered under her breath, "If only Peter lived closer."

"Dad died properly," Lorraine blurted the words out loud. "Fast and unexpected. Just dropped dead. Christmas Day no less! Ha! What an irony! A former Jehovah's Witness dies on Christmas Day."

Lorraine moved slightly on the hard chair trying to get comfortable.

The room was hot. The familiar sounds from the hallway diminished into a distant hum. Soon the heat and her total exhaustion overcame her conscious mind.

Before she could stop them, memories long buried in the past exploded into the present. She was back in the Kingdom Hall. The year was 1958.

2

View From the Front Row

Lorraine's father's voice, strong and charismatic, urged her to pay attention. She opened her eyes and sat up straighter. *I hadn't meant to drift off. I was listening, really, I was.* She looked at her mother, young and beautiful, at the end of the row of chairs. She was crammed between her two brothers, Peter and Dougie, and she squirmed uncomfortably.

Her ass had been asleep for the last twenty minutes and now her legs were tingling. For three hours Lorraine and her brothers sat on armless wooden chairs, straight as stooges. The front row was allocated for them, the Elders' kids.

"Lorraine, keep your hands folded on your lap and listen," her mother warned. "See how good Douglas is behaving." Lorraine glared at her little brother, darts of disgust arcing between them.

Oh yes, Dougie. The perfect one. The one who never questions anything. Dougie who never complains about sitting here for hours on end. She wanted to choke little Dougie. The Elder droned on. Something about 1975. Armageddon was coming. Be prepared.

Lorraine stared straight ahead, eyes wide open; but she was daydreaming. She pretended to be like the other kids in town whose asses were awake and whose legs were running across the road to the park. They were playing or riding bikes or getting dirty and waiting for Sunday supper. *Maybe it would be roast beef.*

The Circuit Servant, the traveling holier-than-thou, gave the Talk. It was never referred to as the sermon, that was a Christian term. *Not allowed.*

Even then, she was pretty sure she questioned the odds — they were baffling.

She tried in vain to make sense of the numbers. The congregation was insignificant compared to others in the rural tobacco growing district of Southwestern Ontario. On a good Sunday, attendance never topped 50. Tonight however, the hall was packed. Probably 70 or so. It was the Memorial Service, or Easter to the pagans.

So, there she was, listening to the big guy talk about those blessed, anointed, chosen ones. All 144,000 of them that will go to heaven after the great battle of Armageddon.

What are the odds? Well, let's say that the total world population is approximately 6.7 billion people. Of those, exactly 144,000 will go to heaven. And, two of them are sitting right behind me. In this Hall.

The anointed ones, George and Bessie Simpson — married, childless and old — were the only ones allowed to partake of the sacred emblems of Christ. Once a year, they drank the wine and ate the bread. Heads bowed, the rest of the congregation passed the drink and bread to the next and the next and the next without partaking, until it reached the Simpsons. They drank, and they tasted.

And we all watch in awe. Lorraine's rebellious side dared her to take a sip of the wine or a bite of the cracker, but as they passed by, she sat numb, staring into space.

And, so it was. For years they went to the Hall at least five times a week; each time they were blessed with the unusual, statistically baffling situation of knowing and seeing and touching the great Brother and Sister Simpson.

They were not really Lorraine's sister or brother. At the Hall all females were Sisters and all males were Brothers. It didn't matter if they were related or not, they just answered to Sister or Brother.

The facts had been touted from headquarters in New York for as long as she could remember. When the final battle occurred, precisely during the lifetime of the millions of people alive in 1914, Jehovah would defeat Satan and the Elect would rise heavenward to rule with Christ.

Following a literal interpretation of the number mentioned in Revelation, Chapters 7 and 14, every Witness knew that only 144,000 were among the Elect, whom were guaranteed to go to heaven as spirit persons without resurrected bodies. The remaining faithful Jehovah's Witnesses would live forever on a renewed, earthly paradise in resurrected bodies. The unsaved whom were annihilated by Jehovah God would cease to exist.

Week after week, and Sunday after Sunday, they heard the same story. Lorraine's parents were strict believers who desired to be accepted into that new kingdom. Fear and compliance drove them to follow headquarters' every ruling.

Lorraine on the other hand, had fierce doubts.

Instead, every Sunday at the Talk, she pleaded with a galactic actuary to help her out. Her mind struggled with the mathematical equation for 144,000 divided into 6.7 billion and then the calculated odds of two of those 144,000 sitting behind her in the hall in Straffordville, Ontario, Canada, population 312.

3

Thicker Than Water

"I want to go home. I'm not doing this!"

"Don't be silly, Lorraine. This happens to all women."

Lorraine glared straight ahead, refusing to grant her mother the satisfaction of a response. The movie wasn't long, but the black and white images of female private parts haunted her.

Every month for my whole life! Between my legs, soiling my panties. Disgusting. Lorraine hated the sight of blood.

She looked around the room at the other Grade 6 students. They were talking comfortably with their mothers. They didn't look embarrassed or upset.

Why don't they look shocked? Perhaps their mothers talked to them about this terrible thing. Mine just prays, bakes cookies and attends the Hall. No time to tell her only daughter about something so important. I hate her.

The nurse rewound the film and passed out information booklets about the PERIOD. She asked if anyone had any questions. No one put up their hand.

But Lorraine had many. *Will I die or get sick and have to go to the hospital every month? Will my brothers and father know when I am stricken with this blood sickness? Will the other people in the class be able to see the blood dripping down my legs?* Her mind raced thinking of all the terrible months and years yet to come.

I'm not going to do it, period.

Her mother, seeing the stubborn slope of her daughter's shoulders, hesitated. *Perhaps I should have warned her.*

*

Lorraine knew it. Feeling the stickiness in her panties, she ran to the bathroom and rummaged into the cupboard where her mother kept the supplies. She tried to make sense of the thin elastic band with the hooks at the front and the hooks at the back. The pad was thick and heavy.

"How do I hook it together?" she muttered. "There aren't any instructions."

Lorraine couldn't call her mother because she was at the table waiting for her daughter to join the family for morning devotions.

Every morning it was the same. Nothing was served no matter how loudly their stomachs growled. Not even juice or coffee.

"Lorraine," her father called, "we're waiting for you. Your brothers are getting hungry. Where are you?"

"I'm in the stupid bathroom trying to hook up this stupid pad to soak up this stupid blood," Lorraine hissed. She stood in front of the mirror with the elastic belt in her hand, mischievously deciding what to do with it.

I'll show her. You want me to come to breakfast? Okay. I'll be right there.

Lorraine took the steps two at a time, turned the corner to the kitchen and waddled to her chair, the foreign pad filling the space between her legs. She plopped into her seat as lady like as humanly possible. The plastic tab of the white belt dangled in the middle of her forehead like an East Indian bindi.

Her brothers reacted immediately. Peter struggled to hide the smirk, which blossomed across his face. Dougie knew better than to utter a word. This was the Reading and he had to hold his temper in check. He couldn't let his mother see that side of him.

His head and heart full of scripture, James did not notice. From her place at the head of the table, her mother, however, was mortified.

"Get that off your head," she ordered.

Lorraine pulled the elastic belt off her head and strung it out like a slingshot before firing it across the room at the cat.

No one moved.

Her father opened the yearbook and began to read.

Matthew 24, verse 14. Lorraine knew it well; in fact, they all did and could recite it word for word. More than any other, this Scripture reading justified every Jehovah's Witness mission. It demanded that they go door-to-door to spread the good news. "And this gospel of the kingdom shall be preached in all the world for a witness unto all nations: and then the end shall come."

Finally, her father finished and closed the book; and yet again the butter had congealed on the cold toast.

4

Dancing on David's Shoes

Lorraine stood at the mirror and inspected her reflection.

Deborah had braided her long, untamed strawberry hair and tied the ends with wide scarlet ribbons. Braids were Deborah's only acknowledgement to style.

But Lorraine was always on the lookout when she wore braids. Like an extra bowl of chocolate ice-cream sitting alone on the counter, braids brought out the tease in Peter. He was fast, and he was relentless.

Deborah did up the last of the buttons on her daughter's dress. The pale pink chiffon overlaid with red strawberries made Lorraine feel like a princess. She couldn't believe she was going to a dance. Although it was in the Kingdom Hall, it was still a dance.

As she twirled in front of the mirror, Peter's long arm grabbed at the streaming ribbons. In one second, he detached the bow. The force of the action released her braid and her hair fell in rivulets down her back.

Lorraine's anger metre went from 0 to 100 in an instant. She sprinted after him, grabbing the plastic bat which leaned beside the screen door.

"You will not get away, this time," she shrieked.

Lorraine caught up to Peter and boxed him repeatedly over the head and shoulders until he was crying and yelling for her to stop.

From room to room, Deborah flew after the two children in a valiant effort to stop Lorraine from inflicting further bruises on Peter. "Stop this instant," she ordered. "Jehovah God is unhappy when you show anger."

Peter cowered against the kitchen counter, tears welling over his eyelids. Lorraine screeched to a halt, her small hands clutching the bat in mid swing ready to smash his forehead a second time.

"But mom," Lorraine sobbed indignantly. "He ruined my hair."

"Neither one of you will be coming to the wedding if this is how you will behave. Let the calm of Jehovah come into your hearts and dispel this anger."

Lorraine could hardly believe her mom. Spouting scripture when what Peter deserved was a good spanking. She glanced at her brother's face, suddenly transformed.

"I'm sorry, sis. I just couldn't stop my fingers when I saw those shiny red ribbons. Sorry. I didn't mean to do it."

Normally, Peter's crazy antics didn't really bother her. She loved Peter. But today was special and she felt her behaviour was justified.

"Lorraine," her mother added, "you must never use violence against your own flesh and blood. Whatever would Jehovah think?"

Lorraine lowered the bat and in a syrupy voice said, "I will try harder, Mom, to make Jehovah proud." She nearly choked on the words. Lorraine promised to behave, and Peter promised not to antagonize her. She did not want to miss the wedding.

Finally, the family walked out the front door, leaving seven-year-old Dougie, who had a severe sore throat, with Deborah's friend, Sister Helen.

Lorraine pranced down the sidewalk. A stiff crinoline beneath the pink A-line skirt made it spread sideways like an upside down strawberry ice-cream cone. Her patent leather shoes clicked with each step. With a self-satisfied smile, she shouldered her black clutch and did a full pirouette. She was off to her first ball.

As an Elder, James was adamant about his family's dress. Twelve-year-old Peter looked very sophisticated in his black suit, white shirt and grey tie. Just before they left the house, James slicked down his son's unruly blond hair with Brylcreem. James looked handsome in his navy pinstripe suit and coral tie. Deborah beamed in her cream dress with rose coloured belt.

James drove more quickly than usual, as they were running late and didn't want to miss the nuptials. The parking lot of the Kingdom Hall was full. Witnesses from all the neighbouring congregations were invited. After all, the Elder's daughter from the Aylmer congregation was the bride.

The Armstrong family sat in the middle row, which commanded a very good view of the podium. Sister Beth took her position at the piano and the congregation stood.

The bride entered from the rear of the Kingdom Hall wearing a beautiful satin gown and long veil. She linked her arm lovingly with the arm of her dear father. The groom stood at the front and gazed down the aisle at his approaching bride.

Lorraine thought he looked nervous. He fidgeted with his wristwatch, turning it over and over on his arm. It was distracting.

"All rise," the Elder began. "Let us pray to Jehovah."

The prayers continued and continued. Lorraine's feet started to ache.

"When is the dancing going to start?" she whispered to her mother.

"Shh, Lorraine. Jehovah is watching."

Elder Lenovz began the Talk. "We thank Him for His guidance in marriage and the joy of raising a family. We offer Him understanding of the roles of Husband and Wife. We bless the bride and groom standing before us here, but we admonish them to remember that Jehovah God is to be obeyed first, then Christ Jesus and then each other."

"Elaine promises to obey God, His Son Christ Jesus, and love and honour and obey her husband, until death."

"David promises to obey God, His Son Christ Jesus, and guide and direct his wife in the name of Jehovah until death."

"Fornication is a sin. Your joining is for procreation only. Be that your intention. Amen."

Lorraine really didn't get that last part but was grateful when the Elder finally stopped speaking. The congregation sat.

"Finally," Lorraine whispered under her breath. Her mother glared at her.

"My feet hurt in these shoes, Mom," Lorraine answered back.

When the ceremony ended, Brother George took his fiddle to the front of the room where he and Sister Beth started the music. The chairs had been stacked and the Hall was converted to a small dance floor.

Lorraine couldn't wait to taste the cookies and cakes that were placed on the table at the back of the room, but the best of all was the dance.

David took his bride's hand. In the centre of the dance floor, they would dance for the first time as husband and wife. They were young, only 18, but they seemed suited for one another. Elaine was vibrant and fun-loving while David was quiet and shy. The congregation applauded. Soon others joined the couple.

Lorraine took Peter's hand and they set out. For the past three weeks, James had taught them the two-step. Both children had fallen easily into the rhythm and their feet never missed a beat. Expertly, Lorraine cupped her brother's left hand in hers and placed his arm at her back. Right. Left. Left and turn. Right. Left. Left and turn. Although it was challenging to do the moves to the beat of Songs of Jehovah on fiddle and piano, they managed.

James and Deborah smiled, proud of their children. Tapping her feet to the trills of the fiddle, Deborah smiled like a school girl. She leaned in to James' ear and whispered, "Now they look like angels dancing together. You would hardly believe she almost broke his shoulder a few hours ago."

"Lorraine has a fiery temper, that's for sure," James offered, "but I wouldn't want her to be anyone else."

Deborah pursed her lips as she reluctantly acquiesced. "At least she keeps things interesting at home."

The groom noticed the ease with which Peter and Lorraine danced and wished he could do as well. When the next song started, David tapped Peter on the shoulder asking permission for a dance.

Lorraine offered her arm shyly. David placed his right arm on her shoulder, his left hand covered hers. He was very tall. Lorraine's gaze rested on the tie pin at her eye level. His steps were jumpy and uncoordinated. He obviously hadn't practiced as much as she and Peter had. Lorraine suddenly felt uncomfortable in the middle of the dance floor with this man.

"You are a very good dancer," he said.

"Thank You, Brother David," she replied. She wondered how someone's hand could possibly sweat so much. *Yuck*, she thought. She could hardly wait to get to the washroom and clean her hands.

David missed a step to the left and Lorraine stepped on his foot.

"I'm so sorry," she said, her face blushing a bright pink.

"That's quite alright Sister Lorraine," he replied as the music ended. The scuff mark on his shoe stood out like a sore thumb.

Lorraine headed to the washroom and washed the sweat from her hands. She turned to look in the mirror and make sure the back of her dress where his hand had rested was not damp.

Yuck, yuck, yuck. He may be tall and handsome, but what a jerk. Can't even dance. And sweaty. Ugh!

Grimacing at her reflection, she washed her hands a second time, just for good measure. As they left the Hall, Lorraine scooped up some confetti to take home.

5

Freedom From the Fuller Brush Man

Paul Boates was a loner, a travelling salesman who got his social fix from calling on customers. He was a Fuller Brush Man and well-suited for the job.

Paul loved his territory. Southwestern Ontario served him well. Customers in rural areas counted the days until his arrival. He was welcomed with open arms from everyone and he did ok financially.

And his Fuller Brush customers were 100% loyal.

Paul especially liked selling to the Jehovah's Witnesses on his route. They brought him into their homes and if he was patient enough to listen to their spiel and take a *Watchtower* or two, he was guaranteed a sale.

James and Deborah Armstrong also looked forward to Paul's visits. They knew he would listen to the Good News of the Kingdom, engage in conversation and allow them to read scriptures about the teachings of Jehovah.

On a warm autumn afternoon, Paul drove his '59 Dodge Wagon up the driveway of the Armstrong home. He smiled to himself as he unloaded two large suitcases filled to the brim with every style of brush and accessory imaginable. Paul was not a tall man, but he was muscular and strong. He lifted the heavy suitcases with ease and carried them to the door.

"Lorraine, Peter," Deborah called out. "Paul is here."

Lorraine and Peter came running. Everything in those suitcases seemed like treasures to them. The brushes for the men were thick-handled and heavy. "Guaranteed for Life," Paul reported. Deborah needed new buffer pads and new brushes for her Viking Floor polisher and Fuller Brush made them as well.

"Stay for a coffee?" Deborah asked rhetorically. She put the fresh grounds in the top of the Corning Ware and turned on the element.

"Kids, I have something you both might like," Paul said, smiling. The kids rushed to his side. Paul handed each of them a small, folding wooden ruler with Fuller Brush Products burned into the topside.

"I have another for your little brother as well," Paul added. Deborah took the third treasure and set it aside for Dougie.

"He will be home from the service soon, Paul. Thank you for always thinking of others."

Deborah poured the coffee and served Paul a warm tea biscuit. He sipped the rich dark liquid and savoured the fresh biscuit while Deborah started into a sermon about Jehovah God's gift of sharing.

"Wooden rulers for the children and new buffer pads and brushes for me. That's all for this month Paul," she said as he pushed the empty cup across the table to her. He packed up the two cases and shook hands with the appreciative threesome. He accepted the most recent copy of *The Watchtower* along with the payment for the brushes. He loved his job.

Lorraine and Peter stood on their tip toes looking out the window and waved good bye to the nice man. Paul threw *The Watchtower* in the back seat with the others. Next stop: Aylmer and then home.

As the dual red taillights of the station wagon disappeared, Lorraine and Peter immediately offered to buff the wooden floors. Deborah agreed. She knew the ritual. Peter would coat the felt buffers with the floor wax and place them on the bottom of the Viking.

"Come on Rainey, jump on!" Lorraine sat on the hump of the steel-bottomed machine and held on to the handle for support. Peter started the motor and off they went: up and down and up and down the hallway over the wooden floors.

Lorraine burst into song, "Yippee we are Free. Yippee we are Free," she sang over and over until the floors were gleaming and Peter was out of breath.

"Soon, you'll be too big to sit on the machine, Rainey. You're getting too heavy to push."

Later that night tucked in bed, Lorraine overheard the conversation between her parents.

"James, are you sure the time we spend talking to Paul when he is here can count toward this month's Kingdom Ministry?"

"Yes, absolutely Deborah. Any time we share the word of Jehovah God, we can record it on our record sheets. It does not matter if we preach the good news of the Kingdom in our own home or from door-to-door. It still counts."

Lorraine shrunk under the covers, livid with anger. *That is just not fair. Poor Paul Boates. He comes here every month with his brushes, and he gets preached at. At least he gets to drive away to freedom after his sixty-minute dose is over.*

6

A Clever Cover-up

"I will not," Lorraine snorted.

"There will be no more discussion," her mother warned. "You will return to the Hall and apologize."

Although the act in and of itself was nothing earthshattering, for Lorraine, it was monumental. She would not cave to her mother's wishes. At the same time, however, Lorraine also knew she stood on very shaky ground. When it came to matters of the Hall, there was little room for disagreement.

The Hall was her mother's second home. Selflessly, she volunteered day after day there. Sometimes she baked cookies for a shut-in Witness. Other times she sat at the bedside of an elderly widow. On Sundays, the heavy scent of sacrifice particularly permeated the house and electrified the air between daughter and mother.

Lorraine knew the order all too well. Jehovah God. Jesus Christ. Her father, and finally the children.

Fourth! Lorraine choked. *We are fourth and still she gets to order me around. Why. Why. Why?*

The Armstrong family was run largely by males and so Lorraine either cared for or answered to males while she was growing up. Peter was two years older and Dougie was a year younger. The pitcher incident involved her younger sibling.

"I don't understand why I should be the one to apologize. Dougie dropped the pitcher, not me," she said, glaring defiantly at her mother.

Lorraine stood ramrod straight. Her eyes locked on her mother's. Her voice had risen twenty decibels since they had returned from the Hall.

At that moment, Peter rounded the corner from the living room to the kitchen. Observing the battle lines drawn across the table, he knew it was time to act. He always felt compelled to rescue his sister whenever he saw her flounder into another black hole of disagreement. He loved his sister more than anything. The two of them were cast from the same mold: outspoken and confrontational, ready and willing to challenge everything.

On Sundays, they often broke ranks and hid behind the Hall when the other children were at lessons. Peter's excuses were always so fantastical, and he delivered them so eloquently and honestly that no one ever questioned their absence. Being the Elder's son might have carried some extra clout, but the children never saw it that way. They simply believed they were in the right and the adults in the wrong.

When Lorraine glimpsed at Peter standing in the doorway, her body relaxed somewhat. He grasped his mother's shoulders, spun her around and hugged her. His eyes, however, bored into Lorraine's. Peter lovingly held his mother at arm's length.

"Mom, I've got a better plan. Lorraine and I will go to the Hall together. We can replace the broken one with our old pitcher, the one with the painted strawberries on it. Two birds with one stone. They get another jug and we get rid of one that we don't even like," he said.

In a flash, Peter removed the pitcher from the cupboard, grabbed his sister's arm, led her out of the kitchen and down the front steps before his mother could say a word.

At the bottom of the sidewalk, they turned left and headed for the Hall. Peter turned to his sister. "Questions, questions, questions," he said. "When will you ever learn that your bullheadedness only angers Mom? Isn't this better than having to read the Bible all afternoon? You and I are free for at least an hour."

Lorraine took her brother's hand. At thirteen he was almost an adult, but on days like this, he was just her brother, the one who made everything all right.

"Thanks Peter. What will I ever do if you grow up and leave?"

"Don't think about that now. The rain has held off and I have ten cents in my pocket. How about an ice-cream for that throat of yours? It's overexerted itself today, that's for sure."

Grinning away her anger, Lorraine skipped along beside her brother. Peter always knew how to cheer her up, but still a dark cloud hung over her. Several weeks earlier in an old trunk in the far corner of the attic, she had found hundreds of Bible Tract pamphlets. Lorraine had heard the Armageddon stories for as long as she could remember and knew 1975 was coming.

She did not know, however, about the 1914 prediction that Charles Taze Russell himself had written about extensively. The articles in the trunk stated that the end of the world would take place in October of 1914. But that September when the First World War erupted, that prediction was moved ahead to 1915, a year before Russell's death. Other predictions followed, but none was as significant as the one in1914–15.

Lorraine squeezed her brother's hand tighter.

"What's bothering you now?" Peter asked.

Summoning every ounce of her courage, she replied, "Why did the world not end in 1915? Mom said that Aunt Jane thought the world was ending, so decided not to have children." Lorraine held her tongue until she couldn't hold it any longer. "The Elders lied, didn't they?"

"Dad explained it to me when I was your age. Apparently, those early times were miscalculations. Something about start and end dates. I never gave it any more thought," Peter added.

Still not completely satisfied, Lorraine stopped at the curb and turned to face Peter. She dug her hands into her skirt pocket.

"You've got to see this Peter," she insisted. "It's really old but I think this will change your mind about some things. I didn't put it back in the box because I was going to show it to Dad at the Bible study." She unfolded the two-page pamphlet and stuck it in Peter's face.

"Look at this picture, Peter. This Awake article is from 1915," she paused for effect. "1915! That's almost 50 years ago. It was wrinkly and old, but you can still read it. Here. Look at the picture. Look at the man's expression. He's smiling, isn't he? And the world is ending. His seven children on the stoop beside him look like skeletons, and he's smiling."

"What can that possibly mean?" she choked. "And see, the name under the title, Charles Taze Russell, the first president of Jehovah's Witnesses."

Peter paused and smiled at his sister. "Too many questions. Too much thinking. Let's just forget about the end of the world and enjoy the afternoon."

Lorraine shrugged and stuffed the paper into her pocket. *I'm not done with all this. Not by a long shot.*

7

Who Made These Rules Anyway?

Lorraine tiptoed into the vestibule and removed her shoes. Peter closed the front door behind her. Together, they entered the parlour and took their seats on the chairs by the window. Breaking the silence, the wicker slats sighed into the quiet. The flush of the outdoors slowly drained from their cheeks.

Lorraine moved her gaze from her parents' faces to Dougie's, each deep in meditation. The lesson was ending. Lorraine knew the signs. Deborah gently stroked Dougie's raven black curls. James reverently held his wife's hands. Their heads were bowed. The Bible lay open on the table.

The ticking of the mantel clock invaded the silence. One minute. Two.

Finally, James opened his eyes and acknowledged the children.

"Thank you both for helping little Douglas today. It is right to care for one another. Jehovah God is happy when families defer to his righteous will."

Lorraine kept her counsel. She knew that this was not the right time to ask questions. Forcing a smile, she nodded to her father.

Slowly, everyday household sounds broke the stillness. As her mother stood up, her cotton shift rustled softly. Her wedged sandals padded quietly across the hardwood floor. The lesson was over. Duty done, dinner was next. They all knew their jobs.

Lorraine set the table. James lifted the heavy roaster out of the oven. Peter helped his mother mash the potatoes and little Dougie placed the napkins by each plate. Deborah stood proudly watching her family work together.

Confrontation averted, Deborah sighed thankfully. For the past several weeks, she had tried to quell more debates than usual. She knew her only daughter pushed her buttons, but lately the questions threatened the faith and that would never do for Deborah.

Where did she come up with these things? Deborah wondered. *And why must she always question everything?* She dried her hands on the towel hanging from the stove. Lorraine shaped the linen napkins that Dougie had been haphazardly left on the plates into stylized roses. Deborah smiled at her daughter's artistry.

How creative! I would never have thought of that. Oh my, how will I ever manage her when she becomes a teenager?

*

Lorraine removed the plates but returned to the table for after dinner conversation. Rare as it was, she loved this time of the day. Thoughts of right or wrong faded into the distance and they were just a family enjoying each other's company. James placed his elbows on the table. Everyone relaxed.

"The chicken was delightful, Deborah. Just enough spice to make it interesting, but not enough to bring out the fire brigade." Deborah smiled at her husband appreciatively.

"My pleasure as always, my dear."

Absentmindedly, James' large mechanic's hands lifted and moved the utensils in regimented fashion beside his plate — all gears and levers. He looked directly at his first born.

"I expect it won't be long Peter, until you and I should get behind the wheel for your driving lessons. Driving a shift is one of the most important skills you can learn, and the sooner the better. What do you think about meeting me at the shop tomorrow after school and we can get started?"

Lorraine's heart sank. *Peter? Driving?* She felt her heart beat faster. The fear of losing her only ally suddenly became a real threat. She couldn't help it. She interrupted her father.

"He's only thirteen. He can't get his license until he is fourteen."

Peter glanced at his sister, shock and anger warring in his brain.

"It's good to start early," he said echoing his father. "And I will be fourteen sometime this year."

Jehovah's Witnesses did not celebrate birthdays, so none of the children knew their exact birthdate, only the year. However, Peter had already secretly chosen a date that he would use on his license. His birthday would be September 15.

Lorraine clamped her mouth shut. She did not expect her brother to be drawn into their father's trap. Growing up. Moving out. Finding a job. Starting his own Jehovah's Witness family.

"Lorraine, I am surprised at you," her mother added. "Are you not proud of your brother? This is 1964 and with only eleven years until Armageddon predicted by the Bethel Overseers, he must become a productive citizen, one worthy of spiritual purity."

There it was again. The Cleansing. The end of the world.

Lorraine couldn't stop them. The words spilled out of her mouth in a cascade of injustice.

"Who made these rules anyway? You can't fool me. I know that Charles Taze Russell's 1914 prediction of Armageddon did NOT come true. So how can we believe this one? I would really like to meet this Charles Taze Russell. I have a few questions for him."

Charles Taze Russell

8

Remnants of the Righteous

Along with many other families who lived on the north side of the Allegheny River, across from the city of Pittsburgh, the Russells — Charles and his parents, Joseph and Eliza, along with his little sister, Margaret — attended the Pittsburgh Presbyterian church.

November had seen an unprecedented number of days of unseasonably warm temperatures, so following the service, the family decided to enjoy the Public Gardens. Charles dropped his mother's hand and skipped along ahead.

"Don't run, Charles," his mother warned. "You don't want to soil your pants."

But Charles knew it was less about him dirtying his pants than it was about her keeping up to an energetic eight-year-old. His mother always seemed out of breath. Her shoulders heaved when coughs wracked her small frame. Her hands constantly clutched a napkin. He obediently slowed his pace.

Joseph wrapped his right arm around his wife and held little Margaret's hand with his left. They found a quiet bench overlooking the brook and for long minutes, nuzzled close against one another, the sun hopscotching from tree to tree. Eventually, Charles pulled his gaze away from the view and turned to look directly into his mother's hollow eyes.

"It's very beautiful, isn't it mother? It makes me feel good inside. Like I do in church."

"Yes, it is lovely. Whenever we come here I am reminded of your three little brothers."

As she spoke, her eyes suddenly changed. Instead of distant and lost, they shone with a manic radiance. Eliza circled her son's fingers with her thin hands and brought them close to her chest.

"You must promise me one thing, my darling," she said. "Don't ever forget that although God's beauty is all around us, the darkness lurks just beyond our Garden of Eden. We must always be good, so as not to fall prey to Satan. If we falter, he will drag us to Hell for all eternity."

Despite the warm sun on his back, Charles shuddered, his young brain unable to reconcile the beauty and the beast of his faith.

Whenever Eliza was overwhelmed by the burden of grief, she closed the shutters of her brain and railed against God for the loss of three of her babes, the latest four months earlier. But losing Joseph Jr., her youngest, to diphtheria had defeated her. Late into the night, in the days and weeks leading up to his death, Charles had heard his little brother's rasping struggle for air. Caved beneath two feather pillows, the sound still assaulted his ears. When little Joseph finally tumbled into exhausted sleep, his mother's soft whimpering filled the silence.

And so, the family spent one of their last Sunday afternoons together. Frail and grief-laden, Eliza died of consumption a couple of months later. At thirty-six years of age on a snowy January 24, three months before the start of the War Between the States, she joined the majority. Young Charles had just passed his ninth birthday.

Devastated at the loss of his wife and charged with the upbringing of two small children, Joseph threw himself into his work. He read the Bible daily and with each passing season looked to Christ for direction. In hindsight,

Joseph's decision to remain in Pittsburgh rather than return to his family home in Philadelphia turned out to be fortuitous. The steel factories as well as the continued improvement of rail routes brought thousands of workers as the call came for more goods: weapons, cannons, rail cars and mile after mile of steel rails.

In 1866, Joseph opened a shirt factory which was so successful that he could hardly meet the demand. More haberdasheries followed. By the time Charles was of working age, Joseph managed a chain of successful men's clothing stores. When young Charles turned twelve, he joined his father's business. Russell's Men's Furnishings was the place to go for the greatest selection of men's wear.

Charles felt stifled in the haberdashery back-office rooms where he scribbled sales receipts, purchased inventory, and signed cheques. As each day passed in a repetition of boredom, he choked on the hollow desert of his life. His faith no longer spoke to him. Neither God's beauty nor Satan's hell moved him.

"Charles, the hack is here. Are you ready for church, son?"

"Not today, father," he answered despondently. Week after week his father received the same response.

*

With the cessation of hostilities in 1865, America was ripe for change. With the South's defeat, Charles felt his country faced a dilemma not unlike his own, but in the case of the country, the Union had remained intact. The security he had once enjoyed within the walls of the church, however, no longer satisfied him. Young Charles made the first of many decisions. It was time to leave the Presbyterian Church.

He was thirteen years old.

Sunday after Sunday, Charles walked the smoky streets of the city silently grieving the death of his mother. Although he felt emotionally adrift without a female's moderating hand, he began to understand that her loss had helped to forge the independent young man he had become. His mother's quiet confidence gave him courage in his darkest moments. Years later, he would say it was her spirit which instructed him to once again search out God. With new eyes, Charles set his sights on The Revival movement.

*

In the mid-19th Century, revivalist faiths spread like wild fire up the Allegheny, down the Ohio, along the Missouri, and into Tennessee and parts west. Along the rivers and then via the railway, the church followed the pioneers.

Held in isolated places, camp meetings attracted hundreds —or even thousands — their main goal: recruitment. Meetings often lasted two or three days and followed an arc of great emotional power. The converts were shown how to observe God in the natural world, and that faith was an intimate relationship between God and the individual. Days of prayer, singing, and preaching emphasized the individual's sins, and the need to turn to Christ and restore the sinner to personal salvation.

Carried on a collective high, camp attendees raised their arms and fell on the ground in a frenzy of piety. Revivalist congregations grew like mushrooms. Early fundamentalist churches promised members a personal relationship with Christ and a deep faith based on the Bible alone.

On a dreary Thursday evening on his walk home from his father's store, eighteen-year-old Charles chanced to buy the evening edition of the Pittsburgh Herald. Not wanting to face his empty rooms, he settled in a quiet corner in the men's smoking room of the Adelphi Hotel on 5th Street. He ordered a snifter of brandy and watched the crowds of visitors and merchants cross the lobby. Busy. Driven. Focused.

Luxuriating in the liquor's warmth, Charles set the glass on a coaster and opened the paper.

He had never read any of the popular evangelical tracts, but on this night, he did. As he read, tears welled in his eyes, and within his chest his heart fluttered with anticipation and hope. The author of the piece, Jonas Wendell, leaped off the page. Charles felt Wendell spoke directly to him. The words melted his stiff resolve. He felt stirred.

An hour later, with a spring in his step, he headed home. His yearnings might have been answered — a faith with which he could connect personally. A faith with strong ties to the Bible.

9

Cult Builders

Charles Taze Russell took the steps two at a time, sluffing off the heavy atmosphere of years of structure and rules. He caught the streetcar towards the Advent Christian Church in Allegheny, Pennsylvania where he had begun attending a few months earlier. Ten minutes later, he tugged the streetcar cord. His heart fluttered in anticipation as he climbed the church steps where a well-groomed young man greeted him.

"Welcome, Charles. I trust you are ready to be inspired. Jonas Wendell's text today is the Second Coming and you can bet his delivery will be memorable, as always."

Charles sat in the second row from the front. Whitewashed walls devoid of papal iconography or statuary reflected the pure simplicity of the Congregationalists' faith. Atop a large lectern rested the most recent translation of the Word of the Lord. Charles turned to the man next to him, a newcomer.

"Welcome Brother," he said. "Let the Word of God enter your heart and mind."

Jonas Wendell's church was the only place Charles felt liberated. As he settled into his seat, he tightened his tie, smoothed his trousers and laid his Bible reverently in his lap. It was the same book he had read as a boy, but Pastor Wendell dared him to see it with fresh eyes.

Since Charles had never been afraid to go where others dared not, it was no surprise that he was consumed with the prophecies hidden in the language of metaphor in the Holy Book.

*

The Second Coming, the Great Awakenings, the Seventh Millennial and many other enlightened dreams of the faithful littered the religious chronicles of the 1800s. Christ's return, both to destroy sinners and restore paradise on earth, was imminent and the Congregationalists believed it would happen in America. Two movements had laid the groundwork for the tumultuous changes that impacted America: The Romantic Revolution and the awakening of Revivalism.

In the late 18th and early 19th centuries, conditions were ripe for young idealists like Charles. Poets, musicians and painters, the rock stars of the day, abandoned reason and intellect in favour of passionate emotion and the exhilaration of the senses. Their rebellion against the formal rules and tradition of the Neoclassical Age validated the creative spirit of the individual.

Their music swelled with political fervor, their poetry transported readers into the farthest reaches of their minds, and their paintings depicted the raw beauty of jagged mountains, tumultuous waves and savage beasts. This same rebellious spirit impacted the heroic efforts of ordinary individuals who led the revolutionary forces to victory over the British.

Following the American Revolution when Americans were forging their new nation, the leaders turned their backs on the skeptical rationalism and deism of the established religions of Britain and Europe. America was a young country led by energetic leaders who looked boldly to the future.

In addition, America's unprecedented natural beauty evoked a fervent emotional response which satisfied the individual's lust for the mysterious, the simple, and the contemplative. Heralded as the Land of Hope, America rang with dreams of freedom and equality. Immigrant ships could not be built fast enough to bring the hordes of humanity seeking the new world.

With the Declaration of Independence ringing jubilantly in their minds and hearts, the Founding Fathers took a bold step in their Constitution's First Amendment. The church and state were declared forever separate, thus setting the stage for a great religious transformation: Revivalism, the second movement to shape the young country.

New immigrants from crowded, dirty, industrial Europe viewed America as a pristine Eden, a perfect setting to recover pure, uncorrupted and original Christianity. By the 1800s, Evangelical denominations, particularly Baptist and Methodists, were the fastest growing religions in the young nation. Their ministry depended largely upon itinerant preachers, known as circuit riders who took their message of salvation to the people in the backcountry and to pioneers settling frontier regions. They were joyously received.

*

"Stand my friends. Lift your arms to the Lord. Confess your sins. Turn your hope to the perfection of our society," Wendell's voice rose, echoing from the rafters and filling the spectators with intense conviction. "Become a Missionary. Spread the word. The time is upon us. In just four short years, Christ will return." His words did not fall on deaf ears.

In the early Revivalist tradition, missionaries shared their stories of Christ's return with strangers and believers alike. Charles gravitated to this aspect of evangelism. With his gift of superb speaking skills, Charles believed he could convince anyone about anything. It was this resolve that led him to dedicate his life to sharing God's Truth.

The spiritual high the congregation experienced at the meeting did not dissipate. Brothers and preachers, missionaries and lay people slapped new converts on the back and pushed the newest writings of the American Bible Society into their hands. Desperately, the newly converted grabbed for the papers.

Charles was alive with fervent energy. He could hardly contain his enthusiasm. Christ's Second Coming, His Advent imminent; Charles vibrated with the need to serve. It didn't matter where, so long as he could serve. In the Temperance Movement, prison reform, the insane, the handicapped — the options were limitless. Charles wanted to be part of the movement to bring others to the perfect state of faith, to ready the world to meet the Lord Jesus. *The Bible. Of course! Deep study of the Bible will be my calling to bring others to the Truth.*

The jostling of the streetcar on the cobblestones relaxed him somewhat, but as he pressed his face to the window his eyes were drawn to the scene outside. In the dark, the sidelights of the streetcar illuminated buildings, stone fences and walkways. Charles watched. Suddenly he sat up and took notice. *It's a blank canvas,* he thought. *A perfect place for silent and passive messaging.* It was a simple, but brilliant idea. Charles figured that if people didn't have time to go to their Bibles, he would bring The Book to them.

He rang the bell a full five stops from his home. He rushed on to the street and into the general store where he bought six boxes of chalk. For the next three weeks, Charles was alive with purpose. Every morning passersby were greeted with lines of scripture scrawled on buildings, fences, borders — anywhere the chalk would adhere. It was the first step in his great quest for Truth.

In the summer of 1870, Russell convinced his father to sell all the haberdashery stores. With close to $300,000 in their pockets, they were able to devote every waking hour to the quest for truth. With some Adventist acquaintances, Russell established a group to undertake an analytical study of the Bible and the origins of Christian doctrine, creed, and tradition. The work filled him with zeal and purpose.

Russell was not particularly bound to the Great Disappointment of 1844 espoused by other Adventist groups like the Millerites. In that year, Baptist Minister William Miller's prediction that Jesus Christ would return to earth sometime between March 21,1843 and March 21,1844 to cleanse, purify, and take possession of all the Saints did not come to pass.

Because of the Millerites' failure, Charles' early missionary work did not focus on end of time prophecies. Instead, he employed his many gifts of hard work, persuasive writing talents, and dynamic public speaking to tell Christ's story. Charles Russell's Bible students hung on his every word, and, in turn, he was transformed as they accepted God's word. He had found his true vocation.

Professing that the established churches had distanced themselves from the Word of God, Bible Student groups popped up all over the country. Dissatisfied with organized religion and empowered with the notion that Jesus Christ alone was the path to Truth, young Christians followed the charismatic

Russell to found missions and Bible student groups all over Pennsylvania. Charles left the Adventist congregation and named himself Pastor.

But Russell was not the only independent preacher of the time.

*

Nelson Homer Barbour, an Adventist pastor 25 years Russell's senior, had been publicly humiliated and branded a delusional zealot when his 1873–1874 prediction of Christ's return to earth failed. Although many of Barbour's Adventists left the movement, he continued to write tracts in the popular Adventist Magazine, *Herald of the Morning*. It was just a matter of time before their paths would cross.

In the winter of 1876, after reading Nelson Barbour's publication of *Evidences for the Coming of the Lord*, Charles financed Barbour to come to Philadelphia to discuss how to proceed in the aftermath of the most recent unfulfilled prediction of 1873–1874.

10

An Unhappy Partnership

"When will this cold snap be over?" Charles muttered to himself as he pushed the bronze plate on the large revolving door to the outdoor platforms. The dry air clenched at his lungs and ripped his breath away.

The 6:50 Special from Syracuse steamed into the station and slowly come to rest on Track 2, its huge engine spewing steam and plumes of smoke upwards to the glass roof, 100 feet above. Charles walked down the platform until he reached the Lincoln Park car. A tall dark porter stood at the ready to assist passengers as they descended the stairs. Charles waited for Barbour to disembark.

He inspected the car's tall gold capital letters. Only the rich and famous could afford the fare on a Pullman car. Charles pulled his hat down over his ears and drew his coat tighter, but nails of cold still worked their way through the fabric. He had been in Philadelphia for a month, and expected to remain for a couple more, but he certainly did not welcome the cold which had settled in with a vengeance. Before Charles had a moment to shift from his left to his right foot, Barbour walked down the steps of the car.

"I would know you anywhere, Charles," Nelson Barbour laughed as he strode towards Charles. "That full white beard of yours is hard to miss. I am thrilled to meet you in person." Nelson Barbour took Charles' arm with both hands and after a long congenial handshake they wrapped their arms around one another.

"Let's get you to the hotel. A good walk will shake out the stiffness of the journey," Charles said, smiling and shivering.

Over dinner, then breakfast and several meals for weeks to come, the men conferred. Charles enlightened Nelson on the nature of Christ's return, known as the Ransom, and the errors of the Creeds. In turn, Nelson enlightened Charles regarding the harmony of Biblical and prophetic chronology. Nelson believed was the Harvest had begun and boldly predicted that the Rapture of the 144,000 heavenly co-rulers would occur on Passover 1878.

For the next several years the two men collaborated and published many articles in *The Herald of the Morning.* Charles followed the tenet that at his return Christ would remain invisible and only true followers would discern His return. Such exclusivity appealed to a wide variety of readers.

But Barbour disagreed.

Barbour argued, "I, too, believe that Christ will return as a spirit since he was resurrected as a spirit rather than a man of flesh and bones, and that only his true followers will discern his return. But I also stand by the fact that those who have been unfaithful to the Truth will be consumed by their sins and destroyed. Our mission is to help others understand this truth and show them the errors of their ways. To bring them into the flock."

"My dear Nelson, the object and manner of our Lord's return must surely be to bless the earth, not burn it up," Charles pressed his friend. "For years I struggled with the existence of a literal Hell of fire and brimstone. There simply cannot be such a place if we believe in God's mercy."

"But Charles, we give our brethren false hope in your view of a Christ who would be benevolent to all of mankind. Sinners must pay. There can be no amnesty with God. When Christ did not return in 1873 nor in1874, my people were heartbroken, and I was completely embarrassed. If we recant on the existence of Hell, perhaps they will not believe us."

"No, Nelson, this is not a time to change what we believe, we just have to figure out what happened. I cannot accept that the chronology was incorrect, but there must be an error in the calculation. We must go back to the

Scriptures to reconsider what they were actually saying about the nature of the first resurrection."

Russell slapped his palms on the table between them, "Of course. How could we be so silly? The invisible arrival of our Lord must have already started. We have the whole concept wrong. When the faithful die, they don't just sleep waiting for new life, they are changed immediately into their new bodies."

And so, it continued back and forth until late in 1880, when Nelson published his tracts about the meaning of the symbols of the Jewish Tabernacle. Charles believed Nelson was in the wrong and wrote articles discrediting Barbour's views and claiming what the true understanding of the symbols should be. When the two men's doctrinal debates took over the content of the articles, the partnership abruptly ended.

In 1881, Russell began writing his own tracts appropriately named the *Zion's Watch Tower* and *Herald of Christ's Presence*. Russell named his Bible group The Watchtower Bible Society recognizing that his followers must watch steadfastly for Christ's return. Finally, to ensure complete control over all parts of the editing process, Russell purchased a publishing company. It was a brilliant move.

Later that same year, Zion's Watchtower Bible and Tract Society became a legal entity when William Henry Conley, a prominent Pittsburgh steel industry businessman was appointed the Society's first president. William Conley, his wife, Sarah Conley, and the Russell family, father Joseph, Charles and his sister Margaret were the five original Bible Students of the Society.

While Charles' growing community of missionaries delivered the teachings of the Bible Society, the publishing company produced and distributed Russell's articles, stories, letters, and prophecies; Russell was a committee of one. All work was signed off by him and by the mid-1890s, he addressed his growing flock as Pastor Russell.

11

The Snake in the Grass

Maria Frances Ackley joined the Bible group in the fall of 1878. She was a bright rising star in the Pittsburgh social scene who believed that her own business career would take off if she surrounded herself with charismatic men of strong character. It was with this enterprise in mind that she applied to work as a scribe at the Watchtower Bible and Tract Society. She was quick with a pen and had a superb memory. By March, Maria and Charles were married.

Marriage, however, did not slow Charles' zealous dedication to spreading the Truth. Russell spoke to congregations and led Bible sessions almost daily. Neither did it produce any children; in fact, many people believed theirs was a celibate union. Such rumours gained credence when the couple retreated into separate apartments in the new Bethel headquarters on Columbia Street in New York, speculating that perhaps theirs was a platonic marriage only.

Maria shared an office with her husband and spent equally long hours with him writing narratives, doctrinal statements or tracts explaining scripture. One evening after working on a piece until she felt it was ready to publish, she brought it to Charles for a final edit.

"My dear, I see here that you have signed your name at the bottom of the article."

"Of course, Charles, why would I not?"

Charles stood, thrusting the papers inches from her face.

"You are never to sign your name on anything. I am the only one with that right."

"But you didn't write it," Maria protested. "This is my work. Marriage is an equal partnership. In work as well as life."

"That interpretation is nothing but so much cotton fluff in your mind. I am the editor and my name — and my name alone — signs all work printed in my magazine. Regardless of who wrote it," Charles spoke with steel defiance. He turned on his heel and strode out of the room leaving the door shivering on its hinges in his wake. It would be the first of many embittered battles between Charles and Maria.

Regardless of the ups and downs of their personal life, some insiders noted that something snapped in his mind following a serious fall a few weeks after the publication argument. Heavily reliant on Laudanum following the fall, Russell often seemed to be in a trancelike state whenever he took the podium to speak to congregations. His voice rose and fell in wild modulations: and buoyed up in a frenzy of urgency for his faithful to go forth and teach all nations the Truth, he spoke for hours at a time. The push to gather more converts consumed his days.

But despite his great successes as a self-professed pastor preaching God's gospel, Charles Taze Russell's life was plagued by controversy. Russell was either in the courts or the tabloids for his entire adult life.

In 1890, his wife Maria accused her husband of immoral conduct and sued for divorce. In1906, in an Ontario court of law, Rev John Ross attempted to prove that Charles Taze Russell was a fraud: that he had never been ordained as a minister, nor could he read Hebrew or Greek, a necessity if he were to understand the ancient texts. Russell's publication of *Millennial Dawn* was disclaimed as heretical by all the established religious institutions.

In 1911, Russell was in Court again, this time to disprove claims that he was personally profiting from the Jehovah's Witness Miracle Wheat campaign. *The Brooklyn Daily Eagle* accused Russell of duping his followers in the sale of the miraculous brand of wheat. The paper published an unflattering cartoon of the religious leader with his wheat. According to the paper, Russell sold the wheat at $1 a pound to hundreds of members of the Bible Society, espousing the wheat would produce five times the yield of any other brand of wheat.

Russell subsequently filed a law suit against the paper's cartoonist for the hefty sum of $100,000. For months, Russell's name was dragged through the tabloids. When the jury found him guilty, he had no choice but to launch a strong defence to salvage his reputation.

Citing Christ's suffering at the hands of imperfect judges two thousand years before, Russell magnanimously accepted the law's sentence. He argued that the court of man was far less important than God's final judgment, and Russell put his trust in the higher eternal court. Glibly, his faithful accepted their pastor's words agreeing that Charles had been wrongfully indicted. Charles accepted such exoneration from his flock with a humble haughtiness.

Although Russell's alleged statements about Miracle Wheat would haunt him and disgrace him during the final years of his life, the wheat fiasco paled in comparison to Russell's confusing and conflicting articles about the end of time and Christ's Second Coming: The Cleansing.

According to Adventist beliefs, Christ had already returned to earth in 1873, and was in their midst, but in invisible form. By their calculations, the end of times would arrive in 1914. Russell concurred with this date based on the scriptural numbers from Revelations 12:6 prophesizing 1260 years marked the period from the beginning of Papal rule in 539AD to 1799AD, the beginning of "the time of the end." Few Witnesses today are aware that 1799 was pivotal to the very existence of Jehovah's Witnesses. It was this concept which began the Enlightenment and indeed the Adventist movement of the 1800s. Russell gloried in his end of time belief system as it heralded God's salvation plan for the entire world.

Using the 115 years from the start of the end of time, Adventists could determine the date of Armageddon to be 1914; it would be the ultimate battle between God and the Devil. In 1914, war, disease, famine and persecution would raze the world. Capitalism and communism would meet in a cataclysmic struggle after which Christ would return to rule his kingdom. And Russell's loyal followers would be ready.

Early in 1904, Russell and The Watchtower Society publicized the 1914 Armageddon date as the Harvest of the Faithful. One hundred forty-four thousand would be raised and the remaining great multitude of the faithful would sleep in death, rather than in a literal Hell, before their earthly resurrection.

From the Brethren in the headquarters of the Organization in New York to the hundreds of worthy Circuit Men and thousands of Elders, the decree was simple: family, friends, job and education came second to the rule of the Organization.

Followers looked forward to the day when the 144,000 anointed would be raised to heaven, while the remaining faithful witnesses would live in a paradise free of poverty, disease, or pain.

And who would not want to be one of God's faithful Witnesses?

12

Fallout

The Brooklyn Daily Eagle offered no respite in their pursuit of Pastor Russell's activities.

In 1911, the paper got wind of the real story behind the separation of Russell and his wife, Maria. The testimony document painted a less than hallowed picture of the Pastor, deemed an amorous jellyfish who floated around looking for unsuspecting young women. Maria claimed she had suffered many instances of mental abuse in a marriage of forced celibacy and cold indifference. Russell naturally denied it all and retreated into the protective offices of The Watchtower and Bible Tract Society. It was imperative that he protect his interests as further documents revealed that he owned 990 of the 1000 shares in *The Watchtower* publishing business.

Charles pounded the table making the cups clatter.

"Now what are they digging up against me? All my hard work! My good name. My thousands of Witnesses yearning for salvation!" His voice raged as he paced frenetically around the room. "Can they not see that I am in the right?" he bellowed.

Joseph Franklin Rutherford waited patiently for the rage to pass. Almost 60, Russell had not weathered well over the years. His long white beard hung matted and full below his chin. Deep lines gouged and mapped his face, a consequence of constant chronic pain and years of dependency on laudanum.

Recently appointed legal counsel for The Watchtower and Bible Tract Society, Rutherford had just celebrated the 5th anniversary of his baptism into Russell's Bible Student Movement. Patiently, the younger man watched his leader rave against the press.

"They don't have a leg to stand on, Charles. Everything they write is hearsay at best. Don't let it trouble you."

"Of course, you are correct, my dear friend and colleague, but still the barbs sting."

"Not unlike the pain our dear Saviour endured, and look at his glorious resurrection and imminent return," Rutherford interjected as a calming argument. "Savour it, Savour it."

Charles closed the newspaper and returned his attention to Joseph, his friend and greatest supporter for more than five years.

"How about joining me in a scotch?" Joseph knew the alcohol would still his friend's anger, and harmony would return to their meeting. Russell waved his arm magnanimously to the well-stocked liquor cabinet. "Choose your pleasure."

Rutherford uncorked the fifteen-year-old Glenfiddich and lightly passed the bottle beneath his nose. The aroma took him back to the early days of his conversion.

"I was thinking this morning about the day I opened your *Millennial Dawn* series," he said. "Your words dissolved the skepticism and salacious contempt I had for religion, any religion for that matter. In my mind, they were all shallow, insincere and hypocritical. And now, here we are together on the greatest journey of all time."

Charles walked across the plush carpet and with a rough grasp on Joseph's shoulder, smiled deeply.

"Yes indeed. The greatest journey." Pausing a moment to collect his thoughts, Charles began slowly. "1914 will soon be here and already the faithful are making choices in preparation for His coming: fathers not planting crops, women remaining childless, businessmen selling their shops. They want nothing to distract them from the hope of resurrection. The Harvest will be glorious, Joseph."

His friend nodded in agreement.

"The world stage is on the cusp of terrible and beautiful change," Russell continued. "European powers are arming themselves against threats lurking in the shadows. Beyond the light, the Asian monarchies are flexing their muscles; and Africa, the Dark Continent, is smoldering. The world is a tinder box. Come it will."

Russell sat, flushed and breathless.

*

And rage it did. Bible students who refused to sign up for military service were persecuted, thrown in jail or killed. During the war, Bible groups were banned in Canada and other countries while many members were convicted under the Seditious Behavior Act in the US.

Russell died on October 31,1916, having devoted most of his adult life to the Bible movement. Although the End of Time had yet again eluded his flock, he sought to guarantee the movement's future with his will, his final tract to his followers.

In the opening clause of Russell's two-page will, he declared his love and Christian good wishes for his Bible House Family and co-labourers in the Harvest work. The remainder of the document outlined his objectives for the future structure of the Organization, particularly with regards to the editorial committee charged with writing the Organization's articles.

Russell donated his journals and copyrights to The Watchtower Bible and Tract Society with the express intent that they be used according to his wishes in perpetuity. The following excerpt from his will shows one of those wishes.

"I direct that the entire editorial charge of ZION'S WATCH TOWER *shall be in the hands of a committee of five brethren whom I exhort to great carefulness and fidelity to the truth. All articles appearing in the columns of* ZION'S WATCH TOWER *shall have the unqualified approval of at least three of the committee of five, and I urge that if any matter approved by three be known or supposed to be contrary to the views of one or both of the other members of the committee, such articles shall be held over for thought, prayer and discussion for three months before being published — that so far as possible the unity of the faith and the bonds of peace may be maintained in the editorial management of the journal."*

Despite disagreements over the election process, Rutherford became president of The Watchtower Bible and Tract Society in 1917. Many bitter disputes followed. Some claimed that Rutherford was not abiding by Russell's wishes by publishing his own work rather than Russell's. In 1925, in a coup over the five Brethren, Joseph Franklin Rutherford — Russell's former friend and legal counsel — became the de facto single leader of the sect.

By 1929 more than three quarters of the Bible student congregations had rejected Rutherford's changes in organizational structure, doctrinal interpretations and congregational practices, which began to appear in the material published by The Watchtower Bible and Tract Society.

In 1931, the remaining congregations supportive of Rutherford adopted the new name of Jehovah's Witnesses and renamed their magazine *The Watchtower.*

Eight years later as another conflict threatened the globe, Bethel headquarters launched The Millions, the largest Jehovah's Witness recruitment campaign of the 20th Century. Kingdom Halls were erected in anticipation of a massive influx of new members.

In the small rural community of Straffordville, Ontario, two young people named Deborah Winters and James Armstrong fell in love at a local barn dance and left their established religions to join the Hall. Their search for salvation, however, would come at an enormous cost.

Deborah

13

Love to share

Deborah Winters wasn't sure what to make of the sounds coming from the basket at the foot of the couch. Her mother and father never used to sit quietly inside the house in the middle of the day. Why now?

"Sweetheart," her mother crooned, "Why don't you come and sit by me on the couch and I will tell you a wonderful story?"

Deborah climbed up between her parents, her eyes on the basket which continued to move gently from side to side. Within minutes, sounds of soft hiccupping and smacking of lips began to rise from the basket.

Deborah nuzzled her body against her mother and began to suck nervously on the long strawberry blond braid which dangled over her right shoulder. Whenever she was nervous, she unconsciously reached for her braid and stuffed it into her mouth.

And she was nervous and excited all in one. She didn't know what to make of the situation at all. Deborah turned toward her mother as she began to speak.

"Once upon a time there was a mother named Christine and a father named Robert who had the most beautiful little daughter whose name was Deborah."

"Just like my name," Deborah squealed with glee.

"Yes, indeed," her mother said patting her daughter's chubby little hands.

"But the mother and father thought the little girl was lonely. That she should have a playmate. Well, it wasn't long before God heard their prayer and they were granted a wonderful gift, a little boy with beautiful blue eyes."

Deborah's own eyes grew larger.

"He was very little when they brought him home to his new house to meet his sister, but even though he couldn't say anything just then, he was very happy to meet her."

"Will I get a little boy to play with soon, Mother?"

"Yes, I believe you will indeed," her mother cooed softly as she kissed Deborah's cheeks. "Are you ready to meet our little Roger?"

"Oh yes."

Robert Winters smiled at Christine. This was the moment. He walked over to the basket and gently lifted out a bundle of something. The dancing cows and horses on the soft flannelette caught Deborah's eyes first.

Pulling aside the blanket, Deborah considered little Roger's pudgy pink face for the first time. He was a perfect doll and she could hardly wait to play with him.

"Deborah, meet Roger Winters."

She came closer to inspect this new creature. This Roger. Her brother. She touched his cheek, his hands and then turned to her parents and grinned.

"I think he will do just fine. When will he be able to play tag and hop-scotch, Father?"

"Well not for a little while, but you will be surprised how fast the time will pass before he will be holding your hand as you take him to school for the first time. Do you want to help me put him to bed in his own room?"

"Yes, of course."

Deborah followed close behind her father trying to grab the blanket which trailed behind him.

"Be careful, Deborah. He is very little and very precious." Somehow, Deborah felt a little bit less precious as the sting of her father's reprimand slapped her face.

Hurt, she turned towards her mother on the couch, but her mother's smile seemed to fly over Deborah's head and settle on the baby in her husband's arms, completely ignoring Deborah.

14

Showers of Tears

With ever increasing difficulty, ten-year-old Deborah lifted her feet one after the other along the sodden path. Muddy water sloshed precariously near the rim of her boots, and whenever the mud pushed hard against the rubbers, her squished feet threatened to escape from inside the boot. With each step she feared her shiny red boots might be sucked into the mud and lost forever.

She raced against time to get home in time to clean her boots before her father stormed through the front door to confront her and her irresponsible behaviour. Deborah heard her father's sharp criticism in her mind, *Why didn't you leave earlier? You must have heard the rain?*

But she hadn't. Not until she stepped out on the verandah at Iris Connolly's house a mile away.

Normally the creek was a burbling little brook which happily accompanied her as she skipped along the path when she went to play with her friend, Iris Connolly. But a quick spring thaw paired with the torrential storm that had barreled across the lake with no warning, created her present dilemma. While they played, the rain had swollen the creek and overflowed its banks turning the path into a quagmire.

Sorry Papa. I was having so much fun that I didn't hear the rain. No, that will never do! He will rage at that.

She slowed her pace a bit.

As soon as I heard the rain hit the windows, I left for home. She experimented with the response. *Yes,* she thought, *much more responsible.*

Deborah passed the fence post at the corner of her yard. Globs of mud flying behind her, she ran up the path to the front door. She stopped to listen. Quiet. They were not yet back from shopping.

Deborah sat on the ledge of the verandah and pulled off her boots. *Nothing that a bit of rain water won't fix,* she laughed breathlessly.

With great gusto, she slapped the boots together releasing most of the mud, and then skipped along the verandah to the rain barrel by the corner of the house. She placed her boots below the spigot at the bottom of the barrel, turned the handle all the way to the right and with her left hand washed off the boots.

A few minutes later, she placed her prized possessions next to her mother's garden shoes by the front door. Hearing her parent's car turn the corner of the drive, Deborah flung herself into the deck swing, picked up her mother's copy of *Harper's Bazaar* and pretended to be entranced with the latest fashions.

As the car pulled up to the house, Deborah's mother smiled. She helped five-year-old Roger from the back seat and carried him across the muddy walk and set him down squarely on the verandah. Robert pinched his son's cheeks as he placed a new model airplane into his hands.

Deborah felt the slight for a split second, then smiled at her little brother.

"Hope you didn't get too wet on the way home, sweetheart?" her mother asked.

"Not at all Mum. I heard the rain start to really come down and left right away," she fibbed. "My new boots kept my feet totally dry."

15

Fiddles and Freedom

Deborah lifted the record and placed it on the turntable. Lately, she had taken a liking to the fiddle. But it wasn't the fiddle alone which Deborah loved. It was the dancing that went along with it.

At seventeen, Deborah fairly flew along the dance floor, her tap shoes in a whirlwind of swoops and points barely touching the worn planks. On a whim, she had joined Iris at the community centre for dance lessons. Old fashioned dance lessons. Deborah and Iris loved to dance the Two-Step and the Polka, but they longed to dance the happy jigs and reels of Ireland. Toe-tapping music they called it.

"What do you think of the new teacher, Deborah?" Iris asked when they rushed to the water fountain for a drink.

"She's wonderful, but every time I leave the house now, I see the look of disapproval on my dad's face. He believes that dancing is bad for the soul. Especially the soul of a Baptist."

"Wasn't dancing really important in the Bible? The Lord of the Dance and all," Iris countered.

"Maybe, but I'm afraid that he will soon forbid me to come to dance lessons. So far, Mother has been able to keep him from making an edict, but I worry."

"Don't. There's nothing wrong in dancing."

"Easy for you to say, Iris. You're not a Baptist like me."

"Well if there is a problem, why don't you become something else? God is God, isn't he? And you're an adult. You can choose for yourself."

Deborah had never imagined such a blasphemous idea, but as the lesson wore on and she tapped and shimmied across the floor, the thought continued to grow. *Yes. Perhaps I can choose for myself.*

*

The posters were up all over town. The Barn Dance was to be the highlight of the social scene in Straffordville. Everyone between the ages of two and ninety-two would be in attendance. Robert had not forbidden Deborah to go, but he had not given her his blessing.

"Dancing out in public like that is sinful," he argued, "and I don't like others seeing you in those sleeveless dresses."

"Oh, Daddy, don't be so old fashioned. This is 1939. The world is different from when you and Mom met. Why don't you come? Roger's already there, I bet, looking forward to dancing, climbing the hay bales and eating corn on the cob. He's almost fifteen and already taller than everyone in the family. He's thinking about joining the Air Force if there's a war. We aren't babies anymore, you know."

As they stared at each other across the kitchen table, the words hung heavily between them. To break the tension, Deborah jumped out of her chair and headed to her room. She turned around at her bedroom door and chimed, "If you change your mind, Iris and I will be at the Barn by six. We don't want to miss one of the tunes. The Haystacks are playing. They have a banjo, two fiddles, drums and a mandolin. I know you would love them. And besides, what could be a better way to spend a Saturday evening?"

16

At First Sight

Deborah and Iris fairly flew up the path to the barn. Against her husband's wishes, her mother had driven the girls to the Johnson's huge barn on the outskirts of town. Christine drove up and down the road looking for a place to park.

"I think this is as close as I can get you girls," Christine said. "Hop out. I'll be back at eleven to pick you up."

"Okay Mom and thanks." Deborah placed her fingers slightly on her mom's hand on the steering wheel. "Don't worry, we'll be just fine. What could happen? Almost everyone here knows us. This is Straffordville after all."

With that, Iris grabbed the small picnic basket from the back seat before heading across the grass to the barn. Christine smiled at them almost enviously as their skirts flew in waves of cotton and crinolines. *Oh, to be young again and worry free,* she grumbled to the empty interior of the car.

Deborah was speechless as she and Iris walked through the large barn doors. The barn had been transformed. It was jaw-dropping amazing.

She smiled at Iris who was equally blown away by the sight.

Along every available wall were bales of hay stacked in countless formations — perfect for climbing on or sitting on. Hanging from the rafters, strings of lights draped across the room high above the dancers below. A raised platform had been erected at the end of the room for the band. Gourds in all shapes and sizes, and vegetables of every colour decorated the apron and cascaded over the edge. Tables draped in red and white checkered gingham cotton and topped with old fashioned lanterns were placed all around the dance floor.

At that moment, the band started to tune their instruments. High pitched strokes of the fiddles and the steady beat of the drum filled the room. Two men dragged over a couple of wooden boxes and set them in front of the fiddlers. On the table nearest the stand-up string bass sat the harmonica, an accordion, a tambourine, an Irish bodhran, and a couple of sets of large spoons.

As the sun fell slowly towards the horizon, the barn filled with dancers. People staked out their places at the tables and then hurried into the centre of the floor. Everyone danced. Children, parents, grandparents. In circles. In pairs. In squares. Alone. The Haystacks hardly took a break. They were anxious to play as many of their new tunes for the dancers and maybe — just maybe — they would rise a notch on the record charts.

For the hours that followed, not one father thought of the impending crisis in Europe. Not one mother worried about her son, brother or husband who might be considering enlisting. The barn and the dance filled the present.

In the soft light from the lanterns, Deborah spied him across the floor. She had not noticed him earlier, but now her attention was consumed by the handsome young man in the brown checkered shirt. She was positive it was James Armstrong just back from school. He was two years her senior and although they hadn't hung out in high school, she knew his family and she knew him. At least in her dreams, she knew him. James Armstrong. Popular. Hard working. Solicitous of his parents and little brother. And here he was at her barn dance.

"What's up?" Iris yelled at her friend against the strains of the song. Deborah did not turn in response to Iris' voice.

"Oh, I see now what's up." Iris followed Deborah's eyes to the handsome young man. "He's mighty cute, for sure. I haven't seen James for a couple of years. Want me to introduce you?"

"Would you, Iris? He probably won't remember me from school. I was two years behind him."

But Iris didn't need to do any introductions. James was on his way across the floor heading right to Deborah. "Well, if it isn't little Deborah Winters. My, but you have grown up real fine."

Deborah's face burned with the compliment. His deep baritone voice rolled out of his mouth, a symphony of sound that set her stomach in a flutter.

"Could I convince you to join me for a dance?" he asked.

"Yes, yes of course. Thank you. I would like that very much."

The remainder of the evening passed in that beautiful glow known only by those who have been struck with a lightning bolt of love at first sight. By the end of the night James and Deborah had danced 25 dances and shared their picnic lunch when they reluctantly stopped long enough to eat.

Brushing shoulders in time with the happy rhythms, James and Deborah clapped and stomped along with the fiddlers who brought the house down with a medley of jigs. Finally, it came time for the last song of the night. John from the band took the microphone.

"Ladies and Gentlemen, we'd like to leave you with one of our most recent tunes. It's new to us, but it's our take on a poem from the Emerald Isle. Charles Joseph Kickham was a Fenian, one of the most powerful voices of the young nationalist secret society in the late 1840s. We think you'll like it.

Let's welcome Poor Paddy Home.

Hurray me boys, hurray,
No more do I wish for to roam
The sun it will shine in the harvest time
To welcome poor Paddy home.

The dancers gathered close to the stage, linked arms and sang along with the band. It was an indelible moment.

*

Following the barn dance, Deborah and James were inseparable. They met in the soda shop after work, they enjoyed afternoon walks along the river, and they took long drives in James' new car. When the sun hovered above the horizon, James stopped the car at the Overlook to watch the brilliant orb smother the dense pines and maples in a final blaze of red and orange.

James placed his arm around her shoulders, but Deborah didn't snuggle in against his body as she normally would do. Instead, she rummaged around her feet for the large bag she had placed on the floormat. Slowly she drew something out of the bag.

Earlier that afternoon, she had bought her first LP record at the Five and Dime, one of the Haystacks recent hits. She shyly offered it to James.

"I thought you might enjoy the tunes."

"Deborah," he whispered, "I haven't been able to put the sight of you that night out of my head. The barn and us swaying to the music. The motion of your dress caught my eye right across the dance floor and lured me to you. Now I'll be able to relive the night we met every time I listen to the songs. You have no idea how much this means to me. And to think I hesitated when Thomas told me about the barn dance. What if I hadn't gone?"

James turned to face the woman who had captivated him. He pulled her close. In the soft crimson of the setting sun, he placed his lips on hers. Her soft mouth blossomed beneath the warm touch of his lips. Urgently, he enclosed her body in his strong embrace.

The next weekend, James rapped confidently on her front door. He smiled when he heard her light step in the hallway. Deborah beamed when she walked through the door to meet him. It was Sunday morning, but neither Deborah nor James was at church with their parents.

"You look beautiful," James whispered as he took her hand in his and brought it to his lips. Deborah relished his touch. Holding her close, the couple walked down the sidewalk to the road where they turned left towards the park. A few moments later, they settled on a seat beside the little pond.

"What a morning," he said turning to Deborah. "And I can't imagine sharing it with anyone but you."

"Yes, it is glorious."

James sighed contentedly as he leaned his hand against the bench. Still holding her hand, he willed the moment to last forever.

To an outsider they were a typical couple enjoying the scenery and each other's company, but on this morning, the conversation took a very different turn. Serious, heavy talk passed between them.

Deborah had finally spoken up against her parents. She had decided to leave the Baptist church, which was the real reason why she was not in church with her parents. She railed against the excessive praise singing, hands waving in the air. Not enough Bible study.

Ironically, James was at almost the same stage in his life. Raised as a strict Presbyterian, he was already searching for a church which based its teachings closer to the teachings of Christ. One that followed the Bible as the only word of Christ. One that expected its followers to adhere to the Bible as their guide to life.

James heard the bells first.

"Do you feel guilty?" he said.

"Not guilty. Different perhaps. I can't remember a Sunday morning when I haven't sat in the pews with my family. I know I've made the right decision though."

"Exactly. It's not that I don't want to go to church anymore. I just need to find somewhere that offers more. The world is crazy right now. All this talk of war. Why can't countries just get along?" James replied.

"Yesterday," Deborah admitted, "my brother Roger picked up enlistment papers. I can't imagine him giving up graduation to put on a uniform and get a license to kill other human beings. It isn't right, just not right. I know war isn't the answer, James, but I don't know what is."

James

17

Garage Battles

James reverently placed the last of his treasures into the box and folded the lid tightly. His tanks, horses, and soldiers; his Dinky toy trucks and cars; and finally, his set of tools: saws, hammers and wrenches. When he next opened the box, he would be living somewhere new and foreign.

For as long as he could remember, Sunday afternoons were spent puttering away in the garage making things and playing at war. A tinker with scraps of this and that, his father had built an entire battlefield out of metal and wood.

His father had painted the flat surface of the salvaged sheet of plywood to resemble muddy fields and grassy hillocks. Huts of corrugated metal served as the soldiers' mess hall, soldiers' quarters and strategy war room. Just the day before they had added an airbase complete with conning tower and runway lights. For father and son, the garage was a world apart, cementing the bonds between them.

It's going to be fine, James whispered hopefully to himself. *Mother and Father said so.* But in his heart of hearts he questioned their words. Many nights when he got up to use the bathroom, he had heard them quarrelling.

It was always the same. They couldn't afford to stay in Tillsonburg. The rent was too high. His father didn't earn enough money. The boys were growing and needed more clothes. They needed their own bedrooms. There was always something wrong with the house and ultimately with his father.

James, however, couldn't understand how his mother didn't see how wonderful his father was. How he could build almost anything from nothing. How he was so patient and helpful. How he never raised his voice at him and his little brother.

*

James and his little brother Christopher climbed into the back seat of the car. As they slid across the seat, the ragged leather of the cushions scraped against their bare legs. They looked at each other and then towards their parents who sat rigid and stone-faced in the front seat.

The young boys took one long look at the only house they had ever known. As the car pulled away from the curb, they said goodbye to 165 Turner Street forever.

Ten-year-old James felt the tears start to burn behind his eyes, but he daren't let them fall. He had to be strong for his six-year-old brother. His brother thought this moving was an adventure. Moving to a new house was exciting. James, however, knew different.

The garage behind the house passed by the window as they rounded the corner. Sunday afternoons with his father flooded his mind. The pain of those memories tore at his heart. Despite his best efforts, James could not stop the tears from overflowing his eyelids and running down his face. He turned towards the door so little Christopher couldn't see him cry. James wondered if he would ever have such fun again.

18

Rebuilding Castles

James collected his report card, shook hands with his teacher, and headed out the classroom door. He was finally going to high school. It was an amazing accomplishment considering he had attended four different elementary schools between Grade 2 and Grade 8, but he was a smart lad and despite the family challenges he kept his head down and worked hard.

But high school wasn't just a sign that he was a young adult, it meant he could finally take industrial arts. James had signed up for carpentry and metalwork, and he knew they would be his favourite classes. He had seen his father struggle with little education past elementary school and that was not going to happen to him.

From age twelve, James had worked after school and weekends at the local fabricating shop. The workers at the shop noted that he listened intently to instructions and took criticism and advice well. The employees could set their watches to James' arrival. Precisely at 4 p.m., James came into the shop for his two-hour shift, and they welcomed his help for four hours every Saturday morning. By the time he was fourteen, James had quite an extensive resume.

Over those two years, James had built up so much experience that he had already decided what his career would be. He would be a tinsmith, a sheet metal worker and a welder. He already had completed his application to the Technical College in Toronto three times over.

Brian was very proud of his oldest son. Despite their many moves, father and son had stayed true to their passion. In each of their homes, the garage was their haven. The projects may have changed as James grew older and his younger brother, little Christopher, joined them, but the time spent together cemented their love and respect for each other.

Before they knew it, James had completed high school and Christopher was about to enter Grade 10, ending their Sunday afternoon sessions.

*

James shook his father's hand, bear-hugged his mother and then placed his hand on his brother's shoulder.

"Now remember, Chris, there is nothing better in this world than being a man of your word. I won't be around for the next two years to drill that into your head. You're on your own in that regard. Listen to Mom and Dad and work hard. Before you know it, you'll graduate too."

Christopher looked straight at his older brother before speaking.

"You've been the best big brother anyone could ever wish for, James. I'll do my best to keep the garage in tip top shape until you get back." His voice cracking with emotion, Christopher struggled to get the last words out, "Wouldn't want you to worry."

James stepped onto the train and turned again to wave at the little trio standing on the platform. His family, the people he loved most in the entire world. He hated goodbyes, especially this one. But the future beckoned and he was ready.

19

Escape

Diploma in hand and a job waiting for him back home in Vienna, the latest home of his parents and Christopher, James threw his suitcase into the baggage locker. He took a window seat near the front of the third compartment just minutes before the conductor called the all aboard.

The train slowly pulled out of Union Station, picked up speed and headed south west. James carefully drew the diploma from his jacket pocket.

Gracing the top third of the paper and decked out in scrolls and gold leaf were the words, Toronto Technical Institute, June 21, 1939. Below the name of the school he read his own name, James Allan Armstrong. It was the umpteenth time he had read the diploma. *James Allan Armstrong is hereby granted tinsmith first class according to the rules and regulations of the Board of Directors.* He ran his fingers reverently over his name.

"I earned it all by myself," he whispered proudly.

As the tracks curved past the factories, smelters, and manufacturing companies, the scenery gave way to rolling hills and quaint villages. At Ingersoll junction, the train turned almost straight south into the farming belt. Through the windows on both sides, James saw large tobacco farms stretching for mile after mile.

It wasn't only the huge fields, but the long greenhouses filled with hundreds of labourers who, hour after hour, sat on benches hunched over the pots.

When the twenty or so pots directly in front of them were planted, the workers stood up and stretched their stiff muscles, moved down a few feet and started with a new set of seedlings. The temperature inside the greenhouses soared into the 90s. From dawn 'til dusk they worked for a meager wage, but still they came. By the hundreds. It was a job.

Ontario hadn't suffered like the prairies during the Depression, but the road to economic recovery nonetheless had been challenging. James pressed his nose to the window. It was late April, planting time. He watched the hundreds of migrant plantation workers bent over the fields. Strapped to each worker's back was a large bag of tender seedlings. He marvelled at how fast a worker could pull a plant from the bag, dig the hole with the little spade, plant the seedling and stomp it down in place. *Five or six every minute, I would guess,* James thought.

Looks like things are really humming now, though, James mused to no one in particular, *and everyone seems to smoke these days. Lots of call for tobacco.*

His parents and 15-year-old Christopher met him at the train station in Tillsonburg, fourteen miles from their home in Vienna. They had to borrow a car from a friend as theirs was repossessed two months earlier. James knew his father would be embarrassed by this latest development. Regardless, James could hardly wait to see his family. Two years was a long time away.

*

Since his return from school, the months had sped by, and before he knew it, July was almost gone. James helped his parents as much as he could, but he was young and wanted to have fun too. Putting in 60-hour weeks didn't leave him a lot of time for socializing.

At almost twenty years of age, Friday nights meant hooting and hollering all the way from Vienna to Straffordville, and sometimes even to Port Burwell on the Lake. Despite the sideways glances from his parents, every Friday at 7 p.m., he either bummed a ride with a co-worker, or hitch-hiked to the bar.

It was on one of those Friday nights that James met Thomas Silverton, a long-time friend from high school who had recently returned from London, Ontario. Thomas and James renewed their friendship, and it wasn't long before they spent every Friday night together.

Thomas had bought a used Chevy coupe which meant the two friends could travel farther afield. Speeding north on Highway 19, James watched the landscape pass. Late summer had spread its golden mantle over the ripening tobacco fields. Everywhere he looked were the soft signs of approaching Autumn.

James wished his own father had got into tobacco. Maybe things wouldn't be so hard now if he had. James struggled to put the negative thought out of his mind and concentrate on Friday night freedom.

Ten minutes later, Thomas turned into the parking lot of the Travellers' Rest Pub. James thought it was very appropriately named. Leaving the tension of his home behind, he felt like a traveller on vacation. Young Beatrice knew the regulars. Before James and Thomas had even placed their jackets on the backs of their chairs, she set two cold beers on the table before them.

"Now that was mighty fast!" Thomas said, winking coyly as she turned to serve the next table.

Beatrice flashed a glance backwards, "Always happy to be of service."

James ordered a dish of peanuts; Thomas a bowl of popcorn. Friday night with all its potential silliness and wild shenanigans lay before them, but James couldn't shake himself out of his serious mood.

"What made you come back, Thomas? Vienna is small compared with London," James asked.

"Just got tired of the crowds and line-ups everywhere. In Vienna I can afford a little house and hopefully find a girl to marry. I've already got my car. First step to settling down. What about you James? Found a sweetheart yet?"

"Not in the cards so far. Haven't had much time to look. You know I work six days a week and hang around with you on Friday nights. I've got an eye on a car though," he retorted.

Thomas took a long pull on his beer before speaking.

"Well, I have a proposition for you. This coming Saturday, there's a barn dance at Straffordville. Bound to be lots of sweet things just waiting for us there. What do you think? The Haystacks are playing. Want to trip the light fantastic? Show off our dancing skills?"

James knew that Thomas would not take no for an answer. And he himself would welcome the opportunity to get out on Saturday night. Living at home had become progressively unpleasant.

He saw how his mother had to skimp whenever she went to the market. After his father's hours at the hardware store had been cut a second time, James noticed that he retreated to the verandah when conversation became too difficult or uncomfortable. James could see the defeat in his eyes and the sadness in his stooped shoulders. Gone was any sense of hope for a better future. James gave as much as he could to help with expenses, but it was never enough. The tension fell heavily on everyone. Despite how fervently they prayed for guidance or solace, God didn't appear to be listening.

"So, are you in?"

"Sounds like a wonderful way to welcome the first Saturday in August," James said. He looked down at his pale-yellow dress shirt. "Probably need to cruise by the Five and Dime for a checkered shirt. Can't go to a barn dance looking like a city slicker."

"That's the truth," Thomas agreed and raised his glass.

"Here's to Saturday night."

For his whole life, James would remember that wonderful Saturday night a month before the conflict erupted. Their meeting was destined. As he peered across the dance floor, James could see nothing but Deborah Winters.

20

Making the Call

The doorbell caused them both to jump.

"That's odd," Deborah said, "I wasn't expecting anyone this morning. No one's home. Except for you and me of course." She giggled, touching his arm. "Do you think someone reported us for being at home alone without a chaperone? Since the barn dance, I'm sure everyone on the street has noticed us together."

"Hardly," James retorted. "This is 1939 and I am certain there are no spies in Vienna checking up on young couples." Deborah jumped off the couch, ran her fingers through her hair and headed to the front door. James cocked his head to listen.

"Good afternoon young lady. I wonder if my wife and I might have a moment or two of your time? We are new in town, but we have news that you might welcome in this time of world strife from leaders who fill us with fearful predictions. If you have been dissatisfied with the words of our religious leaders and are seeking the Truth, perhaps you would welcome the message of the Jehovah's Witnesses."

"Oh, no," Deborah replied, "I don't think we are interested."

"Our theme today," the visitor persevered, "is Peace at all cost. The threat of war in Europe is soon to inflict strife and hardship on thousands of people, ordinary people who do not sanction violence and killing."

"Jehovah God forbids his Witnesses from wearing a uniform or raising a weapon against a fellow human being. Surely you would not want your brother or father to go to war and perhaps not come back? Think of your family without them."

"Well, of course I am fearful of war and losing loved ones," Deborah agreed tentatively.

James walked from the living room to stand protectively beside his Deborah, but as the moments passed he too became interested in what the young couple had to say. Ten minutes later, Deborah invited them inside.

When the clock struck noon, Deborah quietly closed the door and returned to the couch where James sat deep in thought. Three recent copies of *The Watchtower* sat open on the coffee table.

"You know Deborah, their visit is very timely. On Friday, I received my rejection letter from the Army. I knew my chances of being accepted were slim, but I tried anyway. Do my duty for the home country. I guess they don't want any welders in the Corps without 20-20 vision," James said, smiling ruefully.

"I've never found the less than perfect vision in my left eye as a problem. It certainly never affected the quality of my work. Even at school there wasn't any problem." James pulled her close and teased, "Now you won't be able to kiss a man in uniform. All kidding aside, my dear, what this young couple says is most intriguing. What do you make of it all?" James' voice filled the empty living room.

Deborah's soft hazel eyes bored into his. "It seems this is what we both have been searching for. I want to learn more."

21

A Rousing Recruitment

As the late summer sun began to stride across the sky on an ever-increasing oblique angle, Deborah and James spent many happy hours at the Kingdom Hall where they were welcomed with open arms.

Deborah relished the Bible Study groups on Wednesday nights and she especially loved the Thursday night instruction about how to become a missionary for Jehovah.

Even after a long day of work, James enjoyed the men's group which met every Monday night. It gave him an opportunity to delve into the Bible in a fraternal environment. He felt grounded and centred. In fact, he was beginning to think, now that he finally seemed settled in his faith, he might ask Deborah to marry him. After all, they worshipped as a couple and studied the Bible as a couple. He reasoned that it seemed like the next logical step.

Her beauty and quiet demeanour cast a spell over him which remained in his mind for hours after he kissed her goodbye on the porch of the little bungalow on Jones Street and headed home across town. He imagined the caress of her blond curls, soft as corn silk, as they brushed against his cheek when he buried his face in her hair. He felt the rise and fall of her breasts against his chest when he brought her tiny waist into the folds of his arms.

On a particularly long and lonely walk home, James made up his mind. He would ask Deborah to be his wife. He was pretty sure she would not turn him down.

The following Saturday, they had planned a trip into the neighbouring woods to pick pin cherries. The tart little berries were finally ripe and ready to be harvested. Deborah had promised him that he would love her pin cherry jelly.

Neither the berries nor his request disappointed.

James carried two large coffee tins for berry picking. He had drilled two holes at the top of each tin and knotted a yard or so of string from one hole to the other creating a neck strap. That way they would be able to loop the string around their necks with the tin hanging down in front of them, leaving both hands free for picking.

With a picnic lunch basket in her right hand, Deborah walked along by his side. The late August sun mottled the path which wound its way through the woods before them. The day was perfect.

"This looks like a great spot," Deborah announced. "Those trees are covered with crimson red Pins. Shouldn't take us long to fill the cans."

James craned his neck and looked up and around the grove of trees, satisfied with the location. Deborah hung the basket from a dead branch a foot from the ground. "That will discourage ants from sampling our lunch."

"Did you know that these berries have another name as well?" James asked helping Deborah with her picking can.

"I know they are sometimes called bird cherries. I guess because of those long spikes. They sort of look like birds' legs on stilts," Deborah laughed.

"I didn't know that one," James chuckled before continuing, "but they are also called fire cherries. Often, they are one of the first trees to come back after a wildfire." An hour later, their fingers stained with juice and aching, Deborah and James set two full cans on the ground.

"I think it's time to lay out that blanket and rest awhile," James insisted.

"You mean you don't like the outdoors this early in the morning?" she teased. "That's what comes from being so much older than me."

"My dear, it has nothing at all to do with that. I was up all-night thinking about you and missing you. Hard to chug out energy when there's nothing left in the tank."

Deborah blushed at the compliment and then turned around to find a good spot to lay out the blanket.

"Under that tree looks just fine. Better get that basket open lickety-split. Here I've been a slave driver when you're probably starving."

Deborah carefully lifted out a thermos of cold lemonade, two glasses, chicken salad sandwiches and fresh gingersnaps, and laid them on the blanket.

"Here you go. A pin cherry picker's feast," she said, smiling.

While they ate, James felt his heart doing flip flops. He could hardly contain his excitement. *I can't squander this moment,* he thought. *This is it.* He moved closer to this woman who had so captivated his heart. He brushed his fingers along her arms and slowly moved them down to enclose her tiny hands. She turned to face him and looked quizzically into his eyes.

"Deborah, I… Deborah, we have had so many wonderful times together since we met at the barn dance. Deborah, I don't know if I can continue to leave you at home and walk those 506 lonely steps to my house. I can't imagine being without you. I want you to be my wife. And I just know I'm going to love your pin cherry jelly," he added foolishly.

The world stopped spinning as the two gazed at each other, speechless in the moment. Deborah and Iris had agonized over many a cup of tea trying to figure out James' intentions. Iris said to keep looking. Deborah argued that she had met the love of her life, especially now that they shared deep religious bonds. She desired James, and James alone. The memory brought her back to the blanket and the man who had just asked her to marry him.

"Well if you put it that way, I have no choice but to accept," she said, smiling coyly.

"And when the Final Harvest comes, we will enter Paradise together." She started at the words which burst from her mouth. *But I mean it.* Her secret thoughts seemed so right to say to the man before her.

22

Joining the Flock

"It's no use Brian, we can't keep the house," Margaret Armstrong said with a sigh as she twisted the dish cloth through her hands. James' parents once again had come face-to-face with their hopes for a happy future.

"Now that James is home we have to tell him what's going on. I am sure he understands already. Same meals, no new clothes, tax collectors arriving at the door any time of the day and night. Even Christopher is asking questions. Yesterday, he even threatened to quit school and join the army. What, with talk of a war, he said he could make good money and send some home each month."

Brian took his wife's hands roughly in his. He had worked hard all his life and now they might lose everything. How could this happen? How could God let it happen? James entered the kitchen to face his parents sitting mutely at opposite ends of the table.

They had feigned happiness when James announced his and Deborah's intent to marry. James had added for effect that it was time to strike out on his own, especially now with a shop for sale in Straffordville that he thought he might buy. With war coming, he knew he could make a go of it.

"James, when did you come in?"

"Long enough to know how bad things are here. Surely, you don't think I don't know how you have suffered? I'm not a child anymore. Christopher and I are not deaf nor are we stupid, but it is not your fault that it happened, but it is your fault if you give up. There is a new way. New hope. Deborah and I have discovered it at the Hall. Why don't you join us? You'll see. The congregation will lift your spirits and help you understand what is important in this crazy world of ours. The Elder has already agreed to marry us even though we have only been attending for a few weeks."

And so, it transpired on August 28, 1939 with their hands resting on the Bible, that James and Deborah stood before their new Brothers and Sisters, promised to devote their lives to Jehovah God, his son Christ Jesus, and lastly to each other.

At James' urging, his parents and Christopher joined him and Deborah in the Hall on September 3. But on September 3, everything had changed. The talk was all about Hitler's invasion of Poland. For all intents and purposes, this was a declaration of War.

Elder Patterson stood to face those assembled.

"My fellow Brothers and Sisters. Today, we are witnessing a Germany yet again on the move. Again, we will be challenged to face humiliation, derision and possible incarceration when Canada joins the fight. As pacifists, we know that we cannot and will not enter this impending war. Even here in our quiet hamlet, there will be those who glare and accuse us, but we must be resolute in our faith. Jehovah God will preserve us."

As the meeting wore on, young Christopher began to squirm in his chair. With each passing pacifist comment, he felt more and more uncomfortable. His parents might find the Kingdom Hall to their liking, but there was no way he was going to go along with this rhetoric. He was going to enlist. He knew from history class that when Britain declared war on Germany in 1914, Canada was also at war. This time, the Canadian government would have to pass an act in parliament to go to war, but he was sure that would happen. Everyone in his class was speculating Canada would join Britain.

Finally, the Elder gave a blessing to the congregation and they filed out of the Hall each person carrying the heavy burden of being a Jehovah's Witness in a country soon to be at war. Christopher could not get out fast enough.

23

From Bliss to Disappointment and Back Again

"James, James. Are you home yet?" Deborah called racing into the living room of their neat little cottage on Prince Street. Everything had fallen into place as planned. Their marriage had gone off without a hitch, James' offer on the shop in Straffordville was accepted and the same week a sweet rental home across the drive from the shop came available. Life was wonderful.

They had moved in on November 1, an afternoon that rivalled the best of any autumn days they could remember. Southern Ontario could be capricious, but on moving day, she did not play any of her usual tricks. The morning started off crisp and cold with a slight tinge of winter in the air. By noon, with the sun so warm and James working so hard carrying boxes and furniture, he had to remove his jacket.

Deborah worked like a demon to get the kitchen organized, set what little furniture they had in their correct rooms, make their bed and sweep the floor. The rest of the boxes would wait for another day. She wanted to enjoy the first night in their new home with her new husband.

The feeling was delicious. She was the wife of a wonderful, caring man. Mrs. James Armstrong. She still said it out loud as if to pinch herself that it was true.

And then exciting news. For days, she had knocked on every business, restaurant and office door. The expedition had been worth it though. She landed work at one of the largest tobacco plantations on the outskirts of town and she wouldn't need a car as Iris was on the same shift and they could ride together.

Deborah was proud of her green thumb. Ferns, violets and variegated spider plants thrived in her own home. She was confident her gardening skills would easily apply to the work ahead in the hot, humid tobacco greenhouses. She would start at .45 cents an hour. She knew it was back-breaking work in the hot greenhouses and even worse in the fields, but Deborah was not afraid of hard labour.

She heard his step on the porch. Her James was home.

She flew into his arms as he crossed the threshold. Their love continued to grow stronger with each absence. Tonight, was Friday and he too had news, but first he only desired to hold her in his arms.

*

Cuddled on the couch as close as humanly possible, James shared his news first.

"You would never guess who came into the shop this afternoon." He waited while she scrunched up her nose in that characteristic Deborah way as if to say I don't want to play this game.

"Well then let me tell you. The RCAF came to see me today. They called the Toronto Tech School looking for the top sheet metal worker in last year's class. Well, of course you know who that was, right?"

"Let me think," she mused, "Thomas? No? Well, let me guess again." She paused for effect and to stretch out the anticipation. "Does his name start with James?"

Deborah threw herself into the curve of his body and he brought her closer. James laughed until his sides hurt.

"Really?" she asked, "Whatever did they want with my handsome husband?"

"They are looking for instructors at the aircraft plant north of Aylmer. I would make $28.00 a week. Can you imagine? Just for teaching what I love?"

Deborah kissed her husband proudly and then resettled herself on the couch, ran her fingers through her curls and let out an explosive sigh of excitement.

"Well, I have news as well. You are looking at the newest employee at the Verdun tobacco farm."

"Well, it looks like 1939 is going to end with a bang for us. James jumped up and strode across to the fridge. His hand on the handle, he turned to face his wife who was watching him closely. He pulled out two beers.

"Mrs. Armstrong, can I invite you to enjoy something a bit stronger than tea? After all, this is a real celebration."

"Yes, I would be delighted to imbibe," she said, laughing coquettishly. "This is definitely a night to celebrate. I can hardly wait to tell all my new friends at the Hall."

*

The war had once again brought the military service debate to the forefront. Jehovah's Witnesses searched for ways to avoid active service by working in hospitals or ammunitions factories. They argued that they were not going to war. But because they were working at something related to the war, the Organization paid attention.

Bethel ruled on individual cases with an arbitrary voice. Head office believed that if a witness touched the armament when it was made or when it was packed in a box for shipping it was just the same as wearing a uniform at the front line. They levied the decisions with no concern for the consequences.

Jonathon, you must leave the ammunitions factory and find other work. Hospitals are places where you might encounter blood. Andrew, you must look for another job. And so, it went, one Witness after another.

Bethel cited that Jehovah would not want his faithful to do such work and by default the Organization's position was Jehovah's position. These rulings forced hundreds of families to resort to begging for handouts and standing in lines at soup kitchens as they could not feed their families. The struggles were palpable.

Conflicted young men and women spoke with the same voice: *In all conscience, how can I leave my job and watch my family starve while, at the same time by not leaving my job I will be committing the greatest sin against Jehovah?*

Many Jehovah's Witnesses left the Organization during the war years.

*

"Are you sure? There is no way around this? I would not be going overseas or wearing a uniform," James asked.

Elder Patterson was adamant.

"There is no way a Witness can either enlist in military service, or work in an environment which is directly related to the war effort. At the plant you would be manufacturing airplane parts and equipment for tanks and other military vehicles. You must appreciate Bethel's ruling in this regard. There is no appeal, and no questions asked. Many Brothers have been disfellowshipped for not complying. You are just beginning your Kingdom journey, James, and you do not want to jeopardize your future."

Naturally, James did not want to do anything to call his behaviour into question. He and Deborah had begun to make wonderful friends at the Hall and many witnesses came to him for all their fabricating and auto work. In a few short months, he had increased his clientele base by 50%. Things were certainly looking up for the young couple.

"Thank you, Brother Patterson for your time and wise advice. Thankfully you stopped me before I shamed Jehovah. Now, I best be getting home. I must tell Deborah that we won't be moving to Aylmer in the next little while. I think she'll be pleased as we haven't really unpacked all our wedding gifts and she does love our new house here."

James left the Hall and headed home. It was just a short walk down the tree-lined streets, past the elementary school and then left on Jones. He walked with a lilt in his step knowing that he and Deborah were settled. He no longer hung out every Friday drinking beer. Instead he looked forward to spending his evening off with his wife.

The war had settled into a stalemate and all the talk about the boys being home by Christmas had the ring of a pipe dream. He knew that Thomas had joined the Army and would ship-out in February. James wondered if it were against his new faith to go to the Tillsonburg station and say goodbye to his friend before he left. James didn't want to entertain anything that might go against Jehovah or bring his conscience into conflict.

He imagined Thomas sitting on the hard bench seat on one of the many troop trains taking hundreds of young soldiers to the ports of Halifax or Montreal. He was saddened that he would not be on the platform to wish his friend farewell. Many of the young men in town had signed up. They walked the streets when they were on furlough, their pants creased knife sharp and their jackets pressed and clean. Although they were filled with desire to kill the Hun once and for all, it appeared that the day they put on their uniform was also the first time they had shaved.

James turned left on the path through the little park. Every day he walked from town, he passed the cenotaph without a thought, but today, a twinge of conscience flashed in his mind. Not enlisting seemed like he had donned an invisible cloak of cowardice. His eyes rested on the names carved into the granite — hard, cold and dead — the names of those young men who had so valiantly sacrificed themselves for peace.

But that peace didn't last and here the country is again in a global conflict. Of course, James agreed, *Bethel is right. This war is wrong.*

The moment passed, burrowing deep into his subconscious. James took the porch steps two at a time as if desperately trying to outrun a mythical beast of mammoth proportions.

"Is the prettiest girl in Straffordville home?" James called as he crossed the threshold.

"Well, if you are talking about your wife, then she is!" Deborah smiled at the game they made of greeting each other.

"Come here and give me a kiss, you big lug," Deborah said, laughing as she pulled James into her arms.

"Darling, I cannot tell you enough times how Jehovah has made our lives perfect, and how our love for Christ Jesus has brought us so much peace. With my wife at my side life is wonderful."

"Then are you up to making it more wonderful?"

James cocked his head, unsure what she might mean.

"How do you think you might like to be a father?"

Eight months later, when the beautiful baby boy named Peter was placed in his arms, he smiled at his wife lying on the hospital bed spent with joy and said, "I think I will like it just fine. Look at this perfect little human that you and I have created, and Jehovah will help us raise him as a devoted Witness.

Peter

24

The Tin Wizard

Peter folded the waxed paper over twice and rolled it accordion-like down to the top of the bread. His little hands squared off the ends and tucked the paper under his sandwich.

"Perfect. See mom, I told you I could do it myself. Now I just have to get my boots and meet dad at the garage."

"You don't have to go every morning, dear. Don't you want to stay home? Spend some time with Lorraine or help me with little Douglas? You always like to feed him his lunch."

"Nope," Peter replied, but then quickly added, "I do like feeding him lunch, but I love helping dad more."

And with that, he snapped his lunchbox shut, strode confidently across the kitchen and lifted the latch on the screen door.

His father's shop was just a hop and a skip away. It was a perfect set up. A wide drive separated the house from his father's business. James laughed recalling when he and Deborah decided to buy the property.

"Won't ever have to worry about being late for work," he said.

She smiled in that quiet soft way she had.

"No, I suppose not. Very good planning I'd say."

Armstrong's Outfitting and Sheet Metal hummed with activity. Over the years, James had made a great name for himself. Across the entire region, customers came to his shop before anyone else's. They drove the extra distance to purchase quality duct work for their chimneys, repairs for their furnace, or quality welding. If someone needed a custom piece for an oddly-shaped roof gutter or a dented fender, they came to James. No matter what they were looking for, James could make it. He was a wizard with tin.

In fact, James Armstrong was one of only four registered tinsmiths in the province of Ontario. He liked to tell family and customers that he was a rare breed. *I guess I'm one of those hands-on steel dinosaurs,* he thoughts, smiling.

James checked the time. Almost nine. He could almost set his watch to the slap of the kitchen screen door. Seconds later when he looked through the window above his workbench, he spied Peter, lunch bucket in hand, ready to cross the drive.

He may only be six, but by the end of the summer, I bet he'll be able to identify most of the tools and equipment in my shop. Although he's lanky, I already see the future strength developing in his hands. James glowed.

Peter rapped lightly on the heavy shop door. James pulled it aside and waited for the same question Peter asked him every morning.

"Hi Dad. Do you need any help today? I packed my own lunch." James tousled his son's mop of gold.

"Peter. I sure can use your help today. You're just in time. I was just going to put that one through the rollers." Peter's eyes caught sight of the large sheet of metal resting against the big yellow bending machine.

"What is this piece going to be?"

"The Verdun's are building another kiln at the farm. They need ten of them."

Jehovah's Witnesses from as far away as London and Kitchener sent work orders to their Brother James. They trusted him to do an excellent job and provide material for a fair price. As a business man, James knew the value of a client's trust. He strove to be that rock-steady supplier.

Young Peter set his lunch box on the back table and walked confidently to the shelves along the side wall. He picked up the smallest of his father's thick leather work gloves. Although his fingers didn't come near to the ends, when he turned to face his father, he grinned from ear to ear.

"Reporting for duty, dad." For the next few hours, Peter followed his father around like a puppy, loyal and observant of everything his master did. Peter would be going off to school come September, but the summer stretched out lazily before them. James would treasure these days forever.

James lifted the ten-foot sheet of metal from the large wooden cradle while Peter watched intently. He loved everything about the shop: the sibilant squeezing of the rollers as his father fed the metal through them and the soprano strokes of the large mallet when he drove the rivets into the pressed metal to join the ends into long fat tubes.

Peter and Lorraine happily risked their father's wrath about staying away from the rolls when he set them on the driveway for customers to pick up. The "stovepipes to nowhere" as Peter called them were just too tempting. Like kids everywhere who have been warned not to do something, they sneaked out of the house and spent mischievous minutes crawling through the shiny tunnels, their laughter pinging joyfully off the tin walls. James chuckled when he noticed the tell-tale knee divots on the inside of the metal rolls.

Cutting the metal created a symphony all its own. The high-pitched squeal of the blades as his father cut through the metal and the tinkling of the pieces as they cascaded to the cement floor were music to young Peter's ears. All around him was the sound of industry and Peter knew he and his father were part of something very important.

"Are you ready, son?"

"You bet."

"Ok here she comes. Hold it straight. Not too heavy, just enough pressure to keep it from falling left or right. Remember how flexible it can be."

James flipped the switch. The rollers started to turn. Little Peter lifted his arms high above his head and grasped the sheet. His job was to keep the floppy end of the metal from tipping.

James centred the metal between the rolling press. This piece was to be one of the square ends for the furnace. No room for error. Although he was fully involved in the task, he turned his head to watch his young son.

Peter clutched either side of the shining silver. He held on for dear life as it thumped wavelike between his hands. James smiled proudly to himself.

In the shop, father and son were a team. Peter trusted his father explicitly and if push came to shove, James would cross over barbed wire to be there for Peter.

When the last of the sheet of metal passed between the rollers, Peter dropped his hands. His father came around the machine and carried the shiny tube of steel to the cutting table where the shaping details would be done. No cuts. No blood. Only smiles.

For several hours, father and son worked side by side with young Peter following close behind his father, the tin wizard. Each time James completed a piece, he smiled at his son as if to say good job. At twelve noon precisely, James set his mallet and tin snips on his workbench, checked his watch, and glanced across the shop to Peter.

"Almost time for lunch, don't you think?"

James cleared a spot on the bench and pulled up two stools. James patted one twice and Peter hopped up next to his father.

"Let me open your tin of apple juice. I'm powerful hungry."

James' shop served both father and son in those complicated growing up years. Within the walls of the shop, James witnessed the wonderment of molding a smaller version of himself, and Peter basked in the security that his father would always stick up for him and keep him safe.

25

Fancy Pants

That fall when Peter started school, he got a lesson in the eccentricities of females. At the time, his mother was busy training Lorraine to use the toilet. Peter had been a breeze to train; in fact, he never wet his pants no matter how desperately he had to go. Even in the dead of winter when he walked home from the Hall, he was able to hold it. Deborah's daughter on the other hand was proving difficult in this regard.

No matter what tactic she used, Lorraine often left little presents behind the couch, or when she was completely immersed in her playing outdoors, Deborah could see the growing wet circle on her behind. Later that evening, she stated her frustration to her husband.

"James, I am at a loss about what to do about Lorraine. She refuses to come in before she must go to the bathroom. I am forever doing laundry."

"Different from Peter, isn't she? Maybe she doesn't like plain white panties?"

"But the fancy frilly underwear is so much more expensive."

Deborah pushed her body deep into the cane back of the chair and raised her cup of coffee to her lips. She smiled at the idea growing in her mind.

"I think you might have hit on a solution. She loves to wear fancy anything. If I bought a few pairs of fancy pants, she might love them so much that she wouldn't dare wet them!"

On the last Friday of each month after the government cheque arrived in the mail, Deborah scoured the sale ads in the newspaper. Shopping for Peter was always easy: trousers, socks, shirts, long johns and white underwear. Little Douglas was still in diapers, so his toilet training was not an issue, and when he got older there would be lots of hand-me-downs.

Deborah searched the ads for lacey underwear. There in the top left corner was what she wanted. A set of seven panties in a little package: pink, blue, polka dot, white satin all complete with bows and ruffles.

"This is perfect," Deborah exclaimed. "I'll use Lorraine's entire $5.00 baby bonus this month for new underwear. If this works, it will be well worth the expense."

*

Lorraine indeed loved her new panties. Every night she laid out a pair for the next day. They became her special treasures, never to be soiled again. Deborah was thrilled. But good things often bring along their own set of problems.

Lorraine was horrified to think that hanging outside on the line to dry her fancy pants would be in plain view for anyone to see. These were her gems, hers and hers alone. Peter understood the pained expression on his sister's face whenever laundry day arrived. He offered a solution.

"Mother, I have it. When the load of underwear laundry is done, Lorraine and I will hang hers downstairs. Underwear isn't too heavy, and I can reach the line now."

"What a nice thing to do, Peter. I am so proud of you."

Peter dragged the large basket into the basement where he had rigged up an indoor clothesline. Laundry conspirators both, Peter understood that his sister's frillies would dry just as well in the basement out of sight from their neighbours' inquisitive eyes.

26

Colour Coordinated

The rain started early on the Saturday morning in question. The family had just returned from the Hall. Deborah was making dinner. Dougie was playing with his stuffed animals at the kitchen table. Peter was in the shop with his father.

Usually, Lorraine and Peter got along famously, but once Lorraine entered elementary school there were times when Peter's obsessive need to organize his desk seemed like an open invitation for trespassing. In stark contrast to Peter's desk, Lorraine's crayons lay higgledy-piggledy beside her colouring books.

Lorraine lay on her bed engrossed in the latest Bobbsey Twins Adventure; they were visiting their aunt and uncle on the farm. Peter had found the book in the trash in the alley. He had tucked it under his shirt and secretly brought it home. It was the first of many discarded library books that Peter stole for his sister. He knew he had broken the rules by bringing the secular books into the house, but he also knew Lorraine loved reading worldly stories rather than the grim selections in *The Watchtower* or *Awake*. It was their own private rebellion.

The rain pummeled the roof in a steady tattoo. As she raised her eyes from the book and looked around, Lorraine felt the urge for an adventure of her own. Slowly, she set the book beside her and tucked it under the bedspread.

Ever since her brother had moved into Grade 4 and could use pens for the first time, Lorraine was jealous. She hated using gray, boring pencils. She wanted her notebooks to be alive with colour.

She swung her legs over the side of her bed and tiptoed down the hall towards Peter's room. Not suspecting an intruder, the door was wide open. Tossing a glance over her right shoulder, she entered Peter's room. Lorraine knelt on the floor before his little desk and slowly pulled open the first drawer. Peter's pencils and pens were lined up in regimental form. From dark to light and from small to large, his desk drawer was a rainbow of precision, the exact opposite to hers.

She didn't know what got into her, but ten minutes later the carefully sharpened points of three of the coloured pencils were broken, all the pens were in a jumble at the bottom of the drawer, and on the top of the desk, Peter's special Red Robin Tea animal figures were lying on their side. Lorraine sneaked back to her room, retrieved her book from its hiding place and waited.

*

Not 20 minutes later, Peter walked down the hall to his room. She heard the sharp intake of his breath when he discovered the damage. Seconds later, she heard quiet sobbing.

She held her breath.

The sobbing continued. Lorraine covered her ears to block out his heart-wrenching crying, but she could still hear it. She couldn't stand it. Before her mother chanced to hear Peter crying, she leapt from the bed and ran into Peter's room, blubbering.

"I just wanted some colour. My desk looks so dull and messy compared to yours. I don't know what made me do it." Lorraine rushed to her brother and flung her arms around him.

"I'm so sorry, Peter. I love you more than anything." Lorraine squeezed her brother tighter, her shoulders shaking uncontrollably. They fell in a tumble to the floor clutching each other as if their lives depended on it.

Finally, Peter broke away from her bear hug, brushed the tears from his own face and then wiped the tears rolling down her cheeks. His sniffles diminished. He looked deep into his sister's eyes. He knew she really didn't mean to hurt him.

"It's all right Rainey. Sometimes we just do things that we don't plan to do. I know you didn't do it out of meanness."

"No, you're wrong, I must have," she sobbed anew. "Why would I do something so awful to someone I love so much?" Peter grabbed her gently by the shoulders.

"Let's forget it, now. Maybe you can help me put things back together and I can let you use the coloured pens? Go get your Kingdom colouring book."

Thinking that things down the hall were a bit too quiet, Deborah decided to investigate. When she came to Peter's bedroom and sneaked a peek through the door, she smiled in relief. Her two oldest children lay angelically on the floor colouring pictures together.

27

Rain Barrel Street Fight

Peter squeezed a large glob of Brylcreem into his right palm and then quickly rubbed both hands together. Bringing them up on either side of his head, he plastered the gel from the crown of his head to the tip of the duck tail at his neck.

At that very moment, 13-year-old Lorraine rushed down the hall past his room. She pulled up smartly when she saw him at the mirror.

"Where are you off to?"

"None of your business, Miss Nosy Parker." But Peter could never keep a secret from his sister.

"You're going to the Imperial, aren't you?" His silence confirming what she already knew.

"Don't worry, I won't tell. By the way, you look really swell. Have fun," she said. laughing as she ran down the hall to the kitchen. She knew how important it was to keep her mother distracted while Peter was getting ready to leave the house. Deborah had urged Peter to stay away from the park and the hotel. Lorraine remembered her mother's warning: "Punks hang out there. If you're looking for trouble, Peter, it will surely find you down there."

But Peter wasn't worried. He could take care of himself.

Peter reached under his bed and carefully pulled out the brown bag from the Metropolitan store over in Aylmer. A few days earlier, he had spent some of his paycheque on a new khaki shirt to wear with his dark grey trousers.

He ran his fingers over the soft cotton before he undid the pins and removed the collar paper. He shook the shirt out and put it on.

Yes, that looks just fine. He smiled.

He pulled the navy-blue jacket off the hanger and put it on. *Ensemble complete,* he thought winking at himself in the mirror. It was a sizzling night. He expected lots of girls to be out on the streets in various degrees of summer flounce. *Gotta look my best.*

Peter shut the screen door without a whisper of evidence to betray his departure. With a cocky swagger, he hopscotched down the walk to the road. He was "ready to rumble" as they say. He didn't have his license yet, so finding something fun on Saturday night was a bit challenging, but not impossible.

He was planning to meet his buddies Larry and Wayne at the Imperial. Well, not really inside the hotel, because he wasn't old enough to drink either, but Larry and Wayne were. They bought the booze and brought it outside where they would hook-up with Peter. A couple of blocks from his house, he took out his pack of Lucky 7s, the newest one of his sins.

It isn't illegal, he assured himself. *Both mom and dad support the tobacco industry, big time. And the JWs haven't forbidden that. At least not yet,* he grimaced. *That would be my cue to file my Witness walking papers.*

As Peter turned the corner on York Street, The Imperial Hotel rose directly ahead on the right. He spotted his friends on the verandah. Larry beckoned him to meet at the drive just before the hotel. In minutes, the trio of revelers stood together.

"What's up, Lar?" Peter asked.

"Nothing, and I want to keep it that way. Let's find a table in the park." Two six packs in hand, the three men walked down Smith Street towards the river. For years Smith Street had been on a slow slide to decrepit. Until now.

The slow slide had recently been arrested because on both sides of the curbside, someone had placed rain barrels filled with beautiful flowers. It was obvious that the plants were being cared for as they bloomed lush and full. The ugly little street burst with pride in its new glory.

"What's this?" Wayne asked in his usual snarly manner. As he spoke he ran his hand over the flowers in the first barrel on his right. "Well would you lookie here? Some chump is putting colour on the street."

"Just leave it alone, Wayne. I think it looks better," Peter commented quietly.

"Do you now? Well, who asked for your opinion?"

"Come on Wayne," Larry interrupted. "Let's get on down to some serious drinking.

"Yeah, ok, but I'm not much liking these geronemos at all."

The hairs on Peter's neck bristled. Not only did he know who had planted the flowers, he also knew who had dragged the heavy rain barrels from the tobacco plant in the dead of night, filled them with soil and then planted dozens of bright red geraniums in them. He had no idea where his parents found either the time or the money to get them, but he was proud of them for taking the initiative. Peter often heard people commenting about the flowers and wondering who had done such a wonderful thing for their community.

As soon as they reached the riverside park, Larry passed out a cold one to each of the friends. Although they were just a mere two years older than Peter, both Larry and Wayne had good jobs at the tobacco factory and Larry had just bought a used, harvest green Mustang. He had even allowed Peter to drive the car once or twice. He knew how Peter yearned for his own car.

It wasn't long before only one six pack remained.

"So whaz on the 'genda for this evening? Let's raise some ruckus. The dance 'cross town sounds like a good place to crash. Tickets are waaayyy too rish for my blood," Wayne slurred.

"Come on Wayne," Larry replied. "Let's just hang out here and enjoy the beer for a bit. We can cruise the streets later."

"Naw. I'm looking for action, now."

Peter brought out the harmonica that he always kept in his back pocket. "Maybe some chicks might like to join us for a party right here?" With that, Peter launched into "Riding in my Car."

Click clack, open up the door, girls; Click clack, open up the door, boys; Front door, back door, clickety clack, Take you riding in my car.

Soon his buddies were singing along. Several songs and several beers later, Wayne, however, was ready to split.

"Ok buddy," Larry conceded, "Let's see what we can find back in town."

The walk back to the hotel was slower and a lot noisier. When Wayne saw the barrels, he ranted again, but louder this time. "Way too much red. How can people stan' to plan' all tha' red?"

Larry took his friend's elbow and helped him navigate the steps back up to the parking lot. "Time to get you home, I think."

"No way. I'm juzz fine. Don' wanna go home just yet. My old man's still up."

Peter watched Larry and Wayne stumble up the steps into the saloon to play pool and have a few more beers. Peter headed down the road. He walked with a curious lilt, but he was happy. Saturday night hadn't been a complete washout. He lit another cigarette and took a long luxurious pull on the sweet-scented tobacco.

*

"They're all ripped out. Every one of our flowers are strewn across the road. Who could have done such a thing, James? I thought everyone liked them?" Deborah sighed, deflated.

Sitting mum in front of his cornflakes, Peter knew. Oh yeah, he knew. And they would pay. Later that night long after everyone was in bed, Peter rapped lightly on Lorraine's window. Although the rapping had woken her from a deep sleep, she didn't make a sound as she crossed her bedroom to the window. She slowly drew back the curtain to see Peter standing in the flowerbed. She recognized the dark form as her brother, but this was not the Peter she remembered. This Peter was black and blue and purple, but he had a grin a mile wide on his battered face.

"I got them good, Rainey. They won't be pulling up our geraniums ever again. Now I need your help to get me cleaned up, so mom or dad won't know I was fighting."

The next afternoon when Peter walked into the shop to help his father, his father said only one thing.

"Sometimes anger hath a privilege. I am proud of you son, but don't let on to your mother how you got those bruises. You know how she worries."

PART TWO

SMALL TOWN WITNESSES

"Witness: to give or serve
as evidence of a crime"

The Worthy & The Wicked

1

Full immersion

The Armstrongs settled comfortably in the little community of Straffordville far from the congested streets of Toronto and the smokestacks of Hamilton. The family grew physically and spiritually. Peter gained a sister when he was almost three and a brother when he was five. When Peter turned four, James was appointed Assistant Elder, and when little Douglas was born, James graduated to full Elder. Insulating them from the corruption of a big city, the Kingdom Hall became their second home.

The land in Southwestern Ontario offered promise and profit for agriculture. Warm summers, temperate winters and dark, rich soil lured farmers to the district. Influenced by the spike in numbers of people smoking, farmers cashed in and converted corn crops into tobacco fields. The Golden leaves were king. During the War and after the treaties were signed, Straffordville's population, along with many other towns in the tobacco belt, skyrocketed as they welcomed hundreds of new citizens to work in the massive fields harvesting the precious weed.

The 1940s also saw astronomical growth of new Kingdom Halls around the world. The Millions Campaign, spearheaded by Bethel headquarters in New York was a successful recruitment drive resulting in unprecedented growth in the numbers of followers joining the Jehovah's Witnesses. Baptism numbers skyrocketed.

The annual baptism service in which Lorraine and her younger brother, Douglas, were scheduled to be submerged, but it had to be postponed twice. Lorraine had broken her arm in several places in an altercation with Douglas. Her arm throbbed with the memory every time she looked at him. Until the plaster cast was removed, she could not be fully immersed. Lorraine was terrified enough of the water without adding the fearful possibility a weighty wet cast pulling her under. Finally, six weeks later, on a hot afternoon in June, the baptism went ahead.

"Mother, I'm really scared," Lorraine said, almost hyperventilating. "Are you sure they won't let go of me? What if I can't breathe?"

Her mother's reassurance could not calm her terror of the water. On a family camping vacation, Lorraine had almost drowned in the nearby lake. She was only six at the time, but the memory haunted her yet. Her eyes were open. The water waved above her face. She didn't know which end was up. At the last moment, her father grabbed her hair and pulled her to safety.

"Dougie, how can you smile at a time like this?" she scolded her brother. She stared intently at his raven black hair standing out in sharp contrast with the other four Armstrong family members. Any day, she expected horns to rise from his charcoal curls. Over the past two years, Dougie had experienced a major growth spurt. He was almost the tallest in the entire family. He towered over Lorraine. When they sat together at dinners at the Hall, his large feet got caught up in the chair legs and his big hands fumbled with the cutlery. Lorraine wanted to accidentally-on-purpose smash the pointed toes of her patent leather shoes into his knee caps beneath the table.

"I'm not afraid," Dougie gloated, "Jehovah will be right at my elbow, especially now that I am being offered to be a Discreet Slave at Bethel."

"How could I forget, since you remind me of your preferred status every morning before the yearbook Bible lesson? And who am I? Only the sister of Douglas — the chosen one," she said. "At least you get to wear a bathing suit. My dress will balloon with water and I will meet a murky death."

"Enough with the dramatics," Dougie said. "Where's your faith?"

Lorraine glanced away from her brother before he could throw another remark her way. But it got her thinking. She often wondered the same thing. *Why do I continue to contradict everything? I know I have a saucy tongue and it always gets me in trouble, but still I do it. I won't soon forget the time I asked about Charles Taze Russell,* she thought, drawing out his middle name like the strap in a slingshot. *What a disaster that turned out to be.*

The congregation spilled out of the Hall, elated that the weather was beautiful for the baptism. The little lake nearby sparkled and shimmered beneath the spreading oaks. Everyone held hands. The novitiates walked single file to the water's edge. Four Elders took their positions on either side of Lorraine and Dougie, walking the two children into the lake. As the water rose past her knees and then to her hips, Lorraine felt her body tremble.

James gave the nod to Brother Jack and Brother Daniel. "Lift her up. Slowly back. All the way under. Full immersion. Children, there is nothing to be afraid of. This is the happiest day of your lives. This is your promise made before us all, to serve Jehovah God for your remaining days on earth until the great battle of Armageddon. Jehovah will be foremost in your mind, more important than your spouse, your parents, your brothers or sisters. Today you are reborn into a new family of hope."

Lorraine came up sputtering and crying, coughing the water from her lungs. "The water is filthy. I'm choking!"

"Quiet dear," her mother whispered, "You are spoiling the excitement for Douglas, our Bethel Boy."

Lorraine clamped her mouth shut in a vice of torment. She looked from one member of the family to the next, but only Peter nodded as if to understand her anger and that she could trust him to soften the rough edges of her temper. She struggled towards her father who was standing on the shore.

"Now you, son," James directed Douglas. "Walk in as far as you can. Then surrender your body to the Brothers on each side."

The congregation erupted into singing. The Elders chanted the lifesaving benefits of baptism. They rejoiced at the cleansing of the evil and dark sides of the world. "Today," they chimed, "you are free from the clutches of sin and Satan."

But Douglas couldn't get out of the water. For some reason, his bathing suit started to creep down his legs. Soon his buttocks showed pale and white toward the congregation. Feigning shock, Lorraine raised both hands to her face to hide her wide smile. She couldn't have found a better use for her old plaster cast. Only Peter noticed her reaction. But everyone else noticed Dougie. His bare-assed display kept the parishioners totally occupied.

Now what has she done? Peter murmured under his breath.

Peter watched his sister navigate the wide pebbly shore, come up to stand next to him, and raise her arms to welcome the Truth. He nudged her knowingly. She winked back.

"Walk with God," the Elder's voice boomed across the river valley. "Join your voices and welcome Jehovah's newest Witnesses."

As the sweet sounds of the music swelled around the congregation, Lorraine parroted the words. She tried to feel new and pure, and walk in Christ Jesus' footsteps, but when she looked at the people around her, all she felt was suspicion and doubt. She clawed at the errant leaves and twigs lodged in her baptismal dress.

||||| 2 |||||

Aylmer

Seen from miles away, the tall water tower welcomed visitors to the delightful community of Aylmer. Founded in 1899 by an eclectic mix of staunch church goers, resident Mennonites and transient farm labourers, Aylmer prospered.

Its proximity to the United States, the Great Lakes and a direct rail line to industrial cities in both nations boded well for a great future. Houses sprang up overnight, bringing respectability and order to the streets which formed the north-south east-west grid system common in most towns of this era. Smart clapboard homes surrounded by white picket fences marched up and down the streets.

Hundreds of gigantic maples, planted along the roadways when the town was still a village, canopied the streets in the green lush of the future. Each spring, the trees dropped their winged seeds to the ground where wind eddies collected them in large drifts along the walkways. In fall, the leaves wafted to the ground where children searched for the biggest and most perfect specimens. They took them home to press between sheets of paper or to create magical rubbings with rainbows of greens, golds and reds. Transformed into art projects in the final weeks before Hallowe'en, the leaves were seen stuck to classroom windows, pinned in store front display cases and taped on kitchen cupboard doors.

Running east to west, Highway 73 sliced Aylmer in two. It also connected the towns from Delhi in the east to St. Thomas in the west, in a long string of business and residential communities. Although Aylmer was considered the hub of the area, whenever residents of nearby villages came to shop, they felt equally at home in the larger city. Within town limits, Highway 73 became Talbot Street. Coming from the north, Highway 499 intersected Talbot at the core of the grid pattern from which all the streets and avenues radiated. Predictable.

Like so many other towns in south western Ontario, Aylmer experienced unprecedented growth in the post war era. Factories were built beyond the residential areas — the Aylmer Food Processing plant, the Carnation Milk cannery, the glass works and the ubiquitous tobacco plants.

Aylmer boasted a new department store, three garages, milliner's shops, clothing stores, a hardware store and two hotels. Small businesses opened almost every month. Talbot Street was busy every weekday from 9 to 6 and especially on Saturdays when children were off school and municipal buildings were closed. The library saw a steady stream of borrowers charging up the stairs to select the most popular books.

The Grade 4 students were hard pressed to know whether to choose *Charlotte's Web* or *The Incredible Journey*. The girls knew they might cry, but the boys were ready for the experience. Older readers scrambled for *The Martian Chronicles* or *A Night to Remember* to satisfy their urgent need for adventure. *The Cat in the Hat* appealed to all ages. *A Bear Called Paddington* touched reader's hearts, while *To Kill a Mockingbird* illuminated a world which was foreign to the insulated community.

Aylmer was a safe place to raise a family. From September to June, children on their way to school wore down the grass on the paths, which criss-crossed empty lots or parks. From open windows, youngsters heard their friends' sneakers tapping over the wide wooden sidewalks, the clank of the fence latch and then the final run up the steps before ringing the bell.

"Are you ready to go?"

Year round, children's anxious calls rang out: in the late spring, *got your glove*? In the early winter, *don't forget your skates*. The hours after school were filled with games of shinny at the outdoor rink on Fern Street, or pick-up games of softball at the diamond over on Thomas. The seasons defined the sport. Homework was done at kitchen tables just before bed, a last-minute concession to the business of school.

Door by door, street by street, groups of children found their way to school: down Snelford to Talbot, around the corner to Park and then onward to the large playground at the Elementary school. Each day for 200 days a year, clumps of boys and girls from kindergarten to Grade 8 made their recalcitrant trip to the stone building. It was a route they had taken for years. Their friends expected the doorbell to ring at ten to eight, and sure enough it did.

Getting a ride to school was unheard of. Everyone walked. The large elms and maples safeguarded the little charges as they skipped and hopscotched along the sidewalks or hollered down the back lanes, past the caragana hedges vibrant with yellow flowers dripping with fragrant honey.

On Sundays, everyone attended their respective churches. "Dust off the paganism of the week," they laughed. Sew layettes for the poor in Africa. Support the orphans in Kitchener and other large cities. Knit mittens and scarves for the homeless and unemployed in Toronto. Outreach was the rallying call of the organized churches.

The imposing Lutheran frowned austerely down Smythe Street, urging the faithful to recant their sins of the week. The Anglican cathedral's bells rang out for a full 15 minutes before Sunday service. Across the town from the United Church, bells of a higher pitch returned a counterpoint in faith. Further along Mitchell, set far back from the main street stood the Catholic Church. Silver roofed and white-washed, the building exuded purity and goodness. Just inside the front doors and off to the right, the mysterious shadows of the confessional exhorted sinners to cleanse themselves before entering God's shrine.

Aylmer's 2000 residents boasted a strong municipal government. Built in 1887, the white sandstone town hall with its triple Palatinate arches and strong tower was the pride of the downtown. In the town hall, fathers and business owners paid their taxes, and registered vehicles and plans for new buildings. Blueprints for a new school and two banks were filed. The police department along with two holding cells was housed in the back half of the building.

In 1947, Aylmer town council appointed 38-year old Harold Henderson as Chief Constable. He would hold the position for 27 years. When Henderson joined the force, it consisted of a Chief Constable, a Sergeant and two young recruits. Over the years, the number rose to six to service the continued increase in population.

Constable Henderson and wife Hilda lived on John Street a few blocks south of Talbot. Fiercely proud of his town and his staunch English background, Harold worked daily to follow the Christian values instilled in him by his parents. Be kind and generous to others and follow the tenets of the church. Inside the bubble of their community, a scant six miles from Lake Erie the citizens of Aylmer lived a charmed existence.

Several miles north of the town beyond the old Air Force base stood the newly built Kingdom Hall of Jehovah's Witnesses. To anyone of a contemporary Christian church, members of the sect earned many derisive titles: JWs, the JDubs or JoHos. The small number of Jehovah's Witnesses in Aylmer walked a narrow line. Employed as janitors, clerks, waitresses, mechanics, or labourers, the local citizens recognized and reluctantly tolerated their presence, but distrusted their religious affiliation.

Jehovah's Witnesses' staunch refusal to celebrate birthdays, Christmas, or sing the national anthem coupled with their conscientious objections against taking up arms in defence of Canada, bordered on the incomprehensible. For ordinary residents, the activities of the Hall smacked of treason.

3

The Work of Satan

Lorraine hated the uniform: a one-piece navy jumper, front zip and no pockets. With zero style, it was definitely not something she would be caught dead in, but because she loved playing volleyball, she wore it with pride to every practice and game.

And she was very lucky to play at all. Jehovah's Witnesses had strict rules around competition; it was the work of Satan. Jehovah instructed his Governing Body that winning anything by defeating others was a sin. However, playing on an intramural team spoke volumes about how said rules could be broken. Intramural games were not considered rivalry, so Lorraine was allowed to participate.

She played only at her own school and only with her peers. She had to accept the concessions. There were always concessions. She had worked hard to get picked by Coach Morling.

Even though she was short, Lorraine was good at the net. She tied her long curls into a tight ball and wrapped her arms in tensor bandages before every game. When Coach Morling blew his whistle from centre court and yelled, "Armstrong! To the net!" she leaped aggressively off the bench ready to take on any opponent. Fierce determination and pride filled her face. Spiking the ball was her forte and she was committed to the team. She tried not to miss any of the practices except on Kingdom Hall nights when Coach Morling excused her.

If her team did well and was invited to play against the Aylmer Angels, Lorraine was forced by the wisdom of Jehovah God himself to relinquish her position for someone on the sidelines. She dreamed about heading out on the bus with her teammates to play against other schools but knew that would never happen. On those occasions, she slammed the door a little harder when she came home.

Coach Morling pitied her. He understood the reach of the long tentacles of the teachings of the Jehovah's Witnesses. He had seen it many times before with other young Witness children who had come and gone through the school. At monthly teacher meetings, Coach Morling would hear comments from the faculty about the cruelty of students being whisked off to full-time missionary work instead of setting their sights on post-secondary school. Thanks to Lorraine Armstrong, Morling could now offer some insight to his peers on the beliefs of the Jehovah's Witnesses around educating their young.

One day, Lorraine even stuffed a copy of the Kingdom Hall's monthly magazine *Informant* into her bag to bring to school, so she could show her coach the ruling about post-secondary school. She knew her parents might ground her for months if they ever found out, but she felt compelled to justify to her teacher why she missed some practices.

Silently, he read the ruling. Amazement crept into his face.

"Post-Secondary education is not only unwise, it is dangerous," he read out loud. "So, your parents really believe this, Lorraine?"

"Oh yes, without a doubt," Lorraine replied sheepishly. "The Governing Body at Bethel tells us that Armageddon is right around the corner, so there's no sense wasting time going to school. We should be preaching the 'Good News of the Kingdom' and saving others from the ultimate end of the world."

He folded the paper and returned it to her.

"Thank you, Lorraine, for bringing this to me. It helps me understand where you are coming from and makes me realize how much of a sacrifice you make each time you walk into this building."

Lorraine put the article back in her bag and turned to leave. She stopped at the door for a moment, "Thanks for understanding."

Lorraine felt a deeper connection to her beloved coach after that day. Maybe it was because he was childless that he spent so much time with his charges. Lots of the other kids made fun of his too-wide smile and his cheap dentures that exposed perfectly square teeth all the way to the first molars. His red curly hair earned him the nickname "Carrot Top," but Lorraine didn't join in. She silently felt a deep love for the man who called her name to the net.

Decades later, competition was wiped off the list of sins of which young people might be guilty and Bethel changed the ruling about playing sports. This change sparked many heated arguments between Lorraine and her mother. Lorraine was indignant that some arbitrary group of men could dictate when playing sports was disallowed and when they suddenly were allowed. The irony, however, was not lost on her. It was just after Serena and Venus Williams started playing tennis when the Governing Body ruled that it was perfectly okay to compete in sports. Lorraine guessed that the real reason was that Bethel stood to profit in some way from the millions those girls would win.

||||| 4 |||||

The Jacksons

A neat brick dwelling at the corner of Sydenham and Wellington was the modest home of George and Virginia Jackson and their two daughters, Georgia and Mary.

For the most part, the family kept to themselves. George was a baker at the local bakery, and Virginia raised her family and cleaned house for several neighbours. The family attended the Kingdom Hall regularly: two evening Bible studies, Thursday night ministry school, two services on Saturday and Sunday, dinners with their Brothers and Sisters, and they helped keep the contribution box full. Theirs was a humble and simple life.

In her last year of junior high school, Mary didn't have any college or university aspirations. Like her older sister Georgia, she would find a job in town until she married a Brother from the Hall. There was no thought of betterment beyond the role God had ordained for her. Now 20, Georgia had been working at the Dairy Bar since she left formal schooling in October of her Grade 11 year.

Georgia and her sister slept in the two small bedrooms at the top of the stairs, their brothers bunked in the basement. Their parents shared the only bedroom on the first floor next to the living room. The girls' rooms were neat but spartan, each a carbon copy of the other. A bed, nightstand with lamp, and a five-drawer bureau topped with lace doilies was the only furniture. A small, rolled mat lay next to the bed.

Georgia kept a pile of *Watchtower* publications on the lower shelf. Each night before turning out her light, she read one from cover to cover.

Beware of false prophets.

Remain devoted to Jehovah God.

Honour Him through Christ Jesus.

||||| 5 |||||

Pounding the Sidewalk

Door-to-door, Back Call, Bible study, Kingdom Hall: the phrases chimed from the mouths of those who had found the Truth and, in every moment of every day, they were on a mission to share that Truth with non-believers and harvest them home.

In every Witness family, Sunday was the first day of the week, the day to take the message door-to-door. Georgia had already begun her journey to become a full-time missionary. The Dairy Bar had taught her to overcome her innate shyness, and her faith had given her the courage to take the message to the street.

Each Sunday she joined her parents around the table in the kitchen for a simple breakfast, usually toast and jam, before driving to the Hall where they would meet other Brothers and Sisters in the parking lot. There they would match drivers and riders for the campaign.

The pairings depended on the number of people and cars. Usually, an elder would organize the routes, or concessions, that each pair would take. Often, pairs consisted of a mentor and a trainee. Sometimes a mature person was paired with a child, or a regular witness with a new member.

Through the winter, the routes were shortened as the weather impacted how long the members could remain outdoors, but generally, the missionary pairs expected to spend at least two hours preaching the Good News in pursuit of new believers.

The Jehovah's Witness organization was a finely tuned machine with respect to the writing, publishing and distribution of books, magazines and leaflets. The leader of the pair gathered the latest literature in readiness for the unsuspecting householders.

Because the last prediction of the end of the world had not come to pass, The Watchtower Bible and Tract Society articles were no longer authored by individuals. Instead, a group of writers simply named "*The Watchtower* writers" produced the massive number of volumes which rolled off their presses in New York. No single person could be held accountable or blamed for the discontent among dissenters from the Truth.

The driving force of Jehovah's Witnesses was the constant need to recruit converts and drive up the numbers that would share the truth of salvation before the world ended. It was the primary reason why the men, women and children met each Sunday in Kingdom Hall parking lots everywhere around the world.

In pursuit of this goal, members' performance was constantly tracked and recorded. The driver did not approach the householders; instead, he parked the car and waited while the team of Witnesses went door-to-door. His job was to keep accurate records. Every Jehovah's Witness knew that their successes and failures were being tallied on a report card.

The mature member of the pair rang the doorbell. Never did they force themselves upon the householder, but to gain entrance to the house, they asked the same important questions.

Did the householder worry about the lack of kindness in the world? The fear of death? The distrust of materialism and the collapse of the family unit? Would they be interested in reading some of their literature? When the pairs returned to the car, the driver inquired if they had gifted or sold a *Watchtower* or *Awake*, provoking a reason for a call back.

Door-to-door, bell-to-bell. Insistent, perseverant, dogged. There was no doubting the sincerity that guided their steps. They believed Jehovah would reward them for their unswerving faith. Getting a call back was a reason for celebration, not the least of which was earning more points on the report card.

Success was in the numbers and each member had a specific number of points — a quota — to earn each month through door-to-door ministry, leading Bible studies or maintaining the Kingdom Hall. The total of points usually depended on their age or work schedules and family commitments, but everyone worked to please the Elders, and in so doing, to please Jehovah God.

On call backs, the goal was different. Pairs might spend an hour answering questions about the literature left behind the week before. They might offer an invitation to attend a Bible study. These sessions were generally held on Tuesday or Wednesday nights either at the potential convert's home or at a member's home. The new convert's Bible study engagement might last over several weeks or months, but the intent of the slow drip method was always to bring the convert to the Hall.

Once a potential convert entered the Hall, he or she was welcomed with unequivocal acceptance. At the meet and greet, the new member experienced a love they might never have known before. No longer feeling lonely, destitute, unfriended, vulnerable or distraught, they were love-bombed by each member of the congregation.

Thursday night Ministry School taught members how to be successful at the door-to-door calls. The school was scheduled on Thursdays, so witnesses could practice what they had learned at Wednesday night Bible study. Pairs of witnesses went on stage before the entire congregation to role play conversations between callers and householders. This obligatory training was an integral part of the preparation for the Sunday ministry. Through such public displays of personal pressure, members honed their skills to get a better score on their report card.

Georgia enjoyed missionary work, but she often felt overwhelmed by the need to perform. When the door-to-door service was done, she welcomed the return drive to the parking lot where she would meet her parents and go home, set the oven at 250 degrees and put the chicken in a roasting pan for supper.

Then it was back to the Hall for the Talk, the most important activity of the week. Georgia's parents never missed a meeting. Crowded in the back of the Oldsmobile, Georgia and her siblings headed for the Kingdom Hall anticipating an outpouring of Scriptural wisdom. For hours, they were expected to remain silent and engaged in the message being given.

6

Disfellowshipped

Like many other men in southwestern Ontario, Jonathan Stanstorp was a tobacco farmer. For decades his family had planted tobacco on the land north of Straffordville and every fall he harvested the benefits.

He was also a Jehovah's Witness.

In early spring, farmers planted the seeds of the golden leaf in greenhouses. As the seedlings grew, the farmers tended and cared for them as though they were babies: babies that would grow into adulthood and bring riches to their parents.

In the late 1960s, the Jehovah's Witness position on the growing and harvesting of tobacco changed. One year, tobacco growing was a worthy endeavor; the next it was disallowed. The Governing Body in New York ruled that all tobacco was sinful, and the arbitrary mandate came down the pipeline. It was not just smoking tobacco but growing it or working in a store that sold the wicked leaf was forbidden! The Bible and Tract presses were burning with article after article condemning the evil weed. If Jehovah's Witness farmers did not obey, they would sacrifice all hope of surviving Armageddon..

How could the Organization make such a ruling? Witnesses protested to one another in small groups outside the Hall fearing how they would feed their families. But looming fearfully on the other side of the argument was the pointing finger of recrimination. They had no choice but to submit. It was Jehovah's wish. Growing tobacco was the influence of Satan.

Jonathan Stanstorp pushed back. He met in secret with some of the Brothers. By early April, Jonathan convinced Michael Delany and Andrew Marchand to drive to Bethel, New York and face the Holy Jury themselves.

They returned to Ontario completely distraught.

Despite their valiant efforts, they did not gain an audience with the Governing Body; but in a written notice, they had been instructed to destroy the plants, quit their jobs as tobacco farmers and spend more time doing the Kingdom ministry. Within days of their return, the local Elders visited farms to ensure the young seedlings were dug from the greenhouses never to be nourished in the fertilized soil again.

Every Witness farmer pretty much bowed to Bethel, except for Jonathan Stanstorp. Tobacco farming was his life: his father before him and his father before that. The greenhouses teemed with life. Tender leaves snaked upward to the light. His babies were growing. With a rifle across his knees daring anyone to come near, night after night he guarded his future. When the plants matured, he defiantly planted his fields.

Rumours spread like lightning around the Hall. Witnesses spoke about it in secret. The Governing Body sent their directive. Behind closed doors, the Elders ruled.

Unanimously.

On a Sunday late in September, they proclaimed the sentence. Jonathan had no opportunity to air his grievances. He could not argue that his children would starve. He could not speak for many other families who would lose everything. He could not plead that in all good conscience Jehovah God would not want him and his family to suffer.

Jonathan was disfellowshipped. His rebellion garnered him the label of Apostate — the Anti-Christ. Shamed in front of the congregation, shunned by his former Brothers, his friends and other Jehovah's Witness family members, Jonathan, in accordance with the tenets of the sect was denied everlasting life and doomed for eternity. The sentence was cruel and inhuman. "How," he bellowed, "could the Organization do it?"

Such railings gained him nothing.

*

Johnathan Stanstorp didn't know what to do. He had just convinced the bank to lend him enough money to purchase the newest automatic priming machine. Yes, it was a cost of $250,000 but in five years he stood to make it all back and more. The machine meant he wouldn't have to hire migrant workers as primers, boat drivers, or boat loaders. Harvesting would be done by this beautiful machine. But he had signed on the dotted line two weeks before the edict came down from the Governing Body in Bethel.

Late that night he sat desolately in his tobacco field near the kiln and the newly delivered harvester. He had just paid the local crop duster pilot to spray his fields with poison designed to kill the tobacco worms. This would have been a banner year for his farm.

He cradled his head in his hands and wept.

7

Acknowledging Marie

She was pretty. Wore her hair pinned up mostly, in a French roll. She had her own car which was very unusual in the 60s. She had a sense of humor, more than necessary after bearing one spoiled brat of a kid. Marie was her name. Marie Stanstorp. And she was married to Jonathan, owner of a very successful tobacco farm. The same Jonathan who refused to pull up his crops, argued that tobacco had been a part of his life for years and was not folding.

Following the ruling from Bethel and Jonathan's subsequent disfellowshipping, Marie continued to attend the Hall. But other Brothers and Sisters viewed her with great suspicion. Since Jonathan had been censured, Witnesses believed that she too was a traitor to the Truth. Her friends went out of their way to spy on her.

One Friday afternoon while sitting on her porch, Marie was caught smoking. The Elders came down hard on her. She was placed on probation, one step away from disfellowshipping. Probation meant that a person had a one-time chance to redeem themselves. The rules were simple but demanding. Attend all meetings — five a week; sit in the designated seats for apostates — the back row, in the corner. Do not look or speak to fellow Brothers or Sisters.

Probation usually lasted three months. Following the probation period, the Elders decided whether the apostate would be re-admitted to the congregation.

So, for three months, Marie sat in the back of the Hall, eyes down and feeling ashamed. She sat like a statue, isolated and ostracized, without blinking or smiling to her Brothers and Sisters as they entered or left the hall. The chair had a stiff wicker back, but the physical discomfort paled in contrast with the psychological shame.

One Sunday afternoon after the talk, Lorraine followed her mother towards the back of the hall. She recalled Marie looking very sad as everyone passed by her without making eye contact. It was cruel.

But this Sunday afternoon was different. Lorraine and her mother found themselves right in front of Marie, and for some reason, Marie broke the rules. She looked straight at them and smiled. Lorraine saw her mother smile right back and nod her head. She had acknowledged Marie. Proudly, Lorraine squeezed her mother's hand as they walked through the door of the Hall into the street.

*

Johnathan was not as lucky. Several weeks later, he went into the barn with a loaded hand gun. Marie found him the next morning.

PART THREE

CRIMES AND CONFESSIONS

"A statement admitting that one is guilty of a crime"

February 18, 1966

1

Friday Free

In the spring, summer and fall, Georgia Jackson enjoyed her daily walk to and from work, but winter in southern Ontario could be very unpredictable. Blizzards, thaws, rain and ice; she never knew what coat to choose or whether she should wear boots.

February had begun with one of those lovely thaws that teased Aylmer's residents with the promise of an early spring. But there was a change coming. The weather forecaster blasted out his prognostications on the radio as Georgia got ready for work. From her window, wraithlike steam rose from the chimneys. She put her mittens in her purse. Frost was in the air.

For as long as she could remember, Georgia accepted her place in the larger scheme of things. She never doubted the teachings of *The Watchtower* or her parents. She was obedient, respectful, and trustworthy — all fine attributes of one of Jehovah's Witnesses.

At Ministry School the night before, the Elders announced that she would soon be a full-time pioneer. Although the pressure to participate in full-time door-to-door work weighed heavily on her, she put it out of her mind. It was time for worldly work and earning money. When she left her house on the afternoon of the 18th for her shift at the Dairy Bar, her step was a little lighter. It was Friday, her day off from any Kingdom Hall duties.

Despite the chill which had fallen over the town and replaced the morning sunshine, everyone was out and about; in fact, the 18th felt like a holiday. It was a Professional Development day for the teachers, and many students from the elementary and high school were ice skating. Walking alongside the outdoor rink, Georgia watched a trio of girls being pulled by a handsome young man. Shrieks of laughter erupted from their mouths as he catapulted them into a wide crack-the-whip arc.

Georgia crossed to the opposite side of the road, shivered and picked up her pace.

She knew she wasn't a beautiful girl. She didn't make a fashion statement like the other young women of the town who wore smart woolen coats, pleated at the waist, and adorned with wide fur collars. Georgia wore a serviceable blue peacoat, hand-knit patchwork scarves and a matching toque. She didn't complain. Complaining about material things brought reproach from Jehovah.

But as she passed the rink and saw other girls in coloured tights and short skirts blissfully doing figure eights and spirals, the crack-the-whip trio picking themselves up from a wild turn, or boys in hockey jerseys rushing down the ice with the puck, she wished she could have friends outside of the Kingdom Hall. But that was forbidden. She hesitated for several seconds, her mittens grasping the cold chain-link fence, watching and longing. Forbidden. The word exploded in her brain.

A memory seized her before she could suppress it. She was in the classroom again. It was opening exercises. As she had done every morning, she left the room and stood in the hall while the other kids sang "O Canada" and recited "The Lord's Prayer." It was the same for holiday celebrations. The row monitor knew not to place a colouring sheet of Thanksgiving turkeys or festive Christmas trees on Georgia's desk. While the other students anticipated

Santa's arrival and presents, Georgia read her primer. Following Christmas vacation, her mother always kept her and her sister home the first few days in January. She insisted that she needed the girls' help cleaning the Kingdom Hall. Perhaps she understood the effect the holidays had on her children.

A boy whizzed by the fence laughing at his friend. He smiled at her. Georgia wanted to smile back; instead, she hurried along her way.

Walking became treacherous when the snow piled high on the sidewalks. Shop owners were expected to clear the walks in the front of their businesses, but not everyone did. Her walk to the Dairy Bar wasn't far — just four blocks — but they were long blocks.

Every day her mother stood on the stoop to wave goodbye to her daughter as she left for work, and every evening she was thankful when at 7 p.m. she heard the lift of the latch. Georgia loved the moment she entered her safety net. Instead of the required greeting of Sister Virginia at the Hall, she basked in the mutually accepted, "Mom, I'm home."

2

Constable Henderson — On Duty

The Chief kissed his wife goodbye and closed the front door at 287 John Street. At the bottom of the steps, he turned right and strode confidently towards the centre of town. For more than 25 years, he had taken the same early morning walk. This was his town and he was proud of it. Everyone knew him. Business owners welcomed him whenever he had occasion to enter their store. Sally in the Hometown Café and Judith at the Dairy Bar had his coffee or milkshake order started without him uttering a word.

But occasionally, he sensed resistance. A year earlier, he had celebrated 25 years as constable, but despite the accolades, he felt an undercurrent of dissatisfaction. He was 60, the oldest constable in all of Elgin County, and many of the younger officers often hinted that retirement beckoned. Get out on the boat more. Travel with the wife. Casual, innocuous statements, but somehow pointed.

Perhaps it was time to retire, Harold mused. He had a stellar police record. No abductions, murders, poisonings, stabbings or other such heinous crimes that he knew had beset some of the larger communities to the north. No, it was not his time yet. He wanted to build up his pension, so he could enjoy a comfortable retirement.

He squared his shoulders and marched smartly down the road. *Damn such talk,* he thought, *I will leave when I am good and ready.*

As he passed MacGregor Elementary, he tipped his hat at the children in the crosswalk, their coats unzipped despite their mothers' protestations. "But mom, the sun is shining, and it's really warm," they echoed, "not at all like February." Like the children, he felt like removing his coat. It was unseasonably warm.

As he crossed the road and climbed the steps of the Town Hall, the clock in the tower struck nine. Harold wound his way down a narrow hallway and opened the door to Aylmer police headquarters. The force had long before outgrown the space. Files were jammed into boxes piled one on top of the other on sagging bookshelves or tucked under large oak desks. There was talk of building a new town hall and relocating the police station, but so far it was only talk.

At the front desk, Denise welcomed him with his favourite cup of java.

"Just perked," she said, smiling.

"Good morning, my dear. As always, you make my day."

"Morning Chief," Sergeant Harris said, nodding as he placed a file on his superior's desk. "Hope you had a fine weekend. Looks like this thaw will soon be a thing of the past. Weatherman is predicting a massive cold front to blast down from the north and if that weren't bad enough, moist air is forecast to barrel up from the south. We are in for a bit of a mess."

"Hopefully, the ploughs will be able to keep the roads clear," the Chief said. "We don't want another storm like the one in January. Twelve fender benders kept the Smith brothers far too busy and people took even less kindly to skidding into their neighbours."

Following the thaw in early February, the weather had deteriorated. The morning of the 18th saw a raw wind slam across the lake causing scudding snow squalls, bitter wind and frigid temperatures.

3

The Dairy Bar

"Good afternoon, Georgia," Ralph Gladstone from the corner store said, tipping his hat and smiling at the young woman. "Hope you have a ride home tonight. The storm will be whipping up a nasty brew by six or so."

"Oh, don't worry, Mr. Gladstone. I will have no trouble getting home on my own," she said. "I have an extra scarf in my purse and I am wearing my snow boots. Thank you for asking, though." She continued up the road until turning right on Talbot.

Georgia loved working behind the counter at the Dairy Bar. She got to meet so many people; in fact, it was at her job that she really came alive. People were always so happy when they were buying and eating ice cream. In winter, the store also sold brownies and pies, hot chocolate and coffee. On cold days, there was a constant flow of traffic. The circular red leather stools were almost always full: municipal workers from the town offices, mechanics from the garage across the street, women from Daisy's Ladies Wear, students on their way home from the high school, and even once or twice, Constable Henderson from the police department. For Georgia, it was as though the town were on parade just for her.

Due to the particularly cold January, town workers had been unable to take down the Christmas lights along Talbot Street, so a festive atmosphere still lingered along the street. and outside the Dairy Bar. But each time the heavy oak door opened, cold air rushed inside bringing with it a reminder that Aylmer was not out of the woods with regards to winter.

He came through the door at precisely 4:45. Dusting off the flakes of snow from his jacket, he smiled at Georgia, who was standing behind the counter.

David Bodemer and his wife, Elaine, lived on the outskirts of town in the hamlet of Avon. Elaine had grown up in Aylmer, but David was a newcomer. He was sort of a loner who worked on the railway but found a sanctuary after he joined the Hall. He was a soft-spoken man, hesitant and shy about joining conversations. Ministry school was difficult for him. He struggled to remember Bible facts, and when he forgot, he grew flustered and anxious, and his body shook.

Despite these obstacles, Elaine Crooker, the Elder's daughter, fell in love with him and they were married in the spring of 1963. David Bodemer, a handsome young man with a dark mop of hair that fell roguishly over his forehead, was just a few years older than Georgia.

"Hello Georgia. Nice to see you again," he said.

"And you." She hesitated, but then smiled back.

"Getting quite fierce out there."

"I know, Mr. Gladstone warned me about the storm when I walked by his store on the way to work, but I told him not to worry. I have my warm boots." She continued bravely, "You did very well at Ministry school last night. I remember the first time I had to play the caller. It was really hard." She hesitated before asking, "What can I get for you?"

"I would very much enjoy a steaming hot cup of tea. I only have a bottle of coke in the car and I am sure it is frozen by now," he said, laughing.

Georgia fixed the drink and placed it on the counter in front of Brother David.

"I got a fair score from Bert," David offered while he waited for his tea to cool.

"He is a fair Elder, and not just because he is your father-in-law," she continued as she gave the counter a second wipe.

"Thank you, Sister Georgia. He gave me something to work on though. He wants me to make better eye contact and try to read a householder's body language."

Twisting and wrenching her fingers into a tight ball below the counter, Georgia edged away from David. Her heart pounded in her chest. *Fear? Excitement? Embarrassment?* She was not sure which. Ten minutes later, David tied his scarf around his neck, put on his gloves and walked out of the Dairy Bar.

Customers kept her busy as her shift wound down. She collected dirty glasses, mugs and plates, and passed them through to the kitchen where two hardworking dishwashers stacked the clean dishes on large stainless-steel racks. Despite the escalating storm, business remained brisk.

At 5:30, Terry Robinson entered the Dairy Bar. Georgia noticed him right away. Terry was often seen walking the streets or driving aimlessly around town in his car. He always appeared to be looking for someone to talk to or searching for something to do. Today, his seven-year-old son joined him on his vacant rounds. The boy's hollow motherless eyes bored straight into hers.

Terry had lost his wife to cancer several months before and every weekend since, unmoored and adrift, he deposited his son with one relative after another. Georgia felt sorry for the little tyke, abandoned from everything normal. She walked over to serve them.

"Hello Terry, what can I get for you and Jimmy?"

"Well, sweetheart, Jimmy thinks it's a hot chocolate day, don't you son?" The little boy did not answer but continued to stare at Georgia.

"Did I hear a yes?" Terry's condescending tone was not lost on others in the Dairy Bar.

"A small hot chocolate, it is Georgia. We'll sit at the stools. Nice to look out at the snow and the sparkling lights along the Avenue," he said. "Jimmy is off to his Granny's tonight, and I am off to the bar for beer and hockey. In that order. Leafs are playing. Can't miss it."

Georgia brought the steaming mug to the little boy, piled high with whipping cream. He smiled shyly when he saw three full rounds of cream jostling precariously atop the rich brown liquid. His eyes twinkled a warm thank you.

If only I could help him feel happy, she mused to herself as she slipped behind the counter. But before she knew it, they too were gone into the storm.

Her last hour passed uneventfully. She noticed her white waitress dress was spotted with the stains of past pleasure. Chocolate, mocha and vanilla, a veritable smorgasbord of delicacies. *Mother will have to wash it again. It gets dirty so fast*, she thought, smoothing out the creases.

Precisely at 7 p.m., Georgia removed her white waitress shoes and put them in her bag. She pulled on her snow boots, buttoned up her coat and headed for the door. She was glad to be on her way home. It was a raw night. The wind howled around the eaves and the snow crushed against the large store front windows.

"See you tomorrow, Georgia," her boss said, smiling.

"Yes, indeed. Good night, sir."

Georgia shut the door behind her, giving it a little extra push so it wouldn't swing open. As she turned into the street, prickles of snow and ice pellets exploded into her face. She pulled her hood up and hunched into the wind to begin the walk home. Two blocks down Talbot, she ducked into the grocers where she purchased a pound of butter like her mother had requested. She was thankful to get out of the storm for a few minutes. The butter in her purse, she struck out once again for home.

Eddies of snow swirled around her. One block, two. Finally, she could discern the streetlight of her street, Sydenham. She turned south and stepped-up her pace. Her mother expected her to be on time.

Just then she noticed a car stopped ahead of her alongside the sidewalk. She recognized the vehicle. As she came abreast of the car, the driver leaned across the front seat and rolled down the passenger window. She knelt to look inside the car.

"How about I give you a ride the rest of the way tonight, Georgia?"

"Oh, that is very kind, but no, thank you."

"No trouble at all. With a ride, you will be home much quicker. Hop in."

She hesitated, thinking what her mother would say: *How kind of him to drive you home. Whatever were you thinking, Georgia?*

Decisively, she wrapped her hand around the handle and pulled. The wind clutched at the door, threatening to yank it from her, but she held on tight. She stepped into the car and closed the door behind her.

Georgia settled into the front seat, brushed the snow off her hat and placed her mittened hands in her lap. She shivered into the void between them.

"It is very nasty outside," she said, feeling the need to fill the silence. "My coat is covered with snow just from walking two blocks."

"You're safe with me. The car is nice and warm, and I have the radio on. Do you want to listen?"

"I'm not sure," she replied uneasily. She had never been in a car alone with a man other than her father. *Jehovah, what should I do?*

He turned the knob on the radio.

"I like this station. They play the Beatles." The car edged slowly away from the curb. Snow blanketed the windshield so heavily that the wipers could hardly keep up.

"Let's just stop for a minute to listen. *She loves me yah, yah, yah. She loves you, yah.*"

"No. Please, I don't want to listen. I have to get home or my mother will be worried." Despite her comments, he brought the car to a full stop. He turned off the wipers. In seconds, thick snow covered the windshield like a tomb.

Then she saw it. Glistening in the dim light cast from the headlights. She had never seen a man's penis before. It shimmered a deep purple. Her stomach lurched.

He turned to face her. In one fluid movement, he leaned closer and laid his right hand on her shoulder. "You know, Georgia, you are very pretty."

"What?" she whispered, fear and disgrace filling her mind.

"I've watched you grow up these past few years," he paused as if to catch his breath. "Yes, very pretty indeed."

He grabbed her left hand and pulled it down upon his growing manhood. She struggled not to touch it.

"I want to get out. I can walk the rest of the way," her voice parched with frantic dread. With her free hand, Georgia pulled at the door lever, but his hand was quicker.

"Now, that just isn't friendly," he said, chuckling.

She recoiled from him, repelled by his advancements. *Get out. This is a sin,* the message from Jehovah God fired in her brain even before the stimulus of his hand upon her shoulder bloomed into a sensation.

She pushed his arm away, but he held on tighter. He grabbed her right arm and pulled it away from the door handle. He lifted it towards his lips. She threw her body against the car door, but he pulled her closer into his embrace.

"No! No! Let me go!" she screamed, clawing at his collar.

Frantically, he moved his arm across the back seat and dug his fingers into her neck.

"Be quiet," he spit, menacingly.

With his other hand, he covered her mouth and brought her face ever closer to his.

4

Dark Prom

Lorraine returned from Aylmer 30 minutes before the storm hit. It had been a battle royal, but Lorraine had won the privilege of attending her Grade 9 Prom. Deborah had never gotten her driver's license, so Sister Gertie drove Lorraine to Aylmer, six miles away, where the only Jehovah's Witness seamstress lived.

Lorraine could hardly contain her excitement as she fingered the soft tulle cascading over the satin underlay. It was the most beautiful piece of clothing she had ever seen. She could hardly believe it was hers and in a few hours, she would be wearing it in public. The seamstress covered the dress with a plastic case and warned her to hold on tight.

"The wind is picking up and the snow is just around the corner," she said.

It was her first prom. As it turned out, it was also her last.

Lorraine settled in the front seat, but every minute or so, she looked at her dress hanging from the hook in the back seat, swinging invitingly when they turned a corner. On the road out of town, they passed the Dairy Bar.

"Can we stop for an ice cream," Lorraine asked.

"How can you think of ice cream when it is freezing outside?" Gertie said, laughing as she shivered back at Lorraine.

"I love ice cream anytime," Lorraine responded quietly.

"Not today. We need to get home. Storm's coming."

*

Lorraine hurried up the steps of the house, whisked her beautiful dress up the stairs to her room where she took it out of the plastic and hooked the hanger over the closet door. For long moments she simply stared at the dress. It was so beautiful.

She had only an hour to get ready, but it was going to be the most delicious 60 minutes of her life. As she struggled to put on her panty hose, Lorraine realized she was lucky to be going to the prom in the first place. She had already been in loads of trouble by accepting the nomination for Prom Queen and agreeing to have her picture hung alongside the other candidates on the wall outside the gymnasium. *It was a pretty good picture too, if I do say so myself.*

But when James and Deborah got wind of the nomination, they were furious.

"Lorraine, why is it that you cannot remember certain teachings of the Kingdom Hall?" her father asked. "You know that participating in anything that is competitive is against Jehovah's rule. It is against the Holy Scripture."

So, Lorraine promised to withdraw her name and remove her picture. She waited until the morning rituals of "God Save the Queen" and "The Lord's Prayer" gave her the freedom to head to the hallway where she quickly, quietly, and without witnesses removed her photo and her name.

She felt a sharp pain in her stomach as she headed to the locker to conceal the evidence.

Although she would not have a chance at becoming Prom Queen, Lorraine was still determined to attend the prom. Somehow, she convinced James and Deborah to grant her permission to go with Marvin Frederick, a young Brother in their congregation. For weeks, Lorraine and Marvin Frederick practised their dance steps. They felt so excited to be going on a "pretend" date.

Just two years older than Lorraine, Marvin towered over her. He was gregarious and entertaining. And he could dance. Young Brother Marvin might come from the "school-of-hard-knocks" as James would say, but he certainly can "roll-with-the-punches."

And Marvin had had it very rough lately. His mother, Grace, had gone missing just a year earlier. She had attended the Kingdom Hall regularly with her husband, Merlyn, and was a devoted Sister in the congregation family. She never missed a meeting and always maintained her quota of Christian Ministry.

One Thursday evening, however, when Grace arrived for the Kingdom Ministry School she appeared nervous and her face was swollen and red. A slight bruise was turning purple around her eye. No amount of Avon foundation could hide the swelling.

Dutifully, Grace sat beside her husband and her son, Marvin, for the two hours of Ministry School. After the final prayers and songs to Jehovah, she requested a private conversation with Brother James.

Behind closed doors in the kitchen, Sister Grace reluctantly reported that Merlyn had been slapping her lately. If the house were not cleaned to his inspection, she got slapped. If his white shirts were not starched and pressed to his liking, she got slapped. If the roast chicken were overdone, she was slapped again. James listened intently and was shocked at her outpouring of abuse.

"Jehovah God will guide you," he said. "It is only for you to ask His help. Grace, you know that the Scriptures demand that you remain with your husband and be subservient unto him. You vowed to do this in the name of Jehovah and His Son, Christ Jesus. Go back to your home and listen to your husband. Let him guide you through your healing. Pray to Jehovah for His forgiveness."

Grace thanked Brother James for his advice and, lowering her head, joined Merlyn and Marvin at the back of the Hall.

Three days later, Grace Frederick was missing. Brother Merlyn and young Marvin came to James for help. They had searched the house and the barn. Nothing. They couldn't find Grace anywhere.

The search widened. With the help of the congregation, they searched the Frederick Farm thoroughly.

On Monday evening, just 24 hours after Merlyn and Marvin knocked on the Armstrong door, Grace Frederick was found floating face down in the irrigation pond a few miles from their house.

"This is a matter that must involve the police," Brother Armstrong advised the group hovering around the pond. "I know that we always strive to shy away from secular society and defer to our own Judicial Committee, but in this case, we must contact the authorities. It is out of Jehovah's hands."

Marvin had invited many young members of the congregation to skating parties on the same pond in which his mother's body now floated. He would never go skating there again. He stood alongside his father while the small group of men prayed to Jehovah to ask forgiveness for Grace. Taking her own life meant she had lost everlasting life and would have no chance of surviving Armageddon.

*

Lorraine knew that Marvin would soon be knocking at the front door, but she needed to find the perfect accessory to match her prom dress. She tiptoed down the hall to her parent's room and in an instant picked up her mother's old jewellery box. The tiny ballerina that stood inside began to dance when Lorraine opened the lid.

The wooden jewellery box had been her grandmothers' and because Deborah rarely wore jewellery of any kind, the box just collected dust on the dresser. Deborah had never even had her ears pierced.

Lorraine fished through the box and opened the tiny compartment at the bottom. There it was, the perfect accessory. The tiny golden charms of her grandmother's bracelet were still shiny and sparkled in the light. *Oh, it is so beautiful. Thank you, Granny.*

"Done!" Lorraine exclaimed, snapping the bracelet tight and sprinting down the hall to her room. Minutes later, she inspected herself in the mirror, twirling around for effect.

Just then the doorbell rang. She opened her bedroom door and bounced down the stairs. She could hardly wait to show her parents and her dear friend, Marvin. With one hand on the newel post, she swung herself dramatically into the main hall.

Marvin spoke first.

"You look absolutely beautiful, Lorraine," Marvin said, blushing.

"Perfect," James said. "Just perfect, sweetie."

Deborah turned to look at her daughter at the bottom of the stairs, but instead of the expected gushing compliment, Deborah sucked in her breath and spoke with a vehemence that James had never heard before.

"What is that you are wearing on your wrist? Take it off immediately!" Deborah yelled. Lorraine looked down at the beautiful charm bracelet and for the life of her could not understand what she had done this time to anger her mother.

"It's grandma's bracelet. I found it in her old jewellery box. I like it with the dress. What's wrong with it?"

Deborah pounced, "Either you take that off your wrist, or I will do it for you. Do you not remember, Lorraine, that we do not wear the token of a cross?"

The room fell silent as James, Lorraine and Marvin stared at the tiny golden cross hanging from one of the loops on the bracelet.

"We had that lesson just recently at the Ministry School. Did you sleep through it?" Deborah was furious. "The use of the Cross is idolatry. You know that Christ Jesus was executed on a torture stake. Before you even think of leaving this house, I want you to listen to Exodus 20 verses 4 and 5."

Punctuating each word for emphasis, Deborah spoke, "The Roman Catholic Church is an enemy of Jehovah, and their members worship the Cross."

Deborah continued, but Lorraine's ears stopped hearing. She tried not to cry. She had used the mascara sample from Avon that Grace had given her long ago. It wasn't waterproof, the tube said. She envisioned long black smears soon to cascade down her face.

"Deborah, give me the bracelet," James said softly, coming to his daughter's rescue. "I'll take it to the shop and remove the cross. Then you can wear it to the prom."

Waiting for her father to return, Lorraine stood, devastated and embarrassed while her mother retreated to the kitchen. Within minutes, her father was back in the house. He lifted her arm and placed the crossless charm bracelet back on her wrist.

"There. Good as new," he said, smiling. He hugged his daughter, brushing away her tears.

The words were barely out of James' mouth when they heard loud banging on the side door. The tension over the charm bracelet evaporated. James heard his wife open the door and then caught the gasp of shock which escaped her mouth, "Oh no!" Then, "James! James! Come quick! Something terrible has happened."

Lorraine and Marvin were left alone in the living room while James welcomed three fellow Brothers in the kitchen. From the looks on their faces, theirs was not a friendly Friday night call.

"Brother James, please. We desperately need your help, your trucks and your wisdom."

Andrew spoke first. "Georgia Jackson is missing. She was seen after her shift at the Dairy Bar getting into a dark-coloured sedan. That was well over an hour ago."

Georgia was never late. She never went out. She didn't date. Lorraine held her breath.

"We need to form a search party," James said. He called authoritatively to Marvin who was standing frozen in front of Lorraine. "We'll need your help. Grab a pair of Peter's work boots and overalls and change quickly."

Marvin's face blanched chalk-white. It was his mother's death all over again, but James' voice had reached him and brought him back from that dark place. Marvin didn't flinch. He yanked off his prom suit and with shaking hands pulled on the overalls and boots.

Unable to make her feet move, Lorraine remained riveted to the floor. The frantic voices of the men in the next room preparing to launch the search made her shake with fright.

Georgia, her friend, her fellow Christian Sister was missing.

Struggling to keep the tears from falling, Lorraine turned to go up the stairs. Once in the safety of her room, she removed her prom dress. She touched it delicately before folding it carefully in tissue and placing it in a large, old Simpsons-Sears box. She slid the box under her bed.

Compelled to know what was happening, she crept half way down the stairs and peeked around the corner, Prom Night all but forgotten. Marvin had changed from his suit and tie and was already poring over the maps strewn on the kitchen table.

Her father was barking out commands.

"Andrew, go get Brother Albert Crooker at the bank. He needs to know what has happened. I believe his son-in-law, David, is working with him. We need all the searchers we can get. The sooner we get out, the better chance we have of finding her before she freezes to death in this weather."

Then Lorraine heard her mother's frantic voice shrilling up the staircase. She was saying something about a pound of butter, a bottle of shampoo. One neighbour said that Georgia had phoned her mother just before she left work to tell her mom she was going to the Met but would be home right after. Stories tumbled over the wires.

The wrath of winter moved in. High winds drove the snow across the roadway, reducing visibility. The temperature had dropped at least 15 degrees since the sun had set. The men shoved their hats over their ears and pulled on their mitts.

James led one group of searchers across the road to his shop where he gassed up all seven trucks. Within minutes they were heading down the driveway and out on Highway 3 to Aylmer. It would be a long night.

On the way through town, James turned up John Street and pulled off the road in front of the Bank of Montreal. Albert Crooker and David Bodemer were already waiting to join the men. James waved them over.

"Get in and I'll get you up to speed."

James looked over at David shivering in the front seat.

"Where's your coat, David? You're going to be mighty cold in just that sweater."

David replied with a shrug, "Must have left it at home in my rush to get to work. If we swing by Albert's house, I can borrow one of his."

*

The next morning the Armstrong driveway was alive and buzzing with enthusiastic search party Jehovah's Witnesses. Hushed women served coffee and muffins to the sad-faced men who were preparing for the second day of searching. Family members stayed with the Jackson's at their home on Sydenham to offer whatever support they could.

Lorraine wanted to go on the search. She thought it was exciting, but of course being female and close to the age of the missing girl, she was kept under strict surveillance.

"Lorraine, your place is inside making sandwiches and pouring coffee. This is no task for a young woman."

Within a few hours the optimism of finding Georgia alive and well began to wane. She had virtually disappeared. Snowdrifts obliterated any tracks the searchers might follow, and their hopes plummeted along with the temperature.

After Georgia's disappearance, Lorraine was forced to follow new rules.

"Lorraine, you are forbidden to be outdoors after dark and under no circumstances are you allowed to walk anywhere alone." James' booming voice rang threateningly in her ears.

A menacing demeanour tyrannized the otherwise friendly small town. Frightened children imagined unseen danger lurking behind each gnarly maple tree. Darkened back lanes stretched away from the sidewalks into black holes of terror. Exhausted searchers felt fear stick in their throats as hour after hour and day after day they came up empty-handed.

February 18, 1966 changed everything. No one knew if there was some sexual stalker or insane maniac out there terrorizing the rural tobacco growing communities, sneaking around at dusk, looking for little Jehovah's Witness girls who might be on their way home for supper.

Things could only escalate.

5

The Search

Constable Henderson had just finished his Friday evening dinner when the phone rang. It was Davis at the station.

"Got a runaway for you."

Sitting up and paying attention, he said, "Who?"

"Georgia Jackson. You know, that JW girl who works at the Dairy Bar."

The constable relaxed.

"Nothing to worry about tonight, it's Friday. Young people like to go out and have fun. She'll be back before we know it and on her own time. No need to trouble the men tonight. The weather's beastly. Thank you for the update, Davis. You know the protocol; a person isn't deemed missing until 24 hours has elapsed."

At 11 p.m., George Jackson walked into the station. "My daughter is missing," he said to Davis.

"I already spoke with the Chief, sir. He advised that if she is not home by Monday, come back in. Best guess, she's just runaway," he said.

George pushed away from the desk, his eyes flaring with anger. He turned to leave, but changed his mind, challenging the younger officer.

"My daughter is not a runaway," he hissed. "She is obedient and would never run away from her home where she knows she is loved and cared for. She's been taken by one of those transient workers who come through here, or one of those inmates from the Pen in Kingston. She is a good girl. I want you to send out a bulletin and I want you to do it tonight."

Davis realized that Mr. Jackson was not going to back down, so despite the customary 24-hour waiting period and without his Chief's authorization, he sent out the wire.

Kids in the arena that night remembered Georgia's sister and younger brothers coming in to look for her. Under normal circumstances the Jackson children would never be out after dark alone, let alone in the arena. Arenas were off limits for Jehovah's Witnesses. It was about 9 or 10 p.m. Their faces were blanched with that hollow look of a disoriented animal lost in unfamiliar territory.

February 19-March 30, 1966

6

An Eternity of Waiting

Saturday, the 19th and Sunday, the 20th, passed in an eternity of worry. Every male member of the Jehovah's Witness congregations from Straffordville, Vienna and Aylmer were out all day and all night. Trudging through drifts, uncovering garbage pails, peering under porches, hour after hour they looked. From the gravel pit in the north to the fields south of town, teams of searchers covered the fields, lanes and ditches.

Nothing.

How could a responsible young woman like Georgia simply disappear?

On Monday morning, the police finally became involved and began questioning members of the congregations in Straffordville and Aylmer. James Armstrong among them. They interviewed all the men and asked each of them the same questions. Do you know Georgia Jackson? When was the last time you saw her?

Of course, they all had the same answer. Yes. And, the last time we saw her was at the Kingdom Hall.

The search continued. Over the next several days, yellow markers lined the side roads and concessions from Vienna to Straffordville, on to Aylmer and as far away as London. When a road was checked, markers were left to indicate that area had been searched.

Days and then weeks passed. Cold, frigid air hung over southern Ontario and hampered the search. Snow squalls raced across the lake obliterated any tracks that might have led the searchers to Georgia.

On March 2, they finally found something. Georgia Jackson's coat was found off the Glencolin Line near the road. It was neatly folded. There was blood on the collar.

A few days passed before the second piece of her clothing was found. Michael Verbrugge, a member of the Aylmer Kingdom Hall, noticed her scarf near where her coat had been discovered. It too was bloodstained. In tortured responses, the grieving, but still hopeful parents identified the clothing as belonging to their missing daughter.

The congregation held daily prayer meetings for Sister Georgia. Vigils were kept each Sunday evening for the Jacksons who slumped beneath the confusing burden of pain. Not knowing took a heavy toll.

In the congregation, the Elders questioned the behaviour of the police. Why had they done nothing for two days? Are our children not just as valuable as others? Why was the local Police College not called in to secure the area the same day she disappeared? The Jehovah's Witness community had 300 searchers in the area within hours of her disappearance, but the police didn't join the search for days.

The Jackson girl's abduction rocked the small, quiet farming communities. The disquiet spread beyond the Jehovah's Witness residents to families with young women of the same age. Curfews were imposed. Fear hung on the lips of every parent.

For six long weeks, the public held its breath.

7

From A to Z

When the Armstrong children reached high school age, they rode the bus to Aylmer where they attended East Elgin Secondary School, "The East" for short. Of course, Deborah insisted on the practical, useful subjects she wanted her only daughter to take.

She was adamant that Lorraine must learn to type. Nothing, however, could have been farther from what Lorraine wanted to do. Colour and fashion design were where her heart lay, but there was no call for those skills or talents in her Jehovah's Witness world.

"I am only thinking of your future, dear," her mother crooned. "Typing is a necessity, so you can get an office job. No need to trouble your pretty head with thoughts about college. A good Jehovah's Witness does not aspire for such things. Last month's *Informant* is quite clear on such matters: education is unwise, dangerous and unnecessary. If your father hadn't insisted on you staying in school, you would already be a full-time missionary."

Lorraine knew the edict all too well. It was the same one she had taken to her volleyball coach in secret.

"But mom, I do care about college. I want to be something more than just a secretary. I have big dreams, you know," she said. Her arms folded into a figure eight, Lorraine's fingers dug deep into her forearms.

I will not listen. My ears are closed. I will not be a secretary, she repeated to herself.

Angered with her daughter, her mother turned on her heel and went back to the kitchen. Lorraine's eyes bored into her mother's back. For ten long minutes her mind blistered with righteous anger, but in the end her mother and the Hall won. Lorraine was registered in typing class.

At first, Lorraine hated it. Forty students in long rows clacking away at black IBM machines. ASDF JKL; the resting position. They chanted the letters out loud as their fingers stumbled from key to key. Left hand pinky on the A; right hand pinky on the semicolon. The others fell dutifully in line. Pointers waited for the command to jump to the G or H, T or U, or the super hard ones like N or B on the bottom row as the words demanded.

As the weeks passed, Lorraine welcomed the hour from 9 to 10 each morning in room 203, row 4, seat 5. Strangely, at her designated spot she was both anonymous and included. It felt wonderful. For once, she and every one of her classmates were doing the same thing: learning to type.

Line after line they practiced.

"The quick brown fox jumps over the lazy dog" invaded her sleep. But by the Christmas break, Lorraine could touch type 20 words a minute error free without looking. She also began to like the rhythm of the keyboard. *Perhaps mother was right after all*, she thought. *An office job might be just fine.* And then at the end of February, a new student bounded into the seat next to hers.

Georgia Jackson had been missing for almost two weeks.

At one minute to 9, with a big city flourish, Susan Parker swung her legs over the typewriter chair and sat down. The bell rang announcing the start of class, but Lorraine's eyes were locked on Susan's legs. More specifically, the paisley tights she wore. Golden teardrops on a rich purple background danced up her calves and over her knees until they dove beneath the hem of her skirt, four inches above her knee.

Susan's father had taken a job managing the new clothing factory outside of London. Although he commuted to work, the family had decided to live in Aylmer and Susan enrolled in East Elgin Secondary School.

How did her mother let her out of the house? Lorraine wondered as her eyes targeted the thick brown tights on her own legs, visible only to the hem of her skirt two inches below her knees.

Susan leaned in to Lorraine. "Hi, my name's Susan Parker," she whispered.

Lorraine didn't know what to say. *Is she a Witness? Should I talk to her?* But in that moment with the paisley tights daring her, Lorraine threw the rule book away.

"I'm Lorraine Armstrong. Welcome to East Elgin."

"Can we meet at lunch? I don't want to eat alone on my first day."

Lorraine smiled and whispered, "Sure. I have a special place on the second floor. Nice and quiet, but beside a window. I can meet you at the office if you'd like, right after the bell." And then the relentless electronic cacophony of machines cut off further discussion.

*

And so, with talk of fashion and the missing Jackson girl, Lorraine and Susan's friendship grew. Every lunch time in the little nook on the second floor, whispers of Georgia's disappearance brought the girls closer.

"Tell me again about Georgia," Susan asked.

Lorraine had often told Susan what she knew, but this lunch hour she was mesmerized by Susan's crocheted top. It was short-sleeved, soft, and cream puff white with a little body stocking underneath. Lorraine felt the fashion gods taunting her about her very practical long-sleeved cable knit sweater. Still, Susan seemed to enjoy her company despite her lack of style.

Lorraine leaned her head against the window frame remembering the last time she had seen Georgia. The Straffordville congregation had met at the Aylmer hall for Thursday night's Ministry School. It was so hard to believe she was there that night and then gone on Friday. Susan's voice rippled into the memory and brought Lorraine back to the hallway.

"I understand," Susan said taking a bite of her sandwich, "why my parents won't let me go out after dark and why they are always asking me to call them whenever I am going to be late even if I am only going to the Met and back. But I hate it. I like to go shopping after school. All this fear and terror is scrimping my style. I always have to go straight home and get right at my homework."

"When you moved to Aylmer, Georgia had already been missing for ten days," Lorraine grunted ruefully. "She left for home on the 18th from the Dairy Bar, but she never arrived. I was getting the dress for my first prom. Well, once Georgia went missing that never happened. The police still believe she just ran away and will turn up somewhere like Toronto, but my parents are not so sure anymore."

Lorraine adjusted her bra strap nervously before continuing. "That's when the Ontario police brought in a helicopter to search. When they found some of her clothing. Her coat was folded up neatly, but there was blood all over it. Human blood. It's scary. Aylmer is such a nice town. And for this to happen here is unbelievable. Every night, the streets are totally empty after dark. No one walks alone, not even with a dog. If only they could find her."

"Yeah, for sure," Susan mumbled absentmindedly twisting her brightly-coloured scarf between her fingers. "Why don't we go to the Met after school today? I don't want to stay for extra math help. We wouldn't be gone long. Our parents need never know," she said.

The Met. Shopping without my mother. A pair of pretty tights. The temptation was too much.

Since Susan's arrival, Lorraine had been squirreling away money wherever she might find it. She found coins on the streets, she raided her mother's coffee tin for the odd nickel or dime, and on Sunday, she stole the change from the milk delivery. *I've been possessed,* she thought with maniacal abandon.

Taking the last bite of her sandwich, Lorraine peered out the window across the schoolyard. Her hand went to her pocket where she fingered the plastic change purse. Her stolen booty totaled $1.14.

"Yes. Let's do it. Meet you by the office at 4:15," she said.

*

The escapees crossed the playground and shimmied through the opening in the fence at the back of the schoolyard before heading towards town, math help far from their minds.

As soon as they entered the store, Lorraine heard them calling to her. Bold scarlet decorated with pencil thin neon blue stripes: her own pair of beautiful tights. She buried her fingers in the fabric. She caressed the soft cotton against her cheeks. Susan nodded her approval.

Defiantly, Lorraine snapped open the little green purse, paid the clerk, pocketed the goods and with her first real friend by her side, walked out through the wooden doors of the Met.

*

Lorraine met her mother in the hall.

"How was school?" she asked.

"You know, just the same," she lied pulling her sweater close, the tights safely tucked into her waistband.

It was easy, she realized later. Her mother never suspected her 99 cent rebellion. In the big scheme of things, the act itself was nothing. But in Lorraine's world, it opened the floodgates.

8

Deuteronomy 12, Verse 23

Every Thursday night at the close of Ministry School, the Elder stood before his congregation to choose the following week's topic. A hat filled with small sheets of paper on which lines of scripture had been written was placed before him. Brother James stirred the pieces of paper carefully. It would be Lorraine's first time to participate.

Although their daughter had not been found, the Jackson family was in the Hall, stone-faced and riddled with sadness. The horror rested uncomfortably on everyone's lips. But routine was their saving grace. The congregation was happy to return to some semblance of normal.

All eyes were trained on Lorraine. Everyone wondered what the subject matter might be for her first time. Lorraine squirmed in her seat. James lifted the paper from the hat. His strong voice filled the room.

"The topic is Deuteronomy 12: 23."

"Sister Lorraine, you will be the Caller. And as the Caller, it will be your job to convince the Householder to agree that taking blood transfusions is against Jehovah God's will. You will be paired with Sister Gertie. She will be both your mentor as well as play the role of the Householder."

The only thing that stopped Lorraine from puking was knowing that on the drive to Gertie's to practice the Call, her father would let her hold the steering wheel.

The following Thursday, Lorraine knew she was ready. She and Gertie had The Call down pat. She wasn't even worried when her father said that she would be speaking to Witnesses from the three neighbouring Kingdom Halls: Vienna and Aylmer, as well as her own hall in Straffordville. During the practice sessions, she discovered that she had a good sense about speaking in public and because she understood the topic hands down, she wasn't frightened.

Elder James invited Gertie and Lorraine to the front of the Hall. Dougie watched closely from the front row, his eyes pinched suspiciously. He was very curious to see if his sister remembered all the lines or if she got scared and blew the whole thing.

Lorraine and Gertie walked up the little steps to the stage and took their places to begin the dialogue. Lorraine raised her arm as if to knock on a pretend door. She imagined a middle-aged woman answering the door.

"Good afternoon, neighbour. How are you today? My partner and I have urgent news to share with you about a practice which is abhorrent to God."

A long moment of silence filled the hall.

Lorraine paused slightly before continuing. "You believe in God, I assume?"

"Yes, yes of course, but you are one of those JWs," Gertie said, her voice rising significantly, "who won't give blood transfusions. You would rather let your people die." Gertie played the role of the Householder most dramatically.

"How fortunate it is that you have mentioned blood transfusions. That is the very topic I wish to help you to really understand. Do you have a Bible?"

"Naturally! We are Christians. Of course, we have a Bible."

"Well, why don't you bring it here and we can compare what our Bible says about the blood with what your Bible says?"

Playing the Householder, Gertie made the motions of opening a drawer to get her Bible. She returned to Lorraine.

"Here it is. It's the King James version, don't ya know."

"Of course. Please turn to Deuteronomy 12, verse 23." Dutifully, Gertie mimed turning the pages in the Bible and began to read aloud.

"'Only be sure that thou eat not the blood: for the blood IS the life; and thou mayest not eat the life with the flesh,'" she said. Lorraine then opened the New World Translation Bible to the same passage.

"The Jehovah's Witness New World translation of the Bible is more modern and more accessible to all readers. Let me read it to you and you will see that God's instruction about the blood is very clear," she said. "'Simply be resolved not to eat the blood, because the blood is the soul and you must not eat the soul with the flesh,'" Lorraine said confidently.

Gertie seemed astonished. "Oh my, they are the same. And the newer Bible makes the ruling even clearer. I didn't realize God spoke so strongly about this," she said.

"Well, perhaps you would like us to leave you some literature that will help you understand God's ruling. And perhaps we can come back next week to explain anything that might be troubling you?"

"Yes, I think I would like that," Gertie replied.

"This *Watchtower* explains everything in much more detail."

Lorraine and Gertie turned the knob on a pretend door and then faced the congregation. Lorraine beamed with pride as the members clapped.

"I did it," Lorraine whispered to Sister Gertie, hugging her.

"Yes, you did Sister Lorraine. Brother James will be very proud of you." As Lorraine sat down in her seat in the front row, James announced her score to the congregation.

"You remembered the Scripture so well that you didn't have to glance back at your Bible. That is very good. Something to work on is to slow down, pause for effect and always maintain eye contact with your householder. I've given you an 'A' for knowing your Scripture and a 'B' for delivery. Very well done," he said.

"Not bad sis. You nailed it," Dougie said, making sure his mother heard his kind words to Lorraine.

"Thanks, Dougie," Lorraine whispered back. "Coming from you that almost sounds like a compliment." But in the back of her mind, she wondered what Dougie's real intentions might be.

Deborah beamed at her two youngest, growing up loving and honouring Jehovah God. Following the Ministry School, there was a short social event before the closing prayers. Lorraine served coffee and cupcakes to the visiting Witnesses. Across the Hall, she noticed David Bodemer and his wife, Sister

Elaine, from the Aylmer congregation. Elaine carried a babe in arms, while a little boy walked sullenly beside her.

Lorraine hadn't seen him since she served the men in the search party a few weeks ago. Her breath caught in her throat as she forced the horrible memory out of her head. This was to be a happy occasion.

Lorraine watched David closely as he moved across the hall. Instead of walking beside his wife, he seemed to amble behind as if unsure or distracted by the crowds. Finally, he made his way to the refreshment table. Lorraine made a point of pouring his coffee.

"Hi, I'm Elder James' daughter. This was my first time."

"Hello Sister Lorraine. Don't know if you remember me, but I'm David Bodemer from the Aylmer Hall. Elder Bert Crooker is my father-in-law. Remember, you danced with me at our wedding?"

Lorraine started. She remembered all too well dancing with David. *Sweaty, sweaty hands.* She quickly poured his coffee and offered the cream and sugar to get him to move on, but David hung around the table attempting to make further conversation.

"You did very well," he said. "I am always so uncomfortable when I am called upon to do Ministry School practice. I am trying to get better though. Just a few weeks ago I did a practice with Sister Georgia, you know the girl who is missing? It is so awful that we have looked and looked for her, but so far can't find her. She always encouraged me when I made mistakes." A painful cloud came over David's face as he spoke. Lorraine tried to change the topic.

With words like parchment in her mouth, Lorraine replied, "I can't imagine anyone hurting such a wonderful girl. I served at the last Assembly with her."

Thankfully, James called everyone back to their seats for the final prayers and the moment passed. As the consoling words entered Lorraine's brain, all she could think of was Georgia.

Georgia lying in a ditch or a muddy hollow. Georgia held prisoner in a shed or abandoned farmhouse. Georgia faintly calling for help as she is raped and abused.

Bloody, bruised, broken.

The words of the Scripture washed over Lorraine. *What if she is still alive? What if someone is keeping her alive as a cruel joke and is enjoying watching her suffer? What if they find her and nothing but a blood transfusion will save her?*

Suddenly, she couldn't breathe. *What if someone in my family were hurt or abducted and needed blood? After all these torturous weeks of not knowing, wouldn't my parents do anything to save me or one of my brothers?*

Her eyes fell on the passage she had just so skillfully enacted and she felt like she might throw up.

9

Found

Georgia Jackson's body was discovered near thick brush in a wooded area off the Glencolin Road three miles from town late in the day on March 16. The search team thought it somewhat odd that she was found in that spot as they were sure that area had been searched earlier in the week.

She was naked, and the frozen remains appeared to have been attacked by animals. The autopsy indicated that she had been raped repeatedly and likely kept for some time before she was killed. Blunt force trauma to the head might have subdued her, but cause of death was deemed to be suffocation.

Finding Georgia's body was terrible enough for the small community. On the early morning of March 6, ten days before the grisly discovery was made, Lorraine's brother, Peter, was involved in a terrible accident.

His car had careened off the expressway into a ditch filled with steel pipes destined to repair the fences on both sides of the roadway. Two pipes plowed through the windshield. One nearly took off his right arm, the other broke his jaw. The steering wheel lodged in his core and one leg and both arms were crushed. There was no confirmed total of the number of bones he broke. Suffice it to say, too many.

Luckily, the doctor on call when the ambulance brought the unconscious young man in was able to resuscitate him, but he knew after losing so much blood, that if he did not receive a transfusion, Peter would die.

When he got the call at 4 in the morning, James raced to the hospital and met the doctor in the waiting room. The doctor led him into the ER where Peter lay swaddled in blankets. His face, purpled and bruised, didn't resemble the young man who had sat across from him at the dinner table hours earlier. James' shoulders trembled.

"He's still alive, but just barely. He has lost more than half his body's blood volume. He needs a transfusion. We need to act immediately," the doctor said. He rested his hand on James' arm. No words were needed. This was the moment of truth. James had reached a fatal crossroad.

Peter would live or die at his father's command. The terrible debate raged in James' mind. Pressing into his conscious mind was his faith. *I am an Elder. Others look up to me for guidance and help with understanding Jehovah's Word. Do I sacrifice my family in faith for my son?*

James knew that others had struggled with the exact same issue, but when it came to blood transfusions, the tenets of the cult were clear. All Witnesses must declare they would refuse this medical intervention. Witnesses tempted to waiver from this very strict practice received private visits from the Elders who strove to adjust their thinking. Rather than take the blood, Witnesses must remain faithful and die for Jehovah.

But pushing back vengefully against the regulations of his faith, the father-son bond melted his heart. *In all conscience can I witness the demise of my own flesh and blood when there are the means available to save him?*

James set the wooden chair close to Peter's head. He gathered his son's limp and bloody hand, and tenderly brought it to his lips. Through tear-filled eyes, he watched his son, crumpled and damaged on the hospital gurney, struggle to live. With each painful breath, he felt his son slip away from him.

James Armstrong signed the paper.

*

It took the congregation just a week to disfellowship Peter. Even though he was unconscious, they ruled that he had taken the blood, which was both a sin against Jehovah and justification for disfellowshipping.

Deborah wailed for her lost son. She feared for her husband. She felt Lorraine's accusing eyes on hers every time they passed each other. The stench of personal tragedy filled the house with fear, doubt and anger.

10

Dreams

When Lorraine finally returned to school, she could hardly wait to meet Susan for lunch in their special corner on the second floor. As soon as the noon bell rang, Susan ran to their spot. Within a couple of minutes, Lorraine rounded the corner. No words were needed.

Susan rushed to fold her friend into a strong hug. They stood there at the end of the hallway in broad daylight oblivious to anyone who chanced to walk by.

Some older students remembered Peter and silently acknowledged Lorraine's pain, but everyone realized the ramifications of the horrific discovery of Georgia Jackson's body plastered in the headlines of the Aylmer Express. Sleepy little Aylmer had produced a murderer, a sex killer. The town might never recover.

Susan released her friend. "I'm so happy you're back. Must be hard at home," she said.

Lorraine smiled back at her friend, thankful for her understanding. "Peter's still in a coma. He's all covered in casts and bandages. Tubes everywhere. He doesn't look at all like my brother. It's so awful."

The girls shimmied against the wall, took out their sandwiches and started to eat. In the quiet sharing of that meal, Lorraine knew she wanted to tell Susan what had happened to Peter.

"They kicked him out of the church. Disfellowshipped him. He took the blood. The greatest sin of all," she said, and sucked in her breath. "But that same blood saved his life. If my dad hadn't decided to allow the transfusion, Peter would be dead."

Lorraine waited a moment before adding, "Now my brother will be dead eternally. He will never survive the Armageddon and live eternally. But you know, I really don't care," she spat out the words vehemently. "Being a Witness has to be wrong if such a terrible thing can happen."

Susan patted her friend's hand. "I'm proud of your dad. No matter what rule he broke, I would want my dad to do everything he could to save me. Have you seen the Express?"

"No, my mother hid the papers in the locked chest next to the television. I guess she thought it would be too awful for me to read. I know that she was naked and the murderer did awful things to her," she said, trying to stop imagining what might have happened to a fellow Jehovah's Witness just a few years older than her.

"I have it in my bag. Do you want to look at it?"

Lorraine couldn't resist the temptation. She unfolded the newspaper. The article was dead centre on the first page: *Jackson Girl Found.* Lorraine began to read.

"Really? They think she was alive for a while?" Lorraine whispered.

"Maybe she was hidden close by and tried to get the attention of people driving or walking by. Or maybe she was too weak or too far in the bush for anyone to hear her," Susan offered.

"I can't imagine something so horrible. Eaten by animals! Oh Susan, this is sickening. That poor girl. The worst thing is it could have been you or me who was taken that night. Now I take the long way in to town, so I don't have to go by the Jackson house. It is just too awful to think about. Of course, Dad won't let me out on the streets alone."

Lorraine stared for a long while at the photographs accompanying the article before whispering to Susan, "This is the Dairy Bar where Georgia worked." Her strangled voice continued, "I was in Aylmer getting my Prom dress and we almost stopped at the Dairy Bar, but Gertie thought it was too cold for ice cream."

Lorraine tore her eyes away from the paper. "I think I'm going to throw up."

"Don't read any more. It doesn't get any better. And not knowing who did this is what makes it ten times worse," Susan said, sliding the newspaper back in her bag. "Let's finish lunch and forget about it."

But hours later when she was getting ready for bed, Lorraine relived the horror. She pulled the covers tight around her neck. A March storm had blown in over the lakes and the temperature had plummeted.

No reprieve from winter, yet. She shivered, hunkering deeper under the covers.

As the wind blew cold and sleety against her window, she fell into a fitful slumber. Her thoughts became images, and against her will, the images became real. Lorraine watched helplessly as the nightmare scene played out before her.

*

Georgia was alive. She could hear. She could smell. But where was she? Whenever she tried to move, her body rebelled at the effort. Her hands were bound in front of her.

Her skull was pounding and felt ready to explode. The huge lump forming on the back of her head prevented her from lying evenly on the floor. The pain was excruciating. One eye was swollen shut.

Georgia willed her body to move Slowly she crawled across the floor to the wall. With every ounce of strength, she lifted her torso up and peered through the broken window.

His back was to her, but she recognized him as he squatted over the fire melting more snow.

A look of pure terror crossed her face. She opened her mouth wide, but only a parched scream passed between her teeth.

The water. From the snow. She knew what was coming next.

The ice-cold water washed over her. Blood ran from the wounds on her arms, on her legs.

"Have to get you clean again. You have to look pretty for me," he said.

She tried to block his face out of her mind. The blood between her thighs had dried and the stench of her own feces made her sick.

Lorraine's body shook as she tried to hold the terror inside. She scissored her legs together as if to keep the monster away from her. The Monster. Here in Aylmer.

She pulled the pillow over her face and wept. As her sobs lessened, the words came in fits and starts.

"Georgia… Oh Georgia. What did he do to you?"

11

The Funeral

Disfellowshipping meant that Peter was considered dead to the family, a ghost in plain sight. At night before bed, Lorraine begged to understand what kind of religion could inflict such penalties on fellow human beings. She was old enough to realize that her own father might also receive the same treatment.

Souring her world, anger rose like bile.

Despite the strain placed on the family, Lorraine was deeply proud of her father. Doing the morally right thing to save Peter's life had taken great courage, and as the weeks went by, she realized her father's rebellion and Peter's disfellowshipping had set the stage for her own.

While the Armstrong family wrestled with James' brave but sacrilegious act, the Jacksons planned a funeral.

For six weeks, they had hoped to find her, but with the discovery of her body they had to accept the stark reality that Georgia had been maliciously raped, brutally mutilated and murdered. A maelstrom of fear and suspicion infected the congregation at the Hall as well as the community at large. Such horrible things just didn't happen in Aylmer.

James was often angry. His life had spiraled out of the predictable order he enjoyed in February. But the calendar now read March and much had changed. He spent part of every day at the hospital watching for slow improvements in his son's health. Every evening he faced his wife's recriminations. Every night in his prayers, he begged Jehovah to understand.

"We could be wearing black for our own son," he said raising his voice more than the moment warranted. It was a conversation he and his wife had almost every day.

"I know, my dear, that fact is ever in my mind, but how will we carry on with Peter disfellowshipped while at the same time live with the fear that you could be next? What will happen to the other children? How will I face eternity without you?"

*

Georgia Jackson's funeral was held on March 20, 1966. The Armstrongs paid their respects at the Kingdom Hall where they prayed for Georgia's glorious resurrection from the dead after Armageddon.

Lorraine squeezed her father's hand as they walked into the Hall past the accusing eyes of the other Witnesses. Some likely thought James had no business there, but no one dared to question him. They knew all too well that the Armstrongs had been bowed with their own tragedy.

The Aylmer Congregation Servant, Elder Albert Crooker, led the service.

Days passed. The police could find no suspects. As one of the people to have allegedly seen Georgia Jackson that evening, Terry Robinson was interviewed twice. He stuck with his story about seeing Georgia around 8:30 that night. He even laughed awkwardly when he told the officer about nudging her with his car while she crossed in the crosswalk while he waited at the red light. When the bumper almost touched her leg, she pulled her head out of her scarf, looked at him and waved. He waved back.

David Bodemer had seen Georgia at the Dairy Bar the day of her disappearance, but as a fellow Jehovah's Witness Brother in the Aylmer congregation, he was never a suspect. Elder Albert Crooker confirmed that he was with him at the bank the night of her disappearance and David was so distraught that he could hardly speak about the terrible thing that had happened in his own town.

"She was so nice to me," he whispered to his father-in-law.

The police took a vicious beating for how they handled the case. Why did only Jehovah's Witness parishioners mobilize to find Georgia for the first two days? Why did the six constables on the police force not help in the search?

Chief Henderson retaliated angrily, "If 300 Jehovah's Witnesses couldn't find her," he argued, "how could 306 make the difference?" The 24-hour missing person's clause cited by the police did nothing to ease the family's anguish.

Days, weeks, months and finally years passed.

The memory of the events of February and March 1966 dulled, but for decades Aylmer was remembered as the place where a young girl could disappear in full view only to show up six weeks later bludgeoned and thrown in the woods.

Moving On

12

Apostates in the House

1966 settled into its final quarter, the memories of the murder still on the lips of every mother who had a daughter around Georgia Jackson's age. The New Year didn't erase the horror, but gratefully the calendar no longer read 1966.

The Elders at the Kingdom Hall acted more slowly, even prudently with James' disfellowshipping. He was an Elder and a respected business man. Most Witnesses had likely come to his shop for something. They had to tread lightly with James' case. Six weeks after Peter's sentencing, the Elders read the official edict.

"Let it be known, that Brother James Armstrong is hereby disfellowshipped from this congregation. He is dead to us. Please obey the laws of Jehovah God and his son Christ Jesus, and the instruction of The Watchtower Bible and Tract Society. Do not break bread with the Apostate."

Within minutes of the announcement at the Kingdom Hall, The Shunning began.

They drove home in silence. Deborah twisted her skirt into rivers of torment. She had no words of advice or comfort. The air between them had evaporated into a chasm of sorrow. James parked the car and crossed the road to his shop. Deborah slowly climbed the porch steps. She felt the shudder of the shop door as James slammed it behind him. He didn't come out for hours.

James had anticipated clients would take their business elsewhere, but he could never have guessed the scope of the loss. Ninety percent of his customers, friends and his social life evaporated. Orders for kiln pipes dwindled and custom tinsmith jobs vanished as the Witness farmers and wives in his former congregation obeyed the Elders' instructions.

The loss of business meant that James would have to start over, but he believed that he and Peter would survive their ousting and rise above the cruel treatment of their faith.

Although James no longer feared for his son's life, the months stretched out before him in a vacuous stream of emptiness. He had far too much time on his hands. In the lonely hours of his solitary days, his mind often retreated to the dark corners of depression.

James regularly turned to the bottle of Jack Daniels hidden in his desk. He scouted out the book shelves at the Five and Dime in search of cheap pocket novels, but the biggest rebellion came when he started buying Cigarillos.

Lorraine and Peter watched their father as he struggled to embrace his apostate life. He often sat at his desk reading about some gunslinger and puffed away. The Bible — formerly the centre of the family's life — was shut tight on the bottom shelf. The booze and tobacco did not lessen his anxiety, nor did they calm his anger, but they provided him the necessary distance from his past life.

*

That September, Lorraine entered her Grade 12 year, a year all graduates await with optimism. But for her, Grade 12 turned out to be beastly terrible. Peter had been released from hospital in late April, but only because the family made homecare possible.

James had transformed the living room into a veritable hospital room. There was nothing else to do but accept the cards he had been dealt. His son was alive. They would work together to mend him.

Peter's bed was the focal point of the room. Facing the front bay window, Peter had a view of the passing world from which he had been rudely ripped almost a year previously. Two stiff backed chairs stood at attention along the wall next to a night table piled high with medications, syringes, and kidney bowls. When he spoke, his voice rasped through a larynx shattered by the pipe which had almost decapitated him. For eleven months Peter was a hermit on the main floor of the house, and for eleven months the family eased him back to health. Although everyone was on duty, the greatest amount of work fell to Lorraine.

In the accident, Peter had broken nearly every bone in his body. The form lying on the bed no longer resembled the strapping 20-year-old Lorraine once knew. Three limbs sported full casts and his one good leg lay limp and weak beneath the covers.

Every six weeks when his casts were cut off and redone, Lorraine designed brightly-coloured sleeves to hide the stark hospital whiteness of the Plaster of Paris. One month it was red and green Scottish plaid, the next a splash of daisies. Her mother complained about such gaudy additions, but Lorraine retorted with a flair of her arm that Peter loved them.

"Them's fightin' words, Rainey. You know that tone only makes her angry," Peter said.

"I don't care. We must have some colour in this drab, hateful place. No one comes to decorate your casts, so this is the best I can do to make you feel better."

"Thanks, sis. I do like them, and never knowing what you will create next keeps me guessing. You should be a fashion designer. I bet any clothing factory would love to have you work for them."

Lorraine turned on the black and white Phillips and settled next to her brother. With nothing to lose after his disfellowshipping, James had brought the demon television into the home. He was not going to deprive his son from enjoying the worldly programs shown on the odious box. Every afternoon following his physical therapy exercise, Peter and Lorraine snuggled under the

Afghan at four o'clock. When Bat Masterton rode into town on Champion, they forgot the Hall and mother's rules.

One afternoon in early October, Lorraine leaned around the kitchen doorway to be sure her mother wasn't within earshot. She tiptoed back to the bed and whispered into Peter's ear.

"I got a formal invitation from Susan's family. They want me to come for Thanksgiving. The whole weekend. Susan's father owns a big clothing factory in Kirkwood just outside London. Can you imagine me showing some of my designs?" Lorraine covered her mouth to hide her excitement.

"Well, what are you going to say?"

"Yes, of course. Silly."

Peter smiled that old smile, the one she remembered from excursions to the creek where they clandestinely would sail their boats to points unknown. The old Peter was in there still, and when the time came to leave him, Lorraine would miss him dreadfully.

*

When Lorraine came home from school on Friday, she found her mother standing at Peter's bedside. She cringed as her mother's bubbling voice reached her.

"Wake up Peter. It's Friday…" Then she riddled, "Friday, Friday, keep your nose tidy."

She was doing exactly that: wiping the nose of her adult son, his helpless extremities useless at his sides. On Fridays, mother usually did most of the caregiving. Lorraine was off duty except for the laundry. And there was always lots of that.

Peter had a bedside commode, but there were more accidents than the family anticipated, and bed sheets were always in short supply. The family struggled with his transfers to the commode, emptied his leg bag and carefully checked the yellow liquid for signs of blood. They followed the discharge plan to the letter, determined to get Peter mobile.

The silence in the house since James' disfellowshipping was deafening, broken only by Peter's strangled screams of pain when he moved.

Deborah was very quiet and rarely spoke. James went about his business, still suffering from the shock and anger of losing his Brothers and Sisters, his customers, his friends and his wife. He knew that when he signed the authorization for Peter to receive the blood, his son would live, but James had little time to absorb the side effects: that both would be kicked out of the faith that had defined their family.

He knew Peter wouldn't care. He hadn't stepped foot in the damn Hall for years. He had been a rebellious teen. But only weeks earlier James had stood on the dais, leading his congregation in prayer and Watchtower study. He was good at his job. Many of his Brothers and Sisters worked at his shop, but with the sentence, they were forced to quit. When it came, the cut was clean and the loss complete.

Beneath the shroud of evening darkness, Lorraine often watched her father beside her brother, gently stroking his blond head. She heard his whispered words, "I love you, Peter, more than anything."

Members of the Hall still entered the drive to pick up Deborah for the meetings. Their eyes never even glanced up at the shuttered windows of pain.

"Will you join me, Lorraine, this Sunday?" her mother asked. Her inner voice always screamed, *No, never!* But that Friday, she said it out loud.

"I'm never going back Mom," the words came cannonballing out of her mouth. "You can count on that! I will stay and help with Peter. And as soon as Peter is better, I'm leaving forever."

For eleven months, Lorraine lived the roles of caregiver, sister, and consoler. Despite the drudgery of the responsibility, the months passed.

Although her freedom from the Kingdom Hall kept her jailed in the house, Lorraine believed it was a bargain well worth the hardships.

13

The Garden of Even

Peter heard it first and knocked his cane furiously against the wall of Lorraine's room. "Wake up. Wake up, Lorraine," his terrorized voice scratched.

Peter had been sound asleep in his drug induced state, fitfully dreaming about Armageddon. It was the same horrific vision which regularly haunted his disfellowshipped mind. What would the terrible last battle be like? Would it be a fire that would engulf the entire universe or an earthquake that would split the world in two? His eyes fluttered chaotically during his REM sleep.

"Earthquake?" he sputtered groggily. The roar and the vibration finally shattered his dream. "No, that roar was real," he whistled in fear.

"I've got to save Lorraine." He continued to smash the cane against the wall.

Startled by the sounds coming from Peter's room, Lorraine scrambled out of bed and rushed into the hallway. "What is it?" she yelled.

"Armageddon! Get outside, Lorraine. Run. Don't worry about me."

"I'm not going anywhere without you," Lorraine countered.

The shaking continued.

Lorraine peered through the curtains at the front of the house expecting to see smoke and fire, but there was nothing but the sunshine peeking through the dappled leaves. There was just that infernal shaking. And now that she could focus, it seemed to be coming from the back of the property.

Leaning against the railing around the back stoop, Lorraine discovered the source of the shaking. It appeared Armageddon had been confined to Plank Street and Plank Street only. James was rototilling the entire lawn with the industrial tiller from the shop. With each pass of the machine over the sod, its giant blades exposed rich brown soil.

James was building a garden.

The gigantic machine dug into the ground with ease. Sweating and smiling at the newly tilled ground, James face was lit with the fire of determination. When he finally looked up at his startled daughter, he turned off the machine and greeted her. "I'm making a garden!"

Lorraine laughed and returned to her brother's bedside. "Peter, it's going to be a garden. Say it fast and it rhymes with arm-a-geddon." Lorraine saw that Peter was not laughing. He was still shaking from his dream.

For many weeks, Lorraine and Peter had worried about their father. That is until the morning when the shaking started. Without telling anyone, James had decided to build a garden. Not just any garden, a huge commercial garden. Row by row the tiller churned up the soil. James waved to Lorraine, who had returned to the stoop.

"Hello sleepyhead. Welcome to my Garden of Getting Even. No Garden of Eden for me," James said, laughing maniacally.

"Just let them try to take this away from me," he yelled, shaking his fist skyward. "From now on I'll feed my family and find new customers without their goddamn help or interference. A new day has begun."

Deborah never questioned him.

14

Olive Branches

"I'll be back on Monday night," Lorraine yelled over her shoulder to her mom then leaned over Peter to do a quick check on his bag. She hugged him one last time.

"Don't worry about me Rainey. I'll be fine. I'm already using the cane to get around. You deserve a weekend off. Go have some fun with Susan and her family."

Deborah paced quickly into the living room and stood before her children. She placed her hands on her hips as if to demand their obedience or at least their attention. Both Peter and Lorraine turned to face their mother.

"How am I supposed to attend the Talk if you're not here to look after your brother?" Deborah whined.

"I guess you'll have to miss a day. Think you can manage it?" Lorraine quipped sarcastically.

"And why must you continue to hang around with those heathens? You need to find some good Jehovah's Witness friends. Like you had when you came to the Hall."

"No, mom, I don't. I'm very happy with my friends. They are a real family. It's Thanksgiving and I intend to spend it with Susan. Her gramma is coming down from Toronto and Susan's parents are cooking a big turkey." As an afterthought, she added, "I might even make a Thanksgiving turkey centrepiece for the table. I know Susan's dad, Stan, would really appreciate that."

Leaving her mother standing by the sink, Lorraine walked through the front door into the street and headed for the bus. Next stop, Aylmer. As the bus passed the outskirts of Straffordville, she finally felt her shoulders relax.

*

Stan Parker, Susan's father, enjoyed his daily drive to work. He was very happy that he had decided to buy in Aylmer and commute rather than live and work in London. Highway 3, the quickest route between Aylmer and London, was well travelled and each season provided starkly different vistas.

He rarely took another route. He was sure that his '67 Ford could probably find its way to Linen & Leathers on the outskirts of London by itself. The open road spoke to him in ways other drivers might never understand, but of course Stan was a colours man with a sharp eye for beauty and design.

Autumn had cast its rustic mantel over the entire countryside. From lush greens to vibrant oranges, hundreds of tall maples whispered the subtle change to winter.

We are so blessed to live in such a beautiful area of Ontario, he thought.

As he turned on to Number 40 south to Aylmer, a shock of raging yellow police tape stubbornly clinging to a tree trunk caught his eye. And suddenly it was March 1966 again.

A portion of the tape must have been missed by the police. Waving demonically in the wind, the yellow terror distracted commuters in both directions. Stan couldn't help it. He slowed down as he passed the girl's final resting place.

Just when you think you've moved on, some small thing brings it back into the room. Aylmer will be in mourning for a long time, Stan thought.

The event had shaken the community to its core. He remembered how distraught Susan had been.

She couldn't have done it without Lorraine. Their friendship carried her through that tough time. And now it's been over a year since the Jackson girl's battered body was found. Stan sighed. *And still no arrest has been made.*

Every night when he walked through his front door, he thanked God that his daughter was safely in her room or making iced tea in the kitchen with her mother. If anything happened to his Susan, it would destroy him. But still a nagging terror lurked deep in his brain. He knew that the monster who had killed Georgia was still on the loose.

"Nothing is going to bring Georgia Jackson back," he whispered into the empty car, "But that family. That poor family."

Stan unconsciously rubbed the itching psoriasis on his elbow.

Oh, that damn elbow. Always gets me when I'm stressed. Wish it would just clear up for good.

Stan's thoughts returned to the murder. *How can the family wake up every morning and walk past her empty room and not know who killed her? No closure. No justice.*

Usually, Georgia Jackson's murder didn't figure so largely in his mind, but the yellow tape had brought it front and centre and today was different for other reasons.

Lorraine Armstrong was coming to Stan and Margaret's house for the weekend for Thanksgiving dinner. Stan was excited for Susan, and yet he still had some anticipatory stress. He was very aware that Lorraine had never been allowed to stay with non-Witnesses before, but he also knew this would be respite for Lorraine. Stan knew how the Armstrong family life and routine had come to a screeching halt after Peter's accident.

He shook off his worries. The visit would be full of fun and laughter, since Stan's mother-in-law, Pearl, the most adored person in the world, would also be joining the family. A fine role model, Pearl. She not only had wisdom and gracious class, she was also lots of fun.

Stan pulled the car into the carport and hurried inside.

"Welcome home dear. How was the drive?" his wife called out as she did every evening when he returned home.

"The usual," but then he paused. "The police haven't removed the last of the yellow tape from the trees yet. It's been over a year."

"Sweetheart, come here." Margaret pulled her husband close.

"I know what memories that tape brings back. It was horrific and still is. What with there being no suspect." Margaret gently caressed his face. "I also know that you worry about our Susan and indeed any other young woman who might become a victim of such a sick individual. But this is Thanksgiving and we have much to be thankful for. Put it out of your mind. The truth will come out. Eventually."

Suddenly two bundles of creative energy flew down the stairs into the living room.

"Hi Daddy!" said Susan.

"Hi Pumpkin."

Susan gave her dad a quick squeeze and then just as quickly released him. Stan smiled at Lorraine standing next to his daughter.

"Hello Lorraine. So glad you could come."

"Thank you, sir, for inviting me."

Susan barrelled ahead, "Lorraine just arrived, and Grammy should be here any minute. Her train was due 30 minutes ago and it's only a ten-minute taxi ride."

Turning to her friend, Susan added, "Lorraine, I can hardly wait for you to meet Pearl. You will love her. If you think we've got a handle on talent around here now, you just wait 'til the three of us get together. Grammy's bringing some of the latest fabrics and leathers from Toronto and we are going to cut some serious patterns. But first let me give you a tour!" Susan laughed as she led her friend through the house.

Lorraine could hardly believe her eyes. There were books and magazines everywhere! Real books! Hard cover and well-read soft covers were nonchalantly scattered on the coffee table. And stacked up on the end tables were *Junior Bazaar* and *Chatelaine* by the dozen. Not a *Watchtower* in sight! Lorraine couldn't wait to grab a magazine and look at the latest fashions.

Next, Susan led her to the guest bedroom. A beautiful floral wallpaper border accented the frothy pink walls, while a pink and white coverlet with matching decorator pillows completed the ensemble.

"Just drop your bag. This is your room, hope you like it. I just finished the bedspread and the pillow covers last night and wanted to surprise you," Susan said, giggling.

Lorraine could hardly breathe — it was so beautiful. "I love this room," Lorraine gasped.

Susan grinned. "It's part of my Sleep-in-Comfort signature collection. By the end of the weekend, you'll know how to make them, too. Easy-peasy!"

In comparison to the décor of Susan's home, the Armstrong house was modest and dull. Lorraine's home reeked of sterility. With every breath, her family sucked in the grief and pain imbedded in the very air.

Hanging limp and always bunching together when she tried to move them on the fake iron curtain rod, Lorraine's functional yellow drapes with foam backing to keep out the light looked cheap and tacky. Nothing matched. The pale green her mother had insisted she would grow to love still made her nauseous.

Lorraine shook her head and tried to block out thoughts of home and concentrate on the next 48 hours of realness. Every room she entered exploded in a whirlwind of colour and laughter.

The doorbell chimed just as the girls entered the foyer. Susan bounded to open the door. Her grammy had arrived.

Lorraine stood hesitantly behind Susan, but when Pearl saw her granddaughter's friend, she enveloped her in a big welcome hug.

"So, you must be Lorraine," Pearl said, smiling as she stepped back and held Lorraine at arm's length. "Susan has told me so much about you and your interest in fashion. This weekend is going to be a blast."

Pearl was one of those grandmothers that every girl dreamed about having: soft spoken, energetic, youthful and truly interested in young people. Beautifully framing her face, a mass of grey curls burst from beneath a Parkhurst angora tam. Dozens of freckles and lots of laugh lines suggested that joy ruled her personality.

Pearl had risen to the position of the wise family matriarch and was respected by everyone. She dished out her guidance graciously, never boastful or I-told-you-so-ish. Exuding a warm and generous mind, everyone had grown to count on Pearl.

And when it came to style, Pearl was a *fashionista*. Not giving her a moment to even wave a greeting to Margaret or Stan, the girls trundled Pearl and her suitcase to her room. To the delight of the girls, the contents of Pearl's suitcase spilled out in a cascade of brilliance. Gaudy pinks and purples, lime greens and oranges, and soft suede transformed the bedspread into a patchwork of colour. Susan and Lorraine began arranging the samples of linen, lace and cottons into piles. They could hardly get their sketchbooks out fast enough.

*

All day as the girls created, sewed, and stitched, they inhaled the heady smell of roasting turkey. Lorraine guessed small onions and carrots were in the roasting pan, hugging the big bird. She could only imagine what delights awaited at the table. The hours passed in a flurry of creativity. At 6 p.m. on the nose, Margaret called them to dinner.

Lorraine felt her heart skip when she rounded the corner into the dining room. This was it. Her first Thanksgiving dinner. She could hardly believe her eyes. The large mahogany table held a feast of epic proportions. From the golden turkey to the tomato aspic and the delicious dishes in between, her taste buds drooled in anticipation.

Lorraine took her seat and marvelled at the size of the bird resting on a huge decorative Thanksgiving platter in front of Stan. Everything was new to Lorraine's eyes: charming salt and pepper shakers shaped like turkeys, cream and sugar containers fashioned after haystacks and corn, and to top it all off, dinner plates of brilliant glossy orange decorated with fan shaped napkins.

Set in the middle of the table between two tall orange tapers, was a turkey centrepiece, its feathers fanned behind its body and a large red wattle hanging beneath its beak. Lorraine smiled as she returned the stare from the beady little eyes trained on her. After all she was new to this Thanksgiving stuff. She closed her eyes for a second and tried to imagine what a Christmas table would look like here.

The imagination of festive dinners abruptly left her as Stan announced, "Bon appétit."

Instinctively, Lorraine bowed her head. The room became quiet.

Stan looked around the table smiling, "Please raise your glasses to the cooks! Thank you, Margaret and Pearl for this Thanksgiving Feast! And Lorraine, welcome to our table."

I love how they pray! At home it's always ten minutes of thanking Jehovah God, Jesus Christ, the Disciples, the guidance from Bethel, the guidance from the Elders and the leadership from Brother Clifford. Lorraine could never remember a time when she ate hot food.

Grinning from ear to ear, she proudly clinked her glass of soda against all the other glasses. She stifled a giggle as she desperately tried to understand why Jehovah's Witnesses were strictly forbidden to make toasts at the dinner table. She would have to look that one up sometime, as she struggled to remember why it was a sin.

Seated beside her friend, Lorraine followed Susan's lead. What fork to use. What was that red berry sauce? And stuffing. Glorious stuffing, made with real butter. The meal stretched out in a tapestry of happiness.

"So, what can we expect from you ladies, tonight?" Stan inquired. "All we've heard all afternoon is the whirring of the sewing machine. Accompanied naturally, with lots of giggling."

"Daddy, you know we can't divulge our *Line* until after dinner."

Lorraine and Susan's stomachs ached from all the laughing. Lorraine had no idea families had so much fun together or enjoyed each other's company so much.

Margaret carried away the dinner plates and brought in the pumpkin pie. The crust was thick and fluted around the edges. The shiny surface was just crying to be smothered in mounds of whipped cream.

"Don't eat so fast, Susan!" Stan said. "Your mother and Pearl took hours to make this feast, let's enjoy it."

But the girls could hardly wait for the dessert plates with the last crumbs of the pumpkin pie to be removed so everyone could gather in the living room for the Fashion Show.

"Sorry Dad, we're just excited to show you our *Line*," she replied.

"Yes, of course. How inconsiderate of me. I know how impatient that fire of creativity burning inside can be."

Stan turned to his wife, and reminisced. "Remember when she was five and we gave her that little pink plastic sewing machine for Christmas? My goodness, she was determined to make that thing work."

Margaret nodded warmly in reply. "We knew even then, didn't we?" she said.

Susan smiled at the memory. "That was a great gift, Dad. And it wasn't long until I had my own real machine."

Pearl interrupted with a laugh, "But I also remember, Susy, when you came to Toronto when you were in Grade 7, I think, that you used my old treadle machine."

"Of course. How could I forget? That old Singer really challenged me. I found the folded green instruction guide in the drawer and taught myself how to fill the spindle type bobbin and how to run the thread from the spool to the needle. That was hard, but I did it all by myself. Designing my own pattern and sewing that pair of shorts in one afternoon was great. I had forgotten about that. They had a turquoise background with large slices of watermelon all over. It was so much fun."

Stan smiled at his daughter. She was no longer that little five-year- old, but her love of what she could do with fabric had helped her choose her life path.

"From the time you were a toddler, sweetie, you were always fascinated with bits of material I would bring home from the factory," said Stan. Susan reached across the table and patted her dad's hand.

"The acorn doesn't fall far from the tree, I guess."

15

The Gem Named Pearl

With dinner done and the dishes washed, the girls and Pearl retreated to the sewing room to make the final adjustments with the *Line.*

"Grammy, your idea to have a fashion show is just the best. Let's move the couches along the wall so we have a runway for the models," Susan said excitedly. "Lorraine's shift should go first. The bright orange leads in nicely to the soft taupe culottes with the green piping along the pockets and hem. And then we can close with the avocado Nehru shirt."

"Sounds like a great plan," Lorraine concurred. "I've got the script. Can't have a fashion show without enticing narration."

Pearl tossed a quarter and closed her palm over the coin.

"Heads" said Lorraine.

"Tails" replied Susan.

"Aren't you the lucky one, Lorraine! Go put on your first outfit," said Pearl, smiling.

Lorraine rushed to the bedroom to pick out the first piece. *And the coin toss! That was stellar. I can only imagine the look on mom's face.* No form of gambling was ever permitted in the Armstrong home! It was strictly forbidden as the work of Satan. Tossing the coin would have made her mother turn inside out with shock. But lucky? That was a sin unto itself. According to her mother, there was no such thing as luck. One could only be fortunate.

Lorraine chose her first outfit, one of Susan's brilliant designs. It was an orange and blue shift with an empire waist. It had a draw string inside the bodice to enhance the breasts. Lorraine tied it as tight as she could. *Mom's not here. Why not?* The outfit complete, she slipped her feet into Susan's gold Mary Janes with the sparkling toes and headed to the living room.

As the family shouted a group "Ta-dah, Ta-Dah!" Lorraine turned the corner and faced the audience. Susan raised a soup ladle like a microphone and the show began.

"Here we have our model wearing an exclusive design by Daniel MacIver." Lorraine paused at the threshold of the room and twirled. Everyone applauded. She sashayed across the living room and gushed, "Please feel free to touch the fabric."

Susan continued, "Our garments are all hand-washable and pre-shrunk. This beautiful dress can be worn with cinching at the bust line or simply draped for a relaxing fit." She smiled at Lorraine when she saw how tight the empire string was drawn. "What a great look." Lorraine did a cute curtsy and left the room to change. It was Susan's turn.

Sporting a rust three-quarter sleeved top over beige culottes, Susan stood at the end of the runway, then circled 360 degrees to accentuate the peek-a-boo back. The soft taupe culottes swayed seductively like curtains ruffling in a warm autumn breeze as she turned. Susan and Lorraine had purposefully fashioned the clothes with a bit of risk. They wanted their *Line* to be noticed.

Lorraine was back for the finale, pairing an avocado Nehru shirt with flared black tweed bell bottoms. She bowed and invited Susan to stand beside her. Wild applause and a standing ovation ended the show.

*

The next morning, Susan and her parents said their goodbyes to Pearl, but she planned a return visit for the girls' graduation in June. She left behind a whole box filled with leftover leathers.

On as many Friday nights as she could, Lorraine joined Susan on their next big project. For weeks, they experimented making small drawstring purses. Susan's favourite was the ones with thin strips of leather dangling from the bag. The girls felt like cowgirls living rough and ready in the Wild West.

"What if we tried making a dress with the same fringe?" Lorraine suggested. "Don't you think every teenager would want one?

Susan laughed, "Dale West would look stunning in our exclusive design. I think we will have to send her a sample as soon as it comes off the docket."

When the weather turned cold, they designed baby moccasins with hand stitching all around. The results were not too shabby at all.

Sketchbook after sketchbook bulged with experimental designs, and bits and pieces of fabric littered the floor of Susan's room in the process. It seemed obvious that Susan and Lorraine would someday make the fashion industry proud.

"I think there is a market for our products, you know, Susan. We just need to find our niche and advertise the hell out of it."

*

Following graduation, Susan started work at her father's factory in London as an apprentice designer. It was all she had ever wanted to do. She encouraged Lorraine that the time had come for her, too, to head for the big city.

True to her word, Pearl offered Lorraine a room in her house in Toronto and an apprenticeship at Sea Run Clothiers. If she wanted it, she could start in September.

The thrill of leaving oozed into Lorraine's veins, offering her hope.

16

Mending Marjorie

Lorraine left them standing at the train station, Peter waving weakly with his good arm. The other still hung useless and limp, but he had made wonderful strides over the past year. He was walking with a cane and learning how to feed himself. He no longer wheezed when he spoke.

Lorraine was saying goodbye to all of it and all of them. Her father instructed her to hold her head high and be proud of her accomplishments. Mother's instructions were canned, "Find a Kingdom Hall nearby and at least go to the Sunday afternoon Talks."

Lorraine's eyes bore into her mother's. *What do you not understand about never?*

She held her Father for long minutes, kissed Peter's cheek, turned on her heels and climbed aboard. At the top step, she stopped to wave to her father and her brother. As the train picked up speed, she realized this was goodbye to a way of life that had stolen her youth. She was determined it would not steal her future.

The latest *Style* magazine tucked in the bottom of her tote fortified her. As the great engine came to life, Lorraine glanced back. Two toots on the whistle and Tillsonburg faded into the past.

Life would go on for them in that broken house. Peter with his broken bones, her father with a broken marriage and her mother with a broken heart.

Lorraine knew that her mother's heart was broken not because her daughter was leaving but because her only daughter had left the Truth and Jehovah.

Good riddance, Lorraine sighed as she walked down the aisle, swaying as the train gathered speed.

"Hi sweetie. Come and sit down," Pearl said, smiling as she patted the seat beside her.

Thanks to Susan, her saviour and dearest friend, Lorraine was going to a new job and a new life in Toronto. Susan had thought of everything. She knew Lorraine was a naïve 18-year-old from Straffordville, so she had arranged for Granny Pearl, to accompany her. Lorraine heaved a deep sigh of relief as she literally fell into her seat. Pearl gave Lorraine a quick hug and squeezed her hand.

"From the look on your face, I can tell you haven't had a bite all morning. Too excited, too worried and just too damned tired. I just happen to have a picnic lunch right here under my seat. Egg salad, your favourite. Let's sit back and enjoy the trip."

Pearl opened two green bottles of sparkling ginger ale. As the bubbles tickled her throat, Lorraine toasted the future. It was the start of her life without Jehovah.

Joining the clothing industry was a dream come true. Some people lambasted it by calling it the rag business, but Lorraine refused to embrace that term. It was all about fashion.

Dressing people in fabrics and styles that made them feel like real somebodies was magic. New clothes brought joy to people overwhelmed with all kinds of burdens: sadness, heartache, loneliness. Discarding the old was like refilling a vessel with hope. Lorraine welcomed the challenge.

*

In Toronto, she was teamed up with another designer around her age, a beautiful blond girl named Marjorie. From the very first meeting, they seemed to click and after several weeks, co-workers noticed their design synergy. Marjorie and Lorraine became close.

Marjorie was creative, fun and worldly. She paired colours that were not even on the same palette. She was a risk taker and a looker. She took line-dancing lessons.

During their coffee breaks they hung out at the large open space at the end of the massive factory far from the noise of the hundreds of sewing machines, Marjorie would start swinging her hips, practicing the lesson from the night before.

"Come on Lorraine. You can do this!"

Lorraine watched Marjorie's feet closely. Right foot out, heel down, tap three times. Then back and the same with her toe. Repeat with the left leg. One, two, three and back again. Marjorie moved in and around the sewing tables, laughing to the tune of "These Boots were made for Walking" singing in her head.

*

On the morning all was divulged, Lorraine was concentrating on a sketch, a modern design which had invaded her sleep and would not be stilled. The design seemed to pulse to her own heartbeat as she traced the pant lines.

Lorraine imagined Liza Minelli wearing it. It would stun the Papparazi. It was a simple one-piece style which could be worn three ways: a palazzo pant, a dress and a cape. With the seams and darts and bling in just the right places, it could rival anything created by Brenda Beddome, another up-and-coming designer just two blocks away. With this new one-piece though, Marjorie and Lorraine would rise to the top. They would pitch this to Ribkoff and then sell it around the world. Their brand would scream versatility paired with beauty.

While Lorraine hunched over the design table, Marjorie came in with the new bolt of fabric in her arms. She was thrilled with the shipment. She laid the fabric down and laughed out loud.

"Lorraine, watch this. Last night's line dancing class married some great moves together. It's right foot, left foot, tap and then a slide and clap."

She makes it look so easy, Lorraine sighed. She wondered what song played in Marjorie's head. The rehearsal finished, Marjorie unrolled the fabric on the table. Red and orange parallel stripes intertwined with lime chevrons and black circles flashed into Lorraine's eyes. The cloth danced in place and then slowly rose from the bolt. It made its way toward Lorraine forming a snake-like rope around her neck.

Then it transformed into the tights she had bought with the stolen milk money. The tights crawled up her arm, across her shoulder and moved for her neck threatening to strangle her. Lorraine's eyes rolled up and she felt herself choking before succumbing to the black abyss.

"Wake up Lorraine. Lorraine! Wake up!" Marjorie knelt beside her friend, gently holding a damp cloth on her forehead. Lorraine was on the floor, clammy and soaked with sweat.

"What happened?" Lorraine whispered groggily.

"When I lifted the bolt of fabric to show you, you fainted flat out. I guess you like it?"

High school typing class. Red-striped tights hidden in a waistband. Blue neon stripes sparkling underneath her thick brown stockings. Soft caressing cotton under her scratchy woolen nightie. The deception invaded her conscious mind and she was back in her parent's house, guilt-ridden and helpless.

It was time to tell the truth.

"Help me up Marjorie. Sit with me a minute, can you? There is something I need to tell you. It is the only thing you don't know about me and I need to share it. I must, or I cannot continue to be your friend." Lorraine took a deep breath before continuing.

"It's my past. Who I was. I was a Jehovah's Witness," Lorraine said. She waited for Marjorie to say something, but she just sat quietly as if waiting for the next shoe to drop.

"That life comes back to haunt me when I least expect it. I have nightmares all the time, but this is the first time at work."

Lorraine continued, "When I was in Grade 10, my friend Susan — you'd really like Susan, she's in fashion too — from typing class owned a pair of really cool tights. I stole the milk money 'cause I wanted to be like her. I was dowdy and shy." Lorraine's tiny shoulders shook with the admission.

Marjorie gathered her friend in her arms. "Shush Lorraine, everything will be okay." And then she whispered in Lorraine's ear, "I was one, too."

For long minutes they held each other and wept.

"But how come you are so happy? How can you dance?"

17

Apostates All

"The group meets once a month," Marjorie said. "They are all Ex's. We share stories and offer support. Come with me on Thursday and meet these people. They will help you to dance, too."

Although she was excited to meet other former Jehovah's Witnesses, Lorraine felt unduly anxious. She had arranged to meet Marjorie at the corner, so they could walk together. No snow had fallen, but the air had a definite bite to it. Lorraine noticed some valiant leaves still clinging to the trees which lined the street.

Like gladiators entering the ring to an unsure fate, Lorraine followed Marjorie up the steps into the back room of the library on Dufferin Street, an anonymous looking building graced by large oaks behind a sturdy stone fence.

A wave of nausea came over her, but she willed it away. *There's no reason to be afraid. They must also have demons that haunt them. They will understand,* Lorraine pleaded with herself.

The meeting room was pleasant enough, plant filled and peaceful. Soft evening light bathed the six warm mahogany chairs set in a circle near the bank of windows overlooking the gardens. A few others stood near a table with coffee and freshly baked shortbread cookies.

Marjorie linked her arm through Lorraine's and led her confidently across the room towards a woman busily greeting others. When she saw

Marjorie, she excused herself from the little group, and with a broad smile turned to Marjorie.

"So, you convinced her to come. I am very glad," the woman said.

"Yes, so am I. Heather, I would like you to meet Lorraine. She left the Hall two years ago." Heather embraced Marjorie and then turned to Lorraine.

"You have come to the right place, Lorraine. Welcome. This room has been a sanctuary for many Ex-Jehovah's Witnesses struggling with the transition and the demons which haunt them. No one judges. Everyone understands." Four pleasant, ordinary people greeted Marjorie and Lorraine. Coffees in hand, all six took their seats.

Lorraine sat next to Steve. *He looks just like a kid,* she thought. *A frail little skinny boy.* His hair was unwashed and his clothes unkempt. His words came out in breathless gasps as if he expected an Elder to raise an arm in judgment.

When he was 18, he had got his Jehovah's Witness girlfriend pregnant. The girl's parents moved out of the province. Steve never knew where. He lost his job at the tobacco farm. Following his disfellowshipping, his parents, grandparents and little brother disowned him. The couple sitting next to him who had offered him a room, spoke.

"Steve is looking for work," the woman said. "He thinks he has a son."

"I'm following a few good leads at UIC this week," Steve said. "I'm hoping that one of them turns into solid work. I don't want to be a burden to anyone, but Toronto's a big expensive city when you have no job. Without this group, I might have walked the walk for the last time across the Glen Cedar Bridge. I suppose there could be far worse ways to end it all," he added grimly.

Heather interrupted kindly, "We are so glad you did not take that walk, Steve."

The couple next to Steve was Beverly and Ralph. Up until two months ago, Ralph was an Elder in the Bayview Hall. The Bayview congregation was quite famous in Jehovah's Witness circles. Around that time, Michael Jackson had come out as a Jehovah's Witness. It was the talk of the town.

Ralph and Beverly, now in their fifties, had been staunch Jehovah's Witnesses since birth. Their two grown up girls married Jehovah's Witnesses and each family had two small babies. Ralph and Beverly enjoyed four delightful grandchildren. Sixty days ago, their pleasant life as they knew it ended.

In his position as Elder, Ralph had questioned an article in a recent edition of *The Watchtower.* It didn't make sense to him that the Governing Body would yet again endorse a policy advising against educating children beyond public school. It was 1968 after all. Yes, of course, he knew that Armageddon was imminent, but Ralph and Beverly argued that the kids still needed an education.

The Congregation Servant called a meeting. Ralph and Beverly were declared Apostates. The arm of the Organization reacted quickly. Within a week, they were disfellowshipped. Within two weeks, Ralph and Beverly's daughters moved away. A month later, Ralph and Beverly received letters stating they would never see the grandchildren again. "Don't even try to look for us," the note stated.

Ralph managed to keep his part-time job at *The Toronto Star.* Two years earlier, in preparation for Armageddon, he had chosen to work only part-time in order to devote more hours going door-to-door spreading the gospel of Jehovah. Beverly used to clean houses for other Jehovah's Witness Sisters, but that work disappeared, and the bottle became her best friend.

"The hours are so long and dreary," she whispered.

Beverly pressed pictures of her grandchildren close to her chest. Her shoulders shook in quiet defiance. She reached her hand across the space between the chairs and rested it on Steve's forearm.

"We couldn't bear the empty house. We are blessed to have Steve with us," she said. No one spoke. Beverly kept her head bowed, the shame at odds with the pain.

Marjorie cleared her throat softly before beginning. "I was one of the lucky ones — a runaway with some place safe to run. The Jehovah's Witness chains fell easily from my body once I settled in the blue gingham spare bedroom at my aunt's house." She smiled at the memory of the checkerboard of her childhood bedroom, "But I still miss my family. Nova Scotia is a long way away, and to grow up without them is hard."

Lorraine understood exactly what Marjorie meant and how hard it was to forget. Although life in Toronto was full of busyness, Lorraine felt strangely empty. She had made friends, but she often found herself condemning their behaviour, their shallow conquests or their hollow beliefs. *What's the matter with me? I hate everything about my former life, except of course my brother Peter and my father.*

She raised her eyes to the group. It was her turn to speak.

Lorraine's stomach churned in knots and her heart raced, but she wondered how she could feel sorry for her situation after listening to Steve, Ralph and Beverly. She took a deep breath and began.

The years, the pain and the loss fell unchecked from her lips.

Patrick

18

The First of Many Firsts

Lorraine hung the stockings on the mantel of her first home on her first Christmas. Lorraine's husband, Patrick Watson, snapped a picture. 1971 had been a year of firsts: Christmas, husband and a baby on the way. She smiled contentedly as she gently laid her hand around her growing belly. As her fingers softly cradled the new life beating inside her, she saw a wonderful future stretching into a distant horizon. It had been a rocky road, but she regretted nothing.

Patrick moved the big La-Z-Boy on an angle beside the fireplace. "Come and sit, sweetie. Time to just relax and enjoy the fire. We'll likely be snowbound tomorrow, but we'll be snug in our nest, right here on Elm Street.

Lorraine patted her husband's hand lovingly. Yes. This was their nest and she was making a baby. "It's certainly been quite the couple of years. How different my life is from that day I left the family at the train station."

"And how wonderful my life has been since I offered a beautiful young woman my Martini olive," Patrick replied, grinning.

Lorraine smiled at the memory. "Hmmm, I was pretty naïve back then for sure."

She reclined her head against the thick plush of the chair. Unannounced, the summer of 1969 swirled before her.

*

While the world was glued to their televisions to watch Neil Armstrong's moonwalk, Marjorie, Susan and Lorraine were going on a buying trip to Montreal.

Several months before, the three designers had met in Toronto for a clothier's conference. Lorraine was thrilled that Marjorie and Susan would finally meet each other. By the end of the weekend, Susan welcomed Marjorie into her life with open arms. The best friend couple soon became a best friend trio.

But July was the big Montreal Fashion Buying Show, one of the biggest in the country. All the top designers and clothiers would be there. And best of all, the three women were on the guest list. They were flying Air Canada and staying at The Grand. It would be a weekend of "firsts" for Lorraine!

Susan had come up from London by train a day early and stayed with Lorraine. They enjoyed lots of time to catch up on life and projects.

"You've got a wonderful place here, Lorraine. I love the little bistro table set and the view across the park isn't half bad. You've really settled in."

"Sometimes being so far away from Peter and Dad is hard, but my busy life at work compensates and brushes away the loneliness whenever it sends its battering ram into my conscious mind. Marjorie and the Ex-Jehovah's Witness meetings have really helped, too." Lorraine abruptly reached for the carafe and offered Susan more coffee.

"None for me. The crepes were amazing, and I've already downed three cups. We'll have to pee even before we get to the airport. And speaking of airport, let's get cracking. Marjorie should be here in about 30 minutes."

Susan set her tapestry bag by the front door and then came back for Lorraine's bag that was leaning against the bookshelf. She pulled on the handle but fell over in shock when she couldn't lift the bag with one hand.

"We're only going for the weekend, not a month!" Susan said. "Whatever have you got in here?"

"I've never flown before. I thought I might need everything," Lorraine hollered.

"What? You've never been on a plane? Oh yes, let me guess. You're that naïve little JDub girl from Straffordville, population 314. Am I right?" Susan laughed.

"Yup, that's me," Lorraine said, giggling at her friend. "Truth be told, I don't think I've seen an airplane close up. Been living in a cave for the last 18 years of my life, don't you know; but I'm ready to leave my bearskin behind and come into the 20th Century. Should be quite the adventure, don't you think?"

"You are the best sport, Lorraine," Susan said as she hugged her friend. "Marjorie and I are going to have a blast introducing you to the 20th Century."

Susan unceremoniously unloaded all the unnecessary sweaters, pants, skirts and blouses from Lorraine's suitcase. "All you need is three dresses, two pairs of pumps and a couple of tops and pants, plus all the female beauty necessities," Susan said, chuckling. "We want to be ready for anything and everything, but not break our backs carrying them."

Air Canada flight 35 arrived in Montreal ahead of schedule. Giddy with excitement, the women hailed a taxi outside the airport. Minutes later, they pulled up in front of The Grand Hotel. Lorraine stepped out of the taxi, grabbed her suitcase and wheeled it into the lobby where she stopped dead in her tracks. The opulence of the chandeliers, the gold tracing on the windows, and the rich burgundy carpets mesmerized her.

"Nice eh?" Susan quipped. "Nothing like this in Aylmer, that's for sure. Almost outdoes the Royal York."

"You can bet on that. How did we ever luck out? This is amazing. I don't think I will get a wink of sleep. If this is what the lobby looks like, what will our rooms be like?"

The girls' rooms did not disappoint. They had a three-room suite, each room with a king-sized bed. Satin bedcoverings and thick towels hung on gold racks.

"Now this is living," Marjorie said, whistling as she parachuted her slim body into the voluminous duvet. She flung off her shoes and wriggled her toes under the chenille throw at the bottom of the bed. "God, I could stay here forever."

Susan would have none of such sitting around in the room. Montreal was the fashion capital of the country and she could hardly wait to roam.

"Relaxing comes later, ladies. Let's get changed and hustle down to the bar for a cocktail. You never know who's hiding in the shadows of the candlelight. A Whiskey Sour or a CC and ginger would hit the spot right now. Maybe we'll even see Joseph Ribkoff himself!"

19

The Next "Must Have"

Lorraine and her friends were far from the only buyers looking to find the newest product that would put their stores in the spotlight and pull in healthy profits. The Grand was chock-a-block with designers, plant owners and clothiers.

The vendors were staying in the same hotel, setting up their lines in the third floor rooms. Opening night was the line viewing. Retailers were invited to preview the clothing and then schedule meetings with select reps the next day.

Patrick Watson was satisfied with his decision to book a suite. He could showcase the men's line on one side and ladies' wear on the opposite end. This was BTREE's first Montreal Fashion exhibition and he wanted to find the right buyer to represent the line in Toronto.

Some of the reps had dubbed him the Silver Spoon Kid. Coming as he did from a well-known family of clothiers, he had taken to the industry early on. When he was still in elementary school he often modelled at shows, and when he got older, he travelled on buying trips with the company.

When Patrick's parents died suddenly in a horrific traffic accident when he was only 21, he was more determined than ever to keep the business going. His Nan and Granddad pitched in and helped the business stay alive while he was finishing his marketing degree at McGill, but once he graduated, he took the helm.

His marketing and design sense had paid off. In three short years, BTREE had become an international brand. It sure hadn't hurt that The Beatles chose his silk Nehru shirts for their main stage concert in London. The group's decision to outsource to Canada had set the brand on fire and the company grew to employ 300 more sewers at the Spadina plant alone.

He believed BTREE fashions would be the most impressive of the entire show. The Watsons were ahead of their time as they scouted out fabrics that were all natural: raw silks, pure cottons and 100% linen for both men's and women's fashions.

He not only felt the energy of his BTREE products, he knew the country had never seen anything like it; it was a win-win situation. The Grand was packed with excited buyers, and Patrick was confident the right retailer would be there and would want to sell it. He did a final sweep of the room, then closed the door and headed for the bar.

The lounge was already buzzing. Almost every tall swivel stool at the long mahogany stand-up bar was occupied by buyers and vendors, men and women full of anticipation.Serving from their well-stocked bar, two bartenders rushed from patron to patron satisfying their anxious beverage needs.

Quaint lanterns on round tables placed in a cozy arrangement on the main floor of the bar cast a soft glow, inviting passersby to come in and enjoy a beverage.

Lorraine, Marjorie and Susan stepped off the elevator and headed to the packed Bay Side Bar. They saw him at the same moment. Recognition flirted with amazement. Lorraine's eyes were drawn to the grey pinstripe suit and burgundy tie, tasseled leather loafers and matching burgundy dress socks. "Style," she whispered. "Pure style."

At the bar, oblivious to the apparent stare down, Patrick nursed a Martini. Three olives on a fancy toothpick stood upright in the glass.

The women literally drank in the scene, but Susan was the first to speak. She whispered in Lorraine's ear, "See that fellow at the bar? That's Patrick Watson from BTREE. He's rich and his clothes are amazing."

"He's not a bad looker either," Marjorie said, laughing. "I think we should plan to get in to see his clothing line first!"

The women scored a table a few over from Patrick. They ordered their drinks and while they sipped, they planned the evening viewing strategy. But Lorraine could hardly tear her eyes away from the pinstripe suit long enough to make her drink order.

"Okay Lorraine, you have to get your game face on. Get out of the clouds and down to business. By the way, when are you going to have a real drink?"

"Hmm, I'm not quite ready yet. When the time is right," she said. "Not sure what I might turn into with alcohol in my frenetic ex-JDub system." Lorraine chuckled.

Comfortable in each other's company, the three women sank into the supple leather of the round tub chairs. It was a moment to savour as they gazed at the mighty St. Lawrence churning eastward towards the ocean a thousand miles away.

"Susan," Lorraine's voice shattered the moment, "After we're done, maybe you and Marjorie should check out Langil's line in room 345 while I go to BTREE in 367. You've both worked with BTREE before, so you know what to expect. It's all new to me. I really want to immerse myself in it before you join me." Lorraine tried to suppress the image of Patrick Watson's tasseled loafers and wavy blond hair that fell untamed over his right eye. "That way we can cover more ground," she lied.

*

Lorraine walked silently across the carpet in room 367. She noticed how energetically the product spoke to the buyers as they passed the tables, racks and hangers. She was absolutely blown away by the colours, the textures and the bold styles.

As she stroked the soft flowing fabric on a maxi dress, Lorraine suddenly remembered a Sunday Talk at the Kingdom Hall in her former Jehovah's Witness life. The Elder was denouncing The Beatles as the demons of Satan and the industrial world the master of evil. She stood transfixed at the beautiful tag on the garment. A small photo of The Beatles wearing the exact same BTREE shirts smiled back at her.

I see no evil here. No demons of Satan, she silently mocked.

At that moment Marjorie and Susan joined her.

"You won't believe what BTREE has created. I've only been here an hour, but already I see at least 12 items we should carry at Sea Run," Lorraine said, almost tripping over the words and displaying her favourites.

"Susan, I'm sure your father will want you to bring these into the London market. Marjorie, I am confident our team will take our advice and bring it to Toronto."

"I agree," Marjorie replied. "Our market is right for this line. The margins are good and if we commit to a strong opening order, we will get free shipping on our first purchase." They filled in the appointment sheet on the table taking the first time slot for Saturday morning.

As they viewed other lines of clothing and footwear, Lorraine could not get the image of The Beatles and that sermon out of her mind.

*

At 10 the next morning when the women entered suite 367, Lorraine found herself face-to-face with Patrick Watson. He had changed from the grey pinstripe suit and burgundy tie that she had held in her dream the night before. Now he wore one of his famous silk shirts and a casual pair of Khaki pants, suede shoes and NO SOCKS!

"Ever the professional." Susan spoke first, interrupting Lorraine's fantasy. "Good morning, Patrick. My name is Susan Parker from London. We viewed the line last night. I would like to introduce you to Lorraine Armstrong and Marjorie Saunders from Toronto. We represent Sea Run Clothiers and we are very interested in your clothes."

Patrick joined the women beside a large table stacked with order forms and display brochures.

"Pleased to meet you, ladies." Patrick's eyes quickly took in the bright florals and wide lapels of their dresses.

"I can tell you have an eye for the flamboyant, but practical. Design that speaks with authority as well as fun and frolic is guaranteed to appeal to a wide buying clientele from all walks of life. You've certainly got my attention." Patrick's glance rested on Lorraine's face a fraction of a moment beyond a casual interest.

"We need to be exclusive," Susan said. "If we give you a large opening order, can you commit to Sea Run Clothiers becoming the main distributor for BTREE fashions?" Patrick looked from Marjorie to Lorraine and back to Susan.

"I think we might just have a deal."

Patrick smiled and shook hands with his newest trio of buyers. Over the next two hours, Lorraine, Susan and Marjorie blew the budget on BTREE.

*

Patrick decided on a powder-blue sports jacket, with lapels and elbows detailed in black leather. The coat was the newest style in the men's collection of the Linen and Leather line. His crisp white shirt, accented with a narrow black bow tie, was perfect for the Gala. Black pants and tasseled patent leather loafers completed the ensemble. Satisfied with his choice, he entered the elevator and pushed "L."

Patrick chose a table for four and waited for the women from Sea Run. It was the Retailer Host Night, and everyone came to the meet and greet. He was not disappointed. His newest clients marched into the ballroom dressed to the nines. Patrick waved them over.

"Join me for a cocktail?"

Susan immediately ordered a vodka and tonic. Marjorie chose a wine spritzer. Patrick looked at Lorraine for direction.

"I don't really drink," she cooed, "but I'd love to give it a try."

Susan opened her mouth, but clamped it shut when she caught Lorraine's expression.

"I believe this might be the right time," said Lorraine, smiling shyly. She turned back to Patrick, "Can you suggest something I might like?"

Patrick picked up the thin-stemmed Martini glass filled with tempting red liquid. He pressed the elegant glass to her lips. Lorraine took a sip and then another. Patrick offered her the soaking olive which she gladly accepted.

"Slow down, girl. It's not juice," Susan warned.

"But it tastes so good and the olives are amazing. Yes. I'll try one of those," Lorraine said, smiling at Patrick.

20

Caught

In the wee hours of Sunday morning, Lorraine woke up in the luxurious king-size bed. She caressed the silk coverlet for long moments before summoning the courage to open her eyes.

Her head was pounding crazily. Her mouth felt like a desert and her breath — aagghh —smelled like a cross between burnt garlic and sour pineapples.

"Yuck." She opened her eyes a slit and tried to focus on the clock. "Shit, I'm late."

Suddenly, she was wide awake. She sat up in a rush, threw her legs over the side of the bed and landed face first on the plush carpet. Shielding her wounded ego, she got herself upright and padded to the bathroom.

Why didn't the girls wake me? I can't miss the farewell breakfast. I must see Patrick.

*

"Well, well, sleepyhead," Susan teased when Lorraine opened her bedroom door. "Didn't hear you come in last night. You were certainly tearing up the dance floor. How's your head?"

"I've never had an allergic reaction to olives before," Lorraine replied, naïvely running her fingers through her dishevelled mop of hair.

"Well, I'm thinking the olives had nothing to do with how you are feeling today," Marjorie said, smirking.

"Come on sweetie," Susan interrupted. "Don't fret. Marjorie and I have already showered, and breakfast is served until 10:30. How about we meet you in the Pelletier Room in 20 minutes? We'll save a seat for you. After our coffees, we can pick up our contracts. They should be ready by 11."

Lorraine agonized over what to wear. She had never been so consumed with her appearance. Her stomach did flip flops as she remembered the touch of his hand on her back as they danced, and the caress of his face as it passed along her cheek when they said goodnight.

Shit! What is happening to me? I can't even think straight. No more olives for this girl.

She couldn't remember what Susan had thrown into her bag, but she hoped things at least matched. Lorraine settled on the purple A-line skirt with a soft cream three quarter-sleeved shirt trimmed with matching purple edging. As an accent, she draped a pale lilac-hued scarf over her left shoulder.

Patrick caught her eye when she entered the vestibule of the breakfast room. *My god she is beautiful,* Patrick thought as he watched Lorraine glide towards the table, the soft lilac scarf fluttering behind her.

"Here she is and none too soon," he said. "The hot dishes have just arrived." Patrick rose to greet her. "Good morning Lorraine, you look lovely."

He pulled out her chair and made sure she was settled before he sat back down. Lorraine placed the stiffly starched napkin on her lap before smiling at her friends. In that moment, she felt more special than she had ever felt in her entire life. She was unable to recall what she ate or what they talked about, but she would never for as long as she lived forget the way she felt when he touched her hand.

*

The loud speaker echoed through the cavernous station, "Express to Toronto, Track 3, departing in ten minutes. All passengers should make their way to the platform, now." The girls shouldered their bags and turned to say goodbye to Patrick.

"It has been wonderful to meet you all," he said, acknowledging the Sea Run trio. "I believe we have forged the beginning of a successful partnership. I have some finalizing to do with other contracts and a couple of tours of clothing plants, so I won't have a chance to come to Sea Run for a few months, but I am anxious to stop in to your outlets in London and Toronto to check on the line and track sales."

Patrick shook hands with Marjorie and Susan before approaching Lorraine. He leaned down toward her face and looked straight into her eyes.

"It has been my greatest honour to meet you, Lorraine. Until next time, then," he whispered into the lobe of her ear as he cradled her small right hand in both of his. Reluctantly, he released her from his grasp and watched as she ran to board the train. Lorraine followed her friends up the steps into the train, turned and waved once more at the man from BTREE.

The train began to slowly move out of the station on route to Toronto. Susan and Marjorie took their seats and waited, breathless with anticipation.

Susan couldn't contain her curiosity for one second longer, "Let it out, my friend, what did he say?"

Lorraine stared out the window following the black cashmere jacket for as long as she could. She turned to her friends.

"Patrick was very happy to meet me," Lorraine began.

"Happy to meet you. What are you saying? He was ecstatic to meet you, Lorraine," Susan gushed.

"He gave you the courage to have a real drink, now that was a coup," she added.

"And," Marjorie added, I've never seen you blush before." Suddenly, she burst into song, "'This could be the start of something big'…"

Lorraine felt the colour rise in her face. "I guess we will have to wait and see," she said. But she could not stop the rising warmth of the memory of Patrick as it rose from deep within her core to her heart.

We will have to wait and see, she repeated silently in her mind.

21

Play Ball

For weeks, Patrick called every day. "Just checking on the sales," he would say. Finally, he was able to free up his schedule the third week of September. He could hardly wait to call Lorraine with the plans.

"You absolutely must come up to Montreal this weekend. I have tickets to a home game of the Montreal Expos against Philly. This Sunday."

"You can stay with my aunt and uncle," he continued. "They are dying to meet you as I just can't stop talking about you whenever I am there for Sunday dinner. You will love them to bits. They live only a mile from Jarry Park, so we can take the bus and not have to worry about the car. What do you say? Peanuts, popcorn, ice cold beer?"

There was no denying Patrick. But baseball? She had no idea of the rules and she knew it was, well, competitive. The logo of the Expos was plastered all over Montreal. Proverbs was clear, her mother reiterated whenever Lorraine complained about having to bow out of tournament games: anything that might make a Brother offended or weakened was banned. *Baseball, a blood sport?* Lorraine wondered. *Why am I even questioning this? I don't give a damn.* But the old rules still slammed into her head when she least expected them.

Patrick enthusiastically informed her that the Expos were the first Major League Baseball team outside of the US. The deal had been a coup for the city and the game was a big deal for Patrick. Almost every game was sold out and whether they won or lost, more than 28,000 fans went home feeling proud that they had seen the Chicago Cubs, St. Louis Cardinals and other baseball greats in their own city.

Jarry Park was the smallest stadium in the Majors and tickets were hard to come by, but Patrick had called in a few favours from some clothing factories and secured excellent seats between home plate and right field.

"I suppose I might be able to come this weekend despite my super busy schedule," Lorraine teased. "I am off Saturday afternoon and could get the 1:00 p.m. express."

"I can speak to your boss about a tour of the BTREE factory on Monday morning," Patrick said. "That way you won't have to take the evening train back to Toronto after the game. All right then, it's settled! I'll be at the station at 5 with bells on." He paused before adding, "You're going to love baseball."

*

The ballpark was alive with an energy Lorraine had never witnessed. Screaming at the tops of their lungs, vendors sold everything imaginable, and fans spouted statistics with every pitch or hit or run. It was a world apart, but she loved it. Free from any rules, sins or commandments, she basked in the freedom.

"You know Lorraine, back in April and May fans had to sit on folding chairs as the bleachers were still on order. Way more comfortable now."

"Patrick when did you learn so much about baseball?" Lorraine knew all too well that neither Peter nor Dougie ever played baseball. Once in a blue moon, they played catch with James in the back yard, but baseball, on teams? Not ever.

"Grew up with it," Patrick said, smiling. I played Little League and my parents never missed a game."

"They came to cheer for you even when you were little?" Lorraine asked naïvely.

"You bet. Sure wish they had been alive to come to an Expos game," he mused sadly. "But they would be proud that the girl I think about every day is by my side." Patrick pulled Lorraine close and brushed his lips against hers. Lorraine's heart leaped at his touch.

Show of affection in public! She laughed. *Oh, my God, wouldn't my mother have at least one line of scripture to spout about that?*

Suddenly the catcher hit a high ball above the first base line.

"See that? A few weeks ago, Willie Stargell from the Pittsburgh Pirates hit one just like it. It sailed over the right field fence and into the swimming pool across the road. More than a home run, that was," Patrick laughed.

Lorraine loved to see him in his element. Normal everyday activities. No door-to-door. No Ministry School. No yearbook. The secret she harboured sent pangs of guilt through her whole body. For some reason she just couldn't open her mouth and tell him. *Later*, she always said to herself. *Later.*

The weekend passed in a flurry of joy. Standing on the platform on Monday afternoon, a Montreal Expo ball cap tucked into her satchel, Patrick pulled Lorraine into a bear hug.

"Thanks for giving me the best weekend of my life," he said.

"I think I just might start following the team. I know some names already. You know Staehle and Fairey. They scored more than once." Lorraine smiled proud of herself for remembering.

Suddenly Patrick's tone changed.

"You know I'll be gone quite a lot through the fall and winter — what with buying shows — but I will call whenever I can. Your number is already on the speed dial of my memory." With that he wrapped his arm around her waist and led her to the train.

"Seems like we are always saying goodbye in train stations. I promise, though, it won't always be this way," he said.

22

On a Platter

Blustery weather scudded across the lake and hung heavy over the sprawling grid of Toronto. Threatening rain and wind meant another wet drive for the thousands of commuters who in all seasons braved the 401. Spring had teased Ontarians with many false attempts, but by March 25, the day Patrick was flying in from Montreal, rain had replaced snow in all the forecasts around the lakes.

But Lorraine barely noticed the wet. Her Patrick would soon be bringing the sunshine of his smile to her front door. She paced from her sitting room to the window and back to the sitting room where she tried to remain composed while she waited.

Her supervisor had recommended she punch out 15 minutes early. Lorraine, however, worked through lunch, not because she felt guilty of the special treatment, but she knew if she hadn't kept working she would have gone nuts with excitement.

And then the doorbell chimed his arrival. She ran to the door, took a deep breath and slowly turned the lock. While still shaking the downpour from his umbrella, Patrick caught her in his arms. Lorraine buried her face in the soft cashmere lapel.

"Finally, a visit with no long-distance charges!" Patrick smiled, running his fingers along her jaw. Like a giddy school girl, Lorraine giggled with absolute joy.

"I have only five hours in town before I leave for Vancouver, so let's move. We're going on a very special dinner date. It's a surprise, so don't ask any questions. Get your coat, the cab is waiting."

They raced down the steps, Patrick in the lead. The rain had become a full-on downpour. Street lights cast long glowing rivulets across the pavement.

The cab turned off Bloor on to Spadina and stopped before a large oak door. In bright orange and red neon, *Yamato,* flashed across the wet sidewalk. Patrick had planned the surprise date weeks earlier when in one of their daily telephone conversations, Lorraine mentioned that she had never eaten sushi or any Japanese food for that matter. Didn't even really know what it was. He hoped the perfectly presented raw snapper accompanied by a warm Saki wine on the side would be a hit with the woman who was becoming such an important part of his life.

"So, this should be an experience," she said, taking Patrick's arm as they sprinted to the front door. "Should I have brought my tums?" she said, chuckling out loud. Patrick returned the smile but once they were inside, Lorraine's fears were allayed.

The tables were dressed in long white cloths and the linen napkins were starched and stiff. She was glad that Susan and Pearl had taught her about formal table settings and felt confident she would use the right fork for the right dish. Patrick steered her to their reserved table by the window. The candle in the centrepiece sent a soft glow radiating across the table.

That's when Lorraine realized there were no forks at all, only ebony sticks tied with bamboo. *Oh well,* she thought, *this is an adventure, remember?*

She had no time to worry about the utensils because just seconds after they had been seated, the waiter placed a carafe of warm Saki between them, turned over their glasses and filled them. The yeasty aroma of fermented rice and delicate spices tantalized Lorraine.

Patrick lifted his glass and gazed deeply into her eyes. "To Lorraine, the most wonderful woman to enter my life, and if my parents were here, they would agree."

They luxuriated in the moment and watched the rain fall outside. Inside they were comfortable and content. The warm Saki did its magic. Patrick reached his arm across the table and took Lorraine's hand.

"You will love Japanese food," he whispered.

The first course arrived. In the middle of a glistening silver platter was a fish — a red snapper she learned later — its entire body expertly drizzled with red curry sauce, greens and julienne carrots.

Lorraine stared at the offering on the plate before her, its vitreous eyes staring back at her; its tail jauntily flipped skyward. Desperately, she tried to curb her nausea.

Clutching her stomach, she scratched out a response, "Could you ask the server to remove the head, please Patrick. I'm so sorry but I simply cannot take a bite of that."

The words hung in the air.

"It's not the fish itself," she mumbled, "it's…" she struggled with the thought. Patrick gestured to the hostess who expertly lopped off the head and set it on a smaller side plate.

So, she quivered, *that's it, the appetizer: a severed head and a body.*

Lorraine breathed deeply to calm her anxiety, but before she could stop herself, she was back at the kitchen table in her parent's home in Straffordville on a crisp autumn morning listening to James read from the morning year-book. She recalled the moment as if James were right there sitting in the seat beside her.

"And that is exactly why celebrating birthdays is the work of Satan," he said. "The very first birthday ever recorded in the scriptures was that of King Herod's daughter. The only birthday gift she wanted was the head of John the Baptist on a silver platter."

Lorraine jolted back to the present and with shaking hands took a large gulp of her Saki. She watched as Patrick expertly used the chopsticks. By pretending it was chocolate birthday cake, she summoned the courage to take a few bites.

The rest of the meal proved to be far less eventful, but none the less a new experience for her taste buds. Lorraine fancied the delicate cucumber and salmon sushi rolls and the spicy udon noodles. The hot ginger and wasabi sauce encouraged her to drink more Saki and the room spun with the giddy delight of a host of new sensations.

"Well done, Lorraine, I'm really proud of you. You made it through your first experience with Japanese."

Lorraine was more than proud of herself, she was transformed.

Finally, I have a birth date to call my own. From now on, she decided, *today, March 25, is my birthday.*

23

Placard Making

As they left the restaurant and headed for the "Just Desserts" bar on the Danforth, Lorraine noticed him standing on the corner.

He was in front of the Bank of Montreal, standing ramrod straight, staring blankly at the people passing by. He didn't say a word. The huge sign of *The Watchtower* hanging in front of him said it all. Lorraine thought it odd that an adult Jehovah's Witness would be doing placard work in the evening.

She couldn't stop herself from staring. Quickly, she grabbed Patrick's arm for support, trying to dismiss the memory.

"You okay?" Patrick asked when he felt her body stiffen.

"Yeah, just a bit wobbly from the wine. Let's walk a little slower and I'll be fine."

They passed the Witness, his vacuous eyes making no contact with those rushing past him in the rain. The memory swept over her like a tidal wave. Physically, she knew Patrick was steadying her, but mentally she was 10 years old and it was Placard Day.

*

They used plain white Bristol board, a three-hole punch and butcher string. Simple.

The Elder chose a line of Scripture for the front and the back. The message was usually something earthshattering, usually a quote from Revelations.

The pre-teens lined up at the production table and helped make their paper garment. Sturdy enough to tolerate the wind and rain, it was cut to fit the height of the model.

Making the white board outfits pleased Lorraine. She could help cut out the two pieces and string them together. She was very particular with her cutting and stringing, making sure the front and back matched perfectly. *If they want me to march around in the stupid thing, it at least better hang properly,* she thought.

Elder Patterson was kind enough to choose a verse from Genesis on hers. "In the Beginning, God created the Heavens and the Earth." Likely, those lines wouldn't make her an obvious target for pity.

The Elder printed the bold letters carefully on the front and back of her board. Lorraine tucked her head between the two sheets and laced up the string on each side. She followed her mother out of the hall and down the street.

Once fitted with the paper garment, the young Jehovah's Witness children would be assigned a street. Marching up and down and up and down without saying a word, the message shouted out to everyone who passed them.

Placard work was more acceptable for the young Witnesses, since they didn't have to speak one single word of the Truth. They wore it. Doing placard work also prepared them for Thursday night Kingdom Ministry School. Once they were no longer shy about showing the heathens the Truth, they were soon ready for the real thing: going from door-to-door.

People passing by would glance at the white board on the front and back of the marching children and hopefully remember the scripture. They might even go home later in the day and look it up in their own Bible. That was the objective anyhow. Make a statement. Make it memorable and make them want more.

Subtle recruitment and retention without saying a word!

24

Maid of the Mist

Patrick picked her up on time. He was never late — hated being late for anything. They often joked about his obsession for being on time. He lifted two small overnight cases and a satchel containing, among other delicacies, two bottles of wine and a large bottle of champagne, into the back seat of the car. They had been talking about a weekend getaway, somewhere other than Toronto.

Always full of surprises, Patrick kept their destination a mystery, and Lorraine loved the guessing game: "Are we turning here? That hotel looks lovely. Look, a winery and they have tours."

As the car sped southwest along the lake, Patrick took Lorraine's hand in his. The escarpment dazzled in the full blush of hunter and emerald greens dotted with yellows and golds.

It had been a magical year since they met at the Montreal buying show. Whenever Patrick was in Toronto, they added a new experience to their repertoire. The theatre, art galleries, museums, ball games. It didn't matter what they did together, as long as they were together.

She had chosen her weekend wardrobe carefully. Navy slacks, a crisp white shirt and navy blazer for daytime accompanied with comfortable walking shoes and her striped tote.

For evening, she selected a black Joseph Ribkoff dress with faux leather trim on the neckline, white pearl earrings and matching necklace. She packed a small beaded clutch to match her black patent kitten heels. *Night one. Done.*

Susan and Marjorie believed that Patrick was The One for their friend. They were just waiting for him to pop the question. In their spare time, they had even started designing her wedding dress. *Why was he procrastinating? Why doesn't he get on with it?* Every time Susan and Marjorie were on the phone with each other, they asked the same questions.

Without a doubt, Patrick was ready to pop the question, but he wanted the moment to be right.

Likewise, the moment had not yet been quite right for Lorraine to share her Jehovah's Witness past with the man who lit up her life. There were moments when he questioned her about her past. He knew she had been deeply upset outside the Japanese restaurant but couldn't discover the trigger. She always scoffed and made light of it by citing too much alcohol or exhaustion from long hours at work. He wanted his proposal to be in the perfect surroundings with no chance of upsetting her.

"I'm tired of the guessing game now," Patrick admitted as the car passed through Beamsville. "We're on our way to Niagara-on-the-Lake to visit two of my small boutiques. I wanted you to see them as well and meet the managers. The girls are charming, and they've got some great merchandising strategies to share. And after that, lunch at a winery."

Lorraine loved the idea. She had read about the quaint town and the small wineries nearby.

"Patrick," Lorraine said, bubbling to get her thoughts out, "I saw a picture in one of Pearl's cookbooks of the winery in Jordan where the dining tables were set amongst the grape vines. I bought the cookbook, just for that picture. I think it's the Vineyards Bed and Breakfast. Maybe we could go there?"

Patrick called ahead to reserve a room and a private table for two with a view overlooking the vineyard. He spoke with the famous chefs and pre-ordered Lorraine's favourite entrée, fresh lamb and mint sauce. The sommelier would choose the perfect wine.

Several hours later they stood side by side overlooking the vineyards. A grand table and satin chintz chairs sat in the corner. The table was set with beautiful flowers and wine.

"It is gorgeous, Patrick."

"And so are you," he gushed as he scooped her up in his arms.

*

Out of the mists of sleep, Lorraine slowly opened her eyes. His grey pants lay in a heap next to the arm chair, the tasselled loafers askew on the carpet. Fingers of daylight wedged their way between the heavy drapes, filling the room with an ethereal glow. She turned to face the man beside her.

Patrick stirred and rolled over grasping her hand and pulling it to his lips. "I can't imagine growing old with anyone but you," he whispered. "My life would be nothing without you. Since losing my parents, I have been adrift and wanting. You have filled that void."

Patrick drew her deliriously close. Rising above her, he luxuriated in the delicious softness of her body, the hardening of her nipples beneath his chest and the warmth between her legs. Electric charges arced between them. His lips sought hers. They made love again before the knock of room service disturbed them.

*

Patrick poured Lorraine's coffee and then with a mischievous smile, passed the small white porcelain dish across the table.

"Hmm. I love croissants," Lorraine said. She lifted the cover. Encircled in a nest of purple satin was a velvet ring box. Speechless, Lorraine raised her head. Patrick smiled.

"I want you, and only you, to be Mrs. Patrick Watson. What do you say to that, Rainey?" The man she loved more than anything in her world got down on one knee.

"Marry me?"

Lorraine knelt beside him. "Not sure if this is the correct posture for an acceptance speech, but yes, certainly, of course and absolutely," she replied.

Patrick watched as she opened the tiny black velvet box to expose the solitaire diamond ring. "It was my grandmother's. She passed it to my mother and now I'm passing it to you."

Around a large central diamond, 17 tiny diamonds clustered together in the most beautiful bouquet. He placed it on her finger. It was a perfect fit. That afternoon they headed across the Rainbow Bridge to the States. Patrick wanted to add yet another surprise to the weekend: slots and bright lights.

"Just look at those colours rising from the Falls and see how the bridge span rises and falls in a rainbow arc? You can understand why they call it the Rainbow Bridge. Rainbows form here all year and several times a day you can hear the bells from the carillon on our side."

"Almost makes me think of the covenant made between God and Moses," he mused. "Lucky we don't need a passport to go to the United States," he added as they pulled up to Customs.

"That's peaceful if you ask me," Lorraine agreed.

Still overwhelmed with the majestic beauty of the river and the Falls, the quayside gambling establishment sent Lorraine's sensory levels into overdrive. As soon as they walked through the doors, her senses were bombarded with sounds and sights she had never witnessed. The place was packed with people. And there was no indication of peace here. The noise was almost unbearable. Hundreds of men and women were sitting at machines, urging them to give them a payback.

Patrick guided her to an empty slot machine. Lights flashed. Bells rang, and a palette of bright reds, greens and yellows filled her field of vision.

"C'mon. Give it a try. It's the newest version of the electromechanical one-armed bandit. Still outlawed in Ontario, though." Lorraine paused. She didn't know what to do or how the machine worked.

"Here — just put this $2 bill in that opening, then pull the lever toward you. Easy-Peasy."

Her fingers quivering, Lorraine guided the bill into the slot. The note slowly disappeared. As the worldly idol was sucked into the waiting demon cavity of sin, Lorraine almost fainted.

With Patrick's strong arm on hers, she pulled the lever. The machine jolted into life. Cherries rolled maniacally before her eyes. The $2 was spent in five seconds.

She couldn't stop herself. She began to shake, uncontrollably. She tried — unsuccessfully — to control the tremors and her head began to pound. She heard the loud roar of Satan laughing at her weakness. *You gambled*, the voice jeered.

"Patrick, I need to leave. I'm not feeling well. I think I'm going to faint." Patrick took his fiancé's hand and steered her out of the bustling casino. They crossed the bridge and drove back to the vineyard in silence.

Peace, quiet and a starlit night greeted them when they arrived. Seated next to her husband-to-be on their deck overlooking the rolling vines and soft cascading fountains, Lorraine found the courage she needed. She had tried so many times to tell him, but she knew the moment was now.

He poured two glasses of wine and wrapped Lorraine's legs in a soft throw. They clinked their glasses and took a long sip.

She had promised to marry this man without him knowing the biggest demon of her past. It was time to pour out her history, the pain, the scars, and the horror.

"Patrick, I love you with all my heart. You know that, don't you? But there's something you must know," she began hesitantly.

What? his eyes asked quietly. He waited.

Lorraine took a deep breath. The words tumbled from her mouth.

"I was raised a Jehovah's Witness. My life was never normal. I have never had a birthday or a Christmas. I have never dated anyone but you. I had never been out to a movie, a Prom or a party until I met you. I need to learn so much. I am awkward. I don't know anything about the world outside of the Kingdom Hall."

Before Patrick could respond, she took another deep breath.

"I've been getting help. Every two weeks I attend secret meetings in Toronto for Ex-Witnesses. We share. We understand each other's pain. There," she paused, "now you know. That's what's wrong with me."

Patrick turned to face the woman he loved more than life itself. He took her small hands in his and looked deeply into her eyes.

"Everything makes so much sense now, my darling. I only wish I had known sooner. But from now on, things will be different. We will face the demons together."

25

Prom Revisited

Lorraine couldn't stop looking at her finger. The solitaire in its nest of diamonds caught the light of the sun streaming in through the bus window on her early morning ride to work. If she looked closely, she could see her own face reflected in the large facets. It was beautiful, and it announced to everyone that she was Patrick's true love.

Wait until I show the girls and Pearl, she thought, with a sigh and a giggle.

Susan and Marjorie were already in town for Thanksgiving at Pearl's, so Lorraine planned a night of champagne and laughter for everyone. She arranged the flutes on the sitting room table beside a tray of crostini and slivered smoked salmon, capers and red onion. She bolted to the door before the bell even stopped echoing through the apartment.

"So," Marjorie asked first, "how was the trip?"

"Amazing. The Falls were out of this world, especially at night."

"And Patrick?"

"He's great," Lorraine said, smiling and inviting her guests inside. In minutes, they were seated comfortably on the couch munching on the appetizers. Her left hand tucked in her apron, Lorraine poured the champagne. Grinning like a Cheshire cat, she pulled up the easy chair. Before anyone could drink, Lorraine shrieked.

"I can't wait another minute!" she said, showing her left hand as a chorus of congratulatory cries filled the room.

"To Lorraine and Patrick!" Pearl toasted her adopted granddaughter.

"We're so excited for you both. Congratulations." Susan said, laughing.

"He certainly took his time!" Marjorie chuckled.

"But it couldn't have been a better place or time. Niagara is so romantic," Lorraine replied.

"Well, we figured as much months ago," Marjorie added. "We've already been to Bloor Street and picked out our dresses. With Pearl of course. So, what are you going to wear?"

"Wait here and I'll show you." Lorraine returned with a tattered old Simpsons-Sears box. Inside, in its original tissue was her pearl-white Prom dress. She had hidden it beneath her bed since the abduction.

"Oh my God, I can't believe you saved that dress after all these years!" Susan yelled.

"I never got to wear it. Dad kept me home. He said that no young Jehovah's Witnesses would be dancing on that night. They would all be home, guarded under the watchful eyes of their parents until Georgia was found," said Lorraine. "I was devastated, but I kept it because I wanted to wear it someday, for something special. What could be more special than my wedding day?"

"Try it on, Try it ON!" Susan ordered.

*

Marjorie, Pearl and Susan waited while Lorraine tried the dress on for the second time. She entered the living room for the reviews.

"It's a little snug at the waist," Susan said, "but we can easily fix that."

"But it's sleeveless," Lorraine frowned.

Pearl jumped to the rescue.

"You simply must wear my long white gloves. Remember, something borrowed. The gloves will come over your elbow and with the delicate pleated rushing along the sleeves, they will look perfect with your wedding dress."

"No one will see the scars. Even if you take off your gloves, I'm sure no one will notice," Pearl added.

*

The Monday after Thanksgiving, Pearl, Susan and Marjorie set to work. With straight pins sticking out between her teeth, Pearl started making the necessary adjustments to turn the Prom dress into the most beautiful wedding dress anyone could ever imagine.

"I am going to make you a long veil, Lorraine. What do you want to wear as your headdress? Maybe a pearl fascinator or a jeweled headband? I can attach the veil easily to either one," Marjorie said with a flourish.

"It's going to be a simple wedding at City Hall remember," Lorraine added. She questioned all the fuss they were making, but they were adamant.

"The venue won't change the importance of the day," replied Pearl.

Lorraine removed the long silky gloves and rubbed the inside of her right arm absentmindedly. The widest scar was still shiny, red and tender. The healing was taking longer than the doctor anticipated.

Lorraine tried to erase the image of her demon brother, Dougie, out of her head. *Why did he hit me that day? Why must I carry these scars while he has none? Sometimes I wonder where he lives or if he is married or has children. I'm glad he's dead to us, him on his Witness high road. Who cares?* Lorraine thought dismissively, with a smile and a nod to the future. There was no room for such negative thoughts on the most important day of her life.

Patrick's eyes nearly dropped out of his head when he met his bride at the top of the steps. A long train with silk covered buttons attached at the waist flowed behind her. Susan and Marjorie arranged it carefully when they entered the courtroom. Accenting Lorraine's strawberry blond curls, the rich headband of silk and matching covered pearl buttons held the veil in place.

When she took her father's hand to escort her to Patrick's side, she felt her heart would burst with joy.

26

A Mix of Salt and Sweet

Patrick had booked one of the small private salons at the Royal York for the post ceremony dinner. There would be six in total: Mr. and Mrs. Patrick Watson, Susan, Pearl, Marjorie and James.

The red gules of the stained-glass windows and rich wood paneling provided the perfect ambience for the occasion. Warmth and love seemed to emanate from the very furniture. Lorraine took James' and Patrick's hands in hers and brought them to her lips.

"You have been my rocks. Patrick, since Montreal; and Dad since the accident. I would never be the woman I am without you both. And to Pearl and my two best designer buddies, who have rescued me from the dark valleys more than once. Thank you."

James spoke first.

"Congratulations to my beautiful Lorraine and her handsome husband. Sweetie, you look magnificent."

"Thanks Dad. So much."

Patrick raised his glass for the toast to the bride.

"To my beautiful bride, Lorraine, and to our future as husband and wife."

*

A week later, Patrick and Lorraine drove James to the station. Like old times, Lorraine clutched her father in a tight bear hug that turned her fingers white at the knuckles.

"You've no idea how glad I am that you were able to come, Daddy. I wish Peter could have been here, too."

"I know, but he still hasn't been cleared to travel," James said. "It's been such a long road — almost four years — since the accident. He sends his best and lots of love. He's here in spirit."

"And Mom?"

"She couldn't find her conscience clear to join me."

"And that is probably for the best, but still I worry about you, Dad. It must be so hard for you in that house — the accusing stares, the loss of your soulmate and the venomous criticism from your youngest son, even if it arrives in the letters he sends to Deborah."

"It isn't all bad, though," James said. "She can still make my heart skip a beat when she sashays across the kitchen carrying a steaming pot of stew. I chose her, and she chose me and together we chose to become Jehovah's Witnesses. And you and I have learned the errors of that decision."

James patted his daughter's hand reassuringly. "I truly believe, sweetie, that she'll come 'round. I need to somehow assure her that the chains that hold her in that prison of misconceptions and mind controlling coercion are destroying her. Regardless, she is still my everything. Sometimes the hours are long, but I keep on with the odd job and of course my growing collection of Westerns."

"All right, but get out and get some exercise," Lorraine said. "You've always been active. You can't sit all day."

"Don't you worry about me one iota. You've got a husband now, and a new house. There's so much excitement in the Watson family that you won't even miss me. Enjoy making memories together."

As the train whistle shrilled into their conversation, James said, "I'll try to get up for Christmas one of these years. Just you wait and see if I don't."

27

Ex's Round Table

Lorraine almost broke a glass in her rush to leave. The dishes had taken longer than usual to put away, as her tummy was getting in the way of easy maneuvering. She still had three months to go, but already she had outgrown everything and had to reach out to Susan and Marjorie for the new "Preggie Line," as they called it.

Tonight was the first time that Patrick would join her and Marjorie at the Ex-Jehovah's Witness meeting. They had planned it for weeks. He was ready to share his wife's pain, no matter how exposed or brutal the reality.

Heather greeted them at the door. Lorraine recalled the day two years before that she began the journey with Marjorie. She could hardly believe it was really two years.

"So, this is Patrick?" Heather said, extending her hand. "Welcome. Welcome. We've heard so much about you for a long time."

"I am very glad to be here and support my wife. I am beginning to recognize the look which comes over her when something flips the switch and she is back in the Kingdom Hall being punished for her sinful behaviour. I try to head off the dark chasm into which she spins when that happens."

Marjorie took Patrick by the arm and led him into the meeting room. "We've got our four regulars as well as a young woman from just outside Aylmer. Maybe Lorraine will know her," Marjorie said.

Heather invited the members to grab coffees and sweets and take their seats. Following introductions, the meeting began. The regulars gave some personal background and talked about how they had weathered the Christmas holiday.

"I had the most amazing Christmas with Patrick. It was our first in our new home and of course the first with a little person kicking away every time I reached up to put a decoration on the tree," Lorraine said.

"Patrick helped me with all the traditions. It was overwhelming, but wonderful. I think we had more tinsel and candles and wreaths than the downtown Eaton's store. Almost had to wear sunglasses inside but," she said touching Patrick's arm, "it was amazing. The best was hanging the stockings on the mantel. I can't describe the freedom I felt. And it was in no small part because of the courage I receive from this group."

Marjorie wiped her eyes. She knew exactly what Lorraine was talking about. She had not met a partner, so Christmas didn't have quite the same warmth, but her cousins from Nova Scotia had come to visit. It was the first time she had seen them since she left the Hall. Maybe her mom might be next.

Lorraine took her friend's hand. "Don't give up hope," she said. "Next Christmas, you'll see."

"Yeah, I hope so. Holidays are hard, especially as you learn what you missed all your life. I was just thinking about your wedding. Thank God it wasn't a JDub service," Marjorie said. "We might have had to dunk Patrick and wreck those gorgeous loafers of his." Marjorie's bubbly personality always provided that needed break as the conversation swung between heavy loss and redemption. Heather raised her arm generously, inviting the newest Ex-Witness to the circle.

"Hi everyone, my name is Andrea and I'm a former Jehovah's Witness. I lived with my parents in Avon just outside of Aylmer, but they moved the same year I left the cult. It wasn't a pretty parting."

Andrea folded and re-folded the napkin on her lap.

"Take all the time you need, Andrea." Heather said kindly. "We understand this is difficult. No one here will judge because everyone has been where you are today. We know it has taken a great deal of courage to seek help, but that is what you will get here."

Andrea raised her eyes and looked at Lorraine.

"I got pregnant by a non-Witness. I was 17 at the time and in love. Really in love. Grant was starting law school in London at Western that fall, and I was going to join him."

Andrea's shoulders slowly relaxed as she told her story.

"My parents demanded that I confess my fornication to the Elders and accept the punishment of the Judicial Committee. When we stopped for gas on the way home from the Kingdom Hall, I ran away. I had a small amount of change in my purse, so I called my boyfriend's parents and told him where I was. An hour later, he rescued me. I haven't been back since. My little girl will be three this year. And my parents have never seen their granddaughter."

Lorraine spoke first.

"I know that area of Ontario really well. That's where I was imprisoned for 17 years. It took an accident and a murder to get me out the door."

"What school did you go to?" Andrea asked, her eyes widening with interest.

"It was Aylmer. I went to East Elgin. My brother Peter was in a horrible accident and he lost a lot of blood. Dad said yes to the transfusion and then they both got kicked out. It was right around the time that Georgia Jackson was murdered."

Andrea stiffened in her chair so abruptly that she startled the rest of the group.

"I received a letter from the only friend in Aylmer who still writes to me. You will never believe it. They caught Georgia Jackson's killer. He confessed to the Jehovah's Witness Elders."

David

28

In the Yard

"I can't ma, I'm busy."

"Young man when I ask you to do something, there's no such word as can't. Get inside, now."

David looked at the little carcasses, their legs clawing skyward where he had cut them open to expose worm like tendons and chips of bone. With the toes of his sneakers, he kicked clumps of ground over them and ran towards the house.

"What have you been up to out there? David's mother shrieked while drying her hands on the dishcloth.

"Just playing, ma. I got me two red ones. They weren't paying attention and I shot them between the eyes with my sling shot."

"That's good hunting, then, son."

"Where are they now?"

"Just dead in the garden, their four little legs peeking out of the dirt. Had to stop them squeaking."

David didn't really have any friends. No one ventured down the long drive obscured by overgrowth and large trees. Some kids remarked that David did weird things in the back yard by the smoker. What they didn't know was that David yearned for friends, but as years passed and companions eluded him, he grew up sorely lacking in skills necessary to navigate the subtle nuances of social behaviour.

For as long as he could remember, David made up games with imaginary playmates. They never talked back, disagreed or fought with him. They were the best friends in the world because he could do whatever he wanted to them and they never retaliated.

When it came to small animals, he didn't so much want pets, he just wanted to ride into their territory slapping his thigh on a pretend horse like the cavalry and scare them half to death. Once they laid down all tuckered out, he raised a flag of victory. He enjoyed chasing his prey, but preferred to play with them after he knocked them unconscious. It made him feel in charge. Powerful.

But he was also conflicted by his actions. He liked the look of any animal's sleek fur, smooth and shiny. When he ran them aground, though, he knew he had spoiled them and that made him sad. He didn't realize that he couldn't have them both alive and beautiful; or dead and beautiful. Either way, they were spoiled.

His mother repeated the order, "Wash your hands. Dinner's almost ready and your hands are probably filthy." David joined his mother at the table.

"Ma, tell me again about Pa. Why did he leave?"

"He got into trouble. That's all you need to know. You were only a year old. There's no changing what happened and now it's just you and me, and I think you ain't suffrin' with just one parent. Especially one who loves you as much as I do."

"Yeah, but..."

"No buts about it. Eat."

Long dark curls fell in waves over his forehead and into his eyes. He brushed them aside as he ate in silence, staring blankly at the brightly painted ceramic salt and pepper shakers. His shoulders tightened with each bite. *You might love me, but I hate you. I hate living here and I'm going to do something about it. Just you wait.*

David stabbed his fork into a mountain of mashed potatoes.

29

Grade 9 Revelations

David endured elementary school.

His torn pants, his long hair, his holey shoes, all worked to single him out. With only a Grade 5 education, his mother struggled. She worked at the Aylmer Carnation plant whenever her unemployment insurance ran out, but there was little money for anything extra. She tried to provide the best she could. Whenever she had money, she spent it on David.

When the Beatles took the fashion scene by storm, David could only dream of the London Look that designers everywhere were pushing. He stared at the ads and catalogues and dreamed. Ban-Lon sweaters or tailored Cadet shirts were too expensive. Terry velour was more reasonable. The year he began junior high, his mother bought him a pair of flared plaid pants. He thought he had died and gone to heaven.

But his greatest dream was to own a London Look peacoat. He ogled the newspaper ads that showed handsome young men wearing them, but at $14.95 owning one was only a dream. Instead, David had to be satisfied with a thick fleece hand-me-down from the thrift shop. In his juvenile mind, it was the last straw.

He made the announcement at supper time.

"I'm going to quit school, Mom. Come June, I'm getting a job on the railway. CNR is always hiring."

His mother thought for a while before answering. Her husband had left school early and for the years they were together, struggled to find a decent job. Maybe the railway would be good for her son.

"At least you'd be bringing in money," she concluded, "and could help out around here instead of struggling with math and English. Really, when will you ever need to know how to write similes? You can do sums and read and write. That's all you need."

David nodded in agreement. "You got that right, ma. No need to stay in school."

But in his mind, he felt a twinge of sadness. He dreamed of being like the other kids with both a mom and a dad who did things together. He wanted a family that went on picnics and holidays together and worshipped every Sunday. He and his mom had never gone to church, but when he heard the church bells calling families to service he wondered what he might be missing.

In the deepest darkness at 3 a.m., David often awakened from terrifying dreams about dying. Drenched with sweat, he lay in his bed wondering if he had a soul; or if he did have one, how he would ever know? He had never gone to Sunday School or even learned any prayers. Although he was able to sluff them off when he was awake, such thoughts cratered a deep well of fear that haunted him when he slept.

"If I don't go to church will I never get to heaven?" he whispered into the blackness.

30

Rejected

On his 17th birthday, David bought his mom a new washing machine with his overtime cheque from the railway. For years, he had watched her struggle with the old wringer in the basement.

"Son, this is the nicest thing you have ever done for me. I don't know how to thank you."

"No need, ma. Kindness is one of the most important rules I've been learning about at the Hall."

The words came out before he could stop them. He hadn't told her about his attendance at the Kingdom Hall because he knew deep in his heart she wouldn't understand.

"What Hall are you talking about? Not the Kingdom Hall, I hope? That group is a nut job religion. I'll have no son of mine believing in that crap. Your own uncle died in Italy in the War and those goddammed J-fucking Double-Yous wouldn't even join up and fight for their own country for God's sake."

"Mom, you've got it wrong this time. A few months back, a nice couple came to the door when you were at work. A father and his daughter. She was real pretty and I think she liked me. They talked to me about God's Salvation Plan for Witnesses and I want to be part of it. I've been going every Sunday that I'm not working. All the people at the Hall make me feel important."

"David, I will say this only once. If they get their hooks into you, you'll never be free again. Don't say I haven't warned you. I think it's best you leave. I appreciate the washing machine. I will think of you every time I use it."

And with that his mother closed the front door on her son.

*

As it turned out, it wasn't the first rejection David experienced in 1963. Despite all the time he spent reading and preparing the scriptures for the Ministry school and the door-to-door ministry, he found the exercises very difficult.

The young woman who he had met standing at the door with her father months earlier took it upon herself to coach David. In fact, her father, Elder Albert Crooker also gave him extra lessons and the Hall was always more than receptive to new and young converts.

David did show some promise. He appeared very devout. His Bible was becoming tattered at the corners from constant use and he became more outgoing. Elder Crooker was even considering offering young David's name as a possible candidate for the Discreet Slave Program at Bethel. He would wait for the Circuit Servant's arrival to present his recommendation.

Every year, each Kingdom Hall Congregation Servant welcomed a Brother from Bethel to conduct an annual congregational check-up. During his visit, he would conduct marriages, funerals and baptisms. He also called the Brothers together in council to address any issues of importance.

This yearly visit was a most important one. Several Slaves had abandoned the Discreet Slave Program at headquarters, so Bethel was on the search for new candidates to fill those spots. Brother Clifford had received young Douglas Armstrong's application from the Straffordville congregation, and he knew that Aylmer was considering submitting David Bodemer's name.

Brother Clifford followed a strict list of examination criteria before making his selection, but the final decision would be made in prayer to Jehovah.

And so, the weeks passed and young David continued his attendance at the Hall. Each Thursday night, he struggled to impress the congregation at the Ministry School, and every Sunday he followed his mentor from door-to-door.

When Elaine served him coffee after ministry work, she always smiled and gave him extra sugar. One day she surprised David when she whispered, "What's a handsome man like you doing without a girl?"

It was a very bold statement, especially for the Elder's daughter, but she liked David and wanted him to know it.

"I don't know," David replied shyly. "I like being alone and working hard. Praying and reading Scripture too," he added, thinking that might score some points with the Elder's daughter who had the beautiful blond curls. He also noticed her dimples that turned up when she smiled.

"I heard Brother Albert talking that the congregation might submit your name to the Slave program," she whispered, knowing that her father would be angered if she knew she was gossiping. Elaine knew it was a sin to gossip.

"Really?" David replied, his jaw dropping in shock. He couldn't imagine being chosen for anything. He couldn't remember winning anything in his entire life.

*

As it turned out, Brother Clifford did not choose David for the Slave Program.

"A bit too slow," he said in confidence to Brother Crooker, "and there's something mysterious about the boy. I don't think he would work out in New York."

The rejection didn't seem to upset David, though. Within a few months, he asked permission to date Elaine, and a year later they were married. They both were 18 years old.

31

Babies – Babies – Babies

Elaine and David celebrated their second anniversary with an announcement of yet another baby on the way. Albert Crooker was thrilled for his daughter, but the responsibility of another mouth to feed weighed heavily on David's soul as well as his pocket book.

He rarely had a quiet moment to himself and it seemed whenever he got his wife in bed, she got pregnant again. She gained weight and her happy curls lost their lustre. He wondered where his lovely bride had gone.

In secret, he looked at magazines he knew were against Jehovah's wishes. The alabaster curves of the young women called to him, begged him to reach for his penis. The magazine beauties gave him what he wanted. They didn't get pregnant, age or get fat.

In public, however, David appeared the perfect husband and father. He worked hard at the railway and he took odd janitorial jobs at the banks. Life passed in a regimen of diapers, baby food and Ministry school work.

But the dark side itched at him.

One evening at Ministry School he was paired with young Georgia Jackson. She was about David's age, almost 20, and David liked her shy, kind manner. He often asked for her help with a scripture or how to roleplay it. Her dark eyes seemed like deep chocolate pools begging him to enter and search their depths.

He shook off the lascivious thoughts. *Sinful,* he spit. *Sinful.* David let out his breath slowly, *Abomination.* But he couldn't stop the feelings that overcame him. Suddenly, his manhood grew unbidden between his legs. He grasped his pant legs and shook his foot as if trying to get rid of a cramp.

That night, he hid in the garage for hours. Elaine found him curled up on the floor of the garage. He raised his face from the cold concrete and could see the worry in his wife's eyes.

"Whatever is bothering you, David? Come inside. You know you can always offer your burden to Jehovah and He will help you."

He wanted to believe her, but inside where it really counted, he knew he was weak. David took her hand and followed her into the house.

"The children are in bed, now. Come to sleep."

"Elaine, will you be my Sleeping Beauty tonight?"

"What do you mean?"

"I don't want another baby, but I want you. Dress up pretty like the princess you were when we first started dating and lie like Sleeping Beauty. I will come to you and see you dead and then wake you with a kiss and we can make magic."

Elaine often saw her husband in such moods. He would do something sinful and hide away in silence for days on end, regret consuming him. When he finally had beaten down the demons of sin, contrite he would return to Jehovah and beg for her forgiveness. It was the same with Sleeping Beauty, but she had no idea what prompted that desire.

32

Behind the Mask

On February 27, 1966, nine days after Georgia Jackson disappeared, two boys collecting bottles off the Glencolin Road found her blood stained blue peacoat. It was in a ditch behind a birch tree about six feet in from a fence. The coat was neatly folded. Even though there had been a thaw, it was dry. This fact didn't seem to enter the discussion when the boys passed it over to the search parties. Later that day, David stood with the men as they handed the coat to the officer like an offering. His shoulders trembled with the horrible recognition.

"David, you were one of the last people to see her alive in the afternoon at the Dairy Bar. Do you recognize this coat as Georgia's?"

"Yes, I believe so. Yes, I saw her wearing it at the Kingdom Hall," he said. Brother Crooker put his arms around the young man to protect him from the horrible sight. David welcomed his father-in-law's support.

"Thank you, David. This is very helpful. It is our first lead in the case," the detective said. He placed it in an evidence bag to be sent to the provincial laboratory at Toronto. They needed to confirm if the bloodstains on the collar were human.

"Where is she? Who could ever hurt her?" David whispered.

The officer just shook his head.

Every day for weeks, Albert Crooker led his congregation in prayer. But finding the coat only increased the anguish in the Jackson family. George Jackson telegrammed the Attorney General complaining that the police had not done enough to find their daughter. Finally, on March 3, the police offered a $500 reward for information about the missing girl.

The Jackson's couldn't help but hear the hurtful rumours flying around town that Georgia was fed up with her life on Sydenham Street and took off because they forced her to stay at home. The reluctance of the police to launch searches when Mr. Jackson first reported her missing pained them daily. The police stance that "she'll turn up" did not sit well with the family.

Michael Verbrugge, one of the farmers in the area and a Jehovah's Witness, played a key role in the private searches since Georgia's disappearance. He organized the helicopter search on March 2 after the girl's coat was discovered. Charles Oldham of Payne's Mills flew his helicopter while Verbrugge kept in radio contact with him from the ground. In this way they patrolled six square miles of brush around the Police College north of Aylmer.

On March 10, Verbrugge found the girl's scarf while patrolling the road with two friends, but there was still no sign of the girl. Verbrugge was quoted as saying, If it's one of our people, no Jehovah's Witness will harbour him. We will turn him over to the police and let justice take its course.'

Fearful whispers travelled from Brother to Sister, She was a good girl. She wouldn't hurt a fly. Our Georgia. Where is our Georgia?

On the Sunday two days after her disappearance, Mrs. Jackson clung to the hope that her daughter was still alive. That was the night she received a phone call supposedly from Georgia. She heard sobbing and a muffled voice that said, "Help me mom. I am being held prisoner by two men."

The call turned out to be a prank.

On Wednesday March 16, Talbotville Department of Lands and Forests, conservation officer Lawrence Kelly was driving down Highway 40 towards Summers' Corner when he noticed something about 100 feet from the west side of the road in the field next to a densely wooded area off the Glencolin Line a couple of miles northeast of Aylmer. He decided to investigate.

Her snow boots were still on as were her stockings. Her waitress uniform was pulled up to her neck. Her undergarments had been ripped off. Kelly did not disturb the crime scene. He drove to Aylmer to notify Chief Henderson. The body was identified by Albert Crooker, leader of the Jehovah's Witnesses in Aylmer, and taken to the H.A. Kebbel funeral home in Aylmer before being transported to Toronto for the autopsy.

Lawrence Kelly received $500 for finding Georgia, but even though the body had been discovered, the suspect had not. Immediately, the town voted to approve a $1000 reward for information leading to the arrest of a suspect.

Mr. Heffren, on whose farm the body had been found, was mystified as to why he hadn't come across the body on Monday when he was out looking for poles for a greenhouse he was planning to build. *I must have been only 50 feet from the poor girl,* he thought. *Strange.*

As the witnesses gathered for prayers that Thursday evening, the talk swarmed through the Hall. Michael Verbrugge voiced his concerns to Elder Crooker. He found it odd that the body was found in an area that had been scoured four days earlier.

If the body had been placed there after the Sunday search, Verbrugge surmised, *that means whoever placed it also knew where the Members had already searched. And if that's true, then by the process of elimination that person must have been part of the search party.*

Such a possibility chilled his soul.

The brutal murder affected everyone. Parents closely monitored their young daughters and enforced strict rules whenever they went outdoors. Mr. Jackson himself said that what happened to Georgia could happen to any person's daughter or wife.

Mr. Jackson also understood the logic of why police forces didn't launch massive searches when people were first reported missing. A lot of people did disappear for a day or two and then turned up, but he was greatly saddened that Chief Henderson never seemed convinced that anything was wrong.

The autopsy revealed Georgia had received a sharp blow across the back of her head, which likely knocked her unconscious but was not enough to kill her. The final cause of death was suffocation. The police believed the killer was someone the girl knew and trusted. Someone from this area. A local person.

Three hundred people packed into the Aylmer funeral home where Albert Crooker gave the address. "Georgia," he said, "was a faithful servant who dedicated her life to Jehovah and finished her earthly course faithfully." He affirmed that she would be privileged to come back with the many faithful returning from the dead in resurrection after Armageddon.

Michael Verbrugge wrapped his hand around the cold sixth handle on the simple gray canvas-coloured coffin. He nodded to his fellow pallbearers and lifted Georgia's body. As one, they brought her through the front doors out to the waiting hearse. Verbrugge's jaw clenched with waves of compassion and fiery determination.

A team made up of Inspector A.T. Eady of the OPP, Detective Sergeant Dennis Alsop of London, and two plainclothesmen from St. Thomas and the Aylmer police checked out 40 leads. Each lead just seemed to peter out. The officers felt that no matter which way they turned, they faced a brick wall.

As 1966 passed to 1967, then to 1968, and still no culprit was discovered, the horror of the murder dulled. Perhaps parents just wanted to pretend such a heinous crime had never really occurred. Perhaps they just wanted the memory to disappear. But all the pretending or wishing in the world would not make it so.

David and Elaine welcomed two more babies in short order, making the small house they had rented in Avon far too crowded. They were bursting from the floor to the rafters. David said enough was enough, relegated as he was to the garage most of the time. There simply were not enough beds in the house.

David had fashioned a small cot against the back end of the garage where he built a secret cupboard for his off-colour magazines. Near his cot stood a stainless-steel clothes rack. It held a mismatched collection of coats and parkas which overflowed from the house. David stuffed a dark trench coat between two larger dark coats. Concealed in plain view, the trench coat hung completely invisible in his garage hideaway.

In fact, David had quite a few hideaways. Working on the railway for many years made it easy for him to discover old shacks, huts, granaries or other structures abandoned along the tracks that he travelled daily. He knew how to get to them and get away from them with ease.

But hiding from his growing list of misdemeanours and arrests began to prove difficult. He was investigated for selling stolen property from CNR railcars. Break and Enter convictions soon followed. Late in 1970, he was arrested for exhibitionism and indecent exposure. The Hall was beginning to take notice of these infractions. In the fall of 1971, the Judicial Committee considered perhaps young David had a side that demanded exploring.

*

"David, David. It's only a dream. Be quiet or you'll wake the children. This is the third time this month. Whatever is bothering you?" Elaine hissed into the darkness trying to contain her frustration with her husband.

"It seems so real. The snakes are coming out of the walls and smothering me. I can't kill them, and I can't get away. The room is hot but at the same time cold as ice. As each train car rushes past the shed, I stab at the form lying on the ground. I can't contain the rage. My only purpose is to inflict pain. To humiliate. It's lustful, morbid, and beautiful all at once. I force myself down on the form. Over and over."

David gulped air into his tortured lungs.

"Nonsense. This is crazy. It's just your imagination running away with your thoughts. Maybe you ate something that didn't agree with you? Look. See, there's nothing here. The room is quiet. No train. The children are in their bedrooms. You must try to sleep, David. You've work at 6 a.m. They won't take kindly to you being late a third time this month."

David tried to calm himself. He drank some water, changed his sweat-soaked pyjamas, rearranged his pillow and lay down again. Daylight could not come soon enough.

Slowly, his heart started to return to a normal rhythm. In a few moments he heard the quiet breathing of his wife beside him. In and out. In and out. *How easily she can go back to sleep.*

He tried to will it away, but the razor-sharp horrors of his past continued to slice into the present.

33

Brother Powley Ferrets It Out

"I'll be back in a week. You and the children will be fine. Your dad will be here this afternoon. My aunt really needs me now. I'll be back before the middle of December. That will leave me lots of time to get ready for the Christmas Ministry work."

"Say goodbye to your father, children," Elaine said holding three-month-old Christian. The four other children ran to David's open arms.

David hugged his children and told them to listen to their mother and say hello to Grandpa Albert. Aged from seven years to just three months, he had certainly done his duty to Jehovah. Albert Crooker was more than proud of his many grandchildren, all faithful Witnesses. He missed them since they had moved from Avon, close to Aylmer, but the little house had grown too small and with a small promotion, David had found a larger house to rent in Kitchener. Elaine seemed happy.

David, on the other hand, appeared distant and agitated. He looked like he never slept. Even his fellow workers at the Cement Plant noticed.

*

Albert Crooker enjoyed the drive to Kitchener. He zigzagged on the scenic roads before turning east on Number 28. It was a charming route. There were lots of snow banks this time of year and lots of pagan Christmas lights made the drive even more beautiful. He hoped his daughter had a roast in the oven.

Although he was happily anticipating seeing his family, a heavy matter had arisen at the Hall. Near the beginning of December, a Witness approached him about a discovery he made in his garage. Albert thought that discovery might be related to the rumours flying around the congregation for months, if not years.

Secret admonitions were being levelled at Albert Crooker's inactivity in this matter, and if he didn't act on the rumours, they could result in other Brothers questioning his leadership. As the Elder, it was his responsibility to set up an inquiry. Of course, Brother Powley was the best man to lead it. Albert had already called him to set it up.

Within hours after Powley confirmed he would come to Aylmer, Albert packed a small bag, called his daughter in Kitchener and got in the car. At four in the afternoon, he walked into the arms of his grandchildren. Elaine was pleased to see him.

Later that night after the last of the children was tucked into bed, Albert joined Elaine at the kitchen table. It had been a nightly ritual of tea and toast just before bed. But Albert was unsure how to broach the topic which swirled in his head.

There were unanswered questions five years ago. Inconsistencies in his story. Fears of recriminations. And then people just stopped talking about Georgia Jackson. Crooker thought they had moved on and forgotten.

But this business had dredged it out of the muck and mystery surrounding the girl's abduction and murder. Albert knew his congregation was asking questions. Rumours like that travelled fast. If they had heard those rumours, they would soon be after the real reason for Powley's investigation. And that could be damning.

Albert Crooker smiled as his daughter poured his tea.

"Thank you, sweetie. Good to just have some quiet. Like old times."

He couldn't help but notice the strain on his daughter's face as she pulled up the chair and sat down, visibly exhausted. He always knew when she was hiding something or upset about something. He sipped his tea and waited.

"Daddy, it's been really hard around here. I'm afraid that David might lose his job at Bestpipe just like he did at the CNR. I don't think he's stealing again, but something is really upsetting him. He has terrible dreams and he can't sleep. He keeps talking about snakes in the shed and he claws at imaginary beasts. It's horrible. I think the older children are beginning to notice."

Visibly distressed, Elaine paused before adding, "And you know the other things, the indecent things. David's been seeing a doctor to help him to stop. He's had almost 20 convictions. People are beginning to talk at the Hall. It's so embarrassing Daddy."

"I know sweetheart. He's been a troubled lad, I believe, for quite some time and our refusal to act openly about it may have been most unwise."

Albert paused before continuing with the delicate matter. "I was approached last week by a delegation of my congregation. They want to bring in investigators. They think someone might know something about Georgia's disappearance. They want to interview all the members of the 1966 congregation. I've asked Arthur Powley to head the inquiry."

Elaine took a long minute before replying. "You don't think David is involved do you? The Elders cleared him in 1966 and again in 1968 when the lawyer came from Toronto. This is just dragging up old wounds, Daddy. It's awful. Especially when he is trying to get back on his feet and rid himself of his demons." But as she brought her cup to her mouth, fear and suspicion flashed across her face.

*

David was glad to get out of the house. His aunt in Avon had invited a large group of friends from the Aylmer congregation for a big dinner. It wasn't often her nephew came by and she promised all his favourite foods. His mother had refused to join them, but his aunt had never let his Jehovah's Witness faith get in the way of their relationship. She had come to the Hall the odd time and welcomed David's Jehovah's Witness friends whenever they dropped in.

It was good to walk the streets of his old home town. *Four years is a long time*, David thought. Avon had been good to him for a while. As he turned the corner past the old arena, the vision of the group of girls flashed before his eyes. *They must have been young, no more than 10 or 11*, he guessed.

He wondered if they'd ever seen *one* before. *At least one that was full and ready*, David chuckled morbidly to himself. There was no one around. He was invisible as the air. He undid his belt and dropped his pants. He stepped out in front of them. The girls stopped, surprise filling their faces. He pulled the coat wide. There was no mistaking the three girls' shock.

David did a couple of suggestive moves on his manhood as they stared at his crotch. Then he pulled up his trousers, closed his coat and walked on down the road. He laughed as the girls screamed and ran the other way.

But someone had been there that afternoon, watching. And that someone reported the crime. It became the first charge of exhibitionism on his record. There would be many more. At first, he kept Elaine from discovering the charges. The thrill he got from the exposure always put him in a horny kind of loving mood. She never questioned him when he came to her those evenings in need of her services.

*

David basked in the freedom from his family. No diapers to change and no fights to manage. Just a few beers and a few jokes with friends. The nightmares, however, hadn't stayed in Kitchener. The last three nights they had escalated. He could hardly stop himself from crying out.

He got up and padded to the kitchen where he turned on the kettle. The noise disturbed his cousin Chrissy who came out of her bedroom rubbing her eyes.

"What's up David? Something bothering you? You don't seem to be yourself this visit."

Chrissy was a Witness from the Aylmer congregation. She hadn't been there when David and Elaine attended because she was staying with her father in London, but she was an active member now. And she knew something was afoot. The Elders had been having more meetings than normal and just last week, one of the members came to Brother Albert with news so terrible that they closed the meeting room door when they discussed it.

"Nothing much. Pretty busy with the five little ones. They're all under seven but Elaine is really good with them."

"Yeah, I bet that house you had over on Summerside must have been bursting when you left. It only had one bedroom, right?"

"Yeah, but it had a large garage. I used to bunk out there sometimes when it got too noisy."

"Now that you mention it, the Elders were talking about that garage just last Sunday. The new owners, Jehovah's Witnesses like us, had started some renovations and they had to pull off the old paneling and excavate some of the old foundation."

David poured his tea and set it on the table. His face blanched, abject terror flooding his eyes. Chrissy waited for her comment to register. The only sound in the darkened kitchen was the tinkling of the spoon as David moved it against the china cup.

"You'll never guess what they found," Chrissy said deliberately as she watched David's face deteriorate before her.

"Brother Powley arrived in Aylmer two days ago. Something about an inquiry. What do you think that's all about?"

David couldn't speak.

Chrissy didn't back down.

"You know I have to report you," she whispered.

"You have to tell the truth, David. That is the only way to ask Jehovah's forgiveness. If you don't, you will never live eternally."

David slumped against the table.

*

The inquiry was a quick and quiet affair. After several hours of prayer and questioning late into the night, David Bodemer confessed to Brother Powley, Albert Crooker and Thomas Smith that he had raped and killed Georgia Jackson. Later that same day David's three-page type written confession was given to the Police.

On January 24, 1972 David Bodemer was arrested and remanded to prison to await charges.

Shockwaves 1972

34

Hidden in Plain View

Patrick steadied his wife who had stiffened in her chair as the shock of Andrea's words sank in. He knew how Georgia Jackson's murder had terrified every young girl in Aylmer and indeed every young girl anywhere in southwestern Ontario. The police couldn't keep up with the unsolved cases involving young people that continued to pile up over the years.

A young woman might say goodbye to co-workers and not show up at her house. A boy on his way home from basketball practice would simply disappear. Sometimes their abandoned bikes were found, other times they disappeared leaving no trace. Serial killers, sexual deviants, opportunists: law officers could take their pick of the theories for motives, but still the body count continued.

For almost six years, David Bodemer had gotten away with his crime. The terror for Lorraine was that she had known him, ate with him, danced with him and even prayed with him. The irony was beyond horrific.

Andrea started to cry. She had no idea her statement would have such an impact on Lorraine or anyone else at the meeting.

"I'm so sorry, Lorraine," she stuttered between sobs.

"It's not your fault, Andrea. You couldn't have known. It's okay. Please don't get upset. I just need to get home and put my feet up."

Patrick tucked Lorraine in bed and pulled up a chair. "I'll be right beside you, however long it takes," he said.

They were forecasting an early thaw and for once the weather people were right. The gutters filled with twisting brown braids which intersected each other on their race to the drains. Spring was in the air. It was a time of renewal and new life. Two weeks early, on the first of March, little Danielle Marie Watson took her first breaths.

Like all new parents, Patrick and Lorraine were bursting with pride when they brought her home to 568 Elm Street. Marjorie, Susan and Pearl put on the most designer-friendly baby shower one might imagine, but all the gifts and the smiles seemed hollow somehow. Lorraine was saddened that Patrick's parents were not alive to share in the joy, and she was heartbroken that her own mother chose not to come and welcome her granddaughter.

*

The fight had been one for the record books.

James had held his tongue for as long as possible, but when the birth announcement arrived in the mail, he had to do something. Initially, he gave Deborah the benefit of the doubt. He set the small envelope on the kitchen counter.

It sat for three hours in plain view, but Deborah didn't open it or ask about it. She walked past it several times, and when she was making lunch, she moved it to the edge of the counter. She refused to acknowledge its presence.

James could contain himself no longer.

"Deborah," James argued, "this is childish. You know that is the birth announcement for little Danielle. Lorraine mailed it a week ago just after she got home from the hospital. She said she was including pictures. She dearly wants you to share in her joy."

Then he tried a new technique. "Lorraine is our only daughter and this new innocent perfect life is our granddaughter. Don't you want to at least look at the pictures?"

Deborah turned around from the sink and dried her hands. She stared more into space than at her husband. Finally, she spoke, the words hesitating and tortured.

"This child cannot be blessed by Jehovah. She is as good as dead to me."

James stood ramrod straight before the woman he had continued to love regardless of her selfish and pigheaded insistence in remaining at the Hall. He slapped his hands on the counter. His anger and frustration lashed out into the room.

"But she will not be forever lost to me. I will be leaving in the morning. I cannot wait to see the little darling and congratulate Patrick and Lorraine. If you want to join me, I will be more than happy to have your company. If not, you can go pray at the Hall. Perhaps you should ask for guidance in understanding the difference between expectations of arbitrary and dysfunctional rules and your conscience when it comes to matters regarding those you love and who love you in return."

James left the kitchen and slammed the screen door. He crossed the road to his shop and slammed that door as well.

"My God what can I say to convince the woman?" he cried into the empty room.

*

At precisely 8:00 a.m., James closed the front door of the house and walked to the car.

He eased the car slowly into the road in the hopes he might hear the front door open and see Deborah's form appear on the stoop. He adjusted the rear-view mirror, shifted into first and, with a final glance to the house, edged down the drive.

Inside, Deborah stood at the kitchen window watching James leave. Her knuckles whitened in a vice grip on the sink. The tears welled up and spilled over her eyelids. In an ever-increasing tattoo they fell into the lukewarm dish water.

I love you Lorraine, I really do. I just can't see my way clear. Deborah leaned over the sink, sobs racking her body.

35

Easter Eggs and Chocolate Droppings

Easter was later than usual in 1972, but late on the calendar meant the weather promised to be fine. The warmth brought out bonnets and new dresses, jelly shoes and cashmere shawls. In flower beds, tulips stood four inches and the snowdrops heaped in tantalizing vanilla mounds.

Each morning when they approached her crib, one-month-old, little Danielle smiled back at her parents. This precious new life was the centre of Patrick and Lorraine's lives. Her birth had transformed them.

And it was Easter. Not just any Easter, but Lorraine's first celebration of the holiday, and Patrick wanted to make it memorable. Patrick had good intentions. He scoured the stores for the finest milk chocolate he could find. Her favourite was milk with a crunch of nuts.

"Hard to find that combination in an Easter Bunny presentation," he murmured as he tramped the aisles of Shopper's. *Best to get creative and make up my own combination,* he finally concluded.

So, Patrick bought raisin nut chocolate bars, Crispy Crunch bars, and a few Coffee Crisps as well. He then added a small box of Lindt chocolates wrapped individually in glossy foil.

Now that's a fine collection, he thought, smiling.

James had begged off staying for Easter. He wanted the little family to have their time together. He waved his goodbyes on Friday morning saying he could hardly wait to develop his four rolls of film and show the pictures to Deborah. He was sure they would melt her heart.

Earlier that morning, Susan had arrived for a visit and Patrick insisted the two girls go shopping. He knew Lorraine was itching to hit the stores and buy some new outfits for Danielle. He took advantage of his time alone to find the very best hiding spots in the house.

A couple of Lindt on the top of the wall clock.

Two Crispy Crunch under her pillow.

A Coffee Crisp tucked into her favourite tea cup.

Satisfied, Patrick hid the rest of the loot in Lorraine's slippers. He could hardly wait to see her reaction on Easter morning. And after the big hunt, he would regale her with a gourmet breakfast.

*

The cramps started as they left the shoe department at Sears.

"Oh My God!" Lorraine wailed. "They're back. And with a vengeance! Well, one good thing about being pregnant," she said, laughing wryly, "is not having damn periods for nine months. Do you have any Tylenol?"

"You bet. I'm always ready for pain. Let's head downstairs for a tea and maybe the cramps will subside."

Susan and Lorraine ordered decaf Orange Pekoe, bag in. When the server left the table, Lorraine headed for the washroom. She swallowed two Tylenol and then went into the stall. Sitting on the ceramic throne, she buried her face in her hands. From out of nowhere tears filled her eyes and spilled down her cheeks.

For some reason, Lorraine thought of her mother's awkward attempt at preaching about the period: *"Always carry some pads with you, Lorraine. That way you'll never get caught unprepared."*

Lorraine stuck the paper panty liner to her underwear and went to the sink. Drying her eyes and adding a bit of lipstick helped a bit, but the monthly roller coaster of emotions associated with her period lurked just below the surface ready to ambush her state of mind at any moment.

"I'm back," she announced as she approached the table. "I'm so glad, Susan, you came up to meet our sweetheart and to take me out shopping.

You know my love of the stores started when we skipped out of math help and went shopping at the Met. You've had quite an influence on me, my friend!"

Susan grinned a knowing smile and added, "Patrick is probably waiting anxiously for you to come home. Let's drink up and get you back to your family."

Susan and Lorraine said their goodbyes and promised the next shopping trip to Sears would be more pleasant.

"Let's pick the first of the month from now on," Susan chirped.

"Ha, very funny," Lorraine said, hugging her best friend.

*

Lorraine was exhausted. Side stepping Patrick's welcoming hug she headed straight for the bathroom. Minutes later, she returned and plopped into her La-Z-Boy. Little Danielle was sound asleep in the bassinette. Lorraine put up her feet, leaned back and took a deep breath.

Patrick sensed that Lorraine was on edge, so he prepared her favourite Martini: three olives, no ice. Thank goodness she had chosen not to breast feed. That meant alcohol was not on her no-fly list. Greedily Lorraine gulped the drink, passed the olives over to Patrick and sank back into her chair.

Patrick loved cooking and took pride in fancy plate presentation. When the girls were out, he had prepared a wonderful dinner of grilled salmon, capers and a tossed salad. He had even made a lovely crème brûlée for desert.

"You are so good to me, Patrick. I can't imagine my life without you."

"Nor mine without you. And now we are a real family."

Lorraine fed Danielle and together they tucked her into her crib. She planted a kiss on her daughter's cheek. "Good night, my precious. I won't be far behind you." Patrick pulled the giraffe blanket over his daughter before curling his arm around his wife. Together they gazed at the life they had created. At four weeks, Danielle slept a solid six hours. They had heard horror stories from other young parents that they wouldn't get a good night's sleep for a year. Of course, they were not complaining. For several minutes, they watched their baby's chest rise and fall in the beauty of calm and peaceful sleep.

"She's a miracle in every way," Patrick whispered. "We are so blessed."

"I couldn't agree more, but shopping really drained me. It's got to be an early evening for me, Patrick. I just need a good sleep and I'll be right as rain. You don't mind if I tuck in now?"

"Not at all. Tomorrow looks like another gorgeous sunny day. I think we should try out the new pram and take Danielle for her first walkabout. Show her off on her first Easter."

"Sounds wonderful," Lorraine whispered as she kissed him.

Patrick smiled at the thought of Easter morning and the hunt for Easter Bunny treasures.

*

Lorraine's sleep was fitful. Bad dreams about Armageddon stalked into her unconscious mind again. All night she prodded the pillow in a vain attempt to get comfortable.

When she opened her eyes early on Easter morning, she felt a sticky, messy film on her face. She rubbed her cheek only to find it covered in melted chocolate. Her hair was stuck together in thick chocolate strands.

"PatricKKKKKK," she screamed, "come here!"

Patrick rushed into the bedroom to find his lovely wife sobbing uncontrollably on the edge of the bed, chocolate hands covering a chocolate face.

"How can you possibly make fun of me when I get my period? Yes, sometimes chocolate helps, but this? This is a terrible mocking. How could you?"

Patrick held his wife and explained the ritual of Easter morning and the Easter Bunny. He tried valiantly to defend his behaviour, but seeing his distraught partner in abject agony, made him reel with remorse.

"Do you really expect me to believe that normal human beings actually hide chocolate all over their homes and expect adults and children to go hunting for it? Do I look that stupid?"

At the mention of bunny, Lorraine wailed again. All she could think of was her little Millie, hung by the neck by Demon Dougie.

*

Lorraine got the phone on its third ring. She was busy changing Danielle, so she balanced the receiver precariously under her neck. She had always been a multitasker. She had mastered hands-free talk, years ago.

"Hello. Oh, hi Dad. Yes, Easter was very memorable. I'm sure it will go down in the record books of the Watson Chronicle. Hard to top, I can tell you. I got my first lesson on finding Easter eggs. That damn bunny showed up everywhere in the house. I had to take a shower after his visit."

The day before, she had been spitting mad, but their walk in the park after a long, necessary shower had calmed her considerably. She knew as the weeks and months went by, she would laugh about her experience with the initiation rites of that stupid four-legged hare. Maybe when Danielle was three, she might let a chocolate egg back into her home.

"So, what's up?" Lorraine asked her dad as she rocked Danielle in the cradle her dad had bought for them. "You just left on Friday, so this call must be pretty important."

"As you can imagine, the local rag has been full of David Bodemer. This morning, at his fourth or fifth remand session, the paper announced his trial date. It's set for June 19 in St. Thomas Provincial Court. Looks like a lot of people from Aylmer and Straffordville plan to attend. Your mom's already corralled a Sister from the Hall to drive her. They think it will last about a week."

"Those poor parents," Lorraine said and sighed as a wave of nausea at the horrific memory resurfaced.

At that moment, she couldn't stop the overwhelming desire to hold Danielle close and protect her from all that was bad in the world. She lifted her precious daughter to her chest and set the receiver facing her mouth.

"Here Dad, listen. Danielle's telling you how much she loves you."

Contented breaths and goos sparked across the wire from Toronto to Straffordville. Sitting in his recliner, James' heart burst with joy.

36

Turmoil and Pain

Within a year of the Jacksons losing their daughter, they had moved out of Aylmer and away from the memories which haunted them everywhere they went. They settled in Stratford. Georgia's father suffered a paralyzing stroke and her mother lived in a world of shadows, mind-numbing grief and depression.

With David's confession, the Jacksons not only had to enter the eye of the hurricane of their daughter's death once again, but in addition to their personal grief they had to face the realization that one of their own — a fellow Jehovah's Witness — had broken the greatest of the commandments, the taking of another's life. That harsh truth wreaked havoc on their minds.

But their daughter had not only been murdered. A monster had inflicted horrific desecration and sexual violation on Georgia's body both pre- and post-mortem.

The worst part of the fallout from David Bodemer's confession was that the Jacksons were forced to return to 1966 and remember how he appeared so distraught when she disappeared. The police didn't interview David then because Albert Crooker provided an alibi. The police believed Albert and never considered David a suspect. Likewise, Georgia's parents had no cause to doubt his sincerity.

Perhaps the shock of her death blinded their eyes from seeing that David could have been the only possible suspect. He had a car similar in colour to the one that allegedly picked her up, and he had been in the Dairy Bar that afternoon before her shift ended. But in 1966, all that was dismissed or somehow irrelevant.

Adding to his appearance of innocence was the fact that he was a member of the Jehovah's Witness search party. In fact, several weeks into the search, David was on the team that discovered articles of her clothing on two separate occasions.

Although David seemed to be above reproach, there were some people — even back then — who sensed that something appeared out of place.

The Jehovah's Witnesses who were interviewed knew that Georgia would never get into a car unless she knew the person and wouldn't consider him a threat. To be in a car alone with a married man without chaperones would have been a stretch for a God-fearing young woman like Georgia, but she knew him as a father of two delightful children. Harmless.

The night had been frigid cold with a storm brewing, so maybe Georgia would have been grateful for the ride. After all, it was only a few blocks. What could be the danger?

After the confession and the arrest, Detective Dennis Alsop consulted the personal notes he had diligently written in the Jackson folder five years earlier. This time he looked at the case from a different perspective. Since 1966, a spate of unsolved murders had taken place all over Southwestern Ontario, especially in Middlesex and Elgin counties. He searched for signatures, similar MOs and psychological markers.

As he searched his notes, holes began to appear in the timeline of the alibis as well. The police had difficulty nailing down David Bodemer's whereabouts the night of February 18. Albert Crooker was not positive of the time his son-in-law joined him for his janitorial shift at the bank, only that he was there when witnesses came by around 10 p.m. looking for volunteers to search for the missing girl.

In the Aylmer courthouse at his first of many preliminary hearings, David Bodemer was remanded into custody. The Jackson family, Deborah Armstrong and her friend Helen Montgomery were in the courtroom to hear the charges.

37

Courtroom Groupies

The preliminary hearing held on January 25, 1972 was over in just minutes, but the shock of seeing the 26-year-old in handcuffs left an indelible impression.

The small courthouse on Talbot Street was crammed with curious residents and Jehovah's Witnesses. They had lined up outside the front door for an hour before being led inside. Amid hushed whispers, they took their seats. Some came to speak with the Jacksons and offer support. Others just sat mutely. The shock that one of their own citizens was a confessed murderer weighed heavily on their minds.

When the car drove up to the back door of the courtroom, David covered his head with a brown scarf to hide his face from photographers and the public. He was quickly ushered into the courtroom by three plainclothes policemen and settled in the prisoner's dock.

His hands and feet shackled, he walked with eyes cast down. He didn't look at anyone in the room. Elaine sat in the back row clutching her father's arm. She hadn't seen him since his arrest the day before. He looked more haggard than usual. His hair was disheveled and his face unshaven. With vacant eyes, Elaine stared at the man, a confessed killer, the same man who was the father of her five children.

David stood silent and sombre when the judge entered the courtroom. He pushed aside some of the dark hair which had fallen over his eyes like a shield. He wore a simple plaid shirt. He stole a quick glance at the faces of those sitting in the courtroom. When he saw his wife, he started to shiver uncontrollably. Within seconds, he felt the tears burn behind his eyes. He looked at his wife sitting straight and cold, shame and shock filling her face. Hot guilt burst the dam and spilled down his cheeks.

Provincial Judge Fred R. Barnum walked up to the dais and took his seat. He read the papers on the desk and with a stroke of his gavel, formally remanded the suspect to re-appear in court in St. Thomas the following morning. Within minutes the whole event was done.

Sobbing audibly, David was led away.

*

The little courtroom in St. Thomas was packed. At 10 a.m., Detective Sergeant Dennis Alsop of the London OPP detachment escorted the prisoner into the courtroom. David shielded his head and face with a coat and scarf to block out the photographers' flashbulbs and stares of the onlookers. The accused stood in the box to hear the judge's statement. He was remanded into custody until February 3, 1972. On February 3, the suspect was again remanded to February 10, but this time into custody to undergo a week-long preliminary psychiatric examination.

When he appeared in court on February 10, he was remanded yet again: this time to the Mental Health Centre at Penetanguishene for a complete psychiatric assessment. This decision came on the recommendation of Dr. J.K. McNeil, a psychiatrist at the St. Thomas Psychiatric Hospital. Bodemer confirmed that his defence lawyer, David Little, had discussed the matter with him and the suspect understood the nature of the proceedings.

At the hearing, Detective Sergeant Alsop reported to the judge that a car sought by police had been found in a Kitchener auto wrecking yard. The 1957 Meteor four-door sedan had been the object of an intensive police search. He hoped to find some connection between the car and the crime.

Every 8 days for the next several months, Bodemer was remanded into custody. Finally, at the preliminary hearing on April 28, 1972, Judge Barnum concluded there was sufficient evidence to hold him for trial with the charge of non-capital murder. The judge also issued an "exclusion of witnesses" order so witnesses could not hear one another's testimony. At that same time, they were sternly cautioned not to discuss the case among themselves.

On the morning of Monday June 19, 1972, the first day of the trial of Bodemer v. Ontario, a seven-member all-male Grand Jury returned with a true bill on the charge declaring that there was sufficient evidence to warrant putting the accused on trial. Their deliberations had taken only 40 minutes.

*

Helen parked the car by the old hardware store down the street from the courthouse. She urged Deborah to hurry so they could get a good seat. Neither one of them knew what they were in for during the trial, but they knew they didn't want to miss it.

The weather was beautiful for the 30-minute drive from Aylmer to St. Thomas, but that was the only spot of joy that June 19.

"Deborah. Look, there he is. Look at him," Helen said.

It was the first time either of the women had seen David since he had left the Aylmer Hall in December 1966. He looked stooped and weathered even for a man who had just passed his 27th birthday.

Helen whispered into Deborah's ear. "He doesn't look one bit sorry. Can you believe what poor Sister Virginia is going through, especially with her hubby in such poor shape? If it weren't for her friends at the Hall, I don't know how she could cope. Of course, her family is a staunch support."

Deborah nodded in agreement, but then paused to think about her own life, so different from loyal Sister Virginia and her family. Deborah's husband, son and daughter disfellowshipped years ago. Douglas contacted her sporadically from British Columbia, leaving Deborah adrift in a morass of loneliness and self-doubt. *And then this murderer, a Witness himself, capable of doing such a horrific act. What was the world coming to?*

The Crown was scheduled to call around 40 witnesses. Virginia Jackson was the first.

Deborah didn't know how the woman managed to stand up and face the Court. Her eyes were glazed and sunken. It was a wicked thing that she had to relive the events surrounding Georgia's death, but to do it face-to-face with the man who took her daughter's last breath seemed inhuman. And then to hear what he did to her! Deborah could hardly imagine such cruelty.

The Crown alleged that on the night of February 18, the same night Georgia disappeared, a woman heard a car idling on her street. She was sure she heard a woman screaming and then a man yelling. The sounds were silenced with the slamming of a car door.

"If only that woman had called police, they could have followed the tracks in the snow and Georgia would still be alive," Helen commented.

If only, Deborah mused.

Crown Attorney Douglas Walker argued that in the alleged altercation on Centre Street just two blocks from Georgia's house, David Bodemer struck Georgia on the head with a frozen soft drink bottle when she resisted his advances. Allegedly, Bodemer then drove the stunned girl to somewhere out of town where he confined her, assaulted her and, while holding his hand over her nose and mouth to prevent her resistance, she died of suffocation. How long he may have kept her body before placing it where it was found was undetermined.

Helen grabbed Deborah's hand when Virginia began to speak.

"Deborah, I can't watch. Maybe we should leave," Helen said as she sniffled into her Kleenex.

"Be strong. I want to hear everything that happened and know that David deserves to go to prison for this crime," Deborah replied.

Virginia held her composure during most of the questions, but when the lawyer asked the mother to identify her daughter's coat, she couldn't stop the tears. She slumped back in the chair as if trying to get away from the blue peacoat she had bought new for Georgia that winter.

"Yes, that was the coat she was wearing when she disappeared," she whispered.

*

Over the next couple of days, Helen and Deborah spent more time in a coffee shop than in the courthouse. Postponement followed postponement until, finally, late in June the jury was dismissed. The lawyers then moved into a "voir dire" session where they argued over the admissibility of certain pieces of evidence. The courtroom was emptied, and spectators left to their own devices.

The items in question were the statement Bodemer made to members of the Jehovah's Witness sect on January 24, 1972, and the second confession made to Detective Sergeant Alsop.

Finally, after all the delays, the jury was recalled at 4 p.m. on the afternoon of Thursday, June 22. Albert Crooker, their own Elder, was first to be called back to the witness box for the cross examination. On the stand two days earlier, he stated that Bodemer was with him on the night Georgia disappeared.

When the defence lawyer asked the question again, Albert Crooker admitted that he wasn't sure of his claim until January of the present year after police and other persons had talked with him following the arrest of his son-in-law.

Crooker told the Court that "it may have passed my mind" whether Bodemer was with him that night or what time he arrived. In 1966, he said unequivocally that David joined him at the bank that Friday sometime between 7:30 or 7:40 to lend a hand. Like other witnesses since Bodemer's arrest, Albert appeared similarly confused and provided different answers to the same questions asked at the coroner's inquest in 1966.

The defence lawyer was also quick to point out that Crooker was replaced following a series of congregational meetings held immediately after his son-in-law's arrest. He might have a great deal to worry about.

Constable Rupert from the OPP drove from the town's main corner to the locations where Miss Jackson's body and coat were found and back into town in less than 32 minutes. This proved that Bodemer could have killed the girl soon after abducting her at 6:30, make it back to meet Crooker at 7:30, and be there when searchers dropped by to ask for help in looking for the missing girl. A perfect alibi. Crooker left the stand visibly disoriented.

Crown attorney Walker stood to face the Court holding the three typewritten pages that were compiled on the evening of January 21, 1972 in Bodemer's home in Kitchener.

Helen whispered, "Listen, Deborah, they're going to read his confession."

Walker turned deliberately to face Bodemer in the prisoner's box. Walker turned to face the crowd and began to read slowly and clearly so all could hear the self-proclaimed actions David took that snowy February 18, 1966.

"When I picked her up by Spicer's Bakery, I was only going to drive her home. I had no thoughts of killing her or doing anything else to her. When I parked on a side street later, I don't know what got into my mind to put my arm around her or to hit her with the pop bottle when she struggled. I don't remember some things that went on that night."

"Let me continue," Walker said.

"Once she was knocked out, I drove to a side road south of town and parked again just as she came to and began screaming again. I placed my hand over her mouth and nose in the hope she would faint and stop screaming."

"While his hand was over her face, ladies and gentlemen, David Bodemer raped her, repeatedly. The accused's statement declares that when he removed his hand from her face, he realized that she was dead, and he became frightened. He then drove to another area east of Aylmer and dragged the body into a wooded area some distance from the road. When he returned to his car he realized her coat was still there and he drove to another area before stopping and putting the coat behind a tree."

Later that night he returned to his rented home in Avon, a village north of Aylmer, took his own bloodstained coat and a glove Miss Jackson was wearing from his car and stuffed them in a hole in the foundation. He then wiped the blood off the seat of his car using snow and a rag."

Walker turned deliberately to the jury.

"These are not the actions of a man who doesn't know perfectly well what he was about. In fact, this man knew undeniably that he had done wrong. He even confessed the rape and murder to his wife the night before he confessed to his Jehovah's Witness superiors."

Deborah knew that Arthur Powley had been in Aylmer most of January on congregational business. When the news of Bodemer's confession came out, she finally understood why.

Late in December 1971, Arthur Powley had been made aware of rumours that some member of the Aylmer congregation was responsible for the Jackson girl's disappearance and death, and in the interests of the safety of everyone in the church, he was recruited to get to the root of the problem.

With the assistance of Circuit Overseer Charles Ross from Toronto, the two men began interviewing all the male members of the 1966 Aylmer congregation to see what each remembered about that night.

Since many members had moved out of Aylmer since 1966, the two men travelled to several Jehovah's Witness congregations outside of Aylmer. David Bodemer had re-settled in Kitchener in December 1966, so the team travelled there to meet with him.

On Friday, January 21, Powley and Ross interviewed David at his home in Kitchener. Even though Bodemer was not a suspect in 1966, there appeared to be inconsistencies about his whereabouts on the night of February 18.

Powley, however, returned to Aylmer satisfied with David's responses. Three days later, he received a frantic phone call at 1:00 a.m. from Albert Crooker. Bodemer wanted to talk with him right away.

"See? Albert Crooker knew something. I'm sure of it now," Helen whispered. "This should be interesting," Helen added, nudging Deborah as Mr. Powley continued his narrative.

"When Mr. Ross, Mr. Crooker and I arrived around 10:30 that same morning, we found young David sitting at a table in the kitchen with his head cupped in his hands, sobbing. When he regained his composure, I offered a prayer for the Creator to help him to bare his heart and tell us what was troubling him. He hesitantly launched into a confession about the murder and rape of Georgia Jackson. My colleagues took notes and then called the Overseer in Kitchener to come to the house and type the confession. This was three weeks after I began my inquiry."

Under cross examination, Mr. Powley added that he had warned David on his prior visit that "if there is a person in our midst who has done this thing, he should come forward. If he doesn't, he will be caught sooner or later anyway because the angels will ferret him out when God executes his judgment on the wicked."

Under questioning, Powley also revealed that he often used such scriptures to exhort members of the congregation to divulge information which they might have held back previously.

Deborah felt her skin crawl. *It is always fear they use against us. Fear to keep us quiet or to trick us to tell on others.* She could name many other of the many brutal machinations in the Organization's arsenal of suppression. All arbitrary, vindictive and insidious.

David had indeed committed a most heinous act, but Deborah understood the very real fear that had consumed him and kept him silent for years. Within months, he had ditched the car and gotten out of Aylmer. The memories were probably too raw.

Defence lawyer Little asked Powley if Bodemer said anything in response to his question.

"Yes, I remember it verbatim. He asked me if such a person would lose his life at God's hand if the confession were not made to members of the sect. Naturally, I replied emphatically, yes. That's right."

Powley went on to explain the urgency of his statement. "Witnesses believe that we're approaching the end of the system that if a person has done something condemned in God's will and it is still kept secret when God executes his judgment, then that person will be ferreted out and die. Others in harmony with God will live through the Day of Judgment."

"I also believe," Powley added, "that his guilt had been eating away at him for a long while. It wasn't the first time that he had been linked to February 18, 1966. In 1968 members of the Jehovah's Witnesses suspected him of having knowledge of the disappearance. Especially after his congregation overseer learned of the growing number of minor criminal offenses of which he was guilty. Toronto lawyer Glen Howe, Chief Counsel for the Jehovah's Witnesses in Ontario, questioned him and he denied any such knowledge. The matter was effectively concluded, and David continued to live a free man."

"Thank you, Mr. Powley, you may sit down."

*

On the morning of June 26, Helen drove to the Armstrong house anxious to get on the road to St. Thomas. It was likely to be the last day of testimony.

Helen backed on to Plank Street before turning right on the old Heritage Line. The trial had filled her mind for the week. She could hardly sleep in anticipation of the next day in court. She turned to Deborah and smiled almost gleefully.

"So, what will happen today do you think? Will he be executed? He's already disfellowshipped so I guess it doesn't matter. He will never enter Paradise on either account."

Deborah winced at Helen's insensitive comment.

"No. David is being charged with a non-capital crime, so he won't be executed, but he surely will be locked up for a long while."

"I hear that Elaine has already filed for divorce. No one could blame her, and under the circumstances, I'm sure it will be granted." As she turned west on Highway 73, Helen added, "What kind of example is he for his children. Disgraceful."

Deborah settled into the seat and explored her friend's words. Despite her own husband's disgraceful disfellowshipping, James continued to be a good role model and a loyal husband. *Surely Helen didn't think of my James in the same light as this murderer?* She filed the idea into the farthest corner of her brain for future consideration.

Before they knew it, Helen and Deborah were back in the courtroom for the final arguments.

Two psychiatrists and a psychologist identified David as a sexual exhibitionist, immature, quiet and passive. One offered that a passive exhibitionist such as David would be incapable of rape. Another doctor stated that David was out of contact with reality and showed a tendency to make up stories and harbour delusions, while a third doctor said David would be incapable of making up a story without being detected. The story lines would be too complicated for a man of his less-than-average intelligence.

The Defence called only five witnesses. The brief two-hour defence was simple: Bodemer made up the confessions because he was Bible thumped. The Jehovah's Witness sect suspected David of the crime and threatened to disfellowship him if he didn't confess, and disfellowshipping meant that he would not have a chance at Everlasting Life, a terrifying prospect for the young man. At no point in the trial did the Defence call Bodemer to the stand.

The Crown argued that David's confessions came from the strongest sense of guilt within his heart and mind and gave him his first ray of hope in six years of everlasting life. Powley's warnings would have been a powerful inducement to a guilty man to confess. Walker also stated that the confessions were too detailed and proved too accurate to have been made up by simply looking at press clippings as the Defence had suggested. David Bodemer had to have been there. David Bodemer killed Georgia Jackson.

*

"We know he's guilty," Helen announced giddily, "now let's hear the verdict, so we can finally put this thing to rest."

"It's certainly been quite the week," Deborah added quietly.

"All rise," the Sherriff's stiff voice filled the room. The judge entered the court to give his summation and the charge to the jury.

Justice Campbell Grant stood to address the Court. After six days of testimony, several of which had been spent debating the admissibility of the confessions, the judge explained that while a person's confession or statement isn't always true, there has to be some ulterior motive when a man involves himself in a serious criminal offence of which he is innocent. There were two confessions and each fit well into the pattern of the girl's disappearance and death. There was no evidence before the Court to support the Defence's allegations that Bodemer's confessions were fabricated based on newspaper clippings.

Judge Grant continued, saying that all evidence indicated the girl was raped and smothered to death, and whomever committed the crime lived in the Aylmer area and was known to Miss Jackson. He commended the actions of the sect leaders in attempting to get to the bottom of the crime and turning Bodemer over to the authorities.

Following his summation, Judge Grant gave his 105-minute charge to the jury. In it he stated that his first thought was that the only verdict possible was one in relation to the non-capital murder charge facing the accused. At the urging of the Defence, the judge pointed out that a verdict in relation to the lesser offence of manslaughter could also be retruned.

Shortly past twelve noon, more than 100 people packed into the Elgin County courthouse as the jury filed into the adjoining room to commence its deliberations. The courtroom fell quiet. Only hushed whispers and muffled sighs could be heard.

The jury returned at 2:15 p.m. to ask the judge to read the Criminal Code definition of murder again. They left the room and returned two minutes later to announce their verdict. Deborah clutched her friend's hand and held her breath. The air in the room hung suspended in time.

One by one, the all-male jury took their seats. The head juror stood and faced the Court. In his hand was a small paper. He took a deep breath before speaking.

"Your Honour, we find the defendant guilty as charged."

Mr. Justice Grant replied that the life sentence is mandatory in a charge of non-capital murder. He thanked the jury for their work adding, "It would have been difficult to understand your coming to any other verdict."

David did not noticeably react to the pronouncement, nor did his wife or most of the other spectators who had filled the seats in the week-long trial.

As he left the prisoner's box, Bodemer made no eye contact with anyone. He appeared relieved that the whole business was over.

The transfer was scheduled for 4 p.m. on the day of his conviction. The judge gave David one hour to say farewell to his family. The family entered the small provincial jail which had been David's home since January and registered at the front desk. Within minutes the prisoner, under heavy guard, was brought from his cell.

Alongside the children, Albert and Elaine stood in a tight semicircle around the prisoner. It was the first time they had touched each other for six months.

Albert wished him well and stepped back to let his daughter say goodbye. She shook his hand and brought his body close to hers. The two oldest children wept as they hugged the man — a stranger now — that they called father. The two younger children clutched at their mother's skirt afraid to come to the man in handcuffs. The baby slept in the stroller.

David faced years of pain and suffering. His doctors had provided his new keepers with prescriptions to help with the delusions. His wife placed his worn Bible into his hands in the hopes he might find redemption in its leaves. And then the Sherriff gestured to the little group that it was time to leave.

The family was left standing on the steps watching the van get smaller in the distance. "Daddy, I don't know what I'm going to do now," Elaine said. "And with all these precious little ones."

Five hours later the van passed through the front gates of Kingston Penitentiary. On a glorious summer day, David Bodemer's new custodians locked the door, shutting out the wind in the trees and the waves on the lake.

38

Christmas Eve 1972

James tilted the chair back as far as it would go and put his feet on the desk. The cigarillo had burned down to the butt, its sweet smoke making circles above his head. It had been quite a year. *David Bodemer in jail. My little granddaughter almost walking.*

He closed his latest book and smiled. *Ben Cartwright sure knew how to manage his boys.* James loved reading his ever-growing collection of the Bonanza cowboy series.

Things were so different now that he was an Ex-Witness. The freedom to read a western novel, have a smoke and a sip of Jack Daniels. *Ah, I'm living the good life!*

It was Christmas Eve and James was alone. Deborah would be at the Kingdom Hall all evening planning for the door-to-door work on Christmas Day. She was always at the Kingdom Hall. He didn't expect her until much later, maybe after midnight.

He knew from experience that Christmas Day witnessing work brought in more dollars than any other day of the year. James always wondered about that, but he didn't question the take. On Christmas, the pagans were celebrating and always in a giving mood. More *Watchtower* publications were sold on Christmas than on any other holiday. He imagined the young Witnesses in the congregation primed and ready for their work.

James closed his eyes and reminisced about counting and rolling the change from all the Christmas Day profits. He rather missed that. He and the other Elders always enjoyed reaping the rewards of Christmas Sales and preparing the report for the Circuit Overseer.

James wondered if Brother Clifford would be pleased with this year's haul. Would they turn over hundreds of dollars from their tiny congregation as they did when James was an Elder? Thoughts of Brother Clifford swirled through his brain. He could recall the conversation all those years ago as if it were yesterday. In an insistent, almost demanding tone, he had turned to his wife and said, "Deborah, you mark my words. If Brother Clifford selects Douglas for the Faithful and Discreet Slave Service that will be the best day of my life! Brother Clifford is fair and honest. We could do far worse than him as a role model for the congregation."

Becoming more pensive and thoughtful, James added, "And, if anything should ever happen to me, I want Brother Clifford to conduct my funeral. You know, my dear, I believe I will put that in writing, so you won't have to worry about it when the time comes."

"Of course, Sweetheart," she agreed. "Brother Clifford it will be, but no more talk about that tonight. We have enough to think about if Douglas is off to Bethel in a few weeks."

James brought the chair back to a sitting position, while another wave of nostalgia flooded his mind. For some reason finding the letter about Brother Clifford consumed him. He must find it.

"Now where did I put that letter?"

He opened the third drawer of the desk, the one that held his important papers. It seemed to shake and waver as he pulled it towards his body. He leaned over and began rifling through the stack of papers.

"Ah, here it is," he whispered breathlessly.

He reclined the chair, lifted his reading glasses from the front pocket of his shirt and lit the last cigarillo in the pack. The smoke columned toward the ceiling. As he began to read, he tapped the empty pack of cigarillos on the desk.

Tap, Tap.

The taunting of the smoke curling above his head suddenly brought his friend Johnathan Stanstorp into hazy view. His eyes must be playing tricks on him. Johnathan was long dead. Marie found him in the barn.

Nonetheless, James was very pleased to see John. He recalled the times when John would come over and the two of them would enjoy a cigar. Usually on Fridays. James missed his friend.

Tap, Tap Tap. James smiled.

"Hey Johnathan, want a smoke?"

"Sure thing."

They both lit up and took turns making jokes about tobacco being banished from the flock.

"New rules, my friend. The Governing Body is at it again," said James.

Banning tobacco was backed up by just two scriptures. The Elders read the verses in Romans and in Matthew, repeatedly until the tobacco farmers and their customers banished the Golden Leaf.

"How 'bout you Romans and Matthew? Why don't you come join us for a puff?" Johnathan and James sarcastically morphed the two Scriptures into two more smoking buddies.

Romans wailed through the shop, "Smoking is worshiping an idol" he chanted. Matthew followed with, "Don't smoke, and Love your neighbours as yourself."

"Yup that's why we can't smoke, James. You are an idol to tobacco and I am your neighbour."

And then the four of them just laughed and laughed, and then took another puff. James always imagined that Matthew was a jokester while the imaginary Roman was older but wiser.

"So good to see you Jonathan. Been missing you these past years. Not too many of my friends come by. Disfellowshipped, you know."

James leaned back into the soft leather of his chair and pressed his hands into his chest. He tried to ease the stitch or whatever was bothering him. He put his second half smoked cigarillo back into the pack.

Maybe I should stick to just three or four a day, he thought, smiling sheepishly. "What's your take on that, Matthew?"

And then the pain filled his upper arm with a burning he couldn't quite explain. He frowned and rubbed his left arm trying to purge out the prickling numbness. If there had been a mirror in the office, James would have seen the left side of his face drooping and saliva running from his mouth.

'Debvor…,' his lips shaped her name, but his brain was already lost in the black hole of unconsciousness.

39

Keep Those Fuckers Out

Lorraine helped her mother choose the suit in which they would dress James for his coffin. The many years of holding the position of Elder in the congregation afforded him a large wardrobe of pinstripe, navy and black. Ties and shirts were also abundant. Never a bow tie, just the conventional long tie. Not too colourful. Never red.

The tears streamed down Lorraine's face as she fumbled through the closet in her parent's bedroom. Deborah sat on the edge of the bed, silent and in shock watching her daughter with a vacant look.

"Why don't you go lie down, mom. I'll finish." Deborah shuffled out of the bedroom into the living room where she crumpled on the couch. Since her husband's death, she hadn't been able to lie in the bed they had shared.

Unable to sleep but a few hours a night, Deborah's doctor had prescribed a sedative. It wasn't long before the pills took effect. Lorraine peeked into the living room to see her mom curled up on the couch in the fetal position, oblivious to her surroundings. They could select the suit when she woke up.

*

Deborah's boots crunched on the snow as she made her way home from the Kingdom Hall. The snow had piled up in snowdrifts beside the stone fences on her walk home. She shivered against the cold. She knew it was well past midnight. The Christmas Eve ministry work had gone on later than expected. She very cautiously lifted the latch and entered the front parlour. Thinking her husband was already in bed, she took her time putting away her galoshes and hanging up her coat. She stood several minutes in the kitchen, just listening. The house was funereally silent.

Deborah filled the blue ceramic kettle, her favourite, and placed it on the element. She pulled down one of her new green mugs. A cup of tea at midnight would be most refreshing. She might even sit at the window and watch the snow fall.

But when she entered the den, such thoughts crashed to the floor with her tea cup.

*

"Mom?"

"Mom?" Lorraine asked again. "What about the navy suit and light blue shirt with the paisley tie?"

Deborah looked across the room to her daughter, and in a voice like parchment, whispered, "That will do just fine."

Lorraine couldn't get the thought out of her head. Elder Clothes — navy, black, pinstripe. She moved the hangers along the rack in a futile attempt to conjure up the man himself, that strong, proud individual against whom she had measured all other men.

She shook her head and returned to the task, but the thought persisted. On the day she was selecting the outfit for her father's wake, she was imagining a new clothing line. The pun brought a much-needed smile to her face. She could hear her father's hearty chuckle as he repeated, "Elder clothes, I like it, sweetie."

Lorraine and Deborah selected a pair of navy socks and Lorraine shone her father's shoes. She knew they hadn't requested shoes for the body, but Lorraine wouldn't have him going barefooted. The outfit must be complete. She gathered everything together and placed it in a small bag to load in the car for its final journey to the funeral home.

Lorraine's emotions were chaotic. Although she was bowed with sadness, she was reeling with anger at the same time. James' dying wish was very clear. *Deborah, Brother Clifford is the most admired and respected Circuit*

Servant in our District. If anything should ever happen to me, I want him to offer the service.

Lorraine and Deborah initially thought the task of arranging the funeral service would be straightforward, but things spiralled out of control as the day of the funeral drew closer.

Lorraine called Brother Clifford as her mother had instructed. She informed him of James' sudden death and the instructions he had left for the officiation. At first, Lorraine was surprised and then appalled at his response.

"My dear, Lorraine," Clifford replied magnanimously, "This request needs to be taken up with Jehovah God. I will ask Him in prayer for His instruction on officiating at a service for a disfellowshipped Brother."

The next morning at 10 a.m., Lorraine got the Clifford-through-Jehovah response.

"HE has guided me, and I am not to offer this service to a former Brother."

"But I have already printed the memorial cards," Lorraine wailed.

"Jehovah God has spoken to me through my prayers," he repeated and hung up the phone.

Lorraine hunched over in her chair and for the first time since she arrived, she cried. She wailed. "I hate these people! Who could possibly do such a horrible thing at a time like this?" she yelled, stamping her feet defiantly. "Well then, none of the bastards are coming to my father's funeral!"

The planning of the funeral fell to Lorraine, Patrick and Peter with minimal input from Deborah. On December 30, Lorraine contracted Harmony Funeral Home to prepare the announcement and then headed out coffin shopping.

Harmony House Funeral Home
Straffordville, Ontario
Sunday January 8, 1973
Officiating ~ Brother Lyle Clifford
Ecclesiastes Chapter 7:1
"The day of Death is Better than the Day of Birth."
The Book of John, Chapter 14
Family Reflections ~ Lorraine Armstrong

Prayers to Jehovah ~ All
Burial,
St. Luke's Cemetery immediately following the service

A basket case of emotions, Deborah remained at home.

The basement of the funeral home was filled with coffins. So final. So hard. So cold.

"What would you like for your loved one? We have solid oak or maple which can be lined with any coloured satin linings. With silk and gold trim."

Lorraine fingered the small puffy pillows. She didn't like any of them. She inquired if there was a box made of tin.

"No," the funeral fuddy-duddy said. "Tin is not an element we use to inter our loved ones."

Lorraine thought that James would be proud to go to his eternal rest in a tin box. She imagined it with rivets on the edges and folded down and pressed corners.

In the end, they picked an oak highlighted with dark tones and lined with white satin. Lorraine thought the satin would match the navy suit, and the paisley tie would go nicely with the gold trim of the liner.

James was on display in the funeral parlour for one day. Lorraine and Peter's friends all came, so did all the former Witnesses that were disfellowshipped over the years. Many of James' former customers came. It was a homecoming for the sinners and apostates.

"If any Witnesses try to get in, kick them out," Lorraine instructed. "After what Clifford did to us, none of those bastards are allowed in!"

Deborah's medication had kicked in and she was fast asleep on the sofa. She heard neither her daughter's wracking sobs, nor her promise to keep the Witnesses away.

Peter and Lorraine frantically searched for a replacement for the asshole Clifford. They remembered a tobacco farmer who had moved to the area several years earlier. Mr. Philip DaGrotten. He was Hungarian and a simple man, but James really got on with him whenever he came to the shop to get his tobacco kiln pipes.

"I'm calling him," Lorraine said. "Peter, check the telephone book for the DaGrottens in the area. There can't be very many."

In fact, there was only one. And he was home.

*

Lorraine drew the curtain of the viewing room for privacy. As the light slowly drained from the mid-winter sky, Lorraine and Deborah approached the coffin to say their final goodbyes to their well-dressed James.

Lorraine wondered what her mother was feeling. His loss was so sudden, so surreal. No lingering death. No time to watch her husband wither and waste. He just up and left.

Deborah looked down at her husband and took his hand. "I WILL see you again," she whispered.

Lorraine knew what that meant. In that moment as she lowered her lips to kiss her husband, Deborah forgot the teachings of the Truth by desiring to see her James again. For that instant, she had shed herself from the Armageddon messages and the rulings about the Chosen Ones.

"Mom, you will see him again," Lorraine said passionately as they entered the parlour to hear the words of Mr. DaGrotten, the non-Witness officiant.

Philip DaGrotten saved the service. He did a pretty good job considering, and as per Lorraine's instructions, avoided any reference to Jehovah. He announced to the congregation of apostates and friends that James was a good, hard-working man and was known to read the Bible. Philip must have thought it better to say Bible than pocket western novels.

40

Adjust Your Thinking

As they do with all families, years pass in a comfortable parade of predictable routine: first tooth, first steps, first garbled attempts at words, walks in the park, first day of kindergarten, birthday celebrations, and holidays. Patrick and Lorraine watched their little angel grow and with the start of each new year, Lorraine celebrated a cleansing of the good kind — one more year free of the cult.

But always lurking below the surface was the unpredictable: a trigger that sent her spiralling back into the cesspool. There were still many moments when the memories and fears of the years with the cult overwhelmed her and she was frozen in space.

Patrick marvelled at his wife's strength to break the chains that made her believe everyone else was in the wrong and only Jehovah's Witnesses were in the right and so blessed that they couldn't imagine breaking the edicts issued from the Elders. Patrick and little Danny, however, helped her weather the emotional storms that set off the tornados in her mind.

Patrick was her rock. Her anchor. Without him by her side, she might have faltered. He was always supportive of her decision and never failed to confirm her choice. And when the bad clawed its way to the surface, he was there.

On a particularly snowy Sunday afternoon in February, eight-year-old Danielle selected some sheets from her new package of Grams' special writing paper. For as long as she could remember, on the first Sunday of every month, she had made something for the grandmother she had never seen. Lorraine shared the few photos she had in an old blue photo album of her parents and siblings. Danielle always had fun pointing her pudgy fingers from face to face and saying the name. Lorraine often wondered where Danielle came up with the descriptors she added while peering into the eyes of the family frozen in Kodak black and white.

"This is my grandpa who became an angel on Christmas. This is my grams who can't come to see me 'cause she doesn't drive. This is my wonderful Uncle Peter who brings me chocolate every time he comes to visit. And this is my evil Uncle Dougie who lives in the frozen north."

Each time she looked at the photos, Danielle made up some new but horrific behaviour for her evil Uncle. Lorraine shook her head and wondered about her daughter's vivid imagination. Too many cartoons, perhaps. With each of Danielle's wicked giggles, Lorraine shuddered as she stared back at her younger brother's face.

"All right sweetheart, let's get this letter going. It's only a month until your birthday, so we have to make a special invitation to Grams."

"Do you think she might come? After all, she is the only grand person I have. If I make something special, she simply can't say no. I'll add some of my best Cabbage Patch stickers. They should do the trick."

"Those stickers might just convince her to come and see us. I know you would love making cookies with Grams. She has the best recipe for macaroons."

*

Deborah heard the mailman lift the letter box and slide the mail through the slot. The envelopes fell in a pile just inside the big oak front door.

She recognized the one from Danielle, immediately. Three cabbage patch stickers trooped along the seal on the back of the pale green envelope. She laid the bills on the kitchen table, but with a bounce in her step, she carried the coloured letter in her right hand and headed to James' office. She placed the key in the lock and entered the room.

The big leather chair still sat before the desk. As she did every time she entered the room, she ran her hand along the back of the chair where James often rested his head when he was perplexed about something. She could still smell his presence. Even the faint linger of cigarillo smoke. Still, after nine years. How she missed him.

She sat in James' desk chair. The soft leather wrapped her body like his arms. "It provides some comfort at least," she whispered into the lonely space. She placed the letter on the desk and fumbled in the drawer for the letter opener.

She never opened the letters right away. Instead, she leaned back in the chair and spoke out loud to James.

"So, the February 1981 letter from Danielle just arrived today. She put some stickers on the back of the envelope. See dear?" Deborah lifted the envelope into the air.

"My, but she prints so well." Deborah turned her head to look around. "Pretty soon, there won't be much more room on the walls for pieces of her artwork or her letters."

With shaking hands, Deborah opened the letter and read the message aloud to her James. "It's an invitation to her ninth birthday party next month, dear. She reminds me that I am her only grand person and that I just have to come see her new puppy."

Deborah set the paper back on the desk and sat back in the chair.

She could hear him just off to the left, that I-told-you-so tone filling the room. *Deborah, you must go. Danny is the sweetest little thing. Even though I only saw her as a babe in arms, you have brought her alive to me each time you come into the office. You can do this. You are a strong woman, a loving woman, the one I sought across the barn dance floor.*

Deborah smiled at the memory. "I think you're right. It might be time, James." She pinned the latest letter in its place next to the January letter, kissed her granddaughter's name and left the room.

As she slid the key to James' office into her apron pocket, she heard steps on the front porch. With a quick knock, Peter flung open the door and stepped into the entrance way.

"Hi Mom. Just stopped by to look at that furnace. Sorry I haven't been over sooner, but the shop keeps me busy all day and the three little ones keep me on my toes from the moment I get home."

"Don't worry about me," Deborah said, laughing. "I can always make a fire in the Jotel stove in the kitchen. And make a strong cup of tea."

Peter hugged Deborah and laughed at his mother's martyred response. "Nothing's too much trouble for my mom. I know you've said it seems to be making a lot of noise every time you turn up the heat and that it's not pumping out much warm air. I aim to find out why it's running at less than capacity."

Each time Peter came over to his parent's house, he tried to convince Deborah to join him on his next trip to Toronto. He made buying trips for the shop at least every six weeks. He could drop her off at Lorraine and Patrick's and pick her up a month later. She would have lots of time to get to know her granddaughter, plus she would get out of Straffordville.

While Peter worked on the furnace, Deborah paced in the kitchen aimlessly. She didn't know how her son might react, but she had made up her mind.

*

Sunday afternoons were family excursion times for the Watsons, but the mornings were spent at home. Danielle loved Sundays because she was welcomed in her parents' bed where they snuggled and read stories together. Lorraine cherished Sundays far from the tentacles of the Kingdom Hall. Patrick liked to keep his girls guessing, but they knew they would take the streetcar downtown and, depending on the weather, it was either an indoor or outdoor activity.

On colder days, they relished the galleries, children's theatres, museums, aquariums or malls. On warm days, they went to Exhibition Park or Casa Loma, but their favourite was a walk down Bookseller's Row. The heart of Toronto was a bustling energetic place to be.

And Danielle was a part of that life. In a snuggly, in a stroller, at the end of a teddy bear harness, and finally holding her parent's hands and driving them crazy by reading every sign, everywhere, Danielle was the centre of their world. Words and images tantalized their young daughter. Patrick and Lorraine were more than proud.

On a Sunday near the end of February, the Watson family were making a full day of it. They surprised the staff at Sea Clothiers in the Eaton Centre and then walked around the corner to Queen West. The weather was cold, but brilliant sunshine and little wind made the walk pleasant. Danielle wore a soft cashmere hat with ear mufflers.

"You're so wrapped up sweetie, you remind me of Heidi from the book." Danielle laughed at her mother's comment. She loved imagining herself as a character from the books they read together.

"And Heidi is one of my favourites," Danielle replied as they hurried along the street filled with shoppers.

In the early 1980s, Queen West was the intellectual hub of Toronto. Shoppers could count more than a dozen bookstores between Simcoe and Spadina. In fact, the area was lovingly referred to as Bookseller's Row.

A few weeks earlier, Patrick had received a call from Marjorie about a book that she said he absolutely had to purchase for Lorraine. At the last Ex Jehovah's Witness meeting, everyone was talking about it. A former member of the Governing Body of Bethel had been disfellowshipped for writing it.

Patrick planned to settle his wife and daughter in the children's section of Steven Temple Books and look for Raymond Franz's *Crisis of Conscience*. Knowing his wife, she would likely devour the book in less than a week. He hoped that whatever the former Jehovah's Witness had to say about Bethel, it would aid her own healing. He was also pretty sure that everyone at the Ex-Jehovah's Witness group would spend many a session discussing the heresies of this most recent high-profile apostate.

*

"I think I've got it fixed, mom. You shouldn't hear any more crazy sounds, and you should be warm," Peter said. He went to the cupboard for a cookie. "Just taking my payment," he said, reaching into the jar. "Can't pass up a macaroon or two."

As he munched on his cookie, Peter noticed his mother's agitation. Whenever she twisted the dishcloth between her hands, something was on her mind. He waited for her to speak.

"I've been thinking, Peter." She paused. "When is your next trip to Toronto?" Peter almost choked on the bits of coconut in his mouth, but he maintained his calm.

"Well, I was planning to go up at the end of the month and stay for a few days with Lorraine and Patrick. It's little Danny's birthday on the 1st so wouldn't want to miss the celebration."

"Would you like some company?" Deborah whispered while the start of a grin spread across her face.

"Mom, I would love company, especially yours."

As he realized the enormity of her decision and the conflict he imagined raging inside her, Peter rushed to hug his mother. "You're going to love that little granddaughter of yours."

*

Lorraine could hardly believe her eyes when she saw her mother standing beside her brother when she opened the front door.

"Brought a lost relative with me. Hope you have an extra bed."

Danielle was the first to react. She ran to her grandmother and gave her a bear hug. "Hi Grams. I guess you really loved my cabbage patch stickers. Now the whole family is here," she chirped.

Deborah brought the little girl close to her chest. Tears welled in her eyes as she clung to her granddaughter. "I'm sorry it took so long, sweetheart."

Patrick turned to his wife as if to say, *I told you she would see her way clear to choose family first.*

Danielle kept her grandmother busy from morning to night. Once she blasted through the door straight from school, she corralled her Grams into cookie making, doll dressing, and book reading. By the end of the first week, it was as if they had known each other their whole lives. In a way they had, thanks to Lorraine's monthly letters and photographs as well as Deborah's recreation of her granddaughter's life in James' office.

*

Two weeks after Deborah's arrival, Patrick thought the time was right to bring out the thick black book with the gold title printed on the spine. He knew that Lorraine would find comfort in the revelations of *Crisis of Conscience.* Patrick thought the title said it all. He often saw his wife crumble under whatever crisis caused her early life to resurface. He understood how her conscience gnawed at her until she had to act on it, and Lorraine had faced those demons by following her conscience and leaving the Hall. *What strength. What amazing strength.*

But choosing to follow her conscience had put her and her mom at loggerheads. For years, theirs remained a love-hate relationship. But as Patrick glanced across the living room at his mother-in-law sitting beside her daughter with her granddaughter on her lap, he felt they had turned the corner on that conflict.

Patrick placed it on the coffee table and Danielle was the first to notice.

"Daddy what is that? Did you buy a new book for the library?"

Lorraine glanced at the heavy black tome lying on the table, her face full of questions. "You're acting very secretive this evening, Patrick. What book is that?"

"One of Marjorie's suggestions. I think you and your mom will find it enlightening. It's the most recent title on the Governing Body's banned index."

*

As Deborah's visit ended, mother and daughter had reached a place in their lives where they could speak openly about the pain of their Jehovah's Witness years. They had both read Raymond Franz's book and had many discussions late into the night, glasses of wine at their fingertips. Lorraine was adamant that she would never return to the Hall. Too many people in her life had already been hurt and damaged. They carried their burdens heavily in their hearts.

Deborah was still in limbo, but Lorraine hoped her mother would heed the message in the book. With the lines of communication finally open between mother and daughter, Danielle was already planning fun things to do when her Grams next came to stay with them.

Crisis of Conscience exposed the arbitrary policy making at the highest levels in the Governing Body. At the stroke of a pen, rulings that thousands of Jehovah's Witnesses had once followed and taken as gospel were thrown out in a new edition of *The Watchtower*. Suddenly the flock had to backtrack and re-learn how to follow Jehovah. The Organization encouraged them to adjust their thinking on the matter in question and move on as if the former edict had never existed, similar to the 1975 Armageddon prediction which came to naught. The Organization argued the exact date had never been a guarantee, only a suggestion. But the suffering inflicted by the fear of its coming was horrific.

Like others who chose to question the Organization, Raymond Franz spared the reader no part of the painful conflict he faced. It had not been an easy decision for him to write the book and condemn the faith he had followed since his teens, but the more he discovered about the false teachings of the religion, the greater his resolve. The word of the Organization had taken over as the word of Christ.

The book was banned reading for all Jehovah's Witnesses and within months of its publication, Franz was disfellowshipped and declared Apostate. No faithful member could break bread with him. The Shunning was complete and abrupt.

*

Peter collected his mom following his latest order run to Toronto. He could tell by the smiles and hugs that the visit had been a success. *Soon,* he thought, *soon, Mom will join us on the other side of the dark cavern.*

From the passenger side window, Deborah blew kisses at all three Watsons standing on the stoop. She settled in for the drive home, but she no longer felt lonely.

She patted her son's hand, "Thank you Peter for giving me the courage to go. Life is looking so much brighter."

"You did it Mom because you knew it was the right thing to do."

Deborah nodded silently. She could hardly wait to unpack the box of Danielle's art and homemade treasures, and lay them on the desk to share them with James.

The letter arrived in her mailbox a scant 24 hours later. It was addressed to former Witness, Deborah Armstrong. Deborah recognized Helen Montgomery's handwriting.

41

Nova Scotia Bound

Lorraine and Patrick always knew Nova Scotia would become their forever home.

Each year, their visits for the Maritime Buying Shows turned into extended stays. Vacationing in the province, they fell in love with the sights and sounds of Halifax, and the wonder of its waterfront, the luxurious hotels overlooking the ocean, and the great restaurants. Lorraine loved the history and the culture. It just felt like home.

On one of those buying trips, they travelled to the South Shore, and like so many others fell in love with Lunenburg. Living on the east coast were the very best days of Lorraine's life. In fact, she reported to everyone she met, "I love it here, it is always peace and harmony and constant joy."

In Nova Scotia, Lorraine felt far away from the memories and horrors of the past. She didn't even know of any Jehovah's Witnesses or of any Kingdom Halls in the area. It felt good to be rid of the very sight of the buildings and the invasion of the cult.

Finally, she was at peace.

*

"She's not looking after herself," Peter pleaded. "She's not eating and not bathing, and she is collecting and hoarding stones. She just sits all day in the corner of the room moving the stones in a circle around her. I can't deal with it anymore, Rainey. She needs to move to Nova Scotia and live with you and Patrick. Or, we put her in a home?"

Recent telephone conversations that Lorraine had had with Deborah were confusing. She did not respond to questions about what she might have had for supper, or where and how she spent the day. Hearing was certainly an issue, but Lorraine had the gut feeling that something other than hearing loss was affecting her mom.

But a home? For my mom?

Suddenly she recalled the horror stories Lorraine had heard about another Jehovah's Witness senior who had been placed in a Nursing Home. Beatrice Long was diagnosed with dementia. Her son, an Elder at the time and the daughter-in-law, a full-time missionary, had no time to care for the aging, demented Sister Beatrice. So, they placed her.

The long-standing rituals of the Truth stayed strong in Beatrice's mind. She refused to eat in the dining hall with any of the other residents, as they were non-witnesses. She refused to attend any of the therapeutic exercises and recreation programs. She remained isolated in her room. She ate her meals alone and tried to remember her prayers and devotion to Jehovah.

Lorraine got all this gossip from Susan's cousin who worked at the Mallory Manor Nursing Home in Aylmer. The home was small, and the staff was dedicated to caring for their residents. They had an outstanding reputation for cleanliness, great food and meaningful recreation. Community outreach programs offered games such as Bingo and Crib tournaments. Everyone in the community was invited. Bingo at the Manor Hall on Wednesday afternoons was especially popular. Everyone in the Home came to play.

Everyone except Beatrice.

Across the fog of memory, she recognized the work of Satan happening around her. She was startled whenever she heard the Bingo numbers being called and when she heard the loud call of the winner: BINGO. When the Elders of the congregation discovered that the residents of the nursing home played Bingo, they intervened.

From then on, the staff was given strict orders that Beatrice be excluded from such events: Christmas, Thanksgiving, Hallowe'en, or birthday parties.

Lorraine shuddered at the stories of Beatrice. The poor woman shrivelled away, alone and confused, while *Watchtowers* and *Awakes* piled up at her bedside.

A Home is not an option for my mother.

"She is not going to a home, Peter," Lorraine replied sharply. "I will come pack her things and bring her to Nova Scotia."

Lorraine kept her promise. It had only been two years since she had seen her. Surely not that much has changed.

*

Lorraine pushed aside the screen door and fell into the kitchen where she saw Deborah sitting at the table, her food untouched. "Hello dear, I thought you were coming tomorrow," she said.

"No, I'm here now Mom, and we are going to pack together for the move."

"Move? Where are you moving Lorraine?"

The distinct odour of urine erupted from the arm chair as Deborah stood to greet her daughter. They hugged, uncomfortably.

"Let's start with the refrigerator, Mom." Lorraine opened the fridge door and almost collapsed from the fumes.

Rancid and rotten, everything. Milk and cheese and bread and slaw all appeared to be moving with mold. Lorraine pinched her nose. *I wonder if Mom still has Vicks Vaporub. Maybe if I rub it on the end of my nose like the cops do when they find a corpse, I can get through this.*

*

Three days later, bathed and dressed in a comfortable shift, Lorraine prepared her mother for the biggest move of her life. Deborah insisted that she allocate at least one suitcase for her *Watchtower*s and her Bible.

That's irony for you. For years those magazines and rules stole her mind, her independent thought, and her life. Now the doctor says that mild to moderate dementia is stealing Deborah's brain. What brain can be left to damage, Lorraine wondered.

Lorraine found a large box of magazines on the front porch. Each month the Elders delivered Deborah's "quota" of *Watchtower*s and *Awake*s. They were piled up in an ever-growing stack with a note on the top with an amount owing to the congregation. The double-dipping travesty of the Watchtower Bible and Tract Society was not lost on Lorraine. First, her mother had to buy the publications with her own money and then after she sold them, she had to send the money back to Bethel.

Lorraine kicked the pile aside and helped her mother down the stairs. Once Deborah was settled in the back seat, she loaded the suitcases into the van. Lorraine leaned in to her brother in the driver's seat so their mother couldn't hear.

"As soon as you get back home from the station, Peter, I want you to promise me something. Use those magazines to start your furnace," she begged.

"Done," he replied.

Peter drove them to the VIA Station on York Street. He helped the frail little woman navigate the marble foyer until they reached the platforms. At the doors, Peter hugged his mom.

"Don't worry mom. Lorraine will take care of you. I'll come to see you as soon as I can." Deborah raised her hand in a slight wave to the retreating black coat of her firstborn.

They got a sleeper car as the trip would take them to Montreal for a stop-over and then on to Halifax. Deborah needed to be able to sleep. Lorraine needed to be able to drink.

The trip was memorable. Deborah was as giddy as a child as she looked out the windows of the observation car. The forest passing by the windows made her feel as though she were literally running through it. The sun reflected the fall colours in dashes and darts of orange and yellow.

The man in the seat opposite smiled, thinking it lovely that a mother and daughter would take a trip together.

"I see that you are enjoying the scenery. It's beautiful isn't it?" he said.

Deborah's response was canned and quick. "It is the work of our creator, Jehovah God," she replied. Lorraine sank in her seat and closed her eyes. Deborah continued to speak to the man. "I am moving to Nova Scotia. I was living in a barn and my daughter here, said 'no more of that.'"

Lorraine's eyes pleaded with the man to understand. "Mom, you didn't live in a barn. In fact, the house was lovely. Peter did an excellent job keeping it up. He came over every weekend to cut the lawn and do any jobs that needing upkeep."

"I did so," she insisted. "There were cows and chickens in the entry way when we left." Shock and pity crossed the man's face as he excused himself and headed toward the bar.

Lorraine shuddered at the prospect of two more days of Jehovah this or Jehovah that. She feared it was going to be a very long journey.

42

Stewed Prunes

Deborah enjoyed the train, especially the observation car where she could chat with all the travellers. She thought it gave her the opportunity to teach the Truth in a lovely atmosphere. She made notes in her small book and kept track of the number of minutes she spent speaking to the passengers. She thought she would make up for the hours of service missed while away from her home. One hundred hours per month was her goal.

Take advantage of every opportunity to preach the Kingdom Ministry the voice inside her head prattled. After the passengers started to complain to the staff, Lorraine avoided taking her mother back to the observation car. Instead, they enjoyed the quiet of their own sleeper car looking out the window watching the world go by. But on the last night, Lorraine did't want to have their food delivered again.

"Let's go to supper in the dining car tonight, Mom," Lorraine suggested. "It's our last night and it will be like going to a fancy restaurant. I have a few rules, however. You must wear running shoes. You'll fall otherwise. And," she added, "passengers must hang on to the rail. Walking down to the dining car while the train is moving is dangerous. Agreed?"

Deborah had always refused a hand. She insisted that her balance was just fine. A history of falls indicated otherwise.

"We won't go unless you promise to hang on to the rail, and that's that."

"All right, I promise," her mom offered reluctantly.

Lorraine chose a lovely pink skirt and matching jacket for Deborah. The skirt was long enough that no one would notice the running shoes. She did her makeup. A bit of colour on her cheeks and some eyeshadow made her shimmer in the soft light inside the train. Even at 79, her mom's strawberry blond hair hadn't dimmed much. Lorraine placed a sparkling barrette just off to the right of the crown of her head.

"You look beautiful, Mom, if I do say so myself."

Deborah smiled at her reflection in the mirror, satisfied with the overall picture.

The Dining car was inviting. The curtains were drawn for the evening meal, and candles placed in the middle of tables flickered on the crisp white linen tablecloths. Signature CNR silverware was placed on either side of large dinner plates. Lorraine felt they were at the Royal York in Toronto or at one of the beautiful restaurants in Nova Scotia.

At the sight of the couples sitting together enjoying a cocktail, Lorraine suddenly missed her Patrick. At the end of every day, they always shared a drink and each other's company. Just one more day, she reminded herself, and she would be back in Lunenburg sitting on the porch overlooking the ocean. She could hardly wait.

Deborah and Lorraine chose garlic mashed potatoes and shaved beef with seasonal vegetables, bread pudding for desert and a glass of white wine.

When the waiter set the plate in front of her, Deborah looked down at the offering and immediately bowed her head. She closed her eyes and began a prayer to Jehovah God. Out loud.

Lorraine ordered a Martini.

While Deborah continued her praise to Jehovah, Lorraine looked around to see if anyone was noticing or listening. A few smiles from those sitting nearby told her it was okay. Lorraine ordered another.

Deborah's prayer took longer than usual. She thanked Jehovah God for the meal and the beautiful earth. She thanked His son, Christ Jesus for giving her the spiritual wisdom of being His follower. But then to Lorraine's surprise, Deborah went on to thank Mr. Pullman himself for inventing the train and having the wisdom to offer travel to those who might otherwise not be able to go places.

Lorraine reached over and patted her mother's hand as she finished with a blessing to all those other travellers and offered them a safe trip.

"Amen," Lorraine said hastily trying to get her mother to move on to her dinner.

Lorraine gulped down the second Martini and finished her meal, just as Deborah lifted her fork for a first bite. She noticed the olives left sitting on the plate by Lorraine's glass. Since the allergy in Montreal, Lorraine shied away from olives.

"If you're not going to eat those olives dear, I would like them."

Lorraine placed all six of the vodka-soaked red-eyed pearl olives on a side plate and slid them over to her mother.

"Enjoy," she whispered.

Deborah did just that. She finished her entire meal, a dessert of crème brûlée, and a wine spritzer topped off with the vodka-soaked olives.

On their way back to the sleeper car, Deborah giggled and sang snippets of a song she remembered from years before. She happily held on to the rail. Lorraine settled her mom into the travelling apartment and looked forward to a good sleep.

An hour later, her mother announced, "I'm not feeling quite right, Lorraine. I might need some help getting to the toilet." She added with a chuckle, "I guess that I really didn't need the Senocot and the stewed prunes for lunch after all."

There was no escape from the explosion from Deborah's bowels. The combination of prunes, olives and laxatives was deadly. In the small, confined bathroom with no windows and a washing sink the size of a dinner plate, Lorraine set to work to clean her mother up.

Please don't let this be my future. Lorraine sighed, tucking her mother into the lower bunk before climbing up the tiny ladder to the cot above.

*

The rain pelted the windows of the Observation Car. Lorraine and her mother decided to stay there despite the poor view and the looks of the other passengers. The rain was comforting somehow. Today was the last day of their journey and tomorrow they would arrive in Halifax.

Deborah strained to watch the trees as they rushed by. Although she appeared lost somewhere in the past, Lorraine heard her mom click her lips together and blurt out, "As soon as we get to Nova Scotia, Lorraine, I want you to call Douglas and give him my new address."

Her strange request came totally out of the blue. No one had heard from Dougie since James was officially disfellowshipped and Peter was kicked out decades ago. Lorraine stared through the window remembering the announcement.

In front of all his Brothers and Sisters and his young daughter, James had been shamed. Deborah, still a stanch believer, sat straight as an arrow and listened as the Elder chastised her husband. She reached for her daughter's hand as the final verdict was read.

Brother Klein had waited until the end of the Kingdom Ministry School before reading the letter. Lorraine remembered how ironic and mean-spirited that was. Her father, a respected and prominent member in the small congregation, was a participant in the meeting that night, leading the opening prayers to Jehovah God.

As James lifted his head, he looked out over his congregation and smiled. He smiled at his family, his wife and daughter, his customers and his friends.

Lorraine shuddered as the edict poisoned the room. She kept her head down to hide the embarrassment and the hot tears of shame. The bile from her pepper sandwich rose in her throat. She tried desperately to swallow it back down.

This is the second worst moment of my life, she thought. *I* HATE *these people.*

She knew that Dougie would get the news fast. The Kingdom Halls across the country had grapevine gossipers that were lightning quick.

"Lorraine! Are you listening to me?" Deborah said again. "I want you to call Douglas as soon as we get to Nova Scotia and give him my new address, so he can write me."

"Okay," Lorraine replied sinking down into the seat of the car. She closed her eyes and let the rocking of the train calm her.

Deborah remained persistent. Her mild to moderate dementia didn't get in the way of her need to let Dougie know of her whereabouts. Just two nights into her new home, Deborah asked once again. After she retired to her bedroom, Patrick and Lorraine discussed the request and tried to think of someone who might know something about her lost brother.

"I've got it," Lorraine shouted. "We can call Marvin Frederick. I'm sure he'll be able to track the little bastard down."

Patrick laughed, "Shhh. Don't let your mother hear you talk like that. But that is a clever idea."

Lorraine dug through her personal directory. She hadn't memorized Marvin's telephone number, but she knew the one she had was current. Ever since the night of the Prom, they had kept in touch.

Lorraine placed the call to Marvin and asked him to be her detective. He promised to get back as soon as he could, and telephoned a week later. As soon as Marvin was on the line, Lorraine placed the phone on speaker, so Patrick could be part of the conversation. "He's still here in BC, somewhere in the lower Mainland. Don't know where exactly, but at least I have a number. Here you go."

Lorraine reached for a post-it-note.

"Rebecca left him, you know."

Lorraine glanced at Patrick quickly.

Wonder what caused that, she wondered. *Must have been something big. Witnesses divorcing is almost unheard of.*

She didn't interrupt Marvin for the gory details. *It's unlikely, he'd know anyway.*

"Apparently, she's remarried," Marvin continued, "and living in Saskatchewan I think. Rumours were she just couldn't stay. Too much sadness in that house."

After a couple of minutes and promises to keep in touch, Marvin said goodbye. When she hung up the phone, Lorraine stared at the numbers. The Devil's number. She knew she would never enter them in her personal directory.

"His number isn't fit for my address book," Lorraine whispered. Her body shuddered as her hand gripped the paper.

Patrick poured Lorraine a glass of wine. She took two big gulps and then sat in her favourite chair overlooking the harbour. "Patrick, I'm not sure I can do this. What if he answers?"

"I'll be right beside you. Just dial. Your mother's sleeping now, and we can fill her in tomorrow. It's best that we do this now."

Lorraine tapped the eleven digits into her cell phone, lifted it to her ear and listened for a ring tone. After three rings, a soft, sweet but barely audible female voice answered.

"Hello?"

Lorraine had her dialogue ready. She took a gulp of wine and a deep breath.

"Hi. This is Lorraine Armstrong. I am calling to speak to my brother, Douglas. His mother is now living with me and she wants him to have her new address."

Lorraine heard an audible gasp on the other end of the line. "Just a moment," the woman said. "I'll get him."

Another gulp of wine and Douglas was on the line. Before Lorraine could utter a word, his rage exploded over the line, ravaging her ear.

"Tell her I don't care where she lives! Tell her she is already dead. Tell her that she'll get a letter from me alright."

Then silence and the line went dead.

Patrick saw the look of utter shock on his wife's face. Then the tears started. He rushed to fill up the empty wine glass and sit with his beloved.

"I'm so sorry, Lorraine. I shouldn't have encouraged you to find him. Please don't let the nightmare start over. Tomorrow, we'll figure out what, if anything, to tell Deborah."

Deborah slept well and was happily enjoying her toast and coffee when Lorraine stepped into the kitchen.

"Good morning dear. What are we going to do today?" She didn't mention a word about Douglas. Not a word. Not that morning or any time later.

Dougie, however, kept his word.

The letter of Shunning arrived seven days after he promised he would write. Dougie only had the Ontario address, so the post office in Straffordville forwarded it.

Thank God I didn't tell him where I lived, Lorraine thought. *As long as I live, she will never read this letter. She will never know the vile hurt that her youngest son has flung at her. His own mother. God damn him.*

Lorraine kept the mail hidden until Patrick arrived home that evening. When Deborah went to her room, Patrick poured while Lorraine searched for the letter opener.

Side by side, his arms around his wife's shoulders, Lorraine opened the it. The penmanship was poor, but the message was clear. Lorraine's eyes fell upon the salutation.

"Dear Sister Deborah,"

"Patrick, he's calling her Sister! How can he do that?"

Lorraine's hands shook, her heart raced, and her mind raged, but she summoned the courage to continue reading.

I understand from the Brothers in Straffordville that you have decided to remain in the same household as an Apostate. As you know, such fraternizing is against the teachings of *The Watchtower* and our Governing Body. We have been instructed by the Circuit Servant who comes to our Hall that you must be formally shunned from us. You are no longer alive in the eyes of Jehovah, nor in ours. We will no longer pray for your safe keeping. Sister Deborah, you are dead to us.

Your Brother, in the Name of Jehovah,

Douglas

43

Demon Dougie

"Who made you in charge anyway?" Lorraine wailed at her younger brother. He might be an inch taller than her, but he was a year younger and didn't deserve to give orders. Dougie was the only Armstrong with dark hair, thick sinister black hair. In Lorraine's mind that meant he was surely the Devil.

"Mom did, and since Peter is working with Dad today, it's MY turn to clean the kitchen!" he yelled. "And you, you little bitch, it's YOUR turn to take the milk bottles to the cellar. So, do it!"

Lorraine wondered where 12-year-old Dougie, the perfect Jehovah's Witness, had heard the word let alone knew how to use it correctly. She was sure she was not a bitch. If anything, Dougie was a bad brother for saying such a word. Unless they were forced to, Peter and Lorraine rarely included him when they played together or sneaked off for ice cream, but they noticed the look in his eyes, pouting and glaring jealously at them as if scheming to find ways to make them suffer.

"Go on. Get going," he hissed authoritatively.

The Armstrongs were one of very few families who had a summer kitchen in the basement, but as nice and cool as it was in the scorching months of July and August, Lorraine had to go outside to reach the cellar where the returnable bottles were kept.

She hated the cellar. Everyone knew that, especially Dougie. From the outside landing she had to walk down four steps to the hatch door. Then she had to yank on the damn thing to open it. Finally, there were five crumbling steps into the cellar itself, the darkest and dampest place in the house: spider webs, skittering rodents, maybe even snakes. She panicked at the thought of having to go down there! Even in broad daylight it frightened her beyond belief!

Stubbornly, she gathered all four milk bottles in both arms. "I'm doing this in one trip," she whispered bravely. "One trip to the cellar for me is more than enough. I can do this."

For the moment, Dougie had won, but she was already scheming ways to get even.

She gathered the bottles and headed for the back door. As she walked past Dougie with her hands full of the precious returnable bottles, he flicked her with the wet dish towel. As soon as she felt the sting, Lorraine lost her footing and fell down the cement steps, glass breaking all around her.

Dougie laughed and laughed from the top step as she lay bleeding at the bottom.

"Ha! That'll teach ya. You little scare-di-cat!" Dougie waited for Lorraine to hurl a string of invectives his way, but there was no sound from the bottom of the stairs.

He stopped laughing when he realized Lorraine was not getting up; instead, a look of absolute horror passed over his face. He knew he had caused her to fall and he didn't know what to do.

Lorraine lay as still as rag doll, staring in shock at her limp arm. From her wrist to her shoulder she was covered in blood. So much blood.

James arrived home at the exact moment of her fall. Neither of his children was in the kitchen where he expected them to be. He quickly took in the situation when Dougie yelled from the back stoop.

"Come quick, dad. Lorraine fell," he lied. James ran across the kitchen and took the steps in one leap to attend to Lorraine.

"What happened sweetie?"

"Dougie pushed me down the stairs. I can't move my arm. I'm bleeding Dad. Help."

James glared at Dougie who stood like a statue on the landing.

"I didn't push her Dad. She fell. I told her not to try to carry all the milk bottles at once, but she wouldn't listen."

"I'll deal with you later, Douglas. I must get Lorraine to a doctor. Call your mother at once. She's cleaning the Hall with Sister Phyllis."

Lorraine's arm was indeed broken in several places and the glass bottles had left wounds deep into her skin right through the muscles. In total, she needed 23 stitches and wore a cast for six weeks.

In time, the cuts would heal, but Lorraine would consciously hide those ragged scars beneath long-sleeved jackets and three quarter-sleeved shirts. The scars which pierced her mind, however, would haunt her for the rest of her life.

44

Rabbit Stew

James selected two chickens from the Mennonite farm of Earl and Jude Walker like he did every Saturday. But this week, he was picking up another animal — a rabbit for Lorraine. The Walkers raised rabbits and James thought a bunny would be the perfect gift to help Lorraine heal from the wounds on her arm.

Proudly, James arrived home and presented the chickens to Deborah for the Sunday meal, and then he called Lorraine outside. "Check the back seat of the truck," he said, "there's a little something for you."

Lorraine reached in with her strong left arm and struggled with the cast on her right, but she immediately felt the small furry bunny and held it tight. Its little pink nose wriggled and snuggled against her body.

"Oh, Dad. She is just beautiful. I'm calling her Millie," she squeaked with excitement.

Dougie watched from the upstairs window. He was still being punished for causing Lorraine to fall. James and Deborah agreed that their youngest son should spend three hours a day reading *The Watchtower* and *Awake* until he could answer all the quiz questions correctly.

Dougie read them with ease and memorized the answers. He knew his parents would be pleased and would forgive him for what he still called the accident. In the dark caverns of his heart, though, he knew as soon as his punishment was served, he would get her back.

Every afternoon in his bedroom prison, he concocted new ways to punish her. His skin crawled every time she brought Millie's pink nose close to hers and crooned lovingly at the wriggling beast. He hated Lorraine, but he hated Millie even more. By the second week of house arrest, he had devised a foolproof plan to murder Millie.

A month later, when Peter and Lorraine had finished the laundry and hung the work clothes on the line outside and the finer linens inside, they wiped the wringer washing machine clean and rolled it back in the corner.

James, Deborah and Dougie had been doing "back call" — witnessing work — and arrived home to see the laundry hanging from the line.

"Thanks kids. You did an excellent job," James said. "So perfectly hung on the line and everything cleaned up."

Dougie's skin flamed with indignation. He was incensed. He had spent the entire morning trudging from door to door, pleasing Jehovah. *Where's my reward? No one shouted, "excellent job" to me.* Douglas stamped to his room to change out of Peter's hand-me-down suit. *I'm just about done with Peter's old clothes and Lorraine's goody-two-shoes attitude. Mom doesn't recognize my hard work,* he cursed under his breath.

From the step at the end of the porch, Lorraine and Peter checked the clothes on the line.

"They will be dry soon, Mom," Peter said.

"When they're folded can we go play with Millie outside on the grass?" Lorraine said, bubbling.

"Sure. Sounds like fun, but first let's get our treats." Peter led his sister back into the house. They tiptoed past Dougie's closed door on the way to the kitchen to get a fresh-baked cookie.

"Guess he's still busy reading. Do you think Jehovah will have any luck with him?" Lorraine asked.

"Well if you think leopards can change their spots, then maybe," Peter replied.

"I wouldn't bet on it," Lorraine laughed.

*

Dougie saw his chance.

He sneaked out of his room and went to the laundry room where Millie's cage was kept. First, he grabbed Millie and then pulled the retractable cord out from the side of the wringer washing machine. He tied the cord around the rabbit's neck as it squirmed and struggled to run away.

"This is hilarious." Dougie couldn't stop laughing as he watched the rabbit squirm to free himself.

The more the rabbit pulled, the harder the cord retracted. Dougie laughed and laughed. Millie gave one last attempt to escape, but the cord won. The wee rabbit smashed up against the machine with a tremendous force.

A quick and bloody death.

Dougie raced from the basement back to his room, grabbed a *Watchtower* and waited.

45

All Praise to Jehovah

His violent behaviour brought reproach from James and disappointment from Deborah. James admonished his youngest by saying that killing Millie was an act spurred by Satan. He would have to be punished. James had kept track of the increasing number of ungodly behaviours he noticed in his son. The older and taller he became, the more difficult he was to handle. And when it caused injury to the other children, the situation called for drastic measures. James asked for support from the Elders who in turn offered prayers to Jehovah asking for direction. It came.

"I am sure you are fully aware, James, that Circuit Servant Brother Clifford will be making his bi-annual visit to the Straffordville and Aylmer Congregations at the beginning of June," said Brother Richard.

"Yes, of course," James said. "It's another opportunity to report on converts, missionary school and all other aspects of the growth of the communities. We have been particularly blessed in that aspect over this six-month period."

"But with respect to your prayers, we think we may have a solution."

James turned to face the other Elders and Brother Richard spoke first.

"For the past several months, we have seen constant proof of Douglas' devotion to Jehovah and his unswerving work at the Ministry School."

"We believe we should consider offering Douglas to the Faithful and Discreet Slave Service at Bethel," Daniel continued.

James couldn't find the words. He was conflicted between extreme pride and extreme dread, but he fashioned his words carefully.

"He will still be 12 when Brother Clifford gets here. Fourteen is the usual age that most Slaves are chosen," James countered.

"But he's a big boy for his age, and so impressive in his Bible Studies," Richard argued.

James mind flashed back to his daughter lying in a pool of blood at the bottom of the cement steps just a few weeks before. Douglas had wilfully and vindictively caused her to fall. *He might have killed her,* James thought bitterly.

"We don't have to decide right this moment," Daniel interrupted. "Let's take this up again in prayer and then see what Brother Clifford thinks when he arrives. Lorraine can be baptised at the same time, so you will have two children to dedicate to Jehovah."

James left the Kingdom Hall meeting and rehearsed in his mind how he would tell Deborah the result of their prayers. James knew that Dougie was useless at the shop work. Clumsy. Even though he was much bigger than Peter, Dougie had not shown interest in the business and was more inclined to read *The Watchtower* than help with the job of preparing metal work for tobacco kilns.

But James was also very cautious. It was not that he doubted Douglas' hard work, he questioned his sincerity. Often, James had caught his son displaying traits hardly becoming of a Discreet Slave. Still, being chosen would be a great honour for the family.

In hushed tones, James and Deborah met downstairs in the summer kitchen, far away from the children. Deborah remained silent as James told her of the proposal put forward by the Elders.

"If Jehovah God chooses Douglas for Bethel, we will have to arrange his baptism immediately," she whispered. "And what about Lorraine's baptism which was delayed due to the accident?"

"Already arranged," James replied. "They can be baptised together."

Deborah listened intently.

"The Elders also said that the Aylmer congregation have offered a candidate, the young Bodemer boy. He may be new to Jehovah, but apparently he's very devout. Shy and retiring, but hard working. Brother Albert from

Aylmer thinks it would be good for the boy. He's 16 already, but anxious to do anything to please Jehovah. Maybe the Bodemer boy would look out for Dougie, coming from the same area and all. Of course, all of this is speculation dependent upon Brother Clifford's decision."

Deborah had mixed feelings. Being offered as a Discreet Slave would mean giving up her youngest and most faithful child to serve in Bethel until the age of 18. He would spend four years in New York and then likely two or three more interning in missions in underdeveloped nations. Of course, he would be honoured to prepare food and clean for the Bethelites and do whatever household chores they expected of him, but Deborah also knew that her Douglas looked at duty through a very narrow and dogmatic lens.

On a more pleasant note, Deborah realized he would have a chance to visit the Watchtower Publishing Company and witness the production of Jehovah's words, or attend a youth assembly in New York.

I am sure he didn't really mean to kill Millie. He was just teasing like he always does. Everyone in the congregation would celebrate. Bethel will transform our son.

"Yes," she said to James, "I agree."

But as she spoke, the white enamel of the wringer washer glared back at her accusingly. The sharpness of Dougie's actions still stung.

46

Bethel Bound

Lorraine was excited when her mother announced that the Sears Catalogue was ready to be picked up at the Post Office. Monthly shopping from the catalogue was one of those rare events that Lorraine shared with her mother. A real occasion.

Each week, they picked out household items and clothing using the budget from the family allowance cheque. Deborah was very good at stretching those dollars. But this month was different. Lorraine didn't have a chance to pick out anything new; instead, Deborah was dog-earring the pages of young men's clothing and travel items.

"Did you find something for me?" Lorraine asked.

"Not this month, dear. We need to concentrate on buying everything little Dougie will need for Bethel. Rather than send him to the Service with hand-me-downs from Peter, I want to make sure he has a fresh new wardrobe and toiletries."

Lorraine went to her room with tears burning down her cheeks. She tried to look at the positive side. He leaves with a fresh new wardrobe... but he LEAVES! That thought got her through the day. She went back to the kitchen and helped her mother choose the "going-away outfits" for Demon Dougie.

The previous week following the Sunday Talk, Brother Clifford made the announcement to the small congregation.

"Jehovah God has guided me," he began. "Together we have chosen a Brother from among you to join the Faithful and Discreet Slave Service for our Governing Body. This young Brother has shown his dedication to our Saviour Christ Jesus, Jehovah God and His Ministry. He has met his quota for hours in the Kingdom Ministry and has set an example for other young Brothers and Sisters. Even in his youth, this Brother made an impression on Jehovah God. I announce the selection of Douglas Armstrong to join the Brothers at Bethel and continue to serve Jehovah working with our Governing Body."

Upon hearing the selection, the congregation stood and applauded and then Brother Clifford led everyone in prayer.

The celebration meant that the Hall had been scrubbed and the floors washed. The only window in the place was cleaned. The Sisters divided up the chores, and the Brothers stacked chairs and placed the fold-away tables around the room. A pot-luck and songs to Jehovah were on the itinerary.

Brother Clifford commenced the prayers and invited the Brothers and Sisters to the meal. When dinner was over, he would personally deliver little Douglas Armstrong to the great city of Manhattan, New York, where he would start his Slave Service at Bethel.

Three weeks after the celebration, the Armstrong Family brought 12-year-old Dougie to the Kingdom Hall. He was nervous. He kept pushing his raven black hair out of his eyes and looking to his parents for guidance. But he was on his own now. Lorraine thought he looked like Daniel about to enter the lion's den. She couldn't help smiling about that.

Dougie stood, trancelike, beside his suitcases. They were heavy. One was laden with suits, ties, crisp white shirts and dress shoes. The other contained his work pants and flannel shirts, t-shirts, socks and underwear. All brand new for work.

The entire congregation joined the Armstrongs in the parking lot. Brother Clifford said a final prayer and then motioned to his driver to open the trunk.

"Dougie's first job," Brother Clifford joked, "is to load his belongings into the trunk." Somewhat surprised that he was expected to lift the heavy cases into the trunk himself, he looked around quizzically and then grasped the biggest one with two hands. It was the first of many orders he would obey over the next few years.

Deborah hugged her son, somewhat longer and harder than normal. James shook Dougie's hand. "Good work son. We're very proud of you," he said.

Lorraine almost wet herself with glee. She hadn't participated in hugs or handshakes but stood back with the rest of the congregation watching her enemy load his suitcases in the long black limo.

Peter was polite. He stepped forward and, following his father's lead, shook Dougie's hand. At three o'clock that afternoon the long black car slowly backed down the driveway of the Kingdom Hall. They watched until it was a speck on the horizon heading north on the Number 19.

It was the last time Peter and Lorraine would see their young brother.

47

Tobacco Heat

Lorraine's world changed when Dougie left for Bethel. Peace and harmony filled the house. Peter went to work each day with James, and in the summer of '65, Lorraine got her first real job working in tobacco alongside Deborah. It was just the two of them with no Dougie anywhere to be seen.

The daily ritual for mother and daughter started at precisely 6:15 a.m. when Daniel Evans' Ford pick-up roared up the Armstrong driveway. Daniel was the lead hand at the Verdun farm and his job was to get the workers delivered on time. Lorraine didn't mind getting up early, and if the weather cooperated, Daniel let her ride in the box.

With fresh pepper sandwiches and a Joe Louis packed in her paper bag, she skipped out the door behind her mother.

"Morning you two," the driver said. "Looks like we'll have a sunny day." With that cue, Lorraine hopped into the back of the vehicle.

When they arrived at the farm, Mrs. Verdun took their lunches and packed them in a cooler on the back porch.

Some workers headed to the field, others to the kiln, and Lorraine and her mother took their stations at the long harvest table next to the saw horses.

Beneath the wooden horses lay bundles of tobacco slats, rough and bare, begging to be dressed in rich green leaves.

The "primers" were already in the field. They came from far way places like Jamaica and Montreal. Locals didn't prime in the tobacco fields. The Verduns and other farmers had to recruit migrant workers, enticing them with the "big bucks" for the back-breaking work. Since primers had the hardest job, they were paid the most. That fact was never disputed among the rest of the workers.

With backs bent and bended knees they plodded forward, reaching with one arm and then the other, plucking the "sand leaves" from the hearty green stalks. When their arms were full, they would carefully lay their bounty in a long wooden boat, loyally pulled by Joe, the Verdun's Clydesdale.

Even though they spoke little or no English, each primer quickly learned the word "hike" to command Joe to stop so they could empty their arms and start picking again. The primers started first and finished first, jabbering away all day in the scorching heat, hand-picking the ripest of the golden leaves.

Lorraine was not allowed to even look at the primers. "Not from around here, Lorraine. Can't be trusted," her mother warned.

Old Joe pulled the boats right up to the table, nudging the next workers in the cue. They were called the boat unloaders. Next to priming, that was the hardest job and unloading from the top was the easiest. They would stack the leaves on the table in precisely the right position for the leaf handlers to pick and hand over to the tier. But when the top layers gave way to the lower half, the boat unloader would bend forward and seemingly grow longer arms to reach the remaining leaves at the very bottom.

Lorraine would steal glances across the harvest table to catch a glimpse of the poor guy's arse as he leaned over, defying any laws of normal kinesiology.

Lorraine and her mother were one of two teams of leaf handers. They stood facing each other with the harvest table on Lorraine's left and Deborah's right. Grabbing exactly three woody stalks at a time, ends even, they passed one hand then the other over to the tier, then started again. They quickly became a synchronized team. The tier snatched the long leaves from the women, knotting each bundle to the slat with baker's string.

When each side of the slat was full, Deborah and Lorraine took turns lifting it from the horse and placing it on the conveyer belt where it rode gently up the steel belt to the waiting hands of the kiln hanger. The muscled worker, balanced on scaffolding, stood at the peak of the trusses in the scorching kiln, and hung the laden slats overhead to dry. His day was complete when the kiln was full.

Lorraine looked forward to the cow bell ringing at noon to announce lunch. Usually the tobacco leaves were dry by then, so she could shed her long black rubber apron and ugly black boots. "They are man clothes, Mom. I hate them," she complained. But Deborah reminded her to be thankful that the Verduns offered the workers protection from the wet dewy morning haul.

Lorraine joined the other workers in the wash-up line. She rolled the hot sticky tobacco gum from her fingers and palms before dipping them in the communal basin. Even though her lunch menu was somewhat repetitive, Lorraine was anxious to open her cooled sweet yellow pepper sandwich. The soft white Wonder Bread hugged the crunchy sliced peppers all morning and the marriage was delightful.

Deborah and Lorraine sat with the other workers and traded stories of finding tobacco worms, green and slimy beasts, camouflaged within the leaves. The crop duster plane droned overhead, ready to spray the field.

"Get that dog in the house," Mrs. Verdun yelled. "You know that chemical is deadly." Daniel stood up and looked for the Border Collie to take him to safety, but the remaining workers didn't move. They were used to breathing in the thick smoke and rancid fumes coming from the plane above. Anything to keep the crops flourishing.

For two months each summer, Lorraine worked alongside Deborah. Her hands bled for the first few weeks, but then they calloused up. Handing leaves over and over, Lorraine was determined to make enough money to buy her school books in September. If she wanted an education, she knew she had to pay her own way.

The bounty of the Golden Leaves kept James in business building tobacco kiln pipes. And tobacco kept the field hands coming back to rural southern Ontario, earning more money than they dreamed possible. The industry attracted "all walks of life" as Deborah said.

Years later, Lorraine remembered those sultry summer days in the tobacco fields. And she never failed to laugh with her own daughter when someone different or unusual walked by. WOLA, they cried in unison breaking out in wild laughter.

Walk of Life Alert.

48

The Grudge

Lorraine already knew that Brother Clifford was a bigot and an asshole. But when he chose Dougie to join Bethel, she happily foisted another adjective on to the growing list of invectives she used to describe him. The words rolled off her tongue with acid precision. From that moment, she also regarded him as Clever Clifford.

Clever, because he knew that little Dougie would be a naïve and unquestioning servant at Bethel. He would follow rules to the letter. *Scary,* Lorraine thought. She, however, knew rules were made to be broken, or at least bent.

The rumours suggested that the Bethel boys were slaves in the real sense of the word. Not just the "Faithful and Discreet Slaves" that were recruited by Bethel to work with the Anointed and Governing Body, but actual hard-working slaves destined to wait on every need of the members living in the House of Jehovah.

These rumours trickled down to Lorraine through Marvin Frederick, a young Brother in the congregation who had also chosen by Clever Clifford. Marvin lasted a year before he bolted. He came back to Straffordville, packed up his belongings one Sunday afternoon and headed west. Before his departure, he visited with Lorraine.

"It was horrible," he reported over a cup of java at the Woolworth's. "They made us get up at 5:00 a.m. every single day. We scrubbed the halls of the

Bethel home and prepared breakfast while the Governing Body Brothers slept. When that was done," Marvin continued rolling his eyes for effect, "we had to help the Governing Brothers prepare for the day. And I mean 'prepare' in every sense of the word."

Some Brothers were feeble and required assistance to get out of bed and to the toilet. Three Brothers were assigned to each slave. The slaves attended to the most needy first.

One of Marvin's charges was an older man named Brother Francis. He was just past 90 which meant he needed a lot of care, but he was also an Anointed One. One of the 144,000. His care was tedious. He required assistance getting from his bed to his walker and then to the toilet. Every day, Marvin changed the fecal-filled diaper and washed the unmentionable parts of older Brother Francis.

"Disgusting," he told Lorraine. "I wiped crap that had hardened during the night, stuck to his legs, bum and balls even."

"Now that you've left Bethel, maybe Dougie will be assigned your dirty old man, Brother Francis. It would serve him right," she howled. "Pardon the pun, but it works for me."

Lorraine really liked Marvin and his rough and rebel attitude. She was glad he came to his senses and decided to run away. Even the night of her Prom that wasn't, Marvin had shown that same strength. Lorraine admired that gutsy side of him.

"Keep in touch," Lorraine said as she watched him head for the car. James offered him a ride into Tillsonburg and from there he hitchhiked to British Columbia.

49

Missionary Douglas

The graduation ceremony was a small, intimate affair. The twelve Bethel Brothers sat around the grand dining table with Douglas seated at one end. Everyone was dressed formally. Dark suits, white shirts, starched and ironed, adorned by long, thin ties.

The high-pitched ring of the hand bell alerted the Slaves in the massive kitchen to bring the food to the table. The Bethel Brothers who had been mentored by Douglas entered the large dining room. They were humble servants and devoted to their earthly Fathers. One by one, they marched into the grand hall, each carrying a dish for the great feast.

They bowed as they passed the abundant platters of food to the celebrants. Douglas knew from experience that the Slaves would eat last, and eat from those same plates, grateful for anything left by their earthly Fathers.

As a side bonus, the young Bethel Boys developed excellent culinary skills. They learned to cook and bake to perfection. They were trained to keep an immaculate kitchen to be worthy of praise by Jehovah God and the Governing Body.

Following graduation, Douglas Armstrong left his Bethel home to begin a two- or three-year internship as a missionary in a Third World nation. The Bethel fathers had chosen Haiti for his first year of mentorship. The following two years he spent in Mexico. Douglas had no input into their decision.

When he turned 19, the Bethel Brothers brought Douglas back to receive his permanent appointment. The President stood to read the proclamation.

"Douglas Armstrong, you have been a devoted Slave and a faithful missionary serving the Governing Body, your earthly Fathers and your heavenly Father, Jehovah. You will now devote your full-time Christian Service work in a small Kingdom Hall in Northern British Columbia. With a congregation of only 30 members, they need help growing their numbers."

Arrangements have been made to have you travel with the District Servant, Brother Walters, to British Columbia. We have set up housing for you and you will share a car with the Congregation Servant, Brother Strickland. Initially, you are expected to do a minimum 100 hours of service per month while working to the goal of 200 hours within three months. Your housing, food and medical needs will be paid for by the congregation. We will reimburse them all costs. Please keep copies of your receipts for all expenses." The President's strong voice carried the command across the room. "Let us pray."

*

The same suitcases that Douglas had packed many years earlier were filled again and destined for his final home on the other side of the continent. Driven in a luxury car by one of the young Bethel Brothers, Douglas and Walters began the long trek. The threesome stopped at Kingdom Halls from New York State to British Columbia. They took turns delivering the Sunday Talks. The Witnesses they met along the journey opened their homes to them.

Douglas was beyond excited to start a new life in the remote, beautiful wilderness. A small town was an ideal setting.

"Maybe it will be like Straffordville or Aylmer. No, probably not," he countered. "Not likely any rapists or murderers among the population. Hunters more likely. And best of all," he sneered, "no more Dougie." He boldly printed DOUGLAS in capital letters on his luggage tag.

*

Douglas was pleased with his new home. It was a tiny grey clapboard bungalow with attached one-car garage and paved driveway nestled on a quiet road not far from pristine forests and walking trails. A large bay window overlooked the front street and a small garden hugged the side wall. And it was just a short walk to the Kingdom Hall.

Although it was older, the little house was welcoming. The members of the congregation had the house freshly painted both inside and out, and had donated all the furniture. Inside the tiny kitchen Douglas found a small round table with two chairs. A green pull-out couch and pine coffee table filled the small living room. A double bed with pine dresser and night table greeted him in the bedroom. The smell of Javex bleach permeated the bathroom. A new shower curtain swung in the breeze coming in from the tiny window.

The Brothers left him to settle in.

Douglas knew he would be expected to lead the congregation in prayer and take part in the Kingdom Ministry School that very evening. He knelt beside the bed in his new home and thanked Jehovah God and his Son, Jesus for the gift of a home and the blessing of the congregation. He asked for guidance in choosing a topic for the evening's Ministry.

They answered.

Douglas chose the topic "Why Has Jehovah Waited So Long to Solve Mankind's Problems?" He selected 2 Peter, Chapter 3:8 to justify his response.

The congregation sat quietly awaiting their new Brother. They watched expectantly as Douglas walked to the stage. He stood to face his little flock and asked the same question he had written in his notebook two hours earlier. And then he began.

"The Creation took just one week in Jehovah's timing, but with each day that passes, we are closer to the vindication that He will choose. However, let this one fact not escape YOUR notice, beloved ones, that one day is with Jehovah as a thousand years and a thousand years as one day. Amen."

He bowed his head, inviting his congregation to do the same.

The prayer ended, Douglas raised his head and his eyes met those of Rebecca King, who was sitting at the back of the Hall beside her parents. He had been introduced to her just before the meeting. They shook hands and she welcomed him to British Columbia. She had heard about his studies at Bethel and then in Haiti. Her parents spoke very highly of the tall, handsome, dark-haired man from the East.

The meeting ended, but the congregation mingled in the hall. Douglas saw the opportunity to chat with Rebecca, as he was instantly enamoured with her deep ebony curls and soft white skin. Small, dainty hands and feet matched her stature. *Likely no more than five feet tall,* he thought. *Short and petite, just like Mom.*

Sister Julia and Brother Harold King invited Douglas for supper the next day. Rebecca could hardly contain her pleasure. She was thrilled that the new Brother was coming to her house.

Just three months later, Douglas approached Brother and Sister King to ask for their daughter's hand in marriage. He was confident she could only say yes as Douglas had already asked Jehovah and He had given His blessing.

Douglas and Sister Rebecca were married in the small Kingdom Hall. That same day Rebecca lost her virginity and her childlike nature. In full obedience to her husband, she did not use any contraceptive. She was pregnant immediately.

To prepare for the new family, Douglas took a part-time job at the lumber mill to help make ends meet. It would be crowded in the small bungalow, but they knew not to complain, for the generosity of Jehovah and the kindness of the congregation had given them a home.

Exactly nine months later, Rebecca and Douglas welcomed their baby daughter, Elizabeth, into the world. They promised each other to raise her as an obedient servant to Jehovah God.

50

The Apple of His Eye

Young Elizabeth Armstrong thrived. She was adored by her mother, but she was the apple of her father's eyes.

Douglas would often bite down on a McIntosh and say, "Elizabeth, you are the apple of my eye. Your mom and I love you with all our hearts." And then he would take extra big bites and munch and munch until little Elizabeth would giggle rapturously.

The small Kingdom Hall provided the young Armstrong family all they needed to grow within the Kingdom Ministry. Douglas maintained his quota of 200 hours of service work per month, and Rebecca cleaned the Hall and baked for the fragile and older Witnesses. Their lives were full.

Eight years later, when Douglas and Rebecca had given up on having any more children, Jehovah blessed them with a beautiful baby boy. They named him Edward.

Edward changed the family dynamics. Until his arrival, Elizabeth slept in a little cot in an area off her parent's room. Although only a thick velvet curtain separated her from her parents, Elizabeth had made the little alcove into a castle. She had a pink bedspread covered with stars and delightful flowers. She had a little bookshelf filled with her stories of Jehovah. Her favourites were dog-eared and soft from use. She was the princess of her own Court.

Elizabeth made friends at the Hall. Two other families had young girls and the three of them became fast friends. Elizabeth, Anne and Sharon did everything together. They sat together and studied together. Occasionally, the Congregation Servant would assign them roles as Householder and Caller for the Kingdom Ministry School.

The years passed like they do for all parents, in a flurry. From diapers to long pants, and walking to running, Elizabeth filled her parents' lives. Edward grew and flourished. They thanked Jehovah daily for the trust He had placed in them to raise the children.

And Elizabeth was a beauty. When she entered school, her long raven hair curled half way down her back. The dark chocolate tresses were a striking contrast to her pale complexion. No one could miss the Elder's well behaved, hard-working little girl.

But whenever Douglas held his son and tousled the blond curls which fell around his ears, or laughed at the freckles that popped out all over his face each spring, he couldn't help but see Peter. Peter's happy smile. Peter's kind and gracious demeanour. Peter's dimples that made everyone laugh. When those feelings found their way into his heart, no matter how hard Douglas begged Jehovah to remove them, the barbs of hatred festered.

Often at the Hall, friends remarked about Edward's blond hair. Where, they wondered, did that come from? Everyone else in the family had such striking black hair. "Must be my Swedish ancestors," he lied. "My dear son has their genes." He laughed, but all Douglas could think about was his blond-haired Apostate siblings.

Why would that upset him so much? Rebecca wondered.

As Edward grew up, he realized very quickly that he was never able to please his father when it came to Jehovah's rules. He always did something wrong. Edward thought they were just trivial things, but his father took great offense: lifting his fork before the yearbook was finished, running in the house and upsetting Sunday afternoon prayers, or playing in the sandbox ten minutes after he had been called to Wednesday night Bible study.

For the first few years, young Edward learned how to obey without question, but as he grew older the tension smoldered between father and son. His

Lizzie was always able to smooth over the bumps in the road between them and offer an escape hatch for her little brother's feelings.

Little Edward watched his older sister when she spoke at Ministry school. He could hardly wait for his turn to come so he could show everyone how smart he was and make his father proud of him. Despite their 8 year age gap, the two of them were devoted to each other. Wherever Elizabeth went, Edward was not far behind.

But all was not perfect in Camelot. When Edward was about three, Rebecca decided it was time for him to leave the bassinette in which he had slept since birth. He was growing so tall, she remarked, that he needed a bigger bed. Of course, the only available bed in the little bungalow was the cot in Elizabeth's castle.

"I know how disappointed you are sweetie," Rebecca crooned, "but it won't be forever. You'll only have to sleep on the couch for a little while until we can afford to rent a bigger house. Then you and Edward can each have your own rooms."

Reluctantly, Elizabeth removed all her pink and purple flowers, clouds and stars, and helped Edward decorate his little cot with brown and green blankets covered with tractors and ducks. Somehow the castle looked sad and dreary.

*

The congregation was proud of Elizabeth and her devotion to Jehovah God. She and her two friends rarely missed meetings and always came on Sunday morning to the door-to-door work. One evening Elizabeth's mother announced that she would soon be old enough to do service work on her own.

Douglas smiled. "You are right Rebecca. The little apple of my eye is almost 12. Her baptism is just two months away. After that, she will be ready."

Elizabeth could hardly wait! Sharon and Anne were older and had already been submerged and they had knocked on doors solo. They told Elizabeth it was not frightening at all. Most people were nice and always bought *The Watchtower* and *Awake* from them. They reached their monthly quotas regularly.

Finally, on a warm Sunday in August, Elizabeth was baptized. Rebecca chose a brown dress with beige lace at the neckline and hem. She tied her daughter's hair in a ponytail to keep it out of her eyes.

"Just pinch your nose dear. It will only take seconds. And, when you rise, you will belong to Jehovah God. Your life will be dedicated to Him."

Elizabeth rose from the water as Brother Ken and Brother Adam lifted her from the pond.

"Congratulations Elizabeth, you are blessed in the name of Jehovah and Christ Jesus," they said in unison.

The small congregation bowed their heads in prayer led by Brother Douglas and then sang a song to their Creator.

Edward toddled across the lawn to his sister. "You looked so bootiful, Lizzie. I can't wait until I go under the lilies."

"Oh, Eddie, you are so cute. I love you to bits, but you're still too young. A few more years. Listen hard and learn your scriptures and you will make Jehovah proud. And me too," she added, as she pinched his rosy cheeks and roughed up his hair.

*

The next Sunday, the three young girls attended the Kingdom Hall and were paired off to go door-to-door. Sharon and Elizabeth went first and then Anne took a turn. Elizabeth was a pro. She took part in the conversation with the householders and proudly quoted scriptures from the New World Translation of her Bible. The Bible, a gift from her parents following her baptism, was still shiny and new.

"Soon it will be worn out just like mine," Sharon said, smiling. As well as Sunday door-to-door, Sharon knew that Douglas would insist that Elizabeth join him each time he went out to preach the "good news of the Kingdom." That Bible of hers would be tattered around the edges in no time.

On Tuesday evening right after the Bible study, Rebecca and Douglas surprised Elizabeth with a wonderful present.

"You have done so very well since your baptism that we want to give you something that we think you will like." It was a present that would alter her young life. "Come to the garage Elizabeth."

She could not imagine what they had planned. Money was tight, and they lived a very frugal life in the small bungalow. Edward traipsed behind his sister, anxious to see the surprise.

Maybe we are moving? Elizabeth guessed. *Maybe I will get my own room and not have to sleep on the couch anymore.* Her mind raced as she followed her parents outside. Her father opened the heavy door and there in the middle of the garage leaning on its kickstand was a bicycle.

It was not new, but that did not matter. Sharon and Anne both had bicycles and Elizabeth could not wait to go riding with her young Christian Sisters.

"I love it" she squealed. "Thank you so much, Mom and Dad. I already know how to ride because Sharon and Anne taught me."

"That is wonderful my little Apple," Douglas said, smiling. "Do well at the Kingdom Hall this coming Thursday night for Ministry School, and we will let you go riding on Friday."

Elizabeth rushed home after school every day that week and studied for the Kingdom Ministry. She memorized her assigned scripture and then worked to explain it.

It was a difficult assignment: Isiah 52:2. "Shake yourself free from the dust, rise up and take a seat Oh Jerusalem. Loosen yourself from the bands of your neck, Oh captive daughter of Zion."

Elizabeth struggled with the verse. For some reason and only really since her baptism, she didn't feel new and fresh. She felt old and tired. Tired of doing Ministry work. Tired of sleeping on the couch. And tired of not having any fun. She felt like all she did was Ministry work. Lately she had been feeling more like the Captive Daughter of Douglas than of Zion. She trudged on though, because if she did well, she would be allowed to go bike riding.

A lot had changed since her baptism. The blood event started a month after her immersion. Elizabeth had accepted the changes in her body when she got her first period. Her mother helped her to understand and how to take care of herself, but she couldn't control her feelings. She felt confused about her life and often cried for no reason.

When Edward cuddled up beside her on the couch, she brushed him away. She saw the hurt in his eyes and before he ran away crying, she pulled him back against her.

"Don't think anything of that my Eddie. You are the best brother I could ever have."

"And you are the bestest sister in the world. Lizzie, now that I can read, you just wait. I'll be up there on the stage with you before you can count ten partridges!" He laughed and snuggled his face into her body.

"You have the absolute best curls. Wish I had some blond," she said, sighing.

"Well, you know, they're Swedish curls. That's what Dad says, so I must be very, very special."

"You are indeed. Thanks for cheering me up. I really needed it."

With that, Elizabeth shooed her brother away and got back to work, but it was hard. Her emotions seemed to be jumping around wildly inside her and she couldn't catch them or control them. Sometimes, she just wanted to run into the forest and hide by the river. Get away from everything. *What's wrong with me?* she wondered.

Brett, a young boy at school, had suddenly taken notice of her. He was tall and played basketball. "You should hang out after school someday, Liz. It's fun to go to the gym and watch the teams play."

Elizabeth had never been allowed to attend any school activities. She had to rush home every day and prepare for her Kingdom Ministry studies. Her reply was the same, "I need to help my mom with supper. Maybe another day."

Thursday night Ministry school went extremely well. With Sharon as her Householder, Elizabeth used the verse from Isaiah to teach the instructions of Jehovah to go from door-to-door and free the non-believers who were held captive by their false faiths.

She did well at Ministry School role play and Douglas kept his promise to the young apple of his eye.

51

Spare the Rod, Spoil the Child

"Enjoy your ride with Sharon and Anne for the afternoon, but make sure you are home for supper!" Douglas smiled as his daughter lifted her leg over the cross bar. "Brother and Sister Cannon are joining us. They are new to our congregation and we want to make them welcome."

"No worries, Dad. We're going to see Sharon's Aunt Carol who lives about five miles down the valley. We'll have cookies and tea, and then head back home."

"Sharon, are you sure it will only take two hours?" Elizabeth asked.

"Yes, I'm sure, Liz. I've done it before. An hour there and an hour back."

When they arrived at a fork, Sharon tried to remember which one to take. "I think we go left," Sharon said cautiously.

"Hope so," Elizabeth replied. She was already feeling a bit nervous about the time, and an hour later, the three girls were not only lost, but time was running out.

"Guess it was the wrong turn," Sharon said. "We have to go back." In the meantime, Douglas and Rebecca were pacing. Edward was lying on his cot. He sensed his parents' growing anger.

"She's only 20 minutes late, Douglas. Don't worry. She'll be home any minute," Rebecca said.

At dusk they still hadn't shown up.

Douglas called Sharon's parents and they too were worried. The girls were not at Anne's house, nor did they arrive at Auntie Carol's house.

"That's it," Douglas announced. "I'm calling the RCMP." Douglas and Rebecca returned home in time to greet the Cannon's for the evening meal.

"The RCMP have the girls' descriptions and they will find them, I am sure," Brother Cannon said. "Let us bow our heads in prayer and enjoy our dinner." Douglas had asked Jehovah to guide his daughter home safely, but Rebecca thought other feelings were bubbling below the surface. Edward was so upset he could hardly eat.

The three young girls had returned to the fork when the blare of the RCMP siren shrieked behind them.

"Elizabeth, Anne and Sharon?" the constable inquired.

"Yes, that's us," they replied.

"Your parents are very worried. I'll radio a dispatch to let them know you're safe. Let's get your bikes in the back and get you home."

"I'll see you tomorrow at the Hall, Liz," Sharon and Anne shouted as they parted ways in front of Elizabeth's home. "Sorry about the wrong turn."

Elizabeth parked her bicycle in the driveway and entered the tiny home as quietly as possible. Dinner was finished and the table cleared.

From the look on Brother Douglas's face when his daughter closed the door behind them, the Cannon's knew it was time to leave. They made a hasty exit saying they were glad the girls were found.

Elizabeth stood like a criminal before her parents. The anger in her father's eyes made her shiver. Douglas turned to his young daughter.

"Go to the bathroom and wash your hands," he said. "When you are finished, report to me in the bedroom."

The Cannons pretended they had not heard the angry voice from inside the bungalow as they hurried along the sidewalk.

Elizabeth was more terrified when she heard her mother begging, "Douglas, please don't do this. We can scold her in other ways, please!"

Douglas brushed his wife aside and pointed Edward in the direction of his bed. The youngster was quick to obey, but he was scared for Elizabeth. Douglas dismissed him and turned to face his wife.

"You are to obey Jehovah God and Christ Jesus and then your husband. In that order!"

Elizabeth knew something was very wrong. Her parents never raised their voices to each other. Their home was always a place of peace and prayer.

Elizabeth went to the bedroom as ordered. Douglas left the door ajar, so Rebecca could be a witness to his discipline. Little Edward huddled under his cot, terrified.

"Are you aware of the scripture, Proverbs 13:24," he growled. "In case you have forgotten, it says: spare the rod and spoil the child."

"Elizabeth, you have a choice. You may receive the lashing on your hands or on your backside. Choose." Her father removed his leather belt, anger and rage spilling from his eyes.

Edward covered his ears and tried not to listen to the voice of the man who didn't sound like his father anymore. Elizabeth chose her backside. She did not want anyone to see the welts. Not Sharon, not Anne and certainly not her teachers.

Douglas raised the belt. A dozen lashes. More. The whipping continued until Elizabeth fell to the floor, unconscious. Rebecca remained motionless on the green couch, her Bible open to Proverbs 13. With the beating, the lives of the young family changed forever.

Outwardly, Elizabeth remained dutiful and quiet. She never laughed in the house. Douglas never called her "the apple of his eye" again. She had disobeyed him and caused embarrassment for him. Unforgiveable.

Elizabeth continued with her Kingdom Studies as she was directed. When her brother wanted a snuggle, she hugged him with a fierceness he had never experienced before. It was like she was holding on to him for dear life. Draining him.

Rebecca walked on tenterhooks, fearful that her husband would hurt her son if he didn't behave just right. On occasion she noticed her son's shoulders slope and quiver when Douglas instructed him. She sensed the restrained anger simmering below the boy's normally calm nature.

As the months passed, Elizabeth began to daydream about freedom. She started to think about what it would be like to stay after school and watch the basketball team. She wondered what it would be like to have friends other than Sharon and Anne. What would it be like to go to a movie or shopping?

After the beating, dreams of a real life were only that, just mirages. She was trapped in a world that stifled life, and eventually her brother's love wasn't enough to keep her there. As her world became narrower and narrower, she could not contemplate an activity outside the Kingdom Hall. She wallowed in depression. She slept longer than usual and didn't care about her hair or her clothes. She didn't even want to sit with her friends at the Hall. She just wanted the meetings to be done so she could go back to bed.

Elizabeth hated sleeping on the green couch and desperately wanted a room of her own. She had no privacy and had to re-make her "bed" into a couch every morning. Her long dark hair lost its lustre. Edward lay in her arms and cried with her. He tried to brush her beautiful tresses and make her better, but he was only six, and didn't know the depth of the damage the beating had inflicted on his sister. But he was intuitive and although the belt hadn't lashed him directly, it had cut to his very soul.

By the spring of the next year, Elizabeth knew having her own room was not the real problem. For some reason, Isiah: 52, the topic of her last big assigned talk, haunted her. Each night the scripture invaded her dreams. "Loosen the bands around your neck," she remembered.

She decided to use his belt. That would show him. She might even open the Bible to the scripture that allowed parents to beat their children. For weeks every day after school, Elizabeth went to the garage to devise the plan.

She stood on the handlebars of her bicycle and tested the rope she flung over the beam to be sure it would hold her weight. She then placed the bike back in the corner where it would continue to collect dust. A perfect prop.

On the last Sunday in November, Elizabeth begged off sick from attending the Hall. Rebecca placed her hand on her daughter's forehead.

"You're not too hot, but I hope the rest will make you feel better. We'll be back at lunch."

"I'll be all right. And Mom. I love you."

Odd, thought Rebecca, *she never says that.*

Elizabeth pulled the blanket over her head and listened as the rest of the family left the house. Minutes later, she sat at the kitchen table to write the note. On the way outside, she picked up her Bible.

*

"Lizzie, Lizzie we're home," young Edward yelled as he rushed into the house. He raced to the couch, which was still a bed. The blanket was pulled up over the pillow, but the cushions hadn't been put back into a couch. Edward continued to search for his sister.

"She must have gone for a walk, son," Rebecca replied, busy at the kitchen sink. "Why don't you go out and look for her?"

Edward ran outside. He threw a few rocks at the ducks that had landed on the lawn. "Bullseye! Got you, you green mallards! Get out of here and get flying south where you belong at this time of year."

Eventually, Edward decided to look in the garage. When he entered the darkened space, he noticed Lizzie's purple coat lying on the floor next to the bike. He looked up and screamed and screamed. Lizzie was hanging from the rafters, her neck cinched in place by Douglas's belt.

Rebecca found the note nailed to her Bible on the floor of the garage.

"I just wanted to be normal, sorry."

Edward stood forlorn and alone in the middle of the garage searching his mother's vacant eyes. His six-year-old mind could not read her expression. Douglas turned on his heel and strode into the house. The family never spoke of Princess Elizabeth again. She had become a ghost. A damned ghost.

52

Sins of the Fathers

The years passed and Douglas remained Elder. Rebecca worked at the Hall and Edward slept on the green couch. Jehovah justified Douglas's stand on the matter, but deep in their hearts Rebecca and Edward bore the burden of the loss.

When he turned 16 and entered senior high, Edward led a double life. He continued to obey his father at the Hall, but at school and on Friday nights, he hung out with new friends from his class. They taught him the rules of football and before the season was out, Edward — or Eddie as his friends called him — was given the star fullback position on the Bobcats. He was tall, strong and he had quick, athletic hands — the perfect combination for a football player. In fact, at one of the final games in October, a scout from the BC Lions had come to watch the young athlete.

Douglas often questioned his son when he came home late, but Edward promised that he would make it up to him and go door-to-door on the weekend. For years, the loss of his sister smoldered in his unconscious mind. Her suicide haunted him. He realized she had chosen the freedom of death over the greater pain of living, but he missed her. How he missed her.

Edward kept his two lives a secret from his father, but he knew that sooner or later, the truth would come out. Grade 11 was when the cat was let out of the bag.

After the Bobcats' championship win, Edward stayed to party with the team. Half the school was there. Some of the girls had set up the food and the drink tables far in the bush past the Mill Lake Road turnoff. Coleman lanterns hung from the branches of the trees. Lawn chairs filled the clearing. When the team arrived, the party began. Hours later, Edward hiked home.

He knew his father would be furious when he sneaked into the house after midnight, but with the courage of a few beer and a couple of uppers, he dared to open the front door. Edward stepped into the darkness, but before he could reach the couch, Douglas approached him. He had been pacing for hours and the anger fuelled the poison in his voice when he spoke to his son.

"Where the hell have you been?"

Edward stood his ground and stared defiantly at his father. He was a good eight inches taller than his father, so he looked down into the cisterns of anger broiling in his father's face.

Douglas reached to unbuckle his belt, but Edward doubled up his fist and held it menacingly at his father's mouth.

"Don't you even think about it. You may have been able to beat the crap out of my sister, but you will not threaten me with Jehovah or Armageddon or any of that rubbish," he said. "You are a shallow, hollow man who doesn't earn his authority. He takes it with a brutal force hiding beneath a glib false exterior. You and all your Hall cronies can go to hell."

With that Edward turned on his heel and left the house. The door shook in its frame as the young man stumbled away into the darkness. Rebecca trembled in her bed.

*

"Hey look who's back," Walter said. "Eddie. Come on. Have another beer. We missed you. Helluva game tonight my friend. We're going places with you on the roster. Coach is already looking forward to next year."

"Hey thanks, buds. And uh, my old man wasn't too happy to see me. Got a bit riled up. I just need a few cold ones to calm me down before I go back to that den of vipers," Edward said, laughing giddily at the reference.

For several more hours they drank, laughed and slapped each other on the back. They let out all the stops. Edward knew, though, that he couldn't go back home without a bit of help.

"Come on guys, just a couple more. I'll keep them for the morning when I have to face the firing squad."

"All right then, but don't take any more tonight," Walter warned. "You've had a few too many beers to put any more of these little blue charms into the mix. Promise? You only got one stomach after all. Only thinking of you, man. Things will be better tomorrow, and if there's still tension, you got some supplies to get you through the day."

"Thanks a bunch. Here's to next year!" Edward smiled as he waved back and wandered drunkenly back to town.

There was no sound when he entered the house. He heard the soft breathing of his parents coming from the bedroom. He slid out of his clothes, peed and fell on to the couch. He flipped on the mag lite he kept beside his pillow. He set the handful of pills on the table. In the light, they gleamed an intense turquoise. *Beautiful,* Edward thought.

And then Elizabeth was in the room. He rubbed his eyes.

Must be seeing things, he thought. And then his mind churned with the memory of his Lizzie. *You got it right, sis and we had to lose you to his fucking belt of oppression*, Edward choked remembering the brutal beating and the hanging death of his sister.

Cover up, he whispered into the chill, *all one big fucking cover up.*

Tears pummeled his cheeks. He realized then that his sister had had no other choice. To continue in the status quo was not an option. *Lizzie, I wish you were here to help me. You always knew what to do. You knew there was no place in this house for real love. Just rules and more rules. But they didn't make us happy, did they? Not these fucking rules.*

Surrendering, Edward reached for the pills.

Rebecca found him the next morning. She knew he was dead before she lifted the blanket.

Charles Taze Russell Jehovah's Witness founder.
Photo in the Wikipedia public domain

Kingdom Hall Straffordville, Photo
Ruth Anne Whicher collection

Wooden Chairs at a baptism in Straffordville.
Photo Ruth Anne Whicher collection

Cellar steps of the Straffordville home
Photo Ruth Anne Whicher collection

Georgia Jackson.

David Bodemer

Photo's Courtesy of the Elgin County Archives, Elgin Ontario

Georgia Jackson grave site,
Aylmer Cemetery, Aylmer,
Ontario. Jill Martin collection

Aylmer Ontario Police
Department

MISSING PERSON

The Council of the Town of Aylmer will pay a

REWARD OF
FIVE HUNDRED DOLLARS

[$500.00]

for information leading to the whereabouts of Georgia Jane Jackson, Aylmer West, Ontario.

Stout Build
Age 20 Years
Weight 130 lbs.
Height 5' 3"
Brown Hair and
Brown Eyes

This person has been missing since February 18th, 1966 and when last seen was wearing a white waitress uniform, green long sleeve sweater, blue overcoat, white head scarf and carrying a red purse.

Blue overcoat and scarf have been recovered.

If located call the Aylmer Police Department Collect at 519-773-3144.

E. H. Henderson
Chief Constable.

Reward poster for Georgia
Jackson. Aylmer Express.
Courtesy of the Elgin County
Archives, Elgin Ontario

PART FOUR

CLOSING ARGUMENTS

"summing up of a case from each counsel prior to the verdict"

2016

1

A Rude Awakening

Lorraine heard soft stirring coming from her mother's bed. Outside the room, the late November sun struggled to light the sky. After changing their clocks back, the evening light had been swallowed by the time difference. It was only 4:30 p.m. and it was almost dark.

Although Lorraine's body had stiffened on the hard-backed chair, the quiet had been a godsend. Slowly, she opened her eyes. Her mother looked up from her pillow and smiled at her daughter.

"Hello, Lorraine. Have you been sitting there long?" Her voice filled the small room, strong and clear. Lorraine lived for the rare moments when her mother came back to the world.

"I've was just thinking about the train trip from Ontario. Do you remember, sweetheart?"

"Of course, I do Mom. How could I ever forget?

"There were so many nice people on the train weren't there?"

"Yes, and we made quite the impression on them if you recall," Lorraine said, grimacing.

"I wonder if I made a mistake taking the train and leaving the Hall?" Deborah said as she kneaded the bedspread in her arthritic hands. "Perhaps I shouldn't have come so far away?"

"Mom, this IS your home. You've been here in Lunenburg for almost 18 years. Remember? Patrick and I brought you here."

And here we are 18 years later. She is four years away from becoming a centenarian and I am still here for her.

Lorraine knew that Deborah was far better off than poor Beatrice Long and even though she lived in a distant world most days, Lorraine was thankful that for the most part Deborah had escaped the clutches of the Truth. There were moments though when the Hall reared its ugly head and sent Deborah into a tailspin into the dark chasm of fear and recrimination. There was no predicting what might send her over the edge.

The door swished open, washing the room in the sounds of the Home. *That time already?* Lorraine sighed.

"I think I'll go now Mom. Tania's here with your night-time pills. Deborah slowly turned to face the nurse. Stiffening, she sucked in her breath sharply and squinted menacingly into the face of her caregiver, a woman with a short-cropped boyish haircut. "Lorraine, who is that?" she growled.

"Mom, you know who that is. It's Tania, your nurse."

Tania was transgendered. She had a lovely complexion and Lorraine always thought her smile lit up the room, but Lorraine knew that her mother would have no part of taking any meds from her tonight.

Oh oh. Here we go. Lorraine reached for her mother in an attempt to quell the oncoming tirade, but she was too late. In an instant, Deborah's mind whiplashed into the past and the haunting memories of the teachings of the Kingdom Hall. Nothing could stop her stream of invectives.

"Wicked and violating the rules of Jehovah God," she whispered to Lorraine. "Get someone else to bring in the pills. The wicked who are defective will be dealt with by Jesus himself," she ranted. "Corinthians, Chapter 6," she hollered to Tania's back as she ran from the room.

"Mom, please don't quote scripture to the caregivers," Lorraine begged. But Deborah was on a roll. "Jehovah God expects exemplary moral conduct on the part of those who will receive salvation," she spouted.

Lorraine took her mother's bony, gnarled hands gently between her own. "It's all right Mom. She's gone. It's just me and you. Please calm yourself now."

Just breathe. Just breathe. Lorraine willed her heart to calm. In minutes, she felt the thankful slowing of her mother's pulse. Lorraine cringed, *How could I ever forget Corinthians, Chapter 6*?

||||| 2 |||||

Siblings and Sanity

Lorraine paced in front of the sliding doors at the Halifax airport arrival area. Peter would soon walk into the terminal. Her stomach was in knots of anticipation. Catching up would take on so many emotions, stirring up both joy and anger.

"Come on Lorraine, no need to be anxious," Patrick said. "You know that when you two get back together, it's like no time has passed. You just pick up where you left off. He's one awesome brother. I've never seen siblings so in tune with each other. Peter is just what you need right now."

"You're right. I don't know why I'm nervous," she said. "We have so much to talk about especially now that Mom's in the home. So much..." Her words were silenced by a sharp intake of breath as she saw Peter walk through the double doors. Her brother, at last.

The flight had been a full day affair what with the drive to the airport, delays due to a late December snow storm in Ontario and plane changes, but Peter's face lit up when his eyes locked on hers. His hair had silvered since their last visit, but it was still full and fell in soft curls all over his head.

He ran to meet her. She didn't even notice the limp which had plagued him for the past 50 years of his life. Peter folded his sister into his arms and held her for long minutes before he pulled away and examined her at arm's length.

"Oh Rainey, you look wonderful. You've no idea how happy I am to be here."

"Patrick and I are thrilled to have you. Every year it gets harder and harder to travel what with our damned arthritic bones and all. It's been too long," she said. The shared worries for their mother and the countless questions about her well-being would soon fill the car on the drive home.

Turning into the driveway, Lorraine placed her hand on her brother's. She whispered into the darkness. "It's too late to go see her tonight and I think it's best we have some time alone before we surprise her. She'll be confused and agitated at first, but I know she will come around."

*

"Hey, sorry I overslept," Peter apologized as he rounded the corner into the cozy kitchen. "Those two hours don't seem much when you're in the air, but down here on terra firma, wow. They really get you."

"Not to worry. You needed the sleep."

Lorraine brought Peter a fresh Keurig espresso before settling on a deck chair on the verandah overlooking the town's delightful harbour. Although the weather was almost too warm to bundle up much, Patrick insisted on cozy blankets. Except for the crazy frigid vortex that smashed through with a vengeance a couple of weeks before, December had been unseasonably warm. The ATVers were chomping at the bit to get their vehicles out on the backwood trails in soft powder. It was only eleven in the morning but already the thermometer read four above.

"Now that," Lorraine said, laughing as she took a sip of coffee, "should make those peepers of yours stand up and take notice."

Drinking their coffee and simply enjoying each other's company needed no words. Finally, Peter broke the comfortable silence.

"Sitting here with you makes the journey all worthwhile. This view. You and Patrick. What about Danny? When will I get to see her?"

"Danielle is hoping to come down from the city on Boxing Day. That will give us lots of time to catch up. Best to enjoy the calm before the storm when she and the twins take over the house."

Lorraine reached over to touch her brother's arm.

"I can't believe it. Just last month, I was complaining that I wished you lived closer and now here you are. Thank you so much for coming. Dealing with mom will be so much easier together."

"Hard to believe that Christmas is almost here. Whenever I flip the calendar on December, my mind plays memory tricks on me. December is unlike any other month."

The haunting and beguiling memories swirled around her. "Can you imagine Dad with the twins? He would really love them," Lorraine said as she laughed and took another sip of coffee.

"You know he'd be pushing 100? I have a tough time imagining Dad old. I guess because we've aged along with Mom. Dad was so young when he checked out and that's how I remember him. But look at Mom. She's pretty amazing," Peter added. "She's made it longer than most people."

"You're right, but Dad feels closer at Christmas. It's when I miss him the most. And so is that damned Jehovah's Witness Christmas Ministry. Remember those days, Peter? Our first solo call?"

Quickly changing the subject, Lorraine gazed over her cup to the harbour. "Look at this weather. All summer was so dry and then with little rain all fall, everyone thought the winter would be crazy hard, but we've only had one hard blow of frigid weather and now they're forecasting rain and wind for the next few days. It's nothing like Southwestern Ontario."

Lorraine pulled her blanket aside and got up from the chair. "While we're in memory mode, I was sorting through some old boxes and found some very interesting stuff. Give me a minute and I'll be right back."

Watching his sister scurry into the house, Peter laid his head back on the pillow to wait. She was back within minutes.

Lorraine set an old accordion file folder on the table in front of them. Peter recognized the black book immediately. The red edges of its pages stood out in sharp contrast to the soft overcast light.

"Would you believe I had mom's Bible all these years? And here, the letter exempting Dad from military service because of his eye? He sure got out of that Witness ruling quite nicely, thank you very much."

Lorraine passed Peter another treasure. "It's Mom's address book. And pictures." Peter slowly lifted one after the other, his reactions arcing from outright laughter to sombre sighs.

"Won't ever forget these damn stairs." Peter paused as he looked up from the grainy black and white. Lorraine unconsciously rubbed the scars on her arms. "That was quite the day. I remember the blood and the screaming. Mom was never quite sure about Dougie following that event, but she still agreed to let him go to Bethel."

"Look at this one, Peter. That's you and Dougie in the front row by the baptism pond. Brings back some really creepy memories."

Lorraine unfolded a small piece of paper filled with tiny script. "But this is the most amazing find. This is the letter from Helen written a day after Mom left the Hall in 1997. They were best friends, Peter. How could she say such things to Mom? It was like the warm water tap of friendship was turned off and the cold tap labelled Shunning was turned on. Although Mom suffered by losing her Hall life and her youngest son," Lorraine added, "I know in the long run, she's happier to be free of it all. Whenever her mind is alert, she knows she is at peace with her decision."

"You've really gone far back with these things. Uncovering our past takes a lot of courage," Peter said sympathetically.

Lorraine's eyes locked on Peter's. "Yes, a lot of courage. Strength I didn't know I had. You know, to face those years, head on."

To lighten the mood, he laughed and changed the subject, "All this family searching must really horn in on your reading time."

"No, not really, I am just more selective about the books I read. Don't have to pick them out of the bins in the alley anymore."

Peter had never been a reader like Lorraine. Yes, he stole the books for her, but he didn't read them. But when he looked around her and Patrick's house, he couldn't help but notice the bookshelves in the library, the office and the living room full to overflowing. Books and more books. On every table or shelf, there were books.

As he put his coffee cup down, the flaming red cover with stark black printing caught his eye. Like blood. "Hey, Rainey. Whatever are you reading now? This looks serious, *Murder City*?"

Lorraine turned her head slowly to look directly at her brother.

"I just got that one. A friend of mine ordered it from Amazon after she watched the program, *To Catch a Killer*. Peter, you will never believe the prologue. It is terrifying. The author, Michael Arntfield, describes the abduction of Georgia Jackson. I could hardly force myself to read the words, but at the same time I couldn't stop myself."

Peter picked up the book. Lorraine rested her hand on his.

"Let me tell you a bit about the author before you read. Michael Arntfield teaches criminology at Western and he was a cop before that. He researched Detective Dennis Alsop's murder files and using modern forensic and psychological profiling techniques, he has re-written the map of countless murders in our corner of Ontario in the 1960s."

As Peter read the prologue, Lorraine waited for the reaction she knew was coming.

"Oh my God! 'The angels will ferret him out.' Remember when Arthur Powley said that during the search? I can't believe someone is writing about Georgia."

"Well, the book isn't just about Georgia; it's about all the murders, solved and unsolved, that occurred when we were growing up. He calls London, Ontario, Murder City. Not a nice label for sure, but the book hooks you and you can't stop reading. With each description of the many murders that occurred in southwestern Ontario, he exposes the dark underbelly of our idyllic little farming communities. It's also a pretty technical book, you know, about serial killers and what motivates them to commit their crimes. He also creates scenarios which suggest that the killers have a signature or stamp in their method of killing or how and where they abduct their victims. It's a fascinating read, but the part that makes my stomach churn is the description of how David Bodemer got away with murder for almost six years."

"Yeah, Aylmer was turned upside down by that murdering bastard! Remember how Mom and Dad almost locked you in the house every weekend and didn't allow you to go anywhere unaccompanied?"

"It was a pretty scary time. Thank God I had Susan and you and Dad.

||||| 3 |||||

Room 65

The next day, Lorraine and Peter drove the short distance up to the Home. She knew Peter was anxious. Lots had changed since he had last seen their mother. Although Lorraine had hardly slept, she put on a brave face for Peter. They parked in the spot that she always parked in. Her spot on the hill.

"She might not recognize you right away, but give her some time. Talk about happy things, or maybe one of the crazy things we did. Especially the things that got us sent to our rooms," she said, laughing.

Please God, don't let the Hall kidnap her today. Not today. Peter is so looking forward to seeing her.

Lorraine grasped her brother's hand as much for comfort as for courage. "There's almost never a day when I come up here than she doesn't speak about the day I almost killed you with the bat. That story brings a half smile to her face."

Rubbing his head in fake pain, Peter smirked at the memory. He lifted first one and then the second leg out of the car. Slowly, he followed his sister into the Home. Immediately, he stopped short. The stagnant air and burnt coffee lingered in the hallway.

"You get used to it," Lorraine said quickly.

"I don't know. It's so hot in here too."

"Yes, I try to get her to the upper terrace whenever I can. She loves to look at the flowers. On special occasions when a Celtic group comes to play, usually during the summer festival, I wheel her into the day room. We sit at the back, so others won't be put off by her sores, but when the fiddle starts, she taps her feet in time with the beat. You could never stop Mom from buying an LP of fiddle music."

They walked down the hall until Lorraine pulled up short by room 65.

"Here we are. Be strong."

Peter rounded the doorway and pulled up a chair next to Deborah. He took her hand and held it lovingly. She was so thin. So very thin. And the sores. Although he had been warned, they were a real distraction. Lorraine walked to the other side of the bed. She spoke kindly.

"Mom, look who's here? I brought you a visitor."

Deborah's eyes were closed, but she stirred at her daughter's voice. In seconds, her eyes fluttered opened. She stared at the man at her bedside, and then moved her head along the pillow to look at Lorraine.

Deborah's forehead furrowed as she searched for her words. "When did Peter get out of bed? Where are his crutches?"

"Peter's been well for many years, Mom. He flew in from Ontario just yesterday and couldn't wait to come to see you."

"Oh, I see. Well then, perhaps we could have some tea and, and I," she paused, "maybe we can read scriptures together." Deborah's thin arms reached for her night stand searching for a Bible that was no longer there.

"No Mom. That won't be necessary," Lorraine added quickly." Peter is here to visit and show you some pictures of his children and grandchildren. How would that be?"

At the mention of children, Deborah was suddenly decades away. Her voice came breathless and strangled. Remembering Douglas always made Deborah exhausted. She tried to move, but her arms felt like lead. Behind her sockets, she watched little lost Elizabeth and Edward float in and out of sight. She tried to touch them, but they were beyond her reach.

"Oh, my poor little Elizabeth. And Edward. Poor Douglas. He was devastated." Tears coursed down Deborah's cheeks as she laid her head back on the pillow in defeat. Then just as suddenly, she tried to sit up. Peter steadied her shoulders and tried to restrain her as she struggled to get out of the bed.

"What are you doing, Mom? Please lie down," Peter spoke quietly to calm her. "I'll get you some tea."

"I don't want tea; I have to call Douglas. He needs my help. Where is Douglas, Lorraine? Please bring him here."

Lorraine pushed the alarm. "It's nothing, Peter. She doesn't know what she is saying. This happens often."

"I do so know what I am saying," Deborah screeched, flailing her arms into the air, her hands scratching wildly at her face and arms. "I want Douglas!"

Finally, the nurse rushed into the room and gave Deborah a quick injection.

"There's nothing more we can do here. Let's go home."

They would return the following day and the day after that in hopes of having a few moments of normal conversation.

"I'm so sorry, Peter."

"Not your fault, Rainey. That damned brother of ours. Damn him to hell and back."

Slowly, Peter's shoulders relaxed, and he unclenched his fists. "What a crappy cocktail! A mix of dementia sprinkled with JW leftovers. I need a drink."

Christmas

|||||| 4 ||||||

On the Porch

Lorraine and Peter left the Home as soon as Deborah had fallen into a deep sleep. His mother's failing condition weighed heavily on Peter's heart. He was glad he had come home, and he would stay as long as necessary.

Peter took his sister's arm as they walked back to the car. Glaring oblique light from a distant December sun skirted across the parking lot before them. Soon the days would start to get longer.

"My glass is empty," Lorraine chimed waving her glass in the air.

"Sorry sweetheart," Patrick called from the kitchen, "we're out of wine."

"What do you mean we're out of wine? Go find Jesus," Lorraine slurred.

Peter threw his head back and chortled, "That will never do. Can't we call in a miracle or two? Where is Jehovah when we need Him?"

"Peter, you are so bad. I think you should be sent to your room like in the old days."

Lorraine continued to wave her glass in the air.

Suddenly, a voice from the kitchen piped up, "Hey, luck is on our side. I found a reserve bottle hidden behind the SOS pads. Here come your top ups!" Patrick chuckled as he opened the bottle.

Peter welcomed another fill up as well as the piping hot spring rolls that Patrick set down on the table. Great food, his sister, and Patrick. Life was good.

"It's funny Lorraine, Mom never caught on why despite all your angry questions about Jehovah, that you really loved going to your room. Locked in there you could read all those books I stole for you from the bins at the back of the library. Wow, that punishment sure backfired."

"And I will never forget the time you tapped on my window all purple and blue. Mom would have killed you if she knew what you had been doing."

"All in the name of family pride, don't you know? The best, though, was your baptism, or rather Dougie's cement-dropping-drawers incident. That definitely took the cake." Lorraine howled as she recalled that afternoon in the pond so many years ago.

"But tonight," she continued, "has to be dedicated to Dad. Christmas Eve always brings him close."

As she basked in her wine, Lorraine listened to the soft tinkling of the halyards echo across the harbour, up to the Home and above the sea into the cosmos. She reached across the table and held her brother's hand.

"Time for a toast," Lorraine said, smiling.

"Patrick, you need to be here too," she called to him. "Dad was part of your life, too. He loved you like a son."

Patrick filled his own glass and joined his wife and brother-in-law. They raised their glasses. The harbour lights sparkled off the crystal.

"To Dad. To James."

"You know, Peter, if Dad's friend hadn't convinced him to go to that barn dance, he might never have fallen for Mom and you and I would never have been born. That night and the music must have been something else. Mom went out of her way to buy a gift for a man she had known only a week or so. Must have been some fireworks don't you think?"

"Yeah, I bet. And whenever we sat around the Sunday dinner table, there was always a record playing some fiddle tune. She probably brought that LP with her."

"I don't think so. I packed everything, remember? I just wish they had gone to church that morning instead of hanging out at home when those damned "door-to-door" people stopped by with their magazines. Might have saved us all a lot of grief."

"Water under the bridge now," Peter mused.

"Patrick," Lorraine added, "get your fiddle. We need a good old-fashioned fiddle tune. How about it?"

After settling the instrument carefully under his chin, Patrick announced, "Okay, here goes, 'Turkey in the Straw' should keep you on your toes. Hope I can keep up with you two drunken hooligans. After all this wine, my fingers might be a bit sluggish, but I'm game."

Lorraine tapped her feet while she and Peter belted out the words. Their voices sailed across the water. They laughed until the tears coursed down their cheeks.

Peter took Lorraine's hand, and in that moment of togetherness, they were children again, seated around the dining room table after the business of the "Year Book" reading was finally done. It was only when music filled the hollow little house and lifted them from the tensions that separated them, did they feel normal.

"Pretty sure Dad was tapping his feet along as well," Peter said as he threw his head back and roared with laughter.

"Oh my God, but that felt good."

"Why don't we sing for Mom tomorrow?" Peter aid. "It is Christmas after all."

"Are you sure?"

"Of course, she'll love it. Music will put her in a happy place," Lorraine added. "We could use some of that."

"You're not kidding."

"Maybe we could sneak in some champagne or wine."

"Maybe some drunken olives," Patrick offered, in the spirit of the conversation.

"Hmm, maybe not the olives," Lorraine said giggling.

"So, what's on the agenda for tomorrow?" Peter asked. "You know, it is Christmas Day."

"My dear brother, in case you don't remember, Patrick and I embrace Christmas like you would never believe. Tomorrow the house will burst with fireworks. Be ready for lights, candles, trees, and sumptuous food. You won't be able to move by the end of the day."

"No worries. I can hardly wait. I don't ever want to remember what Christmas Day was like for us all those years when we were kids. It locked us in a box that our friends could never open or understand. And you can bet hundreds of poor JoHo's everywhere are busy right now getting ready for tomorrow's ministry. The best day of the year, don't you know," Peter said, chuckling.

"Get serious now, Peter. We're both over 60 and still — after all these years — something as innocuous as an offhand comment from a stranger or a story like the one the CBC carried just last month about those young mothers who refused blood transfusions smashes me back into those hard-backed chairs in the front row at the Hall. That cruel and inhuman suffering in the name of Jehovah has haunted us for decades. And you. You wouldn't be here but for Dad's brave decision."

Lorraine sipped her wine before continuing.

"And Mom. Poor Mom is still in limbo. She never knows from one day to the next if she regrets her decision to leave the Hall, or if she believes that she'll survive Armageddon. It's a hard road for her, especially now when her dementia confuses the hell out of her."

Lorraine breathed a long sigh. "Nasty. Just nasty. We've all suffered terribly. Consider the facts alone: while we attended, our little congregation counted three suicides. Who knows how many since we left? And two in our own family!"

"There's really nothing we can we do about it." Peter said. "We can't take on The Watchtower and Tract Society. Others have tried and failed miserably. Case dismissed."

"No, you're probably right about that. I don't know. But something. We have to do something."

Patrick poured another round.

||||| 5 |||||

Bloody, But Unbowed "Invictus" by William Ernest Henley

Late the next morning, Patrick unloaded the dishwasher and started to make brunch. He let Lorraine and Peter sleep in for as long as they needed. He knew four bottles of wine would have left their heads feeling like so much cotton fluff.

After a full read of *The Herald* and two cups of Tim Horton's hangover helper, Patrick heard the shower. Time to put on the bacon.

Thirty minutes later, on the front deck in the lee side of the wind, the trio cuddled under big fleecy blankets with their coffee and Baileys. Lorraine cherished the peace of the moment.

"You know Peter, I've been thinking."

"Oh no, that could be dangerous," Peter replied.

"We really should write a book about our fucked-up lives. We might be an inspiration to other families out there who are in the same sinking boat."

Peter stared at his sister to confirm that she wasn't kidding. No, this was no joke or "after-the-night-before" philosophizing. He recognized that stubborn as a goat look having seen it many times before. Lorraine was dead serious. Peter knew when his sister was on a mission. First Georgia Jackson flying around in her head and all that blood transfusion talk. It was 1966 all over again.

"Stellar, Rainey. Stellar. And I have no doubt it will be a bestseller. Take the lid right off Bethel that would. So, when do we start?"

*

As they sipped their second cup of Tim's, a non-descript beige sedan drove slowly down the street and stopped at the end of the driveway. There were two adults in the front and two teenagers in the back.

Lorraine and Peter exchanged knowing glances. From their own years of Christmas Day ministries, it was easy to recreate the conversation playing out in the car.

Go ahead. You're on your own this time, they imagined the stone cold comment. The woman in the passenger seat motioned to the girl to get out of the car. Lorraine and Peter watched the teenaged girl slowly open the back door of the sedan. They saw the sheaf of pamphlets in her hand. With leaden feet she approached the house, the north wind catching the tassels of her toque. Lorraine suspected that it was likely her first Christmas Ministry job.

The siblings recognized the sad eyes and swollen red face the young girl tried to hide. But then, a few steps from the veranda, she squared her shoulders and just as quickly brushed away the tears from her face. And in that single moment of transition, the young girl's face morphed into that of a determined, perfectly devoted daughter of Jehovah. She climbed the three steps of the porch and stopped in front of Lorraine and Peter.

"Good morning," she began, her green eyes flitting expectantly from Lorraine to Peter.

No amount of Kingdom Hall training could have prepared her for what she was about to hear.

Epilogue

Lorraine left "The Truth" in order to live free. This is her story. She hopes others manacled by the constraints of the Jehovah's Witnesses organization will find the same courage to break out. Redemption is possible.

We Are Free.

You might say that I am dreaming,
You might say that I'm naïve
But all I'm saying is that I'm seeing,
The world the way I want the world to be.

We are free, we are free,
We've broken chains and we believe,
Someday love's all there will be,
Go tell it on the mountain, we are free!I see patience and understand-
ing,I see joy and I see peace,
I hear laughter and sweet forgiveness,
I say goodbye to old beliefs.

We are free, we are free,
We've broken chains and we believe,
Someday love's all there will be,
Go tell it on the mountain, we are free!

Shout it out from o'er your rooftops,
Sing it from the highest hill,
Send it cross the widest ocean,
Never let your voice be still.We are free, we are free,
We've broken chains and we believe,
Someday love's all there will be,
Go tell it on the mountain, we are free!

When the manuscript of *Murder in the Fourth* was complete, Prince Edward Island musician Mark Haines wrote this piece. The lyrics echo the courage of those who, despite all their fears and doubts, have climbed the mountain and broken free from the clutches of a psychologically crippling cult.

References

Arntfield, Michael.
Murder City: The Untold Story of Canada's Serial Killer Capital, 1959–84. Friesen Press: Victoria BC. 2015.

Franz, Raymond. *Crisis of Conscience.* Commentary Press: Atlanta. 1983.

https://www.britannica.com/biography/Charles-Taze-Russell.
Retrieved 2017-11-23

www.jw.org
Official website of Jehovah's Witnesses.

www.unsolvedcanada.ca
Ontario Unsolved Murders and Missing People. 2014. Retrieved 2015-03-25.